Praise for the novels of Patricia Rice

McCloud's Woman
"Intriguing and passionate."
—*Booklist*

Almost Perfect
"Brilliant and riveting, edgy and funny."
—Mary Jo Putney

Nobody's Angel
"Passion, betrayal, and churning emotions make *Nobody's Angel* a terrific way to spend your leisure hours."
—*Romantic Times*

Impossible Dreams
"Patricia Rice shows her diverse talent as a writer in *Impossible Dreams*. . . . [It] will leave readers with a smile on their faces."
—*Murray Ledger & Times* (KY)

Blue Clouds
"Totally engrossing! Fast-moving, great characters, suspense, and love—a must-read!"
—*The Literary Times*

CAROLINA GIRL

PATRICIA RICE

IVY BOOKS • NEW YORK

An Ivy Book
Published by The Random House Publishing Group
Copyright © 2004 by Rice Enterprises, Inc.

This book contains an excerpt from the forthcoming paperback edition of *This Magic Moment* by Patricia Rice. This excerpt has been set for this edition only and may not reflect the final content of the forthcoming edition. Excerpt from *This Magic Moment* by Patricia Rice Copyright © 2004 by Rice Enterprises, Inc.

Carolina Girl is a work of fiction. Names, places, and incidents are either a product of the author's imagination or are used fictitiously.

Ivy Books and colophon are trademarks of Random House, Inc.

www.ballantinebooks.com

ISBN 0-8041-1983-X

Manufactured in the United States of America

First Edition: February 2004

OPM   10 9 8 7 6 5 4 3 2 1

ACKNOWLEDGMENTS

I want to thank Angela Shrader, RN, and Joan Kayse for their invaluable medical information. Any errors are entirely my own. They told me so. And thanks to Roxann Fortenberry and the Carolina and Kentucky Romance Writers for opening networks of information for me. You guys are the best!

And as always, my undying gratitude to Connie Rinehold and Mary Jo Putney for their clear vision and immense patience. Without them, I'd still be chasing the bottle cap under my desk.

❧ONE❧

"You're kidding me, right?" Aurora Jenkins glanced at the nearly empty budget file the head of the tourist commission handed her. "You want me to spin gold out of straw, too?"

Shrugging his narrow shoulders at her disparaging words, Terry Talbert retreated to his desk so she didn't tower over him. "We're all volunteers here, Rora. We have a million-dollar grant, but no one with your financial expertise."

No one else had her big mouth and opened it so frequently, she corrected, mentally kicking herself. She'd just been laid off from her lucrative bank position for opening her mouth one too many times. But this time, she'd done it for her family.

She could fix her career easily enough, but she was pinning her family's future on the state park plan represented by this meager file. Volunteering her time and expertise had seemed the best means of getting on the inside track. Now it looked as if she would have the responsibility of making the park happen. No point endangering this golden opportunity by telling Terry he was a lazy bum.

Shouldering her bag, she slipped the file into it. "I'll start with land acquisitions. Who's this Thomas Clayton McCloud? I've never heard of him." This was a small town and she'd grown up here. She thought she knew everyone.

"Some computer guru the mayor's mother thinks is cute." Terry grimaced in distaste. "You know how things get done around here. "

Yep, she did. She'd just landed this position because she'd been Terry's high school lab partner. Networking, that was called in the city.

"And 'cute' will acquire the land how?" she asked. "With charming smiles and asking if we could have the beach, pretty please?"

Terry snorted. "Not from McCloud. He's a surly bastard. Check him out. He's usually sitting on the courthouse roof at this hour."

Oh, good, surly bastards were right up her alley. A good fight to get the old adrenaline going, and she could put an end to the park right now. *Keep the big mouth shut, Rora.*

"Is it too soon to resign my commission?" Rolling her eyes but not giving back the file, Rory headed for the door. She'd accomplished more impossible feats than persuading budgets out of surly computer gurus who sat on courthouse roofs. Maybe not any quite so colorful, though. The sophisticated city life she'd been leading paled in comparison.

"Don't strangle him until you get the list of landowners out of him!" Terry called after her.

Once she had the list of heirs to that tract, the state could start purchasing land for the park. The sooner the island had a park, the sooner they could bring some tourist money in here to fill her family's pockets, and she could be on her way again. Maybe she would take a job in Chicago this time. The skyline there was spectacular, and the culture and nightlife beat Charlotte's by a country mile. A career move would be good for her.

Walking out of city hall, she nearly bumped into Jeff Spencer, the town banker, conversing with the elderly mayor. They both knew her but didn't acknowledge her existence. Recognizing the attitude, she shrugged and stepped out of their way. She wasn't rocking any more boats these days.

Breathing in the sweet scent of blooming jasmine, she glanced up the oak-lined street to her rural hometown's only claim to a skyline. The gilding on the clock tower of the courthouse gleamed in the bright May sun.

Built shortly after the Civil War, the steepled courthouse was too small and dark to be effective for anything except record keeping, but they still used it for all their criminal proceedings. Not that a place this size had much more than a few drunk-and-disorderlies.

Given her father's rowdy habits, Rory had been on the inside of the courthouse a few more times than she cared to recall—one of the many reasons the town's substantial citizens ignored her.

Walking beneath live oaks trailing gray beards of Spanish moss, she studied the high-pitched roof of the city landmark, easily locating what appeared to be a half-naked Greek god perched at the peak, tampering with the clock's internal mechanism. It looked to her like it would be easier to tackle the job from inside the tower, but who was she to argue with mechanical genius? Or Greek gods? His shoulders alone were awe-inspiring.

The clock never had run properly, not since the mayor's daddy "fixed" it back during World War II, according to town legend. She kind of liked the fact that the clock always ran slow no matter how many times someone set it. It seemed to depict the town's cautious attitude of living one step behind the times.

If McCloud looked as good up close as he did from down here, she'd be willing to climb up there and join him.

Obviously a victim of her sexless life, Rory shook her head at her voyeurism. She had enough complications in her life without adding a man to it. Someday her prince might come, but in the meantime she was perfectly happy building her own castles.

Emerging from the shade to stand on the courthouse lawn, she called up to him. "Thomas McCloud?" She wondered if her voice would carry that far. Climbing the ladder leaning against the side of the building wasn't on her agenda for the morning.

Rory couldn't tell whether it was her voice that caused him to halt what he was doing or if he'd just decided to take a drink. Either way, he slipped his screwdriver into a tool belt, picked up a bottle of water, and glanced downward through his expensive wraparound sunglasses.

Calling his name again, she waved at him to catch his attention.

From her view on the ground, Thomas McCloud could have doubled as a movie star—sun-bleached hair, slim hips, taut, tanned abdomen, and admirable pecs. And all attitude, she'd just about swear, waiting for the movie-star illusion to dispel the instant McCloud opened his mouth.

Shoving the aviator glasses into his thick, wavy hair,

he lifted the water bottle in a salute, took a drink, set the bottle down on a ledge, and pulled his screwdriver out of his tool belt, completely ignoring her. Attitude. She'd known it. The good-looking ones were born with it.

"Thomas McCloud, I need to talk with you!" she shouted at him.

He carefully unscrewed one corner of the clock frame and dropped the screws into a pouch on his belt without once looking down.

She damned well didn't intend to stand here screaming like a jay, making a spectacle of herself. The townspeople already thought little enough of her family without confirming their "trailer trash" reputation.

Rory marched around the courthouse and up the steps. She'd been the one who'd taught her classmates how to climb up into the tower.

She supposed a sensible person would have gone on to the next order of business and hoped to catch one Thomas Clayton McCloud in another time and place. But life had taught her that the timid got walked over and the stubborn got things done.

Besides, he'd ticked her off by ignoring her. She wouldn't have accomplished as much as she had if she'd let people ignore her.

"How you doing, Elena?" Leaning on the counter in the DMV office, Rory greeted the file clerk who'd worked there for decades.

Sliding her purple-rimmed glasses on top of her gray hair, the clerk smiled a greeting. "Aurora, how good to see you!"

Rory waved her hand at the door partially hidden behind a bank of file cabinets. "I need to climb up there and talk to the clown on the roof. Is the staircase accessible these days?"

"He's a sight to behold, isn't he? If only I were thirty years younger." Elena reached behind an antique wooden file cabinet and removed a key from a hook.

"I thought it was only the high school kids who sought attention by climbing up there." Rory accepted the key and started around the counter.

"He never talks to anyone, so I guess it's not attention he's after." She tucked a pencil into the bun of hair at her nape and grabbed a shrilly ringing phone, waving Rory on.

Clasping the key in her fist, Rory wended her way past desks and cabinets and assorted equipment to pry open the squeaking door. She wrinkled her nose at the musty stench emanating from the wooden structure. If the town ever hired a real live fire marshal who actually inspected buildings, he'd probably condemn this stairway. Until then, she needed a broom to clear out the cobwebs.

Checking a nearby janitor's closet and finding a worn broom, Rory thanked the good Lord for people who never changed their habits. She could swear this was the same broom she'd used the first time she'd sneaked up the stairs. Wielding the handle, she brushed aside cobwebs and cleared a path.

The old staircase seemed safe enough. With her sensible heels slapping the wooden treads so he could hear her coming, Rory climbed to the third-story landing and located the vent overlooking the roof.

"McCloud!" she called, rattling the louver until it opened enough for her to see out. "I need to talk with you. You want to do it here or somewhere more appropriate?"

The clock tower was actually overhead, perched on

the peak of the roof, so she had to look up as well as out to see the mechanic. Mostly she could see his long, jeans-clad legs. Apparently amused by her call, he peered over his sunglasses at the open louvers, but she figured he couldn't see her. "There's a ladder in here," she shouted. "I can climb up there if I have to."

"I like a woman with perseverance. Give me a minute to screw down this frame. I'll meet you down at the Monkey."

He didn't possess the honeyed drawl of a local man, but he had a deep, sexy voice that crawled right down inside her and made itself at home. Rory shivered in appreciation, then rolled her eyes.

He hadn't even asked why she wanted to talk with him. *Men!* He probably thought his body was all she was after. Rory watched to be certain he was fastening the frame, then trudged down the way she'd come.

The Blue Monkey was her father's favorite hangout, but it also served short-order meals and didn't mind serving sailors who dragged in from the harbor covered in grease. It would be air-conditioned and not too busy at this hour, so she couldn't argue with his choice of meeting places.

Rory didn't recognize the young bartender, so she was safe in ordering a soft drink without a recitation of where she'd been and what she'd been doing since high school. She sighed at the ever-present contest slogan on the label of the bottle he slid across the bar to her, but she checked under the cap, just in case. Her father's penchant for playing contests had started rubbing off on her since she'd returned home. Something about placing her hopes in the hands of fate appealed when she had no other options.

Flinging the *Sorry, try again* cap to the bar, she turned to study the jukebox. The playlist hadn't changed since Elvis had checked out. She punched in a Simon and Garfunkel song from the seventies and took her glass and bottle to the first booth.

"Bridge over Troubled Water" hit its last wailing note as Thomas Clayton McCloud sauntered in. He'd apparently taken time to scrub off in a rest room, wetting his long, sun-streaked hair. He wore the ash-brown length tied back with a leather thong against his bronzed nape. He'd donned a plaid cotton shirt to cover his bare chest, but with the sleeves ripped off, it didn't do much to disguise his sculpted biceps.

Rory had to bite her tongue to prevent drooling as he slid into the booth across from her, exuding male pheromones. Brains won over brawn any day in her book, but that didn't stop her from appreciating the view when he crossed his sinewy arms on the table. *This* was the town's computer expert?

He lifted his sunglasses, sliding them into his overlong hair. Up close, Rory could see that it had an unruly curl to the ends. The sunglasses had partially concealed a broad nose with a slight downward slope instead of the classically handsome one she'd expected. He wasn't Hollywood pretty, but his long-lashed gray eyes could ring her chimes any day.

"There'd better be a good reason for dragging me down here this early in the day." With a gesture at the bartender, he ordered a beer. The boy knew his brand of choice without asking and carried the bottle over still sweating from the cooler.

Sipping the beer, Clay admired the glory of the full-figured redhead across from him—his fantasy Viking princess sprung to life in Technicolor. She'd twisted strands of her strawberry-blond mane into a knot at the back of her head, but it was too heavy to stay in the pins. One escaped lock curved in a delicate line along her throat, just brushing her red silk shirt. The stiff-collared, no-nonsense shirt didn't bother him, but the gray business suit she wore with it warned he really didn't want to hear what she had to say. He didn't listen to suits these days.

Leaning back against the wooden bench, he took a good chug of beer and waited for her to get past his rudeness. No sense in encouraging whatever maggot had stuck in her craw. Instead, he engaged his mind in admiring the way her luscious lips tightened into a disapproving line.

"I'm Aurora Jenkins," she said with only a hint of the soft drawl of the island inhabitants. "Terry Talbert has put me in charge of developing a budget for the park grant. I have an MBA in finance and grew up here, so I volunteered to help him out for a while."

Raising an eyebrow, Clay continued sipping his beer, waiting for her to come around to what she really wanted.

In the dim light of the bar, her eyes appeared almost violet. They narrowed at his nonresponse.

"I'm developing a budget for the land-planning grant," she continued without voicing an iota of frustration at his stonewalling. "I understand you're overseeing the software development of a program capable of identifying and locating the Bingham heirs. If you haven't pulled your cost figures together yet, I can help you with them."

Clay nearly snorted beer out of his nose. Wiping the smirk off his face with the back of his hand, he leaned forward, bringing them face-to-face across the narrow table. "I do software. I don't do numbers."

"The state requires numbers, Mr. McCloud."

"The state can go screw itself. I'm working for next to nothing and nothing is what they'll get if they don't leave me alone."

"With that attitude, maybe *nothing* is all you have and all you ever will have, Mr. McCloud. Perhaps I should suggest that the state find a different person to locate the heirs?"

"In my experience, you may suggest to them that the moon is blue, and they'll appoint a committee to study the matter and make a decision sometime in the next century. Don't let me stop you." Flinging a bill on the table, Clay slid out of the booth.

It was a damned shame that great body was wasted on a narrow-minded number cruncher, but he was sticking to simple minds and simple tastes these days—even if Aurora Jenkins's curves could tempt Satan.

"The park is imperative to our future, Mr. McCloud. We need a budget to get the state grant. I'll present you with a suggested budget next week," she called after him.

He almost laughed out loud at that. He should have known any woman willing to tackle that spider-infested tower wouldn't give up easily. Turning, he winked at her in his best obnoxious manner. "You'd be better off hunting for the late mayor's missing fortune than to trust the state."

He walked out, letting the door slam behind him.

Missing fortune, her foot and eye. If she could find a fortune, she'd be out of here so fast, his head would spin.

Cursing, Rory fumbled in her purse for some change so she could pay up and leave.

Where the hell did he get that my-way-or-the-highway attitude? Was he born with it? Did someone teach it to him?

Could she hit him over the head with a two-by-four and bash it out of him? There was a reason she preferred the pinstripe-suit crowd these days. She could control her temper better in the secure environment of intelligent people who shared rational goals.

"Clay took care of it," the bartender said, sweeping the bill off the table before she found her change purse.

"Put the money against his tab." Refusing to take anything from the bastard, Rory threw a couple of ones on the table.

She'd have to investigate Thomas Clayton McCloud more thoroughly before she approached him next time. Did he have any business background at all? Did he even have an education? How much did he actually know about programming? It was a real stretch to believe he could find the on switch of a PC.

She bet he found the on switch of every woman who crossed his path. Fanning herself with a file folder as she left the bar, Rory tried to ignore all the hormones exploding like little bombshells in less noble parts of her.

McCloud exuded sex appeal like bees secreted honey. She didn't have the time or the patience to play little-boy games. He could go exude on some other hapless female.

❧ TWO ❧

"What will we do without Daddy's pickup?" Cissy fretted for the ninety-nine millionth time since Rory had returned home after the accident that had temporarily crippled Cissy and their father. "I can't get to the grocery store, much less take Mandy to after-school classes. No one's going to loan me any money to buy one while I'm not working. And Daddy can't produce any papers proving he has an income, so no bank will loan him any either."

"Pops was down at the bar Friday, so someone's helping him get around. Just be grateful he can't ride the Harley with his leg in a cast." Rory steered her small BMW convertible into the interstate traffic leaving Charleston after Cissy's medical appointment. Until her family was—literally—on their feet again, she wasn't going anywhere. They needed her time as much as her money right now. Which meant she had no excuse to go job-hunting and wiggle out of an unpleasant task with the potential to provide her family's future.

Twenty-four hours had passed since her meeting with Thomas Clayton McCloud, and she was no closer to figuring out how to deal with him than before. She was generally good with people, but McCloud . . .

She had better things to do than fret over living testimonies to the dangers of testosterone poisoning.

Her sister stirred in discomfort, and Rory cast her an anxious glance. Cissy had inherited their bear of a father's sandy-brown hair and their mother's slight stature. Rory had inherited their mother's strawberry-blond mane and her father's sturdy size. She had spent many an adolescent evening envying her sister's delicate figure. But right now Cissy simply looked worn thin.

"One of Daddy's bar buddies probably picked him up." With a grimace of discomfort, Cissy pushed the seat back as far as it would go so she could straighten her leg. "Did he tell you about the California freak he's taken up with now? He has Daddy convinced the island is sinking, the fish are poisoned, and the wells will dry up."

Rory shrugged. "He's probably right, not that we can do anything about it except move to the city, where the exhaust fumes give people asthma, the reservoirs are drying up, and the ground is poisoned with lawn chemicals."

Cissy chuckled, winced, and leaned her head back against the high seat. "Sounds like you and Daddy's buddy have a lot in common. Maybe we should all learn to get around on bikes."

"Oh, yeah, I can see that happening." Rory gave her sister's injured leg a look of disbelief. "Rollerblades, too. Then we can put you in the hospital and keep you there."

Without a hint of hesitation, she changed the subject. "I'm thinking of selling the BMW."

She already knew her sister's answer to that, but she had to put forth the suggestion. Rory loved her baby-blue convertible, but it was highly impractical out here on the sandy roads of the island. If she sold it for just half its worth, she could buy two used pickups with the proceeds. She'd spent her savings and severance allowance on their medical bills. The car was about all she had left.

Cissy turned her head to glare at her through narrowed eyes. "No charity," she said firmly. "I have no way of paying you back, and I'm not gonna owe you into eternity. We'll manage. We always do."

Cissy managed because their father called Rory when unexpected expenses cropped up. Her education and her career had kept the family afloat for years. But she couldn't tell her sister that their father's "good sales weeks" came from her. He might sell more concrete birdbaths and lawn ornaments during the summer, but those sales barely held him through the winter. And now the accident that had totaled the truck had also slowed her father's production.

The pink slip in her last paycheck had ended the family's income cushion. Ostensibly, she had been part of a larger layoff, but she knew the true score. She really needed to learn to quit rocking the boat. Proposing that the bank give as much to literacy as they were giving to the new basketball arena had not been one of her better-thought-out tirades. Especially in these tough economic times.

"Cissy, let's be real here," Rory argued. "I need this thirty-grand showpiece like I need a hole in my head. Public transportation is more environmentally sound. I'm thinking of taking a job in Chicago. I can find a place on the train line and buy one of those electric cars."

"Thirty grand? Damn, Rora, spending so much on a car is stupid. You could buy a house with thirty grand."

"Well, I won't get that much if I sell or trade it. And you won't find a house as nice as Mom's with thirty grand,

I promise you. We should put flowers on her grave every day for having credit life insurance on the mortgage."

It was just a double-wide, but it was the only home her sister and niece had ever known. Situated on thirty acres of swamp and sandy soil that had been handed down through generations of their mother's family, the trailer had been their salvation after their mother's death when Rory was only twelve.

It wasn't as if their father had ever owned anything of his own—until their mother died, and he'd built the concrete factory behind the house. Rory had to give Jake credit for ending his footloose life the instant his daughters had needed him.

"You must have got your smarts from Mom," Cissy said. "She sure knew how to pinch a penny and make Abe squeal."

That their father didn't went unspoken. Rory loved her free-spirited father, but she sometimes wondered how he and their mother had ever stayed together long enough to make two babies. It seemed they'd had nothing in common on any other level but bed.

She'd learned her lesson at an early age. Opposites might attract, but they were damned bad for each other. Her father had spent his life hoping to make his fortune by winning a million dollars. Rory had followed her mother's example, preferring the certainty of education and hard work.

Not that work had paid off in the way she had hoped. She'd zip her big mouth once she found a new job. She'd learned the hard way that working within the establishment paid off far better than fighting it. She'd just temporarily forgotten that maxim in a surge of overconfidence.

"You have smarts, too," Rory assured her sister. "You just didn't have the opportunities you gave me. And kids cost a lot. Since I'll probably never have any, I want to help with Mandy. She's already wanting a car so she can work."

"Over my dead body." Arms crossed, Cissy glared at the road.

"Well, that's my thought, too," Rory admitted. "But the time will come. We'd better present a united front, or she'll be weaseling it out of Pops one of these days." Once she had her career back on track, she would personally see that Cissy's fifteen-year-old daughter had the education she deserved. Cissy had provided the home and security Rory had needed while growing up. Rory could do no less for Mandy.

"Or he'll teach her to ride the Harley," Cissy agreed glumly, leaning her head back and closing her eyes. "I don't want to think about it. You need to start looking for a job. Now that the weather's warmer, the tourists will be back, and Daddy can look after us."

If she hadn't known just how badly her family was in debt, Rory would jump on this invitation to escape. But the minute she left, Cissy would attempt to return to work and ruin her health, and her father . . . Rory would rather not even consider what her Harley-riding father would do with a broken leg and no truck.

She might occasionally resent the narrow world she'd been brought up in, but she loved her family and would do everything in her power to support their decision to live in this backwater town, where opportunities were few but life was familiar.

"What if I decide I like it here and don't want to leave?" she teased.

Cissy didn't bother opening her eyes to answer that one. "You never belonged here, kid. You'll be gone before the summer is over."

Rory smiled happily. Oh, yes, she would. She wanted a condo with great big windows overlooking the skyline this time—once she'd molded the proposed park into a certainty.

Turning their swampy land into a profitable tourist attraction would solve all their financial problems.

She intended to make it happen with or without the help of Greek gods.

"What we need is your video game's Viking heroine and Karate Turtle to rise out of the swamp and drive off the barbarian park builders." Jared McCloud stroked the laptop keyboard, testing Clay's latest program.

Sitting on the porch of his brother's beach cottage, Clay crumpled his empty beer can and pitched it at a seagull trying to steal his fries. He checked over the top of his Oakley sunglasses to see if Jared had baked his brain. The redheaded MBA from yesterday had reinforced his conviction that materialistic princesses made lousy heroine material. "Slipped a little deeper into fantasyland, have we? Does married life do that?"

Actually, he envied the contentment his restless brother had found in marriage, but he'd embarrass the hell out of both of them if he said that.

The sun setting behind the cottage caught water droplets in the surf, illuminating them like tumbling silver coins as a wave lifted and crashed against the shore beyond the porch. Jared gestured at the wooded marsh past the beach and rocky promontory on the horizon. "If the state intends to build a park over there, it's only a matter of time before someone buys the swamp and condos shoot up like mushrooms. Cleo wants to plant a minefield between here and there to hold back the tourists."

"Cleo has the right idea." Sitting back in his canvas deck chair, Clay tried not to care. Life was much simpler if he didn't waste energy standing in the way of progress—that was what he'd told himself when the state had offered him a tidy sum to develop the genealogy software they needed to track the descendants and pinpoint the property owners.

He'd figured the easy cash would tide him over while he decided what to do next with himself. He was counting on the state giving up on buying the swamp once he'd unraveled the names of the innumerable descendants of slaves who'd inherited it. Persuading that many strangers to agree on selling would be impractical, at the very least.

Or so he'd thought until Aurora Jenkins had arrived on the scene.

He fought a surge of discontent with nonchalance. "I think I like being a beach bum."

"Yeah, right." Jared snorted in disbelief and tapped the keyboard. "You've changed the edit mode," he exclaimed. "I can point and drag and the sketch goes just where I want. Freaking fantastic! I can finish a drawing in the morning and spend the afternoon kicking back if this works out. You're a pure wizard, bro."

Clay shifted to a more comfortable position in the deck chair and popped open another beer can. "Sure.

Now all I need is a good fairy to wave her wand and fill my pockets with gold, and we're set."

In the absence of any good fairy, Clay leaned over to poke his large finger into the cross-eyed view of his infant niece. "Hey, Midge, how ya doin', drooler?"

Jared chuckled and with a few strokes of the keyboard and trackball, created a plump baby fairy struggling to stay upright on tiny wings. "There she is, your good fairy. Pin her up over your bed at night."

Clay glanced at the screen, grunted, and returned to munching the fries that constituted his evening meal. "Cute, real cute. You've got it right. Midge is the only magic fairy I'm letting near me."

"Her name is *Megan*," Jared corrected. "Meg for short. Why don't you update 'Mysterious'? Use magic fairies instead of Viking princesses this time. Gaming is still a huge deal these days. You don't have to create and sell business programs anymore."

Now that your dot-com failed remained politely unsaid. Clay snorted at this second mention of the sophomoric script that had generated the popular computer game over ten years ago. "I prefer writing about dripping dungeons and slime pits these days. Maybe I could drop a Viking princess or two into them."

"One woman who returns your ring doesn't justify writing off the rest of the gender. Besides, you're good at gaming. I'll help you write a new script. We could use Cleo's menagerie as a starting point."

Cleo's *human* menagerie would be far more entertaining than her animal one, Clay reflected, but his brother wouldn't appreciate his cynicism. Jared's wife befriended everyone from homeless derelicts to rich cartoonists like

Jared. Or beach bums like himself—jilted beach bums
whose ex-fiancées *didn't* return the ring. Diane had liked
that expensive hunk of rock too well.

"You write it, I'll program it," Clay offered laconically, "and we can be the only two people in the world
who ever play it." Peddling backward to adolescence
wasn't on his agenda. He'd meet the world on his terms
or none at all. The anonymity of this island hideaway
suited his new choice of lifestyle: ex-millionaire hermit.
He'd never played well with others anyway.

"You don't have to keep the rights to every damned
thing you create," Jared protested. "There are trustworthy distribution companies out there."

"Yeah, like the one that's ripping off 'Mysterious' as
we speak. Or the MBAs who let my company go down
the hole." *Or the redheaded one determined to turn paradise into parking lots.*

He suspected he would have some difficulty keeping
that one from hunting down property owners even if he
found a million Binghams. He knew the type. Aurora
Jenkins was on a mission from Mammon.

"No, thanks. I'm keeping my fantasies to myself these
days." Brushing off his brother's suggestion, Clay hun-
kered down and chugged his beer.

He might be skeptical about the benefits of corporate
life, but he occasionally fantasized about having a real
life like the ones his brothers had found in marriage. He
was dead tired of living inside his head. He'd even gone
so far as to find a woman and make a commitment, until
the engagement had fallen apart with his company.

He should have known better than to think he could
lead a normal life. He didn't possess a normal mind, as

he'd been reminded once too often. He offered diamonds and companionship, and women wanted companies. Who knew?

Clay eyed the infant in the cradle just to be certain Midge hadn't gone anywhere. Cleo had dressed her daughter in a tie-dyed nightshirt, and curled-up pink toes stuck out from beneath the hem. He thought Midge was pretty incredible and probably the most real thing he knew, but he kept his opinion to himself.

"I don't know why you're so down on women." Jared added a few touches to the drawing, stuck a wand in the baby fairy's hand, and saved the finished product to the hard drive. "They're one of life's joys and wonders. Abstinence makes you cranky as well as cynical."

"Yup, that's me, disbeliever in life's little mysteries. Women have only one purpose, to mess with a man's mind." Clay withdrew his finger from Midge's determined grip.

Jared hooted. "Maybe that's your problem—you think your brains are in your jeans." He handed the laptop back to Clay, then bent over to adjust the blanket shading his daughter from the sun. "When are you going to release that three-D program?"

"I haven't found the right backing yet." Hadn't looked for it, actually. Rather than turn years of hard work over to another thief, he'd let the program rot.

Like him. Over the past few years he'd owned Jags and Malibu property. Women wearing diamond rings and designer bodies had adorned his life and bed. Where did a man go after that?

Finishing off his bottle of water, Jared stood up and stretched. "I know the program works. So what's wrong?"

"I'm keeping risks to myself these days." Clay sipped his beer and glared at the laptop screen Jared had returned to him.

"Cleo's designed a tin devil with a scowl just like yours. If you're not careful, she'll have it popping up in the driveway as a warning sign."

"Tell Cleo I'll pose for her devil if she thinks it will keep intruders out."

"If they build that park next door, we'll not know privacy again," Jared said gloomily. "I'm thinking we'll have to sell."

Clay clenched his teeth and didn't immediately reply. Despite his doubts about halting progress, he had been doing what little he could to discourage the state from buying the beach adjoining Cleo's property. For a while he'd almost convinced them that the genealogy of ownership was too complex to be unraveled—until the lawyers had stepped in and insisted he continue the search. He didn't trust lawyers any more than MBAs.

He was a big boy now. If the park forced Cleo and Jared to sell, it shouldn't matter to him. There was a whole wide world out there. Except that without family or career or home, he had no anchor and no destination.

Men weren't allowed to admit weakness, so he maintained his insouciance. "You're set back from the road. I don't think park traffic will be a problem." Clay opened the document listing the owners that he'd located so far. There had to be some weakness he could use to derail the state's plans. "You've got years to think about moving."

Shrugging, Jared lifted the infant carrier. "I hope so. Cleo will freak if she has to leave that house she's worked on so hard."

Whistling, swinging Midge, he walked off down the sandy path and boardwalk to the island farmhouse where his wife and kids waited. Clay grimaced and studied the waves rather than watch him go. It was all well and fine for his older brother to live in a nest of childish laughter and uproar. His older brother was a cartoonist and had never needed to grow up.

Despite the difference in their ages, Clay had been older than Jared since birth.

There for a while, maybe he'd forgotten himself and indulged in adolescent fantasies of fortune, fame, and everlasting love. After all, he'd achieved two out of three before he was thirty. But he'd learned the fallacy of thinking he could have all three.

Sipping his beer with his feet propped on the porch rail, Clay figured this was as good as it got. It didn't take half a wit to earn enough to keep him in beer and fries for the rest of his life. He had a roof over his head and a Harley in the drive. Maybe he'd find a new career in fixing old clocks like the one on the courthouse. He liked tinkering.

Maybe a little later he'd wander down to the Monkey and see what kind of hell he could raise.

For now, he switched his computer program to "Mysterious" and began battling villains for the life of the Viking princess.

On a whim, he changed her hair color from blond to red.

❦ THREE ❧

"Yes, I know it's five years old, but it has only sixty thousand miles on it. BMWs are good for three hundred." Rory rolled her eyes at the inquisition of the car buyer on the other end of the telephone line.

Sitting on the dinette table, Mandy swung her long legs, giggled, and unscrewed the top on the last of the soft drinks her grandfather had purchased because the label said they could be winners. She automatically checked under the cap, then flung it into the trash with a shrug. Like her Aunt Rory, she had fiery sunset hair. Unlike her aunt, she wore it cropped short, tousled, and bleached. Three studs adorned one ear, and her navel-revealing T-shirt rode high over a tanned belly.

"Look, it's not as if I need the money," Rory lied arrogantly into the telephone. "If you want to steal a car, go steal someone else's."

Even if she wasn't impressing the guy on the phone with her negotiating skills, she was impressing the hell out of Mandy, who watched her through eyes widened in fascination.

"Well, call me back if you change your mind." She hung up and put a kettle on to boil for iced tea.

"Guess you're stuck keeping the Beamer a little longer. Pity." Mandy leaned over to reach the peanut butter jar on the kitchen counter.

"Smart-ass." Rory handed her the jar before she fell off the table.

The screen door slammed open and Jake limped in, using his crutch more to manipulate objects in his way than as a means of locomotion. Her father was a big man with a full head of sandy hair that had faded over time. He maneuvered his bulk through the crowded laundry room, hooked a chair leg, and pulled the chair out so he could lower his weight without bending his injured leg. "I'm hungry."

"Want some of that lasagna I made last night?" Rory opened the refrigerator without waiting for an answer. "Have you thought about that bookkeeping program I told you about? If you open a checking account, you could control your money better." Probably not enough to buy the insurance he needed, though. One more accident like the last, and bankruptcy, here they came.

"Now, Rora, don't get off on that kick again. I ain't makin' enough for the IRS to mess with, and the people 'round here like cash. No fancy books are gonna make us any richer."

She could argue with that. Writing checks would force her father to see where his money went. If he realized how much he handed out to his drinking buddies and sometime workers, he might be a little more careful. He wasn't twenty anymore. He needed to think about his health and retirement.

Right, that was like telling Peter Pan he had to grow up.

Giving up on the topic, she asked, "How's the leg, Pops?"

"I'll be fishing in no time, providin' there's anywheres left to fish. How you doin' with the town council? Found any way of keeping the state out yet?"

"I'm learning," she answered noncommittally, cutting a slice of lasagna to heat. The state park could generate enough tourism to keep her father's company in cash for years. A service station and minimart would be even better, if she could find funds to build one. She had no intention of keeping out the state just because her father thought fishing should be free. He thought she was sabotaging the park with her volunteer work. What Pops didn't know couldn't hurt him.

"Well, you'd better learn faster," he grumbled. "McCloud told me the state's talking of docks and cabins and parking lots down there. We'll have to pay for the privilege of boating in our own damned waters."

McCloud told him that? Whose side was McCloud on? The state was paying him to work for them, wasn't it? "McCloud needs to stick to locating Binghams," she muttered.

"That's just it!" Jake shouted, waving his fork at her. "Talk to your friends on that connivin' tourist commission. I heard them and the bankers. Soon as they've got some Binghams in their pocket, the frigging vampires got it fixed so all they have to do is talk one Bingham into selling, and the whole swamp goes on the block, not just the beach."

"All of it?" Mandy stared at her grandfather in horror. "Even Grandma Iris's?"

"All of it," Jake agreed in a voice of doom. "Even Luke's dock and the Watkinses' shack."

A pinprick of uncertainty perforated the fabric of Rory's confidence. She knew enough about development to hear a kernel of truth in her father's wild accusation. The back of their property ran up against the Bingham swamp. She didn't know if Iris and the others living back there had any claim on the land, but they'd lived there undisturbed all their lives. They were neighbors and friends. They would have nowhere else to go if the state was talking major development.

"The state doesn't have any use for the swamp," Rory said with more assurance than she felt. "They're just buying the waterfront areas to protect the sea turtles and improve the beach. There isn't any reason for them to even know Grandma Iris is out there."

Thomas Clayton McCloud and his anarchic propaganda were a bigger danger to their future. McCloud's outrageous theories would have the whole island in an uproar, endangering the chances of the park being built. State legislators didn't pay for anything that didn't buy them votes.

She wouldn't let an outsider destroy the first opportunity her family had of digging their way out of poverty.

First, though, she'd call Terry to sort rumor from reality. The state park plan she'd seen had called for only much-needed beach improvement.

She didn't mind developing the nearly inaccessible beach down the road, but Disney World in her backyard really would sink the island.

*   *   *

Rubbing his eyes, Clay shoved back from the desk he'd rigged up in the cottage's front room. Finding misplaced Binghams was akin to searching the Internet for passwords. They were everywhere. And they took forever to uncover.

Locating the appropriate stack of data, he added another pile of printouts to it, looked around at the scattered piles of notes, file folders, and program changes he'd made, and decided he ought to invest in a good filing cabinet.

But that would require admitting he was staying here, and he wasn't ready for commitment yet. Commitment required some sort of goal, and he had none. More accurately, he *wanted* none. *Been there, done that.*

Who knew it was such hard work to be a hermit?

He kicked aside an empty beer bottle, scooped up a sweaty T-shirt, and cleared a space for the next stack of papers. If he really wanted to commit, he'd buy a laundry hamper and a trash can.

Among the attic rejects and litter of the room, his flat-screen monitor and high-powered laptop were the only indication of the high-tech life he'd once lived. Childish sketches drawn by Cleo's eight-year-old son, Matty, adorned one wall. Shells and sea oat bouquets left over from previous occupants replaced the expensive artwork he'd once collected. He couldn't say that one lifestyle was any less empty than the other. This one was just cheaper.

Returning to his seat, he switched the computer to his test version of "Mysterious II," took out a couple of rocket ships with a barrage of blue mushrooms, found the missing princess and her lost laser arrows, and jotted notes on two dozen ways he could improve the script.

His stomach rumbled, and he rubbed his bare belly. Cleo had extended an open invitation to dinner, but the kids ate early, and he'd worked through the meal. He glanced around, looking for a clean shirt amid the debris.

The Monkey offered good company and decent food. He could go into town and let his brain cool off.

Of course, thinking about the bar brought back thoughts of Aurora Jenkins, and other parts of him heated up in response to his mental image of sunset hair and a stunning figure that might take a lifetime to explore.

All right, now he needed a good run on the beach. Forgetting the shirt, Clay picked his way across the piles of paper to the doorway. It would stay light for another hour or so. The Monkey didn't get lively until nine anyway.

Stepping onto the porch and checking the lights at Jared's place, he noted a tall figure striding down the wooden walkway over the dune. Had he sunk so low that he conjured up his fantasies now?

With the sun sliding behind the trees in the west, he couldn't make out the face, but he recognized the shape.

Aurora.

Her parents sure knew how to pick a name. Her hair caught and mirrored the reddish glow of the sunset in the same way the aurora borealis lit the winter sky.

He mentally stripped her of her tailored jacket and knee-length skirt, and redressed her in a flowered sarong and bikini top with her hair flowing around her shoulders.

"Mr. McCloud." Arriving on his doorstep, she managed to sound both curt and agitated at the same time.

"Clay," he corrected. "What can I do for you, Miss Jenkins?"

"Call me Rory," she answered with an impatient wave before reaching into her shoulder bag.

She wore no rings, he duly noted. He had a ring fixation these days.

"I've brought some proposed budget figures for software development for your approval." She pulled a file folder from the bag. "They should adequately cover R&D and any equipment. I need to talk with you."

He propped his shoulder against the porch post and crossed his arms over his bare chest, blocking her progress. He didn't do business these days. And he definitely didn't do MBAs. "So talk."

Already disturbed by what she'd learned from Terry, Rory didn't have time for McCloud's schoolboy tactics, even if all that bronzed, muscled torso belonged on a wall poster. He wasn't built like a fireplug, like so many men who worked out. Instead he possessed the lean, sleek lines and powerful sinews of a thoroughbred.

She'd learned to curb her desires years ago. His display of male arrogance easily negated her reaction to his physique. To make herself heard in a male world, she'd learned how to handle ego.

With mockery, she looked McCloud over as if he were a side of beef. Instead of backing off, he flexed his muscles in response, and watched her with amusement.

Heat rose to her cheeks, and she spoke sharply to cover her blush. "There isn't enough light out here to go over these figures, Mr. McCloud. And I really don't think what I have to say should be broadcast to the neighbors." Maybe she ought to rethink her reason for being here. She was used to handling men in business suits, not half-naked statues of male virility.

Proving he wasn't made of stone, he lifted an eye-brow in a provocative leer. "Why, by all means, Miss Aurora. Let's you and me make ourselves comfortable in my office."

He gestured toward the screen door so she could enter first. Not one to back away from a challenge, she brushed past him to step up on the porch. Her skin reacted as if he'd stroked it when her shoulder grazed his chest, and she was pleasantly aware that he topped her by almost a head. Not many men could match her height, especially when she wore heels.

The trash heap he called an office distracted her from her physical response. Books filled the rattan sofa and chair. Papers covered the worn wooden floor. Only the slatted rocker remained empty, largely because everything he stacked on it had slid off and lay between its rockers.

"Shall I get you a beer?"

In classic bad-boy attitude, he invaded her space by leaning a little too close. She could feel his breath blowing the loose tendrils on her nape, smell the beer he'd been drinking, and wanted to turn around and shove him away for the principle of it. But touching this man would mean physical confrontation, and she didn't think she could handle that. Not when all her hormones begged for it.

She swung around, nearly clipping his nose with the folder. "No, thank you. Is that the Mac with the new processor?" Crossing the room, she hit the space bar, and a warrior leaped out of bloodred shrubbery to scream pun-laden epithets at the player.

"I trust you're paid well to play games, McCloud."

Glancing down, she discovered the printouts beside the monitor and lifted a stack. "This is programming language. Are you developing the park program yourself?"

Grabbing the papers from her, Clay crossed his arms and stashed the stack in his armpit. "What can I do for you?" He changed his sexy leer to an irritated male glare and adopted an intimidating stance.

Which Rory ignored. She had more immediate problems than this Macho Man, and she clung to the hope that those printouts proved he actually had brains behind the attitude.

Much as she hated to admit it, she needed his expertise. "Would you stop acting like a jackass and listen? How close are you to finding the Bingham heirs?"

Clay studied her stonily. "I'm generating names first. Then I'll have to hunt down and verify addresses. Why?"

Without asking permission, his uninvited guest removed books from the sofa and took a seat. "Would you put a shirt on, please? We need to talk."

"You keep telling me that." Clay resisted the impulse to strut for her benefit and grabbed a Rams T-shirt. It had ketchup on one ram horn, but it didn't stink. Of course, he'd shrunk the shirt trying to do his own laundry, so he might as well have just painted his chest black for all the good wearing it did.

Her pained expression showed she'd noticed. Feeling decidedly better about that, Clay located his nearly empty beer bottle, finished it off, then took a seat in the rocker, dangling the empty in his fingers. "If you're not after my body, what exactly are you after?"

"Your head, probably, if you don't quit telling tales in the bar." She didn't look ticked, just disturbed as she opened her file and laid it out for him. He suspected her insults might be her first line of defense against jerks like him.

Clay propped his sandals on an assortment of computer magazines on the driftwood coffee table rather than read the file. "Tales?"

"About the state's intention for the Bingham property. We *need* that park, McCloud," she said with an intensity that illuminated the violet of her eyes. "Our unemployment rate is among the highest in the country. The park will preserve the fragile ecology while providing jobs. Small-business development along the roadway is essential. Free fishing doesn't factor into the process."

"Never does, does it?" he asked noncommittally.

"I don't want the locals up in arms and stopping progress," she said with firmness.

Clay figured she was wound up enough to kick him if he asked how this concerned him. She wore sturdy pumps and probably packed a wallop in those lovely long legs. He waited silently, since she seemed intent on doing all the talking anyway. He enjoyed watching the animated way the Viking princess gestured with her hands as she built up steam. Could he add that to the gaming script?

"What concerns me is how the state will use those names you're providing them," she finally admitted, as if unwilling to impart dangerous information until she'd gauged her degree of control over it.

Clay waited her out.

Apparently winning some internal battle, she continued: "I just verified that once the state locates a few Binghams willing to sell, their attorneys can force an auction of the entire swamp rather than buying just the land along the beach."

Shit. Clay maintained his careless pose, idly swinging his bottle back and forth. Mentally he calculated means of checking out that bombshell for himself. He'd hoped to divert the beach sale and hadn't seriously considered his brother's concern that the whole parcel would go on the market. Cleo and Jared might live with a park, but if the entire swamp went up for sale . . .

Appalling images of high-rise hotels adorned with plastic lawn chairs and beach towels dripping from balconies rose in his mind's eye. Good-bye herons gleaming in the morning sun and owls hooting in the dark. Hello blaring rap music and raucous pool parties. For the first time in a long time, the nausea of anger gripped his gut— proof that he hadn't entirely succeeded in separating himself from the real world.

Lacking any reaction from him, Aurora clarified: "The Bingham property is a huge acreage. The state needs only a small portion of it."

"I don't believe it's possible to tell the state which part of the property belongs to which Bingham," he finally answered, hoping to pry her out of here so he could make a few calls. "If you're so concerned, then you're better off telling the state to take a hike." That was his preference, anyway. Leave the island the way it was, the way it belonged.

His careless words finally lit her wick. If she were a firecracker, Clay figured she'd explode all over him right now. Amazingly, he enjoyed the way ire flared behind her uptight facade. He hadn't been so entertained since he'd written "Mysterious."

"We can't afford to lose that park," she insisted— contradictorily, in his opinion. "What I want to see is the state keeping *all* the Bingham land, much of it in its natural state, and limiting development to small businesses."

"Oh, right, like that's gonna happen." He snorted at the idea of any government spending money to preserve swampland.

"If the state doesn't limit access to the Bingham land," she continued with determination, "then they can sell the remaining acreage to developers who could turn the island into condo strips and malls. How do you think that will affect you, your brother, and his family?"

She sure had his number. He'd seen what overdevelopment had done to southern California and knew exactly how it would affect this paradise.

Not that he meant to admit it to one Aurora Jenkins. He worked alone these days.

"I don't see how I can help you." He flung the bottle aside, since she wasn't buying into his biker attitude. He should have known she wasn't stupid. "The state is paying me to do a job. Once I do it, they have the right to do what they will with the results."

Her wide, voluptuous mouth stirred a man's desire even when it tightened in a grim line. Clay studied her tempting lips rather than pay attention to the wealth of emotions flashing across her expressive features.

"You can help me persuade the state to preserve the acreage," she insisted.

"What's in it for me?" he asked, just to see how she would react.

"I should have known that was your attitude." Rising, she stepped over his stacks of junk in her haste to escape his deliberate boorishness. "People who have no concern for others are lower than slugs."

"A man can manage only so many concerns at once,"
he threw back at her, but she didn't turn around. Clay
winced at the slamming screen door.

Well, that should safely remove one tantalizing female
from his horizon. Once he shut out temptation, maybe
he could get some work done.

Would a game throwing self-righteous Amazon war-
riors into dungeons work?

It was either that, or develop an erotic new game involving beds and hot babes.

❦ FOUR ❦

"There you go, Jake, the oil filter is replaced." Standing on the hot pavement beside the glittering chrome of a Harley, Clay wiped his hands on an oily rag. Life was simpler when all he needed was a wrench and strong hands to make things work.

Do-gooders with redheaded tempers required tools and talents he didn't possess.

"Thanks, good buddy. This bum leg is making things difficult." Propped against Clay's bike, Jake leaned over to scratch an itch beneath his purple cast. The sandy color of his ponytail disguised any gray, though his darker beard was flecked with silver.

Wriggling out from beneath the massive machine, Clay sat up and reached for his bottle of water. "Tip the bike on that leg, and you'll be lucky to walk again."

"A man's gotta have wheels." The burly biker lifted his good leg over the motorcycle and bounced up and down on the seat. "It's not like I'm going far. You found out any more about the state buying up the island?"

Wiping the sweat from his forehead, Clay shook his head. "Can't see how you can stop the state from doing what it wants."

Jake threw him a look of disgust. "Come on. Get on your bike and let me show you what I'm talking about. Let me introduce you to a few people."

Clay resisted. Unlike his brother Jared, he didn't have a charming bone in his body. He tended to glaze over after a few minutes of small talk.

Of course, there was always the chance that Jake would merely show him swampland and introduce him to more people like Jake. Not having anything more interesting to do, Clay stood, shrugged on his shirt, and donned his helmet. "Let me drive you. I don't want to see you break the other leg."

He sailed the Harley over the bridge and along the open highway connecting the string of islands Clay currently called home. The low country of South Carolina sat at sea level, with hillocks sporting trees between marshes of long grasses. The road down the center of the islands had been built on a causeway so it wouldn't wash away in a storm, but much of the land around it was more marsh than solid ground.

They drove past Cleo's sandy lane and into a tree-covered territory virtually untouched by mankind—the Bingham swamp. The state park should occupy only the distant acreage near the beach. The live oaks and hardwoods in the center would no doubt be bulldozed for development if the rest of the swamp went on the auction block, destroying the pristine wilderness forever.

About a mile past Cleo's drive, Jake signaled and Clay wheeled abruptly down a sandy path almost hidden behind a tumbledown gray shack that must have once been a fruit and vegetable stand. Remnants of an old wooden sign reading PEACHES leaned against decaying crates.

By the time they reached their destination—a shack almost as weathered and tumbledown as the fruit stand—Clay was covered in sweat and grime and not fit company for anybody.

An old black woman with silver-white hair and a shawl covering her stooped shoulders appeared on the porch. Beside her stood a frail young woman with the same sandy hair as Jake, sporting a cane, and wearing a disapproving frown. Clay ran the back of his arm over his face, hoping to wipe off a layer of crud, and wishing he'd gone home.

"Hey, Iris, I brought you company!" Jake remained seated, waiting for Clay to lend a shoulder. "He's gonna help us keep our fishing."

The old woman smiled understandingly, as if she knew Jake's bluster for what it was and accepted it. The younger woman, on the other hand, regarded Clay with suspicion.

"Clay, this here is Grandma Iris, the best sweetgrass weaver in the South. She's lived all her life here. And this is my daughter, Sandra Ann. Everyone calls her Cissy. Ciss, why don't you show Clay the sea turtle nests?"

Uh-oh. He hadn't figured Jake for the matchmaking sort. Freezing up, Clay assessed his chances of escape.

"Daddy, you're not supposed to be on that bike. And I can't walk all the way to the beach like this. We'll both be crippled up and back in bed."

"Where's your sister, then? Didn't she drive you out here?"

Sister? Jake had more than one daughter? He'd never taken the time to learn Jake's last name or where he lived. Sandra Ann must live elsewhere if she'd been driven over. Where? In the swamp? He'd never been curious about

Jake or his motives before, but self-protection might require that he pay closer attention.

Cissy shrugged. "You know Rory. She had a dozen things to do today. She'll be back in a little while."

"There you are, then." Jake turned around with an air of satisfaction. "Aurora will take you to the nests."

Rory . . . Aurora! Clay experienced a sinking feeling in the pit of his stomach at the same time self-destructive interest flared. Could there be two women with that name in one town?

And if not, did Jake know his daughter was working against him?

Without quite knowing how he'd been roped into this, a short time later Clay found himself accepting a beautifully woven basket with handles from Grandma Iris.

His first inclination had been to run for his bike and get the hell out of there. But Iris had patted his arm and settled into a wicker chair on the porch as if she trusted him to carry out her request without question. He might be working on a reputation as a surly hermit, but he hated to disappoint an old lady.

"The grass isn't far. I can manage." Wielding her aluminum cane, Cissy limped down to the sandy yard.

"You don't have to do this." Clay offered a helping hand, but she brushed him off. Apparently stubbornness ran in the family.

Without wasting words, she headed down a well-worn path that disappeared into an unforgiving thicket of shrubbery. "If the state lets developers dry out the wetlands, the sweetgrass will disappear. Basket making is an African art that dates back centuries, but the marshes for the grass are almost gone."

An undercurrent in her voice showed her reverence for the land and the art, so Clay bit his tongue against any cynical remarks. Striding ahead, he forced a path by holding back branches to let Cissy pass by. He could appreciate people with a passion for what they did.

Which brought his thoughts around to Aurora again. She was equally passionate about the land, except she wanted to make money out of it.

"There aren't many sea turtle nesting grounds left," Cissy murmured as she struggled over the path he cleared. "They return to the same beaches every year and won't nest where there are bright lights. Our coast is one of the last remaining places on Earth where loggerheads nest."

Clay calculated Jake's daughter had to be his own age or a little older, but she appeared worn lifeless. He caught hints of prettiness in her drawn features, but none of the animation he'd enjoyed in Aurora. He didn't see how they could be sisters. Maybe he was barking up the wrong tree.

Clearing the bushes, he helped her maneuver over a tree root, but she shook him off once they reached the sunny marsh.

"The grass starts here and runs down to the beach." Cissy pointed with her cane to the field of knee-high weeds.

He watched her produce a stout knife and bend over to begin cutting the long, swaying grasses. He could hear the ocean pounding against the shore, but a slight rise on the horizon prevented his seeing it.

"The turtle nests are in the dune up by the beach. Just follow this path and watch where you step. It's too early in the season for hatchlings, but sometimes you can see the mother's trail through the sand. They only come in at night and go right back to sea after they lay their eggs."

Leaving Cissy to her work, Clay ambled down the path through the reeds. He knew next to nothing about wildlife, but he'd watched giant turtles on the Discovery channel, and had once considered a trip to the Galápagos. No harm in taking a look around to see what the fuss was all about.

Of course, if it had been Aurora back there looking stunning and vibrant and bossing him around, he'd have to balk just to show her who was in charge. He was starting to anticipate the flash of temper in her eyes and the way her mouth pulled flat when he irked her. Much better to keep a temperamental woman like that at a distance.

He almost walked through the turtle path before he saw it. He assumed it was a turtle path from the immensity and oddness of the way the grass bent and the sand rippled. He traced it back to a hollow in the dune, but there all traces of the path had been methodically brushed away. Intrigued, he circled the hollow. Maybe he ought to research turtles on the Internet. What kind of creature emerged from the sea to lay and abandon eggs in isolation? How many of them were there? What did they look like?

And how would they survive with a shopping mall on top of them?

Grinding more enamel off his molars, Clay stalked back to Cissy. She regarded him without expression, simply waiting for him to pick up the basket of grass before leaning on her cane and heading back the way they'd come. He didn't see how a nearly invisible woman like this could be related to the firestorm that was Aurora.

"Whaddayuh think, McCloud? See anything out there?" Jake bellowed as they returned to the clearing and the shack.

"Interesting," he admitted, assisting Cissy up the stairs and setting the basket on the porch. "But that's not helping me figure out how to stop the state from buying it all up."

"Nah, you'll have to talk to Aurora about that. She's got her head in all those bigwig circles, but she didn't seem to think you were interested."

Well, he wasn't, really. She wanted the state to keep all the land and develop parks and "small businesses." He thought the state should leave nature alone. He didn't see any meeting ground in between. Maybe he ought to ask Jake how Aurora's plans dovetailed with free fishing, but he didn't want to start a family argument.

Clay smacked a mosquito nibbling on his forearm, then swiped his forehead with the bandanna he kept in his back pocket when riding the Harley. "Aren't there zoning meetings or something where you can protest this kind of thing? What about environmental laws? I can't see where I can help with any of that."

Jake swigged from the glass of iced tea Iris had given him earlier. Wiping his mouth with the back of his hand, he shook his shaggy head. "You know how to work them computers. That's more than anyone else around here. Aurora can tell you what to do."

Like that would happen in this century. Deciding it was high time to get out of here before they asked him to walk on water, Clay straddled his bike and kicked back the stand. "I can write the EPA, I suppose. But you can't stop progress. It's gonna happen one way or another." He wouldn't tell them that he was trying. He'd had enough of public failure.

Sitting in her porch chair, efficiently weaving dried grass into a tight circle that would create another of the art-quality baskets adorning her porch, Grandma Iris intruded upon their discussion. "My mama was a Bingham 'fore she married. My brother Billy lives just the other side of town. I'm sorry to say, but he'd sell his soul for a bottle of 'shine. Aurora says all the state gotta do is buy Billy's share, and they can go to court to sell all this. You give the man Billy's name, and this time next year, this gonna be mud and bulldozers."

Oh, yeah, lay the blame on me. Thank you so very much, Aurora Jenkins. There was no doubt left in Clay's mind that there was only one Aurora in this damned town, and he'd better have a talk with her before she had half the populace out to tar and feather him.

If this quiet old lady was one of the Bingham heirs he was hunting, the park was a hell of a lot closer to a done deal than he'd thought.

He hated it when the anonymous names on his computer came attached to real people.

Trailing into the cluttered front room of his beach cottage, Clay wrinkled his nose at the mess and began pulling off his shirt. Maybe it was time to start pulling his act together if he meant to deal with the outside world again.

The outside world—as in Aurora Jenkins. He must be some kind of masochist to even consider talking to an MBA, but that red-gold hair and those amazing lips beckoned him more surely than his ideas for new video games.

Antagonizing Aurora would be far more entertaining than rotting on the porch.

He really didn't think they were working from the same page. He didn't see any reason to change the island one iota. She was talking in terms of finding *ethical* development, as if such a creature existed. She'd be better off looking for a dodo bird.

The phone rang, and, aiming for the shower, Clay was tempted to ignore it. But he had a few feelers out on his software business, and he didn't want to write off any opportunity.

Grabbing the cordless receiver, he started up the stairs. "McCloud here."

"This is Ben Little in the State Parks Department. Our attorneys are prepared to move on the purchase of the Bingham property. How is the program developing?"

Clay halted and leaned against the stair wall. "I'm getting there," he answered cautiously, crossing his fingers as he pictured a gray-haired old lady rocking on her front porch, creating works of art out of weeds.

"Do you have names? Can you fax me what you've found?"

The sun-baked memory of giant turtle paths and rippling sea grasses and reclusive old ladies cracked open a door he didn't want to shut just yet. "Program doesn't work that way," Clay answered tersely. "It starts with names and birth certificates. We won't get to the verification and current address stage until the genealogy is lined up."

"Can't you speed up the process somehow, find addresses on the names you have?" Little asked impatiently. "All I need is one of them to agree to sell. We can have the whole parcel on the auction block in weeks."

Whammo. The lawyers were in full wolf mode.

Ticked that Aurora's wild theory had been confirmed, Clay set his mouth in a grim line and thought furiously. If he refused to turn over the names, the state would simply seek another source—it wouldn't take them long to learn about Iris and Billy. He had to stall.

"I can't guarantee the accuracy," he answered slowly. "I'll have to buy another computer and second phone line to work the current findings while this one is on-line processing the genealogy." As if that had anything to do with the price of eggs, but Little didn't know that.

"Check your budget to see if an extra computer can be funded. We're going nowhere until this is done. I'll get back to you next week." As if he'd just checked off one more item from his agenda, Little hung up with a click.

Well, shit.

Clay clicked off his receiver. With resignation, he realized his little odyssey into obscurity was about to end.

When actually faced with the Slugs from Slime, he simply couldn't hang up his sword and let them destroy the world. Too much time in the gaming world apparently had warped his thinking into believing justice ought to prevail.

Maybe if he confronted the prim MBA first, she'd rid him of his hero complex, and he could return to munching fries on the porch and pretending the rest of the planet didn't matter.

❈ FIVE ❈

After taking a quick shower and donning a clean black T-shirt and jeans, Clay hit the Harley in search of Jake's daughter. Roaring down the island highway, letting the hot wind pump up his warrior mode, he drove past the peach stand marking the road to Iris's. A half mile past the swamp road, he located the wooden cross scrawled in fading red paint with JESUS SAVES that Jake had described in his directions. Sweat dripped down Clay's forehead from beneath his helmet as he navigated the left turn and chugged down a blacktopped lane of aging cottages.

Peeling white paint on clapboards and mildewed siding on trailers depicted rural poverty, but every yard cheerfully sprouted bouquets of color. Tires painted white brimmed over with red petunias and begonias. Trellises loaded with roses and morning glories and jasmine climbed up to porch roofs. Mailboxes propped by old plows, adorned with painted pictures of daisies, sprang up all along the roadside.

Clay slowed as he spotted three deer crossing one yard. Realizing they were some kind of lawn ornament, he roared on, discovering more anomalies the farther he drove. Brightly colored glass balls atop preposterous concrete structures reflected the blinding Carolina sun. Blue concrete birdbaths decorated with red concrete cardinals stood tall in the midst of flower gardens, and nestled among the flowers he began to notice colorful gnomes, or were they elves? He didn't know the difference.

A concrete Madonna held out her hands in supplication inside a cast-iron bathtub cut in two and turned on edge to form a shrine. Concrete rabbits and squirrels posed beside vegetable gardens. He almost fell off his bike swiveling to stare at a tree dangling colored bottles and Easter eggs.

He'd lived in L.A., cruised the beaches of southern California, and had seen eccentricities of every shape and color. He'd just never seen an entire neighborhood dedicated to cheerful bad taste.

He finally spotted a mailbox painted with a row of purple pansies and JENKINS neatly printed above them in red. The mailbox post grew out of the middle of an enormous vine sporting a riot of yellow flowers. He turned his bike up the narrow drive hedged by sprawling shoulder-high azaleas. A tunnel of moss-draped oaks overhung the azaleas, blocking all view of the house. He felt as if he had exited the real world into a fantasy one.

Rounding the bend past the oaks, he knew he'd fallen through a space warp into another universe. An entire yard—more like several acres—of concrete lawn ornaments stretched out as far as his eyes could see. Unpainted statues and birdbaths marched in neat rows toward a long aluminum-sided building in the distance. Along the drive, beneath the bushes, painted gnomes beamed playfully at him. Or in some cases, scowled.

A neat double-wide trailer with white siding, black shutters, and rampant azaleas at its base sat in the midst of a yard full of painted concrete figures. A towering robed statue of a pagan goddess dominated a vegetable garden on one side. Gnomes, elves, and fairies frolicked between gardenias and camellias. Glittering witch balls rested in concrete hands or on pedestals wrapped in concrete vines. Birds splashed in fountains taller than he was.

Stunned, appalled, and fascinated all at the same time, Clay parked his Harley in a gravel parking space and started down the shell path toward the front door. Once the bike's roar died out of his ears, he could hear the melodious tinkle of a symphony of wind chimes. A soft hum wove through the music of the chimes.

Following the path behind a towering camellia, he located a woman sitting on a bench, painting a Disney-esque dwarf. She seemed oblivious to his approach, although the Harley could probably be heard for half a mile.

The artist wore a crinkly gauze lavender shirt that blew in the breeze, revealing a clingy purple knit top with spaghetti straps and generous cleavage. A skirt in the same crinkly fabric of the shirt blew about shapely bare ankles. She was barefoot, although he could see her sandals lying on the path where she'd kicked them off. Her toenails were painted a pale shade of frosty pink.

Banded in a purple scarf, her straw hat shadowed her face, but all Clay's hormones and pheromones had already kicked into life to scream in unison, *This one! We want this one! Puhleeeze!*

Nearly crippled by the impact of the unexpected assault on his senses, Clay halted to steady himself. He wasn't the kind of man easily bowled over by lust, but he couldn't tear his gaze from the roundness of freckled breasts exposed by the artist bending over to paint a red circle on the dwarf's cheeks. He was in trouble here. He felt as if he'd just taken a right jab to the belly and had the breath knocked out of him. In silence, he watched her graceful fingers expertly add the final touch of color.

An artist! Why had he never thought to look for an artist as a lover? Who needed sharp-minded, sharp-tongued career women when soft, creative females could stir all his senses? He'd been looking in the wrong places.

To his relief and dismay, once satisfied with her effort, the vision in purple finally glanced up. Despite the shadow of her hat brim, he could detect a smear of red paint adorning her straight nose. Wide eyes blinked with lashes so long they swept her cheeks. And the mouth . . .

Oh, damn. He'd salivated over that voluptuous mouth just the other night. Even before she swept off the hat with a graceful gesture, he knew he was in trouble.

Aurora.

Leaving her hat on the bench, she stood up, a quizzical look on her face as he stood there gaping like a starstruck teenager. The lavender fabric of her skirt drifted in the breeze, clinging to her curves, outlining her stunningly long legs. She reminded him of tall, frothy drinks laced with strawberries and raspberries, refreshingly tart and cool on the tongue.

While he stood here dripping in sweat in his bad-boy black.

Damned good thing he didn't intend to make a good impression.

* * *

Amusement rippled through Rory at the cynical McCloud's stare of disbelief. He tore his gaze away to examine the concrete monstrosities that had haunted her since she was a kid. As a teenager, she'd been humiliated by her father's trite creations and had hated to bring friends home.

She'd developed the confidence to appreciate folk art since then. With a little wider view of the world, she'd learned that her father's creations far surpassed most manufactured molds. Not that she expected city-bred McCloud to appreciate the difference.

Standing there with his perspiration-soaked T-shirt defining broad shoulders, his helmet tucked under his arm, and the sun beating down on the rumpled waves of his hair, Thomas Clayton McCloud was a sight for the gods. For once he didn't appear to be adopting a pose, although he stood like James Dean with booted feet akimbo while he took in his surroundings through the mask of his aviator glasses.

Since those surroundings included her, Rory suffered a moment's unease. She didn't have the time or patience to deal with sexy misanthropes who didn't care what happened to the people on the island—no matter how much her libido screamed otherwise.

"I thought it was my father coming up the drive. May I help you?" She kept her tone neutral.

McCloud returned to awareness in a blink of an eye. Shoving his glasses into his hair so she could see his slanted cheekbones, he frowned and looked past her shoulder like a child refusing to admit guilt. "You might be right about the state's intentions. I didn't think they'd move this fast."

Sitting down on the bench, she whacked the lid onto her paint can with a little more force than necessary. "You think I lied? For what reason?"

"Hell if I understand a woman's reasons."

Startled, she glanced back up. He was amazingly tall. His lean frame decked all in black nearly blocked sight of the loblolly behind him. She refused to admire the way his sun-streaked hair curled damply against his neck. "Women protect family first. That generally defines their reason for anything."

Maybe she should invite him in for a drink? He looked as if he could use one, but life was complicated enough, and she was wary of his intentions.

"In my experience, women protect their own asses first." He shrugged and studied the dwarf she'd been working on. "Did you paint all these?"

She wiped her hands on a rag. "Hardly. I've only been back here a few weeks. My sister and niece do a lot of them. Pops hires people occasionally. Would you like a glass of water? Tea?"

"Water would be fine."

He looked ill at ease. Not understanding why, Rory led the way into the house. "How did you meet my father?"

He followed her through the shabby sea of green that was their front room, taking it all in without comment. "He's at the Monkey a lot. We talk. Or he does."

Rory figured that at least the trailer was neat, if quaint, which was far more than he could claim about his shack. "That's my father, all right. Since you're the whiz kid who's been telling him he'll lose his fishing if the park gets built, sounds as if you get some talking in."

Apropos of nothing, he replied, "He took me out to see the turtles."

Occupying half the space in the tiny breakfast room adjoining the galley kitchen, Clay McCloud filled it with masculine vitality. Awareness of his presence crawled across her skin, and Rory felt almost trapped as she opened the refrigerator to rummage for bottled water. "The turtles come out only at night, and it's early in the season to see them." She had no idea why they were discussing turtles, but she could be patient.

She handed him a bottle and opened one for herself. He apparently didn't feel the same heat as she did, since he continued to invade her personal space. She inched backward to the other counter of the small galley, tugging her shirt closed over her clingy knit top.

Clay threw his head back and swigged heavily of the water. Fascinated, Rory watched the gulps course down his long throat. When he returned the bottle to the counter, he watched her through wary eyes, and she wondered if perhaps he might be as physically aware as she and just covering it with attitude.

"They're arriving. I think I saw a nest," he admitted, a note of interest behind his reluctant words.

"You aren't likely to ever see one again if the state sells the swamp to developers. House lights confuse the hatchlings, so they wander inland instead of heading for the ocean, giving land predators more time to eat them. One more species down the drain."

"It's going to happen whether you like it or not," he asserted defiantly, taking another swig from the bottle. "Money talks louder than nature. If the beach park happens, so will swamp development."

Maybe it was wishful thinking on her part, but it sounded as if he was waiting to be convinced otherwise. "We need the park," she answered cautiously, feeling her way. "If the state doesn't save the beach, someone else will eventually build condos on it. It's the swamp the state isn't interested in that worries me."

"Even a park will destroy the nests and marsh." Setting the bottle down, McCloud folded his arms combatively over his chest, daring her to disagree with his cynical assessment. "A park will attract people and reduce the habitat."

"Other parks have installed signs and fences keeping people away from the turtles. It's the lights from development that are harmful." She didn't know why she bothered arguing. He wouldn't listen, wouldn't care, and wouldn't do anything about it. She needed to pick Cissy up, and he was in her way.

"What did you think would get built around a park if not condos and hotels—peach stands?" he asked sarcastically. "That will make a difference."

That did it. She didn't have to stand here and take any guff from an outsider who hadn't lived here and wouldn't live here and who understood nothing. He blocked her exit from the kitchen or she'd just walk out.

Poking his chest with her finger—and trying not to think about the unyielding strength of that muscular plane—Rory nudged him out of her way. "Fruit and vegetable stands, concrete monuments, gas stations and minimarts, basket stands, whatever the locals darned well feel like putting along the road. Why shouldn't development benefit the people who live here? Why the dickens should outsiders be the ones who profit?"

"Dickens?" He lifted an inquiring eyebrow but didn't retreat any farther than the stool at the counter.

She poked Clay's chest harder, annoyed that he merely looked down at her, annoyed that she didn't seem to intimidate him in the least. She'd learned to overcome her embarrassment at towering over most men, knew how to use her size effectively when necessary, but he didn't seem in the least bit fazed. "People here aren't stupid. They may lack education, but they know what's good for them, and you don't. If you're not here to help, then you're part of the problem."

Abruptly he caught her by the waist and set her down on the stool as if she were no more than a sack of groceries.

No man had ever attempted to lift her, much less move her. Too stunned to register anything else, Rory almost missed what he had to say.

"You can't bully me like you bully everyone else, Xena, Warrior Princess. If you want help, don't drive it off when it arrives."

She looked appropriately startled, Clay noted with satisfaction. He didn't usually manhandle women, but he figured she'd started it. If they were going to work together, they had to lay some ground rules—starting with leaving his starving libido alone.

He couldn't believe he'd actually suggested they could work together. Impulsiveness was the bane of his existence. They couldn't even agree on what was best for the island except that it wasn't condos.

"Warrior Princess?" she echoed his words in disbelief.

So he'd taken a flight of fantasy. He shrugged it off. "Would you prefer Wonder Woman?"

"How about Amazon Queen?"

He couldn't tell if she was being sarcastic or laughing at him. He grabbed the water bottle and backed off. "My brother is a comic aficionado. Some of it rubbed off."

Damn, but she did look like some kind of queen sitting there on her royal throne gazing down on the peasants. A strand of hair had escaped her long braid and curled along her cheek, softening the firm line of her jaw. He didn't know a thing about women's clothing, but the royal purple knit tank top suited her. Suited him, as well. He had some difficulty focusing on her face and not her cleavage.

She'd been warm and supple and alive in his hands, and he wanted them around her waist again, but he didn't have a clue how to go about it without getting his face slapped.

"How does one graduate from an adolescent who reads comics to an aficionado?" She jumped down from the stool and stalked toward the front door.

Hell, she both irritated and tempted him at the same time. How did she do that?

He really wanted to kiss her. He'd go nuts looking at that mouth of hers without learning how it felt beneath his.

"By making a million or so drawing them?" Knowing he wanted to kiss another MBA should drive him straight to his bike, but he lingered in her emerald Easter egg of a living room, absorbing details he'd missed the first time through.

He'd grown up in a Long Island mansion with professionally decorated rooms of Oriental carpets, designer fabrics, and antiques he hadn't been allowed to touch. He'd moved to California and a streamlined beach house of glass and wood and leather. He knew this room was done in appallingly bad taste from any standard he was aware of, from the green velvet sectional sofa to the cheap walnut bookshelves, but he felt at home here. Which was unusual. He never felt at home anywhere except in front of his computer.

When he didn't immediately follow her to the door, she swung around, her braid flying. "A million dollars? Your brother made a million dollars drawing *comics*?"

He should have known money would catch her attention. Shoving his hands into his jean pockets, he returned his undivided fascination to Xena. *Rory* really didn't fit her. "I don't ask him for financial statements. He's not starving. Now, are we working together or not?"

He'd caught her so off guard that she stared at him with complete unself-consciousness, giving him time to appreciate the impact of purple pansy eyes, long lashes, and a wide mouth parted slightly in astonishment. He liked her with her defenses down. What would he have to do to keep her like that?

"How would we work together?" she demanded, sensibly enough. "You're the one who will provide the state with the list of Binghams and sell us out."

"If I don't give them the list, you won't have your park."

"You don't even believe there should be a park," she countered.

"*I'm* not the problem. You're the one who has a problem if you want to force the state to do things your way. I can just throw out the program, tear up the list of Binghams, walk away, and protect turtle nests by stopping the park." Until the state hired someone else.

He knew better than to believe he had a snowball's chance of halting the park, but there was some tiny chance they might limit development in the swamp behind it—if he and the MBA princess could work together.

At his mention of stopping the park, a look of panic reached her eyes, and he wondered what that was all about. What in hell did she have riding on a state park? Not that he cared about her hidden agendas, of course.

"The county zoning commission," she murmured, drawing back from her dazed state and looking confident again. "They need a recommended-land-use plan."

"I'm not a lawyer, but zoning sounds like a good start." If he was smart, he'd be wary when she started looking confident. "What about the EPA? Aren't the turtles protected?"

She grabbed her purse and pulled out her keys, still not looking at him. "They're loggerheads, threatened but not protected. But we can bring in environmental groups and try for some temporary injunctions until zoning can be decided. Development can't be halted. We need the money out here."

"Along the highway only," he persisted, wanting parameters established. Condos in the wooded swamp next door to Cleo and Jared would destroy their safe haven.

He told himself it was for Cleo and Jared that he did this. He couldn't think of any other reason to be involved.

As if she heard his thoughts, she shouldered her purse and pinned him with her glare. "And what do you get out of this?"

Time with you didn't seem to be the appropriate answer. He probably didn't have an appropriate answer.

Clay snapped his helmet on. She didn't budge an inch but stood practically nose-to-nose with him, waiting for a reply.

"I'm paying penance for my former life, okay? Just tell me if you want my help or not, and I'll get out of here."

Oddly, his heart beat a tattoo while she considered his offer. He really didn't want to get involved, he told himself. He was waiting for her to boot him out so he could go back to his cloistered world and work. He didn't know why he'd volunteered in the first place.

"All right." She whirled around and started for a sweet little Beamer beside the house. "I've got your phone number. I'll call you when I have a list of the zoning restrictions and commission meeting dates. Initial that budget I gave you and get it back to me."

Clay did his best not to grin as she slammed into her car and roared off in a cloud of sand. That attitude of hers worked fine when she was wearing the armor of her business suits, but failed completely in royal purple with paint on her nose.

With a pang of guilt, he realized he'd been judging Aurora Jenkins by her business suits, just as people judged him by his appearance or his job title or his financial statements. He'd learned to deliberately use his looks and bad attitude to steer people away.

So what was she hiding behind her suits of armor?

And why the hell did he itch to find out?

Rubbing his fingers beneath his helmet while surrounded by reflecting balls and laughing dwarves, he wondered if he'd finally let his last screw loose. Jared would laugh his fool head off when he heard about this.

❧ SIX ❧

Unable to justify the expense of a cell phone when the island reception was iffy on a good day, Rory had canceled hers when she moved home. She regretted that decision now as she huddled with the cordless in her bedroom, away from the trailer's other inhabitants, keeping her voice low while she tried to argue with a car dealer in Charleston over the BMW's worth, without success.

Grimacing, she clicked off the receiver and looked up to see Cissy stepping out of the bathroom, robe wrapped around her, hair still damp, watching her with curiosity. Cissy's end of the trailer only had a shower, so she had been using Aurora's tub.

"Did that whirlpool gadget help?" Rory had put the device on her credit card with some vague hope that by next month, she could pay for it.

Her severance package might cover groceries and utilities for a while longer, but somebody in this family needed to start working soon.

"It felt good," Cissy admitted. "I tried to do too much yesterday. Who were you talking to?"

"I'm still trying to sell the Beamer. We need to make an

expedition into Charleston, I guess, pick out a truck and trade it in."

"They'll give you cash back?"

She had no idea. The Beamer was the first car she'd ever owned. But Cissy was looking at her expectantly, and Rory hated to disappoint her. "I'm sure we'll find someone willing to deal. Maybe we can even swing two trucks and some cash. We'll have to think about what's best."

She'd be stranded in this trailer if she didn't have transportation of her own. Trapped. Her breath caught in her throat with that panicky thought, but she shoved the panic aside. Family first. She'd find her way out again.

"Daddy will know someone with an old truck they want to sell," Cissy said with a shrug. "You shouldn't have to sell your car. What do you think of that guy he brought out yesterday?"

Unable to sprawl across the high bed with her damaged hip, Cissy merely leaned against it. She was only three years older than Rory, but she'd stepped into their mother's role with natural talent.

Panic momentarily checked, Rory accepted the part of younger sister that they both needed right now. They'd spent many an evening sprawled across this bed after Mandy had gone to sleep, talking of beaus and life and love.

"Scary," Rory answered without thought. At Cissy's raised eyebrows, she regretted the admission. "McCloud has some weird California notion that we need to preserve the whole island." She might admire his idealism if she didn't think it was selfishness behind his offer to help.

"I don't think that's what I asked," Cissy said dryly. "He doesn't talk much. How did you get that out of him?"

"He talks, when he's so inclined. He saw a turtle nest yesterday and was suitably impressed. You did good." Unable to sit still, Rory roamed the room, tucking away cosmetics and combs and hairpins.

"He's from California. He rides a bike. He hangs out at the Monkey. He's a little too much like Daddy, don't you think?"

"Probably." Rory picked up her budget file and flipped it open. She had too many things to do to discuss men, especially ones whose macho attitude concealed a dangerous level of intelligence. "But he knows computers and has a millionaire brother, so he could be useful."

"A millionaire brother?" Cissy waited for more.

"Something about his brother being a comic artist. I didn't ask questions. I wanted to pick you up before Pops talked you into riding home with him."

"You know better than that." Crossing her arms, Cissy watched her walk around the room. "I've heard about a guy on the other side of the swamp who draws comic strips. He married the owner of the hardware store. Didn't know he was a millionaire. I don't think they have anything fancy over there."

Small-town gossip never changed. The grapevine was useful, but Rory didn't know how much she wanted to get involved. She just wanted to talk with the zoning commission and be done. "McCloud is living in a shack down by the beach behind the old Newsome house. If his brother owns the Newsome place, then they've fixed it up some."

"His kind doesn't hang around long," Cissy warned. "He'll play at helping for a while, then lose a battle and disappear on that hog of his."

Rory knew her sister was speaking from experience. Mandy's father had been a college student who'd worked on the yachts in the harbor one summer. He hadn't been from around here and hadn't been seen since. Outsiders stayed and played for a while, but they seldom lingered. There wasn't anything here for them.

"I won't count on McCloud," Rory promised. "I just need him to hide the names of the Bingham heirs until I get some zoning changes."

"Ain't gonna happen." Standing, Cissy limped toward the bedroom door. "Money talks, and you'll be in the way."

Her sister sounded just like Clay. When had Cissy grown so cynical?

Going back to her budget file, Rory studied the contents, planning some way of presenting her case that would make sense to zoning commissioners with dollar signs in their eyes.

If she'd thought of gas stations and minimarts, there were others out there dreaming even bigger dreams. Best to nip those big dreams before someone started acting on them.

Emerging from Cleo's Hardware bright and early Monday morning, carrying a new wrench to replace one of Jake's he'd broken, Clay halted in the shade of a magnolia at the sight of a familiar head of sun-red hair in the street down the block. Seeing people standing in the middle of the road around here wasn't unusual. Aurora's rigid stance struck him as curious, though. She was wearing one of her business suits again, with her hair all prim and proper, but the image of gauzy skirts and braids was indelibly imprinted on his mind. He'd spent the weekend fighting the urge to see what she was up to, since she hadn't called.

Sauntering in the direction of what appeared to be a confrontation, he studied the other party involved. Tall, blond, and rich, he diagnosed from the expensive cut of the man's suit and the way he stood with hand in pocket, suit jacket pulled back at a GQ angle. Also hot and irritated, he gathered, recognizing the way Mr. GQ gestured curtly with his free hand, stepping away from Rory as she spoke.

Clay got a kick out of watching Aurora's southern version of dynamite, but this jerk didn't seem quite as fascinated. "Get real, Rora," the jerk was saying when Clay came within earshot. "We need a property tax base out there if we're to make any improvements."

He didn't think he should be eavesdropping, but it wasn't as if Mr. GQ was exactly quiet about his tirade. Standing in the shade on the sidewalk, he waited to see how Aurora replied. Given their discussion of last week, he figured she had already started to cut a swath through the planning commission. Unlike him, she seemed to have no problem getting involved or believing she could stop city hall.

"The cost of overdevelopment will be greater than any revenue from your so-called property tax base," she answered heatedly. "Read your economics, Jeff. Building a base slowly and with planning for the future will benefit the area far more."

Clay didn't like the sound of "building a base" much better. What about the turtles? And the sweetgrass?

"The place is a swamp filled with losers and misfits," Mr. *GQ* replied with scorn. "The sooner we're rid of them and building something constructive, the sooner we can have cash flow. I thought you, of all people, would understand that."

"Why, no, Jeff," she answered in mock incredulity, "Ah'm just a loser and misfit, how could Ah *possibleah* understand what's goin' through the minds of brilliant men like yourself? Cash flow! Imagine that. Ah'll be certain to keep that in mind come election day."

Clay could hear the fury behind her syrupy drawl and wondered if it was the insult or the danger to her hidden agenda that raised it. She might tickle his hormones, but that didn't mean she'd fried his brains into forgetting she had something up her sleeve besides turtles.

"You won't be here come election day," Jeff shouted in frustration, "and your swamp rats don't vote. Drop it, Rora, and do everyone a favor. The park will bring in business, and there's no reason to block progress."

Thinking the balled-up fist at Aurora's side probably wasn't a good sign, although he applauded the emotion behind it, Clay sauntered over to join the fray. He wasn't much on politics, but he suspected Aurora's anger didn't bode well for the turtles if she was already antagonizing the people whose aid they needed.

"I'll have to tell Jared the locals call him a swamp rat," he offered as both combatants turned at his approach.

"I'm sure he can turn that into a juicy item for his strip. He wields a mean pen."

"Your brother is a property owner, so he doesn't qualify as a rat," Aurora explained in a tight voice. "Jeff's referring to my father and Grandma Iris and the squatters out there. Homeless people, they call them in the city. Except here they have homes. They just don't pay for them."

He *really* didn't want to get into that. He'd much rather punch smug Mr. *GQ* in his square jaw. He couldn't remember ever wasting energy in street brawls, but he flexed his muscles menacingly, just to keep *GQ* in his place. He couldn't think of anything to add to the conversation, so he just watched the worm wiggle in silence.

Aurora picked up on his vibrations instantly. Clay bit back a snicker at the evil eye she gave him, but she made the introductions without comment. "Jeff, Clay McCloud. Clay is the state's computer expert for the park. Clay, Jeff Spencer. He's an officer of the Community Bank and on the zoning commission."

"The commission is elected?" Clay asked with feigned ignorance.

"Of course not," they both answered in unison, looking at him as if he were an ignoramus.

Again Aurora caught on quickly. Clay didn't think she was admiring his unfastened denim vest or bare chest with the look she shot him, but he smirked as if she had. She rolled her eyes and returned to the debate. He was getting a kick out of matching wits with a woman who could see right through him—and who didn't mind looking.

"Jeff is running for town council. I asked him to support our petition against rezoning the island until an environmental study can be done."

He didn't know they had a petition, but he was sure they'd have one the minute they got out of this street. "Fair enough. I'll get Cleo on it. C'mon, we'll go talk to her. She knows all the swamp rats and every other rodent up and down the coast. Great meeting you, Jeffy!"

Not giving the puffed-up banker a chance to retaliate, Clay grasped Aurora's elbow and all but dragged her out of the middle of the road to the shaded sidewalk. Keeping the momentum, he marched her back up the road to the hardware store. He figured she was too steamed to speak, and he'd like to keep it that way as long as possible.

Actually, he kind of liked holding her elbow and having her match him stride for stride. Upon occasion he'd absentmindedly outwalked frilly women who minced about in high heels.

He was much too conscious of Aurora's in-your-face presence to forget her. Her floral fragrance wafted around him, and he sneaked a peek at the way her thigh-high skirt slid up her leg. He was damned glad she didn't wear jeans like every other woman in the universe. Pity it wasn't a little leather number instead of another of her business suits. If he kept his thoughts purely on sex, he wouldn't have to wonder what in hell he thought he was doing.

"This had better be good, McCloud," she muttered as he shoved open the old-fashioned wooden door of Cleo's store.

Ignoring her threat, Clay shouted for his sister-in-law while steering Aurora through the maze of paint cans and lawn tools to the counter in the back of the store.

A head shorter than both of them, her short copper curls tousled from her habit of running her hand through them, Cleo eyed their approach with the same skeptical expression Clay normally wore. Seeing it, Aurora laughed out loud and pulled away from his hold.

"Hi, I'm Rory Jenkins, and I bet you're Clay's ever-suffering sister-in-law. I'll haul him right back out of here, if you like."

The normally stoic Cleo almost broke a smile at that. Lifting rounded eyebrows in Clay's direction, she held out her hand to shake Aurora's. "Deal. Keep him away from the Monkey, throw him in the harbor occasionally, and I'll do whatever it is you want."

"A petition. We can keep a page here on the counter. I want the zoning commission to hold off on any rezoning on the island until an environmental study has been completed."

"You got it."

Clay glared at Cleo's smug expression as she cleared a stack of advertising brochures from the cluttered counter, but he didn't have to care what anyone thought. He just wanted . . .

What the hell did he want? Certainly not another MBA with a hidden agenda, although he was beginning to suspect Aurora didn't hide much. He just wanted to save the swamp.

No wonder Aurora had rolled her eyes at him earlier. Even *he* didn't believe that. He shoved his hands in his back pockets and held his tongue.

"I appreciate that." Rory produced a file from the bag slung over her back, removed several sheets of paper from it, and set it on the cleared space. "Anywhere else you'd suggest leaving one?"

"The Monkey, Kate's restaurant, and the bookstore. Why don't you give me a few of those? Jared can run them by the schools and the yacht club, and get some of the hunters and fishermen into this."

"You are a saint!"

Clay watched in amazement as she produced still another stack of papers from the bottomless bag. Maybe this wasn't an intelligent idea after all. Cleo and Aurora in one room could ignite explosions.

On second thought, he'd always liked fireworks.

"Bring me back a hamburger. I'll be making a few phone calls." Cleo tucked a petition into a pocket of her tool belt and turned an expression brimming with mischief on Clay. "I leave you in good hands."

He wasn't at all certain who was in whose hands, but he felt a need to assert himself a little more forcefully than usual as Aurora started toward the door without him.

Catching up with her, he took her elbow again, opened the door, and pushed her out. "I think that went well, don't you?" he asked dryly.

"I think I'm going to like working with you, McCloud," she replied, taking off down the street, heedless of his hold on her. "You're so damned predictable."

Predictable? He was a friggin' *genius*. Geniuses weren't predictable, were they? His ex had called him an uncommunicative sphinx in one of her better tirades. Other women had cooed and called him mysterious and enigmatic—or the ones with a vocabulary had, anyway.

He hadn't done a damned thing except take her to Cleo. Maybe he'd better make a few ground rules clear before

they got started—like that she should tell him what in
hell kind of petition they were carrying around, and why.
If he blindly trusted an MBA, he could be signing away
his rights to live and breathe.

❧ SEVEN ❧

"Coffee."

Without asking for her opinion, McCloud steered Rory down the next block, in the direction of the concession stand at the harbor. Unaccustomed to being hustled around in quite that manner, she wasn't prepared with an effective protest. She had a cup of coffee in her hand and McCloud at a picnic table across from her before she could decide if she even wanted coffee, much less whether she wanted to share it with him.

Staring at Clay's bronzed, nearly bare chest, she had to admit she didn't mind sitting here, admiring the view. He didn't have a spare ounce of fat anywhere she could see. She'd certainly never had opportunities like this at the bank. Men in suits were interchangeable obstacles to overcome, but Clay's lean abs stirred thoughts she hadn't had in a long, long time.

Except the family bad luck with the opposite sex had made a large impression on her psyche. She didn't do casual sex. It was a committed relationship or nothing for her, and she and McCloud had no basis for even basic friendship. The man was not only not her type, but he was obnoxious about proving it.

"You had something you wanted to say?" she taunted, since he said nothing. She was used to men who grabbed the conversation and ran, as if it were their goal to keep the conversational ball in their court. Clay's silences made an interesting change of pace. She scratched idly at the vendor's contest ticket that declared she could be an instant winner and uncovered the inevitable *Try again*.

"I thought you might like to tell me about those petitions." He sipped his coffee and watched her through narrowed eyes. "I thought you *wanted* development out there."

A gull squalled from the sandy playground behind them. The outboard motor of a sailboat chugged sluggishly as it backed out of a docking station. People strolled the boardwalk along the harbor and sat at tables on the restaurant patios above. In this idyllic setting, she had no reason to fear the tall man sitting across from her. She supposed she ought to, since he'd just hauled her down here like a dog on a leash.

Only she'd learned from her father not to judge people by their appearances. It would be a lot easier if she could label Clay McCloud a biker or beach bum, sniff, and not give him the time of day. He certainly worked at maintaining the look: sun-bleached, uncut hair, three-day-old beard shading his angular jaw, denim vest, cutoff jeans, and sandals.

But she'd seen his high-tech computer and the programming language and his reluctant fascination with the turtles. She suspected there was more to this man than readily met the eye.

Or she could be fooling herself. She'd done that before.

"I talked to some of the commissioners," she finally

answered when he sat there without saying another word. "They weren't interested in hearing about environmental planning or limited zoning or anything else unless it's backed by money. I figured they might listen if we were more than a few voices screaming into a vacuum."

Clay nodded and sipped his steaming coffee. "From what your friend said, you may get signatures, but you're not likely to have many voters on that petition."

"It's not a legal document. A petition can't change zoning. It just gives us a little popularity edge."

"It also gives the bank and other interested parties fair warning that trouble lies ahead." He sipped his coffee and waited.

Rory winced. She hadn't thought of that. She studied the problem from all angles, then shook her head. "I can't see how it will matter unless someone wants to bribe us not to interfere. People on the island would take the money and *still* sign the petition."

His mouth quirked upward in one corner. "Okay, I'll buy that. But a petition won't convince the commissioners if they're thinking of condos and property tax bases. Short of locating the town's missing World War Two cache, you can't change things."

She didn't believe those old bar stories any more than she believed fairy tales. Even if the town had lost some stolen German spy hoard, no one could find it.

Setting the coffee aside, Rory rubbed her forehead. She'd love to see a small grocery store on the island. It was a ten-mile drive just to pick up food and medicine. In bad weather, that was a dangerous mission. Decent housing was desperately needed. And Jeff had been right:

She did understand about the property tax base the county needed to improve schools.

But big developers would bulldoze all the marshland and woods without consideration of the needs of the people on the island.

She shook her head. "One good hurricane, and the island really would sink if they pave all that land. I don't understand short-term thinking. Take the money now because tomorrow we die?"

There for a moment, she almost thought she saw Clay's eyes sparkle with approval at her sarcasm. He had disconcertingly light gray eyes that contrasted with his bronze coloring, and long dark lashes that spared his broad nose from harshness, giving him an almost approachable look.

He shattered the illusion by grinning. "Because we all live on a yellow submarine?"

And here she thought she was having a rational conversation with him for a change. She offered her innermost thoughts, and he *laughed* at her! Why did she even bother trying?

"Screw you, McCloud." Standing, she heaved her nearly full cup into a trash bin and stalked toward the boardwalk. She had too many things to do to put up with that attitude.

He fell into step beside her without a hitch. "No sense of humor. Do they suck it out of you in MBA school?"

"At a risk of repeating myself, screw you. I don't find anything laughable about my home." She wished she could outwalk him. She wished he'd just leave her alone and go away. What was he getting out of this, anyway? It wasn't as if he'd hang around long enough to care.

Even after she left here, she'd care, wouldn't she? This was her home. She would stay in touch. He wouldn't.

"Have you called the EPA yet or did you just putter around making up pretty pieces of paper this weekend?" he asked.

Rory reacted to his insult rather than ponder her guilt if she left the island for her career. "My mother taught me not to hit," she said calmly enough, not slowing down. "Cissy told me not to hit anyone smaller than I am, which makes more sense. You're not smaller than me. Do they have a boxing ring at the gym or shall I just let you have it right here?"

"I know I'm gonna regret this." Clay took a step ahead of her and stopped.

Rory almost ran him down, but he was too quick. Before she could dodge, he'd grabbed her wrists and pulled them behind her, and they were chest-to-chest, standing beneath the hooves of the statue of the Confederate general's horse.

She didn't stand a chance. It wasn't just Clay's iron-hard grip, although she couldn't have escaped that if she tried. The problem was that she didn't want to try.

"You have the most amazing mouth," he murmured, not in a sensual whisper but with puzzlement. "It's a wonder no one has showed you how to keep it shut."

Since that wasn't precisely an invitation to seduction, she didn't guess his intent until Clay's lips slanted across hers. She almost melted into her shoes right then and there.

Oh, gad. He was amazing in every way. His arms supported her so her weakened knees didn't collapse. His hard chest against her breasts aroused and tantalized until she almost whimpered for more. And his mouth! It didn't tease but deliberately took and tasted and lingered and made her feel as if he could have stood there all day just kissing her.

He made her feel like the most desirable woman in the world. As if she were worth taking the time to learn, one seductive step at a time. They were both breathless when a deliberate cough intruded, forcing them back to the real world of staring passersby and snickering teenagers.

Still keeping his grip on Aurora, Clay glanced up and glared, hoping to chase off whoever had turned off the best kiss he'd ever shared. He didn't want to let her go.

"It's not even noon, little brother. Most people who want to neck in public wait until dark."

Clay contemplated popping Jared, then shoving him into the nearest trash can for embarrassing Aurora. But before he could carry out either action, Aurora jerked from his hands to crouch down beside the stroller Jared was pushing.

"Oh, she's adorable! What's her name? Look at those big brown eyes! Hi, sugar, did you get those eyes from your daddy?"

Clay stared in incredulity as the uptight MBA in her straitlaced business suit morphed into a cooing, sweet-talking, laughing enchantress. Even Jared looked dazed as Aurora shed her suit jacket to give Midge a better grip on the shell-and-crystal necklace plucking sunbeams from the sky and arranging them around her neck—not to mention down a glorious chest clad now in just the thinnest silk.

"Meet Aurora Jenkins," Clay said dryly when she completely ignored their presence in favor of the baby.

He'd had his mind bent and his ears blown out by that kiss, and she acted as if they'd pecked each other's cheeks.

Or maybe this was her way of hiding her embarrassment.

Feeling oddly proprietary at that thought, Clay crouched down on the other side of the stroller. Letting Midge grip his finger, he nodded upward at his brother. "That's Jared, and this is Midge. They belong to Cleo."

"Don't mind me, I'm just part of the stroller," Jared commented from above, watching both of them with curiosity. "And don't let Cleo hear you calling her Midge. Her name is Megan."

Clay had a lot of practice ignoring his brother, but Aurora's cheeks were still pink, and she looked across the stroller at him with uncertainty. "It's okay," he assured her. "He's nuts and doesn't bite."

She giggled at that. Actually giggled. Feeling as if he'd climbed Mount Everest and discovered gold, Clay caught her elbow and dragged her upward.

"Pleased to meet you, Jared," she said in her best business-polite manner. "You have a lovely daughter."

"So did Mrs. Brown," Clay muttered. He didn't know precisely how he felt now that she'd returned to normal, but he didn't mind standing at her elbow, looking down her enticing cleavage while he figured it out.

"Does insanity run in the family?" she continued without any change in her inflection.

Jared beamed. Clay cleared his throat and backed off.

"Not that we've noticed," Jared claimed. "Doubting Thomas simply doesn't believe modern music matches the golden age of oldies. Mrs. Brown's lovely daughter refers to an English tavern song from the sixties."

"Of course, the classics, how foolish of me. I should

have known a man of intelligence and erudition wouldn't listen to anything else."

Clay raised his gaze to the heavens and pursed his lips in a whistle. Okay, she was getting even with him for her embarrassment. He was a big boy. He could take it. He even got a cheap thrill out of it.

"Nah, he's a genius with extremely bad taste in music, that's all."

"Hence the fascination with the Blue Monkey. I understand. The bar is full of geniuses. It was nice meeting you, Jared. If you're ever out our way, please stop by. My father makes a baby rabbit statue that children adore."

Shoving his hands into his pockets, Clay watched Aurora fling her jacket over her shoulder and saunter off, swinging her hips enticingly in the tight red skirt. A whistle inadvertently escaped his lips.

"I'm going to enjoy this, aren't I?" Jared asked rhetorically, not turning to watch Aurora but watching Clay instead.

"Nope, but I might." Without explanation or farewell, he took off after her. Did she really think that after a kiss like that he would simply disappear in a puff of smoke?

He probably ought to, his brain told him. He'd been burned once by her type, and he wasn't the kind of fool to get burned again.

But this was the twenty-first century. He may have had his head buried in a computer for the last quarter of the previous century, but he knew what was happening out in the real world.

He didn't have to propose marriage to have sex.

* * *

Aurora heard Clay behind her but didn't turn around to look. His kiss had scorched her clear down to the bottoms of her feet and probably burned out a few brain cells as well. She couldn't believe they'd done that in clear view of the entire populace of the city, including his brother and niece. *Gads!* Hadn't she learned from her mother and sister?

A brown hand shoved open the plate-glass door of Katy's restaurant before she could reach for it.

"I don't need your help, McCloud," she muttered as they entered. She could tell the locals from the tourists by which ones lifted their heads to see who'd come in. She nodded greetings at several familiar faces, wending her way through the dinette tables without stopping.

"You can't send me up in flames and just walk away like that," he murmured, catching her elbow to slow her down.

"You can't embarrass me in front of the entire town and expect me to thank you for it!" She tugged her elbow free.

"You're just as charming as I am, you know that?" he said in his usual scalding tone.

Aurora glanced up at him incredulously, then swallowed a laugh at his aggrieved expression. At least he was blaming himself as much as her. "Back off, McCloud, you're making a big mistake here."

"Wouldn't be the first time." He grabbed her heavy bag from her shoulder and slipped it over his. "This thing weighs as much as the Rock of Gibraltar. What are you carrying in here? The public library?" Rummaging around in the contents, he found her file folder and produced a petition.

She was used to lugging the bag around, but she wasn't

arguing if he wanted to play Macho Man. She was actually getting a kick out of his attempts to stay on her good side. It had been a long while since a man had spent time learning what she was about. "Give the lady the petition without the commentary. I have work to do today."

The tall waitress behind the counter wiped her hands on her apron and waited expectantly. Clay bent past a row of counter stools to hand her the petition. "Cleo said you might keep this by the cash register and help us get some signatures."

The waitress grinned broadly, didn't take the petition, and waited. Clay squirmed. He shot Aurora a frustrated look. Understanding that McCloud had given Stella his bad-boy treatment, and the waitress intended to make him grovel, Rory contemplated letting her. But she didn't have enough time on her hands for games. And she didn't think Clay was good at groveling.

"It's okay, Stella. I'm cutting him off at the ankles. I need to pass a few more of these around this morning, so if you want to take a jab at him, let's do it now and move on."

Stella delicately accepted the petition between two fingers. "Whaddayuh say, McCloud?"

He growled. He scowled. He shoved his hands in his pockets and copped a biker stance. With Aurora's bag over his shoulder, the effect was lost. Stella grinned more broadly.

"Please," he muttered. "If you want to save the sea turtles."

"Why do I want to save turtles?" Stella waved the petition tauntingly.

Aurora knew half the people in the café were watching, but Clay didn't seem particularly concerned about that. He simply didn't know how to bend a little. She elbowed him out of the way. "You want to save Cleo and me and Cissy and Grandma Iris and the sweetgrass baskets." She pulled another paper out of the bag over Clay's shoulder. "Here's one for Katy. She can put it in the B-and-B. Fry up a burger for Cleo and we'll be back to pick it up."

Catching Clay's elbow, she swung him around and marched him past the sea of staring faces, leaving Stella to do as she wished with the petition.

"I knew there was a reason so many people prefer computers to real life." He removed his arm from her grip as they reached the sidewalk.

"Because computers are mindless slaves that don't talk back?" She tried to retrieve her shoulder bag but he stubbornly held on to it. Brown leather and large, it looked more like a backpack than a woman's purse, but it still didn't look natural on his denim-covered shoulder. "Look, this will be faster if we split up. Take a handful of the petitions and hit your favorite haunts, and I'll hit mine."

"What, and get that kind of reception everywhere I go? No, thank you. The jackass will haul your saddlebag. You do the talking."

He really did look grumpy at his inability to intimidate Stella, and Aurora had to stifle a laugh. Male egos were such fragile things. She patted his sculpted biceps understandingly. "Maybe if you try using sugar instead of lemon, you'll fare better with the ladies."

"Will sugar work with you?" He lifted a skeptical eyebrow.

Hit with the intense focus of those dark-lashed gray

eyes, she almost succumbed to the desire fluttering in her belly.

Remembering her mission, she shook her head. "Nope, and I don't like lemonade either."

She thought she might be lying to herself, but she started down the street trailing Clay McCloud behind her anyway. Having a partner in one of her crusades was a new and rather tantalizing experience. She'd find out soon enough if he could be trusted.

❦ EIGHT ❧

Clutching the letter from Mandy's school, Cissy hobbled in the direction of the ringing telephone. She wanted to ball up the letter and cry, but she'd quit the watering-pot business at seventeen, when she'd had to grow up fast.

Mandy would be seventeen all too soon. She wanted her daughter to have the opportunities she hadn't had. She wanted Mandy to have the whole world at her feet, like Aurora did. It would be worth everything she'd sacrificed over the years if Mandy could rise above her surroundings and make a difference in the world.

The letter in her hand would help Mandy accomplish that. All she needed was five hundred dollars, and Mandy could spend her summer at the university learning all those things her mother couldn't teach her about succeeding in college. There was no question in Cissy's mind that her daughter would qualify for any scholarship she wanted, but clothes and living expenses would always be a problem. If she couldn't come up with a lousy five hundred dollars, how would she provide for all those other things Mandy would need?

She might as well dream of five million dollars when she had five dimes in her purse and no job.

Tripping over a chair leg and nearly falling, Cissy grabbed the phone on the fourth ring. "Yes?"

"Sandra Jenkins?" a male voice inquired.

Except for her father, men didn't call her, and this wasn't her father. "I'm not interested." Annoyed that she'd risked life and limb stumbling through the house for a sales call, she started to hang up.

"Miss Jenkins, you'll be interested in this."

Her hand slowed. Warily, she used her cane to boost her onto the stool and returned the receiver to her ear. "Unless you're offering me a job, I'm still not interested."

She couldn't go back to her department-store position yet—didn't know if she ever could. Her hip ached, and it would be weeks before she could move around fast enough to work properly. The doctors weren't making any promises. She could type, but no one wanted typists in this day and age of computers. She didn't have any talent she could sell except painting her father's statues, and that didn't pay. She'd be reduced to playing the lottery and praying if something didn't turn up soon.

"Better than a job, Miss Jenkins. My name is Ralph Turner. I'm with Commercial Realty, and my firm is prepared to offer you a considerable sum for your property," said the voice over the telephone.

Cissy snorted. "Right. And all I have to do is tour your condo on Hilton Head, right? I think you've got the wrong number."

"No, ma'am, I don't. Our firm is purchasing a few lots along your road to pave the way for a new development. Records show you as the owner of one of the parcels. We're prepared to offer ten thousand an acre, and if you wish, you may take the house with you."

Cissy abruptly slid from the stool to search for a note-pad. *Ten thousand an acre?* She did a rough calculation. There were probably over thirty acres, all told. Totally useless for farming. Good for a little duck hunting back around the marsh but not much else. Ten thousand times thirty acres—three hundred thousand dollars. She'd have to split it with Aurora, of course, but one hundred fifty thousand dollars . . . That was more money than she could bring home in a decade. She could pay for Mandy's education and have plenty left over.

Ten thousand an acre was a totally outrageous price. She might have dropped out of high school, but she wasn't an idiot. She knew what marshland sold for out here. They weren't near the beach or the main highway. She had neighbors all around her. Why her property? "Are you offering everybody that?" she asked suspiciously.

"We need only the one lot in a central location," the voice answered smoothly. "Yours is ideal, but if you're not interested, we'll call our second choice."

"How much time do I have to decide?" She had to ask Aurora. She and Aurora owned the land jointly, but Aurora didn't want to live here and wouldn't mind selling. She didn't know about their father. He didn't own the land, but he owned the building out back, where he lived and made his monuments. They'd have to compensate him for it.

"We need a decision fairly quickly, Miss Jenkins."

She could keep her house. She could find a cheaper lot, move it down the road. . . .

"No, I'm sorry," she answered abruptly, surprising herself. "It won't work. I can't buy more land and still afford to move my house for that kind of money. Thank you, but—"

"You drive a hard bargain, Miss Jenkins. We own some lots farther toward town. We can throw in one of those and use our equipment to move your house as part of the deal. You'd be closer to schools and shopping. The lot won't be as large, but it will be solid ground."

She would hate to leave her neighborhood, but Mandy wouldn't have so far to go to school. "I'd have to see the lot," she answered cautiously.

"Of course. We understand. Is there a good time for me to drive you over there?"

Three hundred thousand dollars. Mandy's education. Maybe even her own. A future. A spike of hope caught her breath and brought tears to her eyes. It had been a long, long time since she'd felt anything like hope.

When it came to Mandy, she had no sentimentality whatsoever for the land her mother's family had owned for generations. She loved her neighbors and loved the security of her familiar home, had never dreamed of leaving, as Aurora had, but she would sacrifice her life for Mandy.

Desperately, closing her eyes and crossing her fingers for luck, Cissy prayed Aurora would agree.

"Around two?" she suggested.

"One of the neighbors brought over some boiled shrimp last night. It just needs shelling. I can toss it with a little pasta and pesto and make a salad; it won't take a minute." Aurora pushed open the trailer's front door. A blast of cold air hit them as she led Clay into the dim interior. Cissy must have turned on the air-conditioning. Cissy didn't like to waste money on utilities. Was she not feeling well?

Concerned, Aurora switched on the overhead lamp to brighten the big front room, but she didn't see her sister napping on the couch as she usually did when her hip pained her. "Ciss?" she called. "Mandy? Anyone here?"

It was after four. Mandy ought to be home from school. Cissy didn't have a car and hadn't told her of any plans for going out with friends today.

"Maybe they're out in the shop?" Clay suggested, dropping her heavy purse on the coffee table. "Listen, I really ought to be going anyway. You don't have to feed me."

Impatiently she ignored his insincere suggestion. He'd followed her around all day, braving the heat and stares and annoying questions with formidable patience. She didn't know any man who would have withstood the endless barrage of talk for more than a few minutes, much less all day. He'd impressed her with his tenacity.

He'd even learned part of her spiel by day's end and had persuaded the owner of the Monkey to set out a petition. For someone as nontalkative as Clay, that was an even more impressive feat. She didn't know whether it was libido or ego that prompted him, or if he really was that concerned about the turtles, but the least she could do was feed him. Their lunch had consisted of inhaling the odor of grease on Cleo's hamburger.

She crossed the green carpet to the galley kitchen and read the whiteboard hanging on the refrigerator door. *Back soon* was scrawled there in Cissy's handwriting. *Out back* followed in Mandy's. Someone had taped a losing lottery ticket to the bottom of the board—a running joke for their gambling tax deduction.

"A friend must have picked her up." Aurora opened the refrigerator and hauled out the bowl of shrimp, dropping it on the counter. "If you'll start on these, I'll start the water boiling for pasta and mix the salad."

At his silence, she glanced up. Clay prodded a boiled shrimp as if it were some new form of computer hardware and he couldn't find the switch.

"You do know how to prepare shrimp, don't you?"

"If they come out of a freezer, I eat them." He picked one up by the tail and examined it closely. "They have legs this way."

Laughing, she snatched it away. "You start water. I'll do shrimp."

"If it had an engine, I could make it work," he offered helpfully, maneuvering around the counter into the galley and helping himself to a pan hanging over the stove.

A man standing in her tiny kitchen captured her attention. His head brushed the pots she'd hung over the counter, and his shoulders blocked all view of the cabinet behind him. Even her father avoided her woman's domain. Mesmerized, she watched him study the size of the pan and the amount of water filling it as if it was an interesting science experiment. She had to take a deep gulp of air to drag her gaze back to the shrimp.

A car crunching the gravel drive distracted her. She didn't know what Cissy's reaction would be to having a male stranger in the house. Living together like this, they'd developed a few unspoken rules. Not bringing men into the house was one of them. She'd like to speak to Cissy first, before Clay's presence caught her by surprise. Crossing the room, she pulled back the sheer draperies over the picture window.

A distinguished silver-haired man assisted Cissy from a shiny white Cadillac. They appeared to be in earnest discussion, so she didn't want to intrude, but she watched with concern. Cissy had quit dating years ago. Potential employers did not drive potential employees to and from an interview. Who could the man be?

She felt Clay watching over her shoulder. "Salesman," he declared with a touch of cynicism. "Do you need a vacuum cleaner?"

She chuckled in agreement. "Maybe Cissy decided to test-drive a Cadillac." Her sister looked more animated than she'd been in years. Fighting back anxiety, she tried to be happy for her. Cissy didn't have a lot to be excited about these days. Maybe she'd won the lottery. That would account for wasting air conditioning on an empty house.

"I'll talk her out of it. Cadillacs are all looks and no go." Clay opened the front door and stepped outside to assist Cissy up the stairs.

"Did they talk to you, too?" she asked excitedly as Clay handed her through the doorway. "What do you think? Are they legit?"

Behind Cissy, Clay shook his head and shrugged. He'd pulled on a T-shirt he'd retrieved from his motorcycle bag earlier, but he still looked more biker than computer wizard. Aurora caught a wary expression in his eyes before he turned to aid Cissy in taking a seat on the couch.

"I don't know what you're talking about, Ciss. Explain. I'm fixing shrimp. Want some?" Food first, to settle the anxiety gnawing at her middle. She didn't attempt to discern which anxiety unsettled her the most. She'd just let time and a full stomach take care of them.

Mandy slammed in through the back door before her mother could say a word. "Who was that in the Caddy?"

Clay looked as if he'd like to bolt. Standing uneasily in the low-ceilinged trailer, his broad shoulders filling the empty spaces between the women, he didn't fit in here. But they were used to their father and worked around him. Aurora shoved a pot in his hands and pointed at the sink. Obediently, he filled it with more water.

"That was Mr. Turner from Commercial Realty." Excitement spilled out with Cissy's words, and her eyes danced with it. "He just showed me a wonderful lot down on Obadiah Lane. It's in a real nice development. The neighbors drive SUVs and have sailboats!"

Rory shoved half the bowl of shrimp at her niece. There wasn't much point in attempting to figure out what Cissy was talking about until she came to the point. "You're planning on moving?"

"That's just it! They'll move us. I don't know about Daddy's business, though." A look of worry crossed Cissy's pale features, but she dismissed the passing thought in favor of another. Sheer happiness lit her from within. "They're offering us ten thousand an acre, Rora. *Ten thousand!* We couldn't get that kind of money anywhere."

Very gently Aurora set her bowl down. Her gaze flew to Clay, who had stopped running water to listen. She saw the same concern in his eyes that she knew was in hers. Clay possessed a skeptical outlook. She preferred to be optimistic, but what were the chances that bolts of fortune really did strike out of the blue—without frying their targets?

"Who's offering that kind of money?" she asked. "And why?"

"I assume Commercial Realty," Cissy said with a shrug. "They want to build something here. They said they'd go to one of the neighbors if we didn't accept the offer, so why shouldn't we be the ones to take it?"

"You have a computer here?" Clay asked quietly.

Aurora indicated the door to the master bedroom with a nod. Cissy had taken over the other end of the trailer when Mandy was born. Aurora had stored her furniture and simply moved into her old room when she returned.

She instantly had second thoughts about allowing this almost total stranger into her private quarters, but her protective instincts overcame any lingering need for privacy. She lived in a trailer, after all. Privacy had been a moot point since she moved back here. "I can't imagine you'll find anything on Commercial Realty, though," she told him. "They're a front."

He ignored that. "Password?"

"Sugarbaby." Aurora grimaced at his raised eyebrows, but neither of them wasted time on commenting. If what they suspected was true, they had a nasty problem on their hands.

Clay strode off in the direction of her bedroom, oblivious to the stares of her family. He had such an easy way of slipping into his shell without regard to anyone else that Aurora almost envied it. Especially now.

Mandy was pattering her mother with questions that Cissy eagerly fielded, describing the lot, the neighbors, the closeness to the harbor and town. Aurora crushed the shrimp shell in her hand.

Maybe the deal was legit. Maybe someone wanted to

build a gas station here. That would be all right, she
thought. Some local fellow with big dreams—he might
even let Pops keep the workshop. It wasn't logical, but
hope never was.

Cissy threw her a worried look when Rory didn't leap
into the excited discussion. But what could she say? The
park didn't even exist on paper yet. She couldn't believe
some outsider had already heard about the park and seen
the potential for development.

Clay had warned her that they would stir things up
with the zoning petition. Having her home bought out
from under her wasn't what she'd thought he meant.

There wouldn't be any way she could tell Cissy no.

She didn't want to tell her sister no. She wanted this to
be legit.

She cracked another shrimp shell and prayed.

"You're not very excited," Cissy finally called over to
her. "Do you think it's a bad deal?"

"I'm afraid it sounds too good to be true," Rory answered cautiously. "I always examine the undersides of
rainbows."

She hated the defeated look that entered her sister's
eyes. Cissy might be the eldest and the closest thing Rory
had to a mother, but she looked to Rory for the money
decisions.

"I knew it," Cissy said in discouragement. "I should
have just hung up the phone. What do you think they're
trying to pull?"

Before Rory could find an answer, the back door
slammed open and Jake entered. "Thought I heard you
come home. Got enough of that shrimp for me?"

The sisters exchanged looks. Even if the offer was legitimate, here was the main stumbling block. Where would Jake go if they sold the land and Cissy moved to a development? He lived in a small set of rooms off the workshop and ate most of his meals here. The statues littering the yard were the only income he possessed. He wasn't old enough for social security, and he'd never saved a dime in his life.

"Sure, Pops. Want to make some of that hot sauce you like? I know you don't like the pesto." Rory reached in the refrigerator for the ingredients, praying Clay came up with an answer soon.

They didn't have high-speed Internet lines out here, and Cissy couldn't afford cable, so any Web search would be slow. He'd have to have magic fingers to drag out information fast enough to give them answers now.

"Got any fries? That'll do me." Jake grabbed the ketchup and Worcestershire and began mixing them in a small bowl Rory handed him.

The silence from the living room was almost deafening. Operating on automatic, Rory found the ingredients for her father's supper, for the salad, for the pesto. Growing up, she'd learned to cook in self-defense, since Jake didn't cook and Cissy was always working. Figuring she ate three times as much as her sister, it seemed only fair at the time. It was a comfort now.

"What are y'all so silent about?" Jake demanded, finally noticing the quiet. "You hiding a man in the bedroom?"

Mandy giggled. Cissy rubbed her nose, a certain indication she was hiding something.

Relieved to find a different direction for her thoughts, Rory opened a beer and handed it to her father. "Yup.

We trussed up your friend McCloud and threw him in the bedroom to use later tonight."

"Don't doubt that." Jake threw back a swallow of beer and set the can down before continuing with a twinkle in his eye. "Heard y'all had a good time at the harbor today."

Oh, sugar. Word traveled entirely too fast in this town. Turning red, Rory grabbed a box of pasta and dumped it into the boiling water. "*He* was having a good time. I just went along for the ride."

"That was some ride," a dry male voice said from the bedroom doorway. Once certain he had the attention of everyone in the room, Clay held up a sheet of paper. "Commercial Realty is apparently the real estate arm of your local bank. It appears they're acquiring property on the island and using the realty as a holding company."

Flying, friggin' maggots. Of course the bank was behind it. They knew about the parkland and had a developer all lined up. She knew how that worked.

Ripping off her apron, she stormed out the back door and slammed the screen.

"Was it something I said?" Clay asked rhetorically, tossing the paper to the coffee table and heading after her.

No one stopped him.

NINE

"Aurora, stop it." After watching her rage up and down the garden path half a dozen times, Clay stepped in front of her and caught her arms. It had worked pretty well when he'd done this before.

This time, though, she glared at him. He threw up his hands in surrender. "Throwing a tantrum won't solve anything."

"You'd rather I exploded all over the trailer? I'd blow the roof off." She stormed past him again, but her step faltered slightly. She swung around, and he could see tear tracks down her cheeks.

Oh, jeez. He couldn't handle tears. He liked it a hell of a lot better when she was storming around town with righteous ire and justice for all in her voice. Or laughing at the foibles of life. Or even laughing at him. That was okay, too. He liked it that she didn't always take him seriously.

He sought for some means of making her feel better and failed.

"Cissy gave up *everything* for me and Mandy," she cried in a voice breaking with tears. "She used to get the best grades in class. She was so pretty, she had boys asking her out all the time. But she had to work and go to school and raise me first, and then when I was old enough to stay home on my own at night so she could finally have a little fun, she got pregnant with Mandy and had to drop out. It's not *fair*, Clay."

"We didn't sign a contract at birth saying it would be." That was as lame a thing as he'd ever said, but it made her wipe her eyes angrily so the tears went away. Tears made him feel helpless. Anger he could handle.

"She deserves something good to happen," she insisted. "I've not seen her so excited in years. She deserves a good life. I'm working on it, but there is only so much I can do. How can I deny her this?" She sounded more unhappy than mad.

Clay watched Aurora rub her hands up and down her bare arms and wished he could do that for her. She'd left off her jacket, and in her silk shell she looked more like a woman than an impersonal suit. He wanted to kiss her until she forgot her problems, but he figured he'd pretty much pushed his luck as far as it would go in that department. She'd sock him one if he tried it again. Rightly so, under the circumstances. He just wasn't certain where to go from here.

His family hid feelings as thoroughly as hers exploded with them. Just call him emotionally handicapped. Dysfunctional.

"You sure you ought to deny her this?" he asked, not knowing a better way of phrasing it. "The bank should be reasonably legit, shouldn't it?" He knew better. He knew banks were out for the biggest bang for their buck like anyone else. But he wanted it spelled out in concrete terms he could understand, not emotional fireworks that left him staggering.

"Banks don't buy real estate on speculation," she said tiredly. "They're acquiring for someone who doesn't want their name involved yet. And if they don't want their name revealed, you can guess it's for a reason."

Yeah, if some place called Sunbelt Development started knocking on doors, land prices would skyrocket, he calculated. "You could try explaining to Cissy what happens if hotels and condos are built out here."

She looked up at him with a hint of desperation. "And make her feel guilty if she still wants to sell? She's thinking of Mandy. How can I ask her to choose between Mandy and what's best for the island?"

Since he was presumably opposing the sale for his brother and his family, Clay couldn't answer that one. "Don't you think she ought to at least make an informed decision?"

"The bastards are picking on Cissy for a purpose, probably because I'm putting those petitions out there. I bet Jeff Spencer is behind this." She hugged herself and looked away. "They figure Cissy is the weak link, that she'll agree to the sale, and once the land is gone, I'll lose interest and leave the swamp alone."

"But the land belongs to both of you, doesn't it?" he argued. "She can't sell without your consent."

She shook her head. "That's what this Bingham thing is all about. The law says all they need is one owner's signature on a sales agreement. They can take that to court and ask for a property partition. My signature is irrelevant. They don't have to offer me anything."

"The court will order your land auctioned to divide it?" he asked in disbelief.

With a look of misery, she nodded. "Cissy doesn't understand that the sales agreement is only for her share. Once she signs, they don't have to offer me anything. They'll simply demand that the court divide the property. The deed doesn't specify which of us owns which part of the land, so the court would have to divide it up in lots and sell it. An auction will generate peanuts because no one else in their right minds would want this land, much less bid against the bank, so there will be only one offer to buy—theirs. Under the agreement she signs, they may pay Cissy ten thousand an acre for half the lots, but they'll offer squat for my half. Unless I can bid against them on the choice pieces, I'll be left with inaccessible, worthless swamp."

"Explain that to your sister." Since he'd had considerable luck with repositioning her earlier, Clay caught Aurora's elbow and steered her toward the back door. She dragged her feet, but he figured she didn't have anywhere else to run. That she actually listened to him filled him with wonder. She didn't strike him as a woman who listened to just anyone.

He had the insane urge to find her a million dollars and solve all her problems. She looked as if he were marching her to the guillotine when he opened the door to usher her in.

The gathering inside slipped away from the back windows and pretended they were setting the table as he and Aurora entered. Clay thought this was the moment to make his exit. He wasn't the kind of social animal who fit well into his own family's get-togethers, much less someone else's. But Aurora took a stack of plates from her sister and handed them to him, and he didn't know how to escape her expectations.

He'd never set a table in his life, but he placed a plate in front of each chair while Aurora stirred her pasta and haltingly explained how the bank could be hoping to stop her rezoning petition by buying their land.

She explained how the state could use the same tactics to auction off the Bingham land right out from under Grandma Iris, giving the heirs almost nothing. After she told them the buyer could pave the marsh clear down to the state park line and cover it in condos, the silence from her audience filled the room and threatened the seams holding the house together.

"Bastards," Jake muttered when she was done. He crumpled his beer can and flung it at the wastebasket. Aurora automatically leaned over and picked the can off the floor where it fell.

Cissy remained silent as Clay helped her into one of the chairs at the table. There were only four, but Jake seemed more comfortable at the counter with his purple cast stretched out to one side.

"If you agree not to sell, will you trust me to make this up to you?" Aurora asked, placing the bowl of pasta and shrimp in the center of the table. "I'll pay you back."

Mandy glanced anxiously from mother to aunt and intelligently reached for the pasta rather than speak. Clay thought he'd rather sit at the counter with Jake, but Aurora handed him a beer and indicated a chair. Awkwardly taking his place with the three women, he tried to stay out of the argument.

"I can't make the home-equity payments without a job

or ask you to spend all your money on us." Cissy poked
listlessly at her salad. "They'll do whatever they want
anyway. You can't change anything."

That had been Clay's belief, but Aurora didn't strike
him as the type to give up without trying. Viking blood,
he decided, watching all her pretty feathers ruffle and the
gleam of battle light her eyes. She could almost make him
believe anything was possible, including waking his
slumbering concern for the world outside his.

Cynicism had slammed the doors of his world long
ago. Aurora battered holes in the doors, giving him
glimpses of new views. Scary, but interesting.

"Don't you see?" Aurora demanded, her graceful fingers flying in forceful gestures, her face lit with animation. "Someone is already running scared if they're trying
these tactics. They don't need our lot if they can have the
Bingham acreage. They're doing this in hopes the money
will shut me up."

"But if they turn the Bingham land into condos, it
won't be worth living out here. Why shouldn't we take
the money?" Cissy was practically pleading, although
she didn't lift her gaze from the plate.

"Mama, I'll get scholarships. I don't need the money
for college. We can't let them sell out Grandma Iris. And
what about Grandpop? Where would he put all his
stuff?" Mandy reluctantly came down on Aurora's side.

Clay watched the frailer sister struggle with her conscience and her hopes and her needs, and couldn't bear
the pain in Aurora's eyes as she watched it, too. Even
Jake kept his mouth shut, but his face looked ashen and
old for the first time since Clay had known him.

Before he could bite his tongue, Clay pointed out the

obvious. "Once the state park is built, the value of this land will skyrocket. It could be worth a few million in a few years, or you could develop a profitable commercial business here with the right zoning." He couldn't believe he was saying this. The state park was an extremely bad idea, in his opinion. Commercial businesses were worse. But he hated seeing anyone looking so downtrodden.

Damn Aurora, but she was twisting his head around to see her side. Her face lit with surprise and pleasure at his new position on their argument. It was almost worth the trouble he was getting himself into just to see her look at him with admiration and approval. He usually got that from women only when he handed them jewelry.

Cissy looked hopeful for a moment, then shook her head. "That's years away. We'll starve before that happens. And it takes money to make money. We don't have it."

Aurora started to speak, but Clay plowed ahead before she could offer to pay her sister again. For whatever reason, he was willing to dismiss her MBA and her hidden agenda and believe that she worked for what was right. He *needed* to do this. He wasn't much on examining motivation, but he figured doing something because it was right might clear some of the bad taste from his mouth left by the greedy tactics of his corporate experts. This was a simple problem, one he could handle.

"I can teach you how to use the computer," he told Cissy. "There are all sorts of jobs you could do with a little training. You won't have to rely on anyone else or wait for windfalls if you have a little knowledge to sell."

The way they all looked at him, Clay thought maybe the roof had come off and God had entered on a sunbeam. Uncomfortably, he reached for his beer. He'd only made a suggestion. It wasn't as if he'd achieved world peace. But Cissy looked as if he'd offered her gold, and Aurora . . .

Ah, hell. Aurora's approval would have him walking on coals if he didn't watch out. You'd think he'd learn to quit jumping into things feet first. It was always a mistake to get involved. She'd have expectations, and he didn't have any way of satisfying them.

"Could you really?" Cissy whispered, as if not trusting she'd heard him right.

His tight T-shirt bound his shoulders, and he twitched uncomfortably. "Computers aren't all that difficult. Some basic word processing and Windows would give you a foot in the door anywhere. Add graphics and you'll be hot property once people learn what can be done with them. I've been doing some work for several area businesses that you could easily take over. There's not much computer expertise out here."

The silence stretched thin, and Clay thought maybe he ought to leave. He wished he had Jared's gift of gab, or his brother Tim's obliviousness, but he didn't. He could feel the power of all the emotions bursting around the room, and he itched to escape. He didn't feel competent enough to be all they expected of him. Anyone could learn a damned computer, after all.

"You think you could teach her how to do one of them bookkeeping things?" Jake asked unexpectedly, breaking the silence.

Clay enjoyed the astonishment lighting Aurora's face. He could watch her light up like that for the rest of his life and never cease to admire it.

The oddly buoyant feeling in his chest at her reaction

caught him by surprise. It was as if all the emotions in the room had coalesced in his middle. He didn't recognize the feeling at first, but he thought it might be happiness. He was feeling *happy* because an old man had agreed to do what his daughter wanted?

The laughter and chatter that erupted would have normally shut him out. His usual mode of operation would be to pull back into his shell, finish his food, and mosey on to his empty house and his computer screen.

But Aurora's family wouldn't let him retreat. Aurora leaped up and kissed her father's cheek, then for good measure kissed Clay's. He wanted a hell of a lot more than a kiss on the cheek from her, but Mandy was jumping up to hug his neck, and Cissy sat there looking worshipful, and all the questions bouncing around had to be answered somehow.

"Are you sure this is what you want to do, Ciss?" Aurora asked as the excitement wore itself out. "It's not the same thing as having all that money in hand. It's kind of like gambling on the lottery."

"No, it's not." Excitement still burned bright in Cissy's eyes. "They can rob me of money, but they can't rob me of knowledge. Clay's right. There's no limit to what I can do once I have some salable skill. I can buy my own house and lot. Will you let me use your computer to learn until I can buy one of my own?"

"You can have the thing if it will help you get Pops organized. I can always buy another when I'm working again." Aurora swung around and pinned her father with a stare. "You did mean it, didn't you? You'll let Cissy put your stuff on paper? You'll get a bank account?"

Clay watched with interest as the older man squirmed, but they had him firmly nailed. Jake grunted and nodded.

"Reckon it's time. If you're giving up that kind of money 'cause of me, then I guess I'd better get my act in order. But I ain't gonna like it," he added for good measure.

"We're not giving it up for you, Pops. We're giving it up because the whole island will be better off if we do. It will take some time to see the benefit." Aurora leaped up again, cleared her plate off the table, and asked, "Anyone ready for strawberry shortcake? I think we should celebrate."

Clay figured he would eat anything stuck in front of him if it brought him closer to spending a few minutes alone with Aurora. She looked positively radiant right now. She could switch from tears and anger to joy and laughter as simply as flipping a light switch.

Sailing around the kitchen with confidence, she produced strawberries and an enormous cake and miraculously created fluffy whipped cream out of a frozen bowl and beaters and what looked like the stuff he poured in his coffee. It was like watching a marvelous new video game unfold. He was dying to push her buttons to see what happened next.

Instead, she pushed his.

The homemade cake Aurora set in front of him melted in his mouth and tasted like heaven. He'd eaten in L.A.'s hottest restaurants and hadn't tasted a thing while negotiating investments and talking software. He didn't think he'd ever tasted anything that could compare with this dessert prepared in a two-bit trailer in the backwoods of nowhere. The people around him didn't seem to think it an unusual event. They chattered on while spooning up strawberries as if this were an everyday occurrence instead of a religious experience.

He never wanted to go back to his diet of beer and french fries again.

Clay knew he was in trouble, but surrounded by all this feminine energy, he simply didn't care. It was akin to living inside a Christmas tree. Aurora sparkled, Cissy shined, and Mandy chimed. Lights glittered off red hair and blond. Floral fragrances mixed with the mouthwatering scents of food. Clay figured Jake would start ho-ho-hoing any moment now, develop a red nose, and climb up the chimney. He hadn't felt this included even when he'd joined Jared and his family at Christmas.

The women showered him with questions, handed him a towel to dry dishes, unself-consciously brushed by him to reach for cabinets in the narrow kitchen, and teased him with their perfumes and laughter. Aurora wrapped a towel around his waist so he wouldn't get his cutoffs wet. Jake handed him another beer. Mandy showed him the graphs she'd created on the school's computer.

By the time everything was put away and he knew it had to be time for him to go home, he didn't know if he wanted to leave. The beach cottage would be dark and lonely and silent. He'd never noticed that before. A computer had always offered him music, companionship, and intellectual challenges, and that had been enough.

With Aurora slipping her hand around his elbow and accompanying him into the night, Clay thought a computer would never be enough again. He wanted to hold the warmth of her against him, feel the brush of her breasts against his side, listen to her laughter. Take her home with him.

"A miracle happened here tonight," she murmured, echoing thoughts he hadn't put into words. "I don't think I can thank you enough. You meant it, didn't you? That you could teach Cissy?"

"I'm probably not much of a teacher," he warned. "I expect people to know what I know, and I get impatient when it doesn't come naturally. I hope you're not setting your hopes too high." He felt a little better spitting that out. He wasn't God. He'd favored the Clay part of his name for good reason. He was all too human and earthbound.

What if he opened the door to step into her world, and she slammed the door in his face? Was it worth the pain and hassle? He didn't have enough experience with real relationships to calculate the risk factor.

"It can't be as bad as me trying to teach her," Aurora asserted. "We fight, and she won't listen to me. I'm not that great at it, anyway."

"She'll still need a car to find a job," he reminded her, treading cautiously. "And she's probably right when she says the bank will do what they want. This place won't be the same if they turn the island into a sea of crackerboxes."

"It's okay. Once I go off to Chicago knowing they don't need me any longer, I can pay her back. You are a saint."

Chicago. She was going to Chicago. Of course she was. She didn't belong here. Oddly enough, that relieved some of the pressure. Whatever was happening between them wouldn't be long-term. They'd let it play out and both would go back to their own worlds when the time came. Kind of like the summer vacations he'd never really taken as a kid.

Relaxing, Clay caught a fist of sunset hair that had fallen from its pins. He couldn't hold Aurora still. It was like trying to trap a rainbow. Her eyes flashed, her mouth curled upward, her soft curves moved closer, and his lips were on hers before he knew what he was doing.

She tasted of strawberries and cream, and he died and went to heaven all over again.

With a sigh of relief and gratitude, Clay hauled her into his arms and kissed her as if he'd never let her go.

☀ TEN ☀

"Is he for real?" Cissy whispered as soon as Mandy disappeared into her bedroom with the phone.

Stunned and spinning from a kiss that had revealed the mysteries of life, Aurora sipped her bottled water and didn't answer immediately. She thought that kiss might have melted the iceberg around her heart to Popsicle-sized chunks, and now she was sailing into uncharted waters.

Only the slowly rising defeat in her sister's eyes dragged her back from her daze.

"I figure McCloud's for real," she hastily reassured Cissy. "I'm just not sure what he's expecting to get out of this." She added this more for herself than Cissy, but her sister grabbed it and ran.

"You can handle him," she said with confidence. "It will be like handling Dad."

Aurora threw her a scathing look. "Like Mama handling Pops, you mean. You know how well that worked out."

Regaining confidence, Cissy shrugged. "If you can handle the big-city fellas, you can handle a biker."

Rory wasn't at all certain it worked that way. The

"big-city fellas" wore suits and talked finance and operated on a safe turf she understood. They didn't tilt her hormones into overdrive by wearing denim vests over naked chests and kissing her as if she possessed the key to their universe. It was mighty hard to resist the kind of power he offered her.

She had to resist. She had goals here, and they didn't include dallying with itinerant beach bums, even ones who could spin a computer faster than a motorcycle. "I think it's more a matter of *you* handling him. He will make a lousy teacher unless you bop him over the head with a keyboard a few times."

Cissy looked blissfully radiant. "I can do that. Do you have any idea how much it *costs* to learn what he's willing to teach me?"

"Not a hundred fifty thousand dollars." Gloomily, Rory sat down beside Cissy, picked up the TV remote, and switched on the news. "What if I'm wrong? What if I can't get the zoning changed?"

"It will still be better than before." Undemonstrative by nature, Cissy gave her an awkward hug. "It's not the money that counts, but what we do with it. If I can send Mandy to school on money I earn, it's far better than selling out our neighbors for a pretty subdivision lot."

Tears prickled behind Rory's eyes as she hugged her sister and prayed she'd chosen the right course.

Clay's heated kiss and the excited clamor in the vicinity of her heart made it impossible to tell whether she was thinking with her head or with her hopes.

She was feeling so lucky, she ought to buy a lottery ticket.

* * *

Deciding he was in no mood to go home and get ragged on by Jared over that kiss in the park today, Clay motored down the road to the beach. If he was insane enough to antagonize the state, rile the local establishment, and become involved in the emotional chaos of the Jenkins family, he ought to at least have some understanding of *why*.

He locked his bike to a wind-gnarled oak and strolled across the boardwalk to the beach. The surf was out, but a breeze rippled his hair as he gathered his bearings and judged the distance to the turtle nests.

Aurora had said he'd be lucky to see a turtle at all. He'd run a search on-line, learned more about the primeval habits of loggerheads, but he needed to learn more. Right now, though, he wanted the real thing, not words. He wanted to know he was diving into a whirlpool for a reason, if only a symbolic one.

Hurricane-ravaged trunks littered this part of the island. Driftwood, brittle pine needles, and decades of dried grasses and leaves gathered behind the roots of trees torn from their moorings. The drought of the last few seasons had left dead trees and shrubs scattered throughout the forested area. New growth interspersed the dead. A state park might revitalize some of the natural habitat. Or not.

He strolled quietly in the gathering shadows of dusk, looking for a likely spot to watch without disturbing nature. How many turtles used this beach? How often did they nest? Was he talking a small population of animals or a large one? Was there any point in fighting for a few of the creatures?

Was there any point in fighting his attraction to a vibrant bonfire of emotion wearing the cold armor of a business suit?

Locating a fallen tree trunk still sporting branches, Clay found a seat where he could look out over the sand and ocean without being seen. Moonlight might be useful. Did the turtles come out in moonlight?

Maybe this was a mistake. It gave him entirely too much time to think. The flat screen of a computer focused his attention instead of letting him drift through his empty life.

It didn't hurt to take stock once in a while, he decided, especially if he avoided his brother's teasing by doing so. Their dysfunctional family had taught them poor communication skills. TJ let everything roll off his broad back. Jared reacted with laughter and taunts. Clay figured he pulled his head in like a turtle and let the world pass on by.

He wasn't certain he wanted to do that anymore.

Watching the shades of sunset darken to twilight, he contemplated turtles, Aurora, and amazing kisses, not necessarily in that order.

By the time he'd reaffirmed his earlier decision that sex was a desirable solution but a relationship probably wasn't possible, his ass was sore from the tree trunk, and his head ached from staring into darkness. He hadn't seen any sign of turtles.

Preparing to slide out from the branches without being slapped in the face by them, Clay sought a safe purchase on the limb in front of him. In that second he spotted the creature crawling from the sea.

In awe, he froze where he was, forgetting his awkward position while he watched the immense loggerhead haul herself from the surf and rise on four flippers to waddle determinedly across the hard-packed sand.

He tried to breathe quietly as she lumbered closer, her destination the softer, drier sand farther up the shore, beneath his feet. Settling back amid the branches, Clay prepared to watch the Jurassic age meet the twenty-first century.

Studying dinosaurs was better than the movies any day. This was the real thing—nature emerging from the primeval ooze for purposes of procreation. Ancient history in Technicolor.

Rory dialed the number of McCloud's cottage again. Nothing. Could he actually be on the courthouse roof this early in the morning? Or did he sleep late and just not answer phones?

Trying not to care, she clicked off the cordless and wandered back to the kitchen. "He's not in. I have to go over a few more figures with the tourist commission this morning. If I run into him, I'll see what he says. He may only work on his computer in the evening."

Cissy offered a bleak smile. "Maybe he didn't mean it. If he packed up and ran last night, there's still time to change my mind. I haven't told Commercial no."

More inclined to fight than accept defeat, Rory figured she'd go after McCloud with a butcher knife if he'd lied to her sister, but Cissy didn't need to hear that. "Don't tell them anything yet. No sense in warning them that their plans have been thwarted. Give me a little time to get ahead of them."

"Remember to stop at Cleo's for another can of red paint," Cissy called as Rory headed out the door. "Daddy can send that big order out next week if I finish the dwarves."

"Will do." Adding another mental note to the growing list in her head, Rory hurried down the front steps into the early-morning sunshine. She stopped to smell the magnolia-scented air and admire the sway of willow leaves over the peony bed. What would life be like out here if a developer succeeded in changing the acreage behind them into a bustling hive of apartment dwellers?

She enjoyed escaping on holidays to this slower life. It wouldn't be the same if she couldn't amble back to Grandma Iris's to buy baskets for Christmas presents, or sit on the beach on lazy summer nights and watch for the loggerheads. They'd lose the herons and cranes that lived on the fish and crabs. She might as well stay in the city without all that.

She supposed life would go on, but Cissy and her father would hate it. They'd end up selling the land and living in some development, where they'd get on each other's nerves. At least they each had their own space out here. She wanted to keep it that way.

Turning the BMW around in the gravel drive, she started toward the road, only to meet a red Jeep entering. Her father had a separate entrance with a sign for his business, but sometimes tourists took the wrong drive. She pulled her convertible to the side of the road and cut the engine.

The Jeep did the same. This close, she recognized the driver. Jared McCloud beamed at her and climbed out to admire her car.

"Nice." He ran his hand over the powder-blue finish, obviously checking out the machine and not her.

"A fascination with vehicles runs in the family?" she asked dryly, wondering what he wanted. "I'll sell you this one, if you're interested."

To her surprise, he looked interested, but then he shook his head. "Love 'em, but can't use 'em these days. Not kid-friendly. Cleo says you have birdbaths out here. Is it too early to look at some?"

"Nope. Pop's already up and about. There are some in the yard, but most of the inventory is in the next drive down. You can park here and wander over if you want."

"Thanks." Lankier than his brother, with a shock of dark hair that fell across his brow, Jared shoved his hands into the pockets of his khaki shorts and threw an uncertain look up the empty drive. "Don't suppose you have a notion where Clay is? He told one of the kids that he'd teach her his graphics program, since it's a school holiday, but he never came in last night."

Rory struggled with a kaleidoscope of emotion at this news. She wanted to say, *So what? Alley cats stray.* But from the look on his brother's face, she thought maybe this particular cat hadn't strayed lately. She ought to be appalled that Jared thought maybe Clay had spent the night here, but after what he'd observed yesterday, she really couldn't blame him.

She didn't know how she felt about Clay being the kind of homebody who caused people to worry when he didn't show up, but she recognized a quiver of fear at his disappearance. Surely no developer was desperate enough to harm anything but the environment?

"He left here after supper last night," she said. "It was before dusk. I have no idea where he was headed."

Or maybe she did. She was fairly certain her family

had unnerved him with their emotional turmoil. Clay didn't strike her as the type accustomed to living in a fish-bowl of chaos. And he'd been so totally fascinated by the turtles that he'd actually—grudgingly—agreed to help in her crusade. The idea of his whereabouts grew a little more feasible.

"The turtle nesting area is down the lane and up the beach a way. He was pretty interested. Do you think he might have—" She cut herself off at Jared's skeptical expression. Okay, so maybe she'd figured Clay wrong. "Have you asked the bartender at the Monkey if he's been in there?"

If Clay followed her father's pattern, he'd probably picked up someone at the bar. She didn't know why she thought McCloud might be different from any other man around here.

"I don't want to embarrass him by asking," Jared said sheepishly. "I'll go talk to your dad. Maybe he can nose around for me. I'm sure Clay's fine and just forgot about Kiz. I'm sorry I bothered you."

Watching Jared return to the Jeep, Rory wanted to call him back, but she couldn't think of anything to say. What did she know about Clay McCloud, anyway? That he kissed with a hunger and loneliness that called to all the empty places in her heart? Or more likely, with a learned expertise that bowled over every woman he touched. She didn't want to know how he spent his nights or that he hurt young kids with broken promises. If Jared was talking about Kismet Watkins, that poor kid didn't need any more rejection in her young life.

She didn't want to believe she'd trusted a man like that

with her sister's hopes and dreams. Watching in her rear-view mirror as Jared picked up a colorful concrete dwarf and grinned, apparently unconcerned by his brother's defection, Rory started her engine and roared out to the road.

Instead of turning toward the main highway, she swung toward the dead end by the beach. One of these days she'd quit believing in lost causes and the inherent goodness of man, but she needed Clay McCloud right now, and she didn't want to give up on him already.

Parking her car in the makeshift lot formed by years of beachgoers, Rory didn't immediately see Clay's Harley. Cursing herself for a fool and an idealistic idiot, she climbed out, glad she'd chosen platform sandals today instead of heels. She might wreck her hose but at least she wouldn't fall and break her neck.

The bike's chrome glittered from a thicket of wax myrtle at the base of a dead oak. Not knowing whether to be glad or very afraid, Rory picked her way past the thicket, along the edge of the sandy dune to the beach. Surely he wouldn't have driven back to town, picked up a twelve-pack, and passed out on the beach. She'd give the man credit for some sense.

The dune gave way to sandy beach and hurricane-lashed shrubbery and trees. She kept a sharp eye out for any turtle trails. The tide was still far enough out not to have wiped away every trace.

She saw the track before she saw Clay. She halted, glanced around to be certain she didn't disturb any fragile nests buried beneath the sand, and spotted a flash of blue on an old tree trunk behind the myrtle.

Telling herself she was insane, he was insane, and the whole wide world wasn't large enough for the two of them, she carefully trod a path along the shrubbery's edge. She halted when she could safely recognize the man sprawled along the wide trunk of a fallen oak, sleeping like the dead.

In repose, he was much safer to look upon than when awake. Dark lashes fanned across bronzed cheeks, and a stubble of dark whiskers colored his angular jaw. Sun-bleached hair rippled in the breeze, and she could almost see the boy he'd been—curious, intelligent, always seeking—maybe never finding?

Silly thought. He was a grown man, a loner who'd chosen to fritter the rest of his life away in a beach shack and make a world out of a computer. Nothing she could relate to. Spying on turtles was an interesting side she'd not expected, but she wouldn't fall victim to hormones and look for excuses to believe a footloose loner could magically turn into the caring, steady man she wanted.

"You'll develop a serious crick in your neck if you don't get up from there," she said loudly when his even breathing broke into a small snore.

The snore halted, but he didn't immediately wake, or give any indication that he was awake.

"Your brother is looking for you, something about a kid you promised to teach?" She hadn't understood the part about the graphics program, but that wasn't important. In her book, breaking promises to kids was on the same level as kicking cats.

One lid opened and a silver eye peered from under it. The eyelid closed again, and a frown appeared between his thick eyebrows.

"I don't see any beer cans, so can I assume you make a habit of sleeping in trees?"

A deep sigh caused his broad chest to rise and fall. "You're not going to go away, are you?"

"Nope. This is almost as entertaining as watching turtles nest."

"Yeah, that's what I figured." He didn't move but seemed to be assessing the number and quality of aches and pains from his uncomfortable resting place. "I take it the turtle went back to sea?"

"One assumes. They usually don't stay for daylight." With a disgruntled exhalation, she relented. She'd spent many a night out here in the summers, watching for the turtles, awed by their massiveness and determination. She couldn't blame a stranger to the area for experiencing the same effect. "Come back to the house and shower, and I'll fix you some breakfast before you go home. You're likely to have a kid waiting on your front porch, certain you couldn't have forgotten her."

"Kismet." He groaned and swung into a sitting position. Narrowing his eyes, he glared at her. "You won't let me hear the end of this, will you?"

"Haven't decided yet. But if you're in the habit of breaking promises, I might call you on it until you die." Without waiting for him, Rory started back to the car.

A man who offered to teach computers to kids and her sister was not a man who fit anywhere into her perception of the world. She either had to readjust her thinking or start running as fast as she could in the opposite direction. She didn't have time to indulge in infatuation.

❦ ELEVEN ❦

While Mandy rustled around the kitchen fixing breakfast, Cissy sat at the kitchen table with a basket of unpaid bills in the chair beside her. Head propped on one hand, pencil in the other, she tried to sum the total of the figures she'd scribbled on a piece of notebook paper, but the number she kept getting was too astronomical to comprehend. Way past the small sum she needed for Mandy's summer school.

Rory had emptied her savings to cover the deductible on Cissy's insurance and to pay part of her dad's enormous hospital bill. Cissy hated that, but looking at the pages of expenses on both bills, her eyes glazed over. Basic math said the balance remaining was larger than the Grand Canyon. And that didn't count the mortgage she hadn't told Rory about—the one with the overdue payment the bank had called about a few minutes ago. After yesterday's revelations, she understood the early-morning call meant they were pushing her to sell. Understanding didn't make it easier.

They'd have to declare bankruptcy. Would they lose the trailer? Dad's factory? She had lost her mind believing she could pull out of this.

All she had to do was pick up the phone and call the realty company. The cordless sat on the table beside her where she'd left it after hanging up on the bank call. She had Ralph Turner's card right here. . . .

The front door opened, and Rory entered, trailing a disheveled McCloud in what appeared to be yesterday's clothes, reeking of rumpled male.

Cissy tried to hide her disappointment. Last night she'd thought Clay McCloud was the answer to all her prayers. He'd appeared roughly respectable, understanding, and talented.

This morning he looked like her father after a bad night in town. She was trusting Mandy's future to a man with twigs in his hair?

"Give me a minute to clean up," Clay was saying as he entered, wielding a bundle of clothes. "I can catch something to eat at Cleo's. I don't want to terrify the kid looking like this. As Cleo says, Kiz has issues."

"If you're talking about Kismet Watkins, yeah, she's scared of her own shadow." Finishing her cereal, Mandy jumped up from the table and eyed them with interest. "You been sleeping on the beach?"

Realizing they had an audience, Clay tried not to appear embarrassed as the long-legged teenager looked from him to Aurora. How the hell did these women live in one another's pockets like this?

"Watching turtles," he replied a little more curtly than he'd intended.

"There's a shower in there." Oblivious to her niece's interest, Aurora pointed to her bedroom door. "Throw your dirty clothes out and I can put them in the machine, or next time you pull this stunt you'll only find dirty clothes in the bike's bag."

Clay thought about protesting, but with an audience watching it didn't seem worth the effort. He should have just driven home, but he was feeling guilty enough about standing Kismet up after she'd finally relented and agreed to learn the software. Scaring her to death with his rough appearance wasn't on the agenda.

He hadn't scared Aurora with his appearance. Once she knew he hadn't deserted Kiz, she'd even accepted why he was there. He couldn't think of too many women who would understand his need to see and understand things for himself.

Entering Aurora's bedroom, he glanced around with interest as he hadn't the day before. The cheap white poster bed was probably left over from childhood. The sleek desk and computer in the corner, though, looked like something he'd buy and must have come from her banker days. She'd talked about her job a little yesterday as they'd trudged from store to store. She hadn't said, but he assumed she'd left her career to take care of her family. Playing the part of caretaker wasn't the behavior of any MBA he knew, but then, Aurora was full of surprises. He was enjoying uncovering all the layers.

Maybe it was just the anticipation. He couldn't remember the last time he'd had to work at wooing a woman into bed. Had he ever?

Her bathroom wasn't large, but it held a tub with a whirlpool gadget attached and a showerhead. The jasmine scent he recognized as Aurora's blended with the potpourri of rose petals on the vanity and the lemon fragrance of her soap and shampoo. He'd never spent time

in a feminine bathroom, but he had no insecurities about
his masculinity, so it didn't intimidate him. He wanted to
explore, see if he could find the secret to unlocking Aurora's armor—only Kiz was waiting, and he didn't have
the leisure.

Using the lemon shampoo and soap, he lathered quickly,
turning on the cold to tame his unruly sex and unrulier
thoughts.

He'd thrown his dirty clothes out the door as instructed
so Aurora could take them away. She was right—he'd
probably have stuffed them back in his bag and forgotten them.

He didn't know if he liked her knowing him that well
when he knew next to nothing about her. Women had always been a mystery to him. They attached themselves
occasionally, offered sex, tried to manage his life, and
when he couldn't be managed, they'd disappear.

Diane had married his CEO after the two of them siphoned most of the funds his investors sank into the
company. He'd sold everything he'd owned to pay back
what he could. After that, he'd lost interest in following
the road to love and fortune, but a man couldn't live
without sex. So maybe he should scout the layout, learn
what made Aurora tick, and build a safe barrier to keep
her out of his life while encouraging her into his bed.

Jerking on his T-shirt and old jeans, wrapping a raw-
hide shoestring around his wet tail of hair, Clay eyed his
scruffy visage in the mirror and shrugged. He'd left the
fancy hair salons behind in L.A., and he didn't have his
shaving gear with him. Maybe he ought to think about
packing a kit in his bag. Until now it hadn't occurred to
him that he might need to be presentable to anyone.

Back in Aurora's bedroom he could hear the low murmur of feminine voices and the clanging of pots and pans from the kitchen. His stomach rumbled in appreciation of the scent of hot coffee and frying bacon. If they continued feeding him like this, he'd have to buy their groceries.

Aurora's closet and dressers were all closed, concealing any glimpse of female secrets. He could poke around on her computer, but it would look pretty suspicious if she caught him. He'd learned her screen name when he'd been in there last night. He'd have to surprise her with a virtual card.

He could program a card with laughing Dopeys and dancing rainbows. Would she get a kick out of that?

Or was she the sort to prefer expensive jewelry?

He stopped in front of the childish white dresser that matched her bed. A curlicued, gilded porcelain clock was the only ornament. No jewelry box.

Her neatness compared to his slovenly haven had him shaking his head. Was there even anything in the drawers? He'd bet that if there was, it was all neatly sorted in stacks by color.

To verify his suspicion, he tugged open a top drawer. The scent of jasmine wafted around him, and a cloud of lace and silk spilled over the edge—underwear!

Grinning, Clay admired the array of colors and frivolities. Who would have imagined this side of the straitlaced MBA? He couldn't resist envisioning Aurora's voluptuous curves framed in—

"McCloud!"

Guiltily he slid the drawer closed, shoved his hands in his pockets, and ambled toward the sound of her voice. "Coming." He wished.

He grinned to himself at the unintentional pun. Jared was the clown in the family, not him.

Aurora appeared in the doorway and eyed his casual pose with suspicion. "Admiring your pretty face in the mirror?"

"Hoping you'd left a rubber band lying around. This thing doesn't stay in. How do you keep your dresser so neat?" As the youngest of three brothers, he had the innocent pose down to a fine art.

Standing in front of her, Clay admired the thick swirl she'd tugged her hair into, but he liked it better down. Before she could come up with a sharp retort, he located the clasp, opened it, and brought the whole red-gold heap tumbling to her shoulders.

Instead of smacking him or backing off, she stayed planted where she was, studying him. "You thought you'd find a rubber band in my hair?"

He wrapped a long strand of red-gold around his finger and admired it. "It's prettier down. Softer."

He thought the tension between them escalated to stellar proportions. She watched him warily but the magnetic attraction trapped both of them. He'd never seen Aurora nervous, even when she'd been facing him down at his place when she hardly knew him. Now, after sharing those mind-blowing kisses, he was excruciatingly aware of womanly curves he wanted to touch and gorgeous eyes watching him as if he were the big, bad wolf.

Maybe it was standing in this bedroom with the froufrou bed and sexy underwear that heated his awareness and her nervousness.

Reluctantly releasing her curl, hoping to appear nonchalant, Clay sauntered past her to the women waiting in the other room.

Aurora hurried to follow Clay. She wasn't into fooling herself, so she had to admit the annoying man possessed a crude charm that rang her chimes. But she didn't have to act on that attraction. All she had to do was look around to prove she didn't need any more problems on her hands.

Cissy was wearing the closed expression she used to shut people out, which didn't bode well for the computer lessons. Was her sister having second thoughts about selling out? Please, Lord, lend her strength.

This morning was not turning out at all like she'd planned.

"Sit down, have some eggs," she ordered before Clay could mess with her mind again. "What time were you supposed to meet Kismet?" Aurora took the frying pan from the stove and dished scrambled eggs onto a plate she'd set out for him.

Clay glanced around for a clock and grimaced. "In about fifteen minutes. Was that Jared's Jeep we passed? Is he still here?"

"Nope. We told him you'd been found, and he went back home." Mandy filled her glass with orange juice and flopped onto the seat beside Clay at the table. "He said he'd tell Kiz you'd be late. You really teaching her computers?"

"Graphics. She likes drawing. Why, you interested?"

Aurora watched as Clay drank his coffee, swallowed breakfast whole, and answered Mandy's questions at the same time. Her cheek still felt warm from where he'd brushed it with his hand when he'd— *Oh, sugar*. She'd left her hair down. No wonder Cissy was looking at them as if they were space aliens.

"Yeah, why don't you come over and keep Kiz company? I think she'd feel better if there was another female there, and Cleo doesn't have time to sit with us. Maybe you'd learn something." Clay finished off his coffee and glanced up at the wall clock again.

His gaze caught Aurora's, and he winked. She fought back a blush. Damn, but she hadn't felt bubbly inside like this since high school. How did he do that?

As Mandy leaped up to change her clothes or fix her hair or whatever it was teenagers did when going somewhere, Clay turned his devastating attentiveness on Cissy.

"Is there a good time for us to start your lessons? It's probably not wise for you to track through the sand to my place. I can bring my laptop over here, but if we need to print anything, we'll have to borrow Aurora's printer."

He glanced at Aurora for approval, and she tingled all the way to her toes. Incapable of coherent thought, she nodded.

"I don't want to start something you can't finish," Cissy said with unbecoming surliness. "I don't need charity."

Broad-shouldered, unshaven, and all male, Clay appeared taken aback by her sister's rude declaration. "It's not charity," he said cautiously. "It's keeping developers away from my brother's land until we have a better plan. I'm not a quitter. Are you?"

Rory held her breath, uncertain what had happened with Cissy between last night and now but praying she wouldn't back out. Another time she might marvel that Clay hadn't taken offense, as most men would. Right now it was Cissy who held her attention.

Her sister looked torn. She glanced at the bill basket, glanced back to the end of the house where she and Mandy lived, then met Rory's eyes. With a shrug, she picked up her coffee cup. "I keep my word if others keep theirs. You just let me know when you have time, and I'll be here."

"At four." He rose from the table.

Trying not to choke on her relief, Rory followed Clay to the door. "Thanks," she murmured so her sister couldn't hear. "There for a minute, I thought she'd changed her mind."

"She's entitled. That's a heck of a lot of money they're waving around." He held the door for her so she could follow him outside.

It was early yet, and heat hadn't taken hold of the air. Rory breathed deeply, trying not to let her awareness of Clay disturb her thought processes. Even through the layer of her perfumed soap she could detect the all-male scent of him. She didn't think it safe to look too closely at how the soft cotton of his shirt hugged his chest.

"I really can pay her bills, one way or another." She crossed her fingers behind her back and said a little prayer of hope. She would demand a signing bonus with her next job.

"All right. I thought maybe I could come back here this afternoon, and after I work with your sister, you and I could go someplace for dinner and talk about this zoning thing." He brushed a strand of hair from her face and tucked it behind her ear.

She recognized the expectant look in his eyes. He wanted more than talk. She probably did, too, but she wouldn't give in to hormones. She'd learned how to diet at an early age. Food and sex weren't all that different— stick to the kind that was good for you and avoid the tempting but worthless sorts.

"If you come over around four," she heard herself saying, and hoped she didn't sound as breathless as she feared, "I can fix dinner while you and Cissy work. Pops likes to eat early. We can feed both of you. Maybe Cissy will feel more charitable if she thinks we're contributing something."

He looked as if he'd like to argue, but Rory held her ground, doing her best to appear complacent and beyond argument. It apparently worked. A corner of his mouth crooked up in a half smile, and though he didn't kiss her, he made her feel as if he had.

Her heart picked up speed—she *wanted* him to kiss her, even if they were being watched from the windows.

"I'll bring steaks. I don't know how to grocery shop, so if you need anything else, tell me."

"We don't need steaks. I have a garden full of greens and a freezer full of fish." They'd learned to can and freeze as kids or they'd have starved.

"Steaks," Clay insisted. "And maybe some big fat potatoes."

"The new potatoes are ready to dig," she protested.

"Big fat potatoes," he replied, as if she hadn't said anything. "With sour cream and butter. And all those other little things they throw on. I'm not in L.A. anymore and don't have to eat nouveau cuisine."

She wasn't entirely certain of the relevance, but the

pleased look on his face was that of a child in a candy store, and she quit arguing. Hadn't he said he usually never tasted food?

Maybe he'd regained his appetite.

As he walked away with that long, jaunty stride of his, Rory tried to ignore her own newly aroused appetite, but by the time Clay McCloud had mounted his Harley and rode off, she was planning the evening meal and praying she wasn't on the menu.

❊ TWELVE ❊

With Kismet's lesson done for the day and time on his hands before he could reasonably visit Aurora again, Clay settled down to finish the task of locating Bingham heirs. He didn't know what he would do with the information once he was finished, but the state had paid him a nice chunk of change. He couldn't completely disregard his job, although the temptation was there.

While the printer spewed a long list of names and addresses, Clay opened up his e-mail program and typed in Aurora's screen name. To balance out the evil emerging from his printer, he typed, *You remind me of starry, starry nights. Come play on my planet anytime.* He hesitated before sending off that nonsense, but she didn't know his screen name and couldn't prove it came from him.

Opening the door to involvement was akin to opening Pandora's box. Sexual involvement he could handle, especially with Aurora. But he wasn't so self-absorbed as to not realize women like her wanted more than sex.

So sending anonymous romantic e-mail was akin to pulling petals off daisies. If she understood the message and knew it was from him, she was a winner and worth the effort of whatever complications ensued. If she thought the e-mail was spam and tossed it, she wasn't his kind. Daisy-petal picking made as much sense as anything else in his life these days.

He'd gambled on less before. This time he just wasn't certain which alternative was the prize.

Catching the last piece of paper spitting from the machine, he switched off the printer, glanced over the list of names, and shuddered. If just one person on this list knew he was an heir, he could sell out all the others. He might as well be holding a two-ton bomb that could explode the whole island into a developer's paradise.

He could still sell the information. Get a check from the state, another from some developer, sell the genealogy program to the Mormons or libraries, and head back home to New York or L.A. Or set off for Tahiti. Cleo and Jared could live anywhere. Aurora didn't have a hope in hell of saving the island from development. She and her sister ought to take the money and run.

But they wouldn't, so he wouldn't. Stupid of him, but there it was. He didn't need the money. He didn't need New York or L.A. or Tahiti now—

The phone rang, dousing his fantasy of setting up shop in the South Pacific. Tripping over a stack of file folders, he glowered at the organized chaos that was his front room. If he was staying, he'd have to do something about the mess.

If he wanted to bring Aurora here, away from the prying eyes of her family, he'd better do a hell of a lot of somethings.

Stepping over a box of reference material, he grabbed the phone before it leaped off the wall and came after him. "Clay here." Gazing around, he looked for some-where to stash his potentially explosive printouts.

"Thank goodness!" Urgency rushed Cleo's usual clipped tones. "Can you come sit with Meg for a while? Matty fell off some playground equipment at a friend's house, and I don't think it's serious but—"

Clay cut in before Cleo passed out from lack of breath. "I'll be there in a minute. Hop in the car and go."

"Thanks!" She slammed down the phone before he could realize the ludicrousness of his offer. He wasn't his brother. He didn't know a damn thing about babies.

How long could it take for Cleo to hie into town, pick up Matt, and run back here? One little baby shouldn't be that hard. Glancing down at the valuable papers in his hand, he shrugged and shoved them into the first open drawer he found.

That done, he jogged over the sand and boardwalk and up the hill to his brother's home. Heaven only knew where Jared had gone. His brother could arrive home before Cleo had time to reach town.

Cleo was looking frantic as she paced the porch, torn between her daughter sleeping inside and her son, hurt, in town. At Clay's approach, she dashed down the stairs, truck keys in hand. "She should sleep another hour. There's a bottle in the refrigerator, but she just ate a cou-ple of hours ago. Jared's in Charleston on a video call with some movie producer. I don't know when he'll be back."

Clay grabbed the door of her truck and held it open so she could climb in. "They'll both be fine. Just be careful and give me a call to let me know how Matt is." He hadn't the heart to worry her with his incompetence. Cleo never panicked except when it came to the kids.

"I hate doing this to you. . . ."

He shut the door while she fastened her seat belt. "I know how to call for help if I'm in over my head. Midge is in good hands."

"Meg. Megan." She threw the truck in gear and roared down the drive.

"Midge," Clay insisted to the cloud of dust she left behind.

If Jared could handle a baby, surely he could. She was a cute little thing.

The cute little thing was wailing her heart out as he entered the house.

Okay, don't panic. How hard could it be?

The nursery was whimsically decorated in bright blue walls, with a cloud-painted ceiling dangling swinging butterflies and dragons. Entering, Clay prayed Midge would quiet down before he reached the crib.

She didn't. In fact, her little face wrinkled into lines of rage and turned red as she reached a particularly demanding note.

He needed a checklist. When machines froze up, he worked through a series of corrections until he had them working again. He simply needed to figure out what made Midge tick.

He offered his finger. She batted it blindly and squalled louder. *Strike one.* Seeing the key in the carousel thing hanging over the crib, he turned it until the musical notes of "Pop Goes the Weasel" wrecked his eardrums. She didn't buy that either. He didn't blame her. He'd try her on a little Billy Joel next time.

Babies liked movement, like cradles and cars. Tightening his jaw, Clay studied the situation. She was down in that crib pretty far, and she was wriggling and flailing like a beached turtle, but she was a bitty thing. All he had to do was slip his hands under her and lift and hope she didn't wriggle so hard she tumbled out of his grip.

He worked one hand under her padded bottom, got a good whiff, and winced. "Midge, don't do this to me!"

At the sound of his voice, she quieted and stared up at him.

Excellent. Talking worked. Pity he couldn't talk her into changing her own diaper. Or find Kismet and Mandy to help, but they'd taken off for the beach hours ago.

Well, if he could clean and change an oily engine, surely he could figure out Midge's chassis.

For the first minute or two, Midge was apparently so bemused by his awkwardness that she forgot to cry. But he apparently took too long figuring out the best means of removing the soggy mess around her bottom, and her wails returned with renewed vigor.

"Give me a break here, Midge," he muttered, ripping at tapes and trying to hold on to her while she kicked furiously. "I've never needed an instruction manual, but I sure could use a Help file right now."

She wailed louder.

"I only like bikes that roar," he warned as she continued caterwauling after he'd rigged a dry diaper around her, leaving the messy one for Cleo to clean up.

Cleo had said she'd just eaten. Did that mean she couldn't eat again? Until when? Hell, he hadn't thought to ask.

Midge's wails were too pitiful to tolerate. Feeding usually shut kids up. It wouldn't hurt for her to eat early.

"All right, I think I've got this now, kid. Hang on." Burped milk down his front and a wide-awake Midge waiting to see what he would do next, Clay slipped the straps of the baby carrier over his head and let her hang down his back like a backpack. "Let's go for a walk. And if that doesn't work, I'll take you out on the Harley and teach you to ride."

He'd almost dropped her when Cleo had called to report she had to take Matty into Charleston to have his swollen finger X-rayed. She'd given him a hurried list of instructions he couldn't write down because Midge was pulling his hair, and he couldn't disentangle her fingers or find a pen. Most of the instructions had made sense at the time. He wished he could remember what they were now.

Figuring Jared easily owed him a month's free rent—had he been paying rent—Clay jogged out the front door, hoping the fresh air would relieve the stench of baby puke.

He prayed Jared would arrive before four. He hated to call Cissy and tell her he couldn't make it. She'd not looked happy with him this morning.

He wished he had more experience in seducing women, but the challenge of persuading Aurora Jenkins into bed could be just what he needed to shake him out of the doldrums.

The idea of waking up to a firecracker like Aurora captured his imagination. Did she wake up waving a gavel of justice? Would she wear frilly nightgowns like her underwear or practical nightshirts like her suits? She presented a challenge so unique that he hungered to explore far more than the physical.

That realization rocked his world. Usually, once he released a little pent-up sexual energy, women bored him, so he didn't expend much time or effort in learning about them. Maybe settling for easy women had been his mistake.

Midge bounced on his back as he jogged along the shady edge of the beach where gnarled oaks and pines grew, reminding him that he was supposed to be taking care of her, not indulging in sexual fantasies.

Ahead of him was the rock jetty that marked the edge of Cleo's property. He knew from the maps that the state park would start beyond the jetty. Jogging past the rocky outcropping, he ran along part of the Bingham estate, but this acreage had no road access—which was why he stopped short at the sight of a surveyor's stake.

He ran the beach every morning and knew the stake hadn't been there yesterday.

At the sound of voices deeper in the thicket of woods, he jogged inland. Kismet's family lived back here somewhere. Maybe he just heard the kids.

Humidity and mosquitoes were a deterrent. Blackberry thickets abounded. Halting, worried about the infant on his back, Clay scanned the wooded area ahead, searching for some sign of human life-forms.

He located the yellow hard hats of the surveyors walking toward him just as he was about to leave.

"You working for the state?" he called, unwilling to take Midge any deeper into the marshy area.

Tucking a pencil into his shirt pocket, one of the men glanced around until he saw Clay. Shrugging, he picked up a piece of his equipment and folded it. "Nah. Just some builder." He squinted closer at the carrier on Clay's back. "You know you got that thing on backward?"

Clay didn't much care how he had the carrier on so long as it kept Midge burbling happily. "I didn't know this land had been sold."

"Doesn't have to be sold, far as I know. Just needs to be under contract." Losing interest in the conversation, the surveyor returned to packing up his instruments.

Under contract. With a sinking feeling, Clay jogged back down the path to the beach. Aurora wasn't going to like this at all. Neither was Cleo. And what about Kismet's family? If some developer had found one of the Bingham family to sign a contract, what would happen to the Watkinses? As he understood it, the kid's family lived a precarious existence. They'd never survive if they were thrown out of their home.

Falling back on his usual motto, he decided he had his problems; they had theirs. Since he didn't know how to solve either, he would simply let Aurora know what he'd seen. She would know where to scout around and find out about a pending contract.

He hated the idea that she might give up her fight to preserve the wetlands and the turtles. How would he ever get to know her then?

Did he really want to know a warrior princess who leaped into the fray as surely as he avoided it?

Oh, yeah, he really did. There wasn't any way this side of heaven that he was letting Aurora walk out of his life without knowing more about her. He wanted to get inside her head and see what made her tick. So much for daisy-petal picking.

If he called her and told her about the surveyors, would she come over to see the stakes for herself?

He wondered if she knew anything about babies. Maybe she could figure out how to pry the kid out of this harness and into bed without a screaming fit. And then they'd have a little time alone. . . .

One step at a time, McCloud. Slow and easy.

Opening the refrigerator door to discover a selection of soft drinks of a kind she didn't drink cluttering her shelves, Aurora swore under her breath and began unloading them onto the counter. Each bright red label announced, *Grand prize—one million dollars. You could be a winner!*

If she were a winner, she would be in Chicago, with a six-figure income and a condo overlooking the skyline. She'd be in charge of her life instead of facing bankruptcy and losing the only real home she'd ever known.

If she were a winner—dreaming up another spectacular fantasy, Aurora opened one of the bottles, poured the drink into a glass of ice, and added a lemon to dilute the sugary taste—if she were a winner, she'd buy Cissy a new house. One with a guest cottage for her father.

She'd invest in a gas station and minimart in the front yard so Cissy wouldn't have to go into town to work. . . .

Oh, what the heck. Instead of flinging the cap into the trash where it belonged, Aurora checked under it.

Grand Prize Winner! appeared before her disbelieving eyes.

The phone rang, saving her from fainting. Clutching the bottle cap in one hand, she grabbed the phone receiver with the other, waiting for it to pour forth maniacal laughter and a voice crowing, "April fool!" Her father's cronies had weird senses of humor.

At the sound of Clay's voice, she almost passed out again from sheer relief at the quick trip back to reality. His curt report of surveyors in the marsh snapped her back to the disastrous world with which she was all too familiar. Someone had bought the Bingham tract? How?

Telling Clay she'd be over shortly, Rory hung up and looked at the cap in her hand with disbelief. She felt like an idiot for believing for even a second that she could solve all her family's problems with a plastic bottle cap. She'd probably won a carton of soft drinks.

Not inclined to take chances, she flipped on a fluorescent cabinet light to peer under the cap again. Her fantasies had probably short-circuited her brain. Surely no one ever won a million dollars in these contests.

The cap's message hadn't changed.

So—that didn't mean anything. She could still have just won a Nintendo or a Barbie doll.

Finding the kitchen scissors, she carefully peeled back the bottle label. She scanned the fine print, locating the 800 number to verify winnings. Did she really want to play the fool and call that number?

Lifting the instructions to the light, she read the details, but her hands started shaking and she had to reread the label several times. The directions for claiming free drinks were intricate and involved caps saying *Free six-pack*.

The details on claiming the grand prize simply said to call.

She had nothing but pride to lose in trying. She could sacrifice pride for a chance at a million dollars. Suspending disbelief, attempting to achieve an air of insouciance, she picked up the phone as if she were calling for carry-out pizza and dialed the 800 number.

First ring.

While waiting for someone to pick up on the other end, Rory idly played with lists of things she could do with a million dollars.

The hospital bills were only a hundred thousand or so. No problem.

Second ring.

Heck, she could buy trucks for both Cissy and Pops with less than forty thousand.

Third ring.

Taxes would probably be four hundred thousand, dang the IRS.

Fourth ring.

Should they set aside the remainder for Mandy's education or invest in a gas station and hope it would pay tuition?

Starting to laugh at herself over the dilemma of riches, ready to hang up since no one seemed prepared to answer, Rory shut up the instant a recorded message began to play. As the message talked on, she slowly slid down the wall, harboring the bottle cap in a fist against her chest. She might have to hold her heart inside her chest if it pounded any faster.

She'd won a million dollars!

She owned a bottle cap worth *a million dollars*.

Cold shivers shot down her spine every time she tried to grasp it. She let the message replay a second time.

She was a millionaire.

She was shaking. Things like this didn't happen to her. She didn't even know how to *feel*.

Tears filled her eyes and laughter filled her lungs and she could hardly hold herself still.

Clicking the cordless off, she tried to think through the haze of euphoria. She was the family financial expert. If the prize was really, really real, she had to make the decisions, and she couldn't afford any errors.

She had to consider Mandy's education, her father's retirement, the mounting medical bills, the mortgage, the day-to-day expenses that were never quite covered by Cissy's minimum-wage job, the pickup truck they no longer had. . . . The list could go on into eternity. Her need for cash to move back to the city and finance a new apartment hovered right about at the bottom—after she contributed 10 percent to charity.

It was an overwhelming responsibility, one that could make her weep in frustration. She'd never had any idea how difficult being rich could be.

She laughed out loud at that—probably with hysteria—and turned on the phone again, a rush of adrenaline shooting straight to her head.

She wanted the bottle cap in a safety-deposit box before her luck changed. Then she needed to find a lawyer to help her consider all the tax ramifications and set up a trust fund before she cashed in her prize. If she had a prize. She wouldn't believe it until she had it in hand. She wished Cissy were here instead of at Iris's. She needed a reality check.

Calling a college friend, she obtained the name of a good tax attorney in Charleston.

Talking to the lawyer popped the first of her fantasy bubbles. He was even more skeptical than she at the likelihood of collecting a million dollars from a bottle cap.

Setting up a date to bring it in, she called the bank about a safety-deposit box. All the local boxes were full.

She needed to take the cap to Charleston, but the city was over an hour away, and she'd promised Clay she'd come over. Actually, picking up a phone and calling her was so inconsistent with his uncommunicative nature that she decided she really had ignored his urgency for far too long.

She had to continue as normal. Even a million dollars—or half, after taxes—couldn't buy the Bingham tract. She couldn't let riches go to her head.

After frantically searching for a safe hiding place, she stuffed the cap in her underwear drawer and dashed out to the car. She needed Clay's pragmatism to bring her back to earth. She'd take flight otherwise.

Driving down the highway with the Beamer's top down, and the Carolina blue sky for her ceiling, Rory couldn't believe she was hiding a million-dollar bottle cap in her underwear drawer—and driving up McCloud's lane as if his sensible patience were the answer to her prayers.

Or maybe she was here because some yahoo calling himself a Purple Knight had sent her a love note, and she really wanted to believe the enigmatic man who had spent the night on the beach watching turtles would talk to her about starry, starry nights. She longed for a man with a touch of romance in his soul, instead of the ones she'd known who had stock certificates in their blood.

She ought to have learned by now. A sweet-talking Purple Knight was about as trustworthy as million-dollar bottle caps. For all she knew, the message was spam from a con man selling real estate on the moon—

Rory hit her brake and stared out the windshield as she

turned into Cleo's drive. What the dickens did McCloud have on his back? A baby? The sight was almost enough to drive all thought of the bottle cap out of her head. Almost.

The infant carrier was little more than a knapsack against Clay's broad shoulders. An awkward knapsack given that it was on backward, but who cared with all that broad expanse of muscled chest exposed by a T-shirt pulled taut by the weight?

"Cute albatross," she commented, swinging her legs out of the car as Clay opened the door for her.

"Humor, har, har." Offering his hand, he assisted her from the low-slung sports car. "I think the albatross is supposed to hang in front."

"So's the baby carrier."

She wasn't a small woman, but Clay pulled her upright with ease, while wielding a backpack full of baby. She squinted at the sleeping infant, trying to piece together the conflicting images of bad-boy biker in long hair and tight shirt with the innocence of the babe on his back.

She wasn't ready to raise her hopes any more than they already were by sharing her news, if it really was news. Babies and Clay McCloud were an excellent distraction.

"She's supposed to cuddle up against your chest." She wanted to reach over and lift the sleeping infant from her awkward position, but she knew nothing about babies. She was mightily impressed that McCloud did. And that he looked quite comfortable in this interesting new role.

"Is that why I can't lift her out of there? How in hell is it supposed to go on?" He strained his neck attempting to look over his shoulder. "She's still there, isn't she? She's mighty quiet."

Laughing inwardly, somehow relieved that he wasn't as adept as he appeared, Rory studied the situation. "She's sleeping. Here, let me unstrap this thing. The poor little mite is practically falling out." Taking a deep breath, Rory stepped close enough to unbuckle the main harness cutting into Clay's muscular shoulder. The opportunity to hold the baby while touching Clay excited her in more visceral ways than a prize that might not be real.

"And you don't think it's a terribly uncomfortable position for me?" he asked in aggrieved tones.

She knew better than to listen. He was looking down her blouse and wrapping her hair around his finger again. She was already tingling enough without his encouragement.

"I saw a utility truck out on the highway as I drove by." She tried sticking to business as she unfastened the buckle.

She and Clay both caught the strap to prevent it from falling. His rough hand covered hers, and she felt the contact all the way to her toes. "There wasn't any name on it."

"It's probably not local. The bank wouldn't want gossip starting." He swung the carrier off his shoulder. While she held it upright, he expertly removed the sleeping baby and cuddled her across his shoulder.

In awe at his seeming expertise, Aurora followed him up the shell sidewalk. "I can't believe Cleo trusts you with her kid when you can't even put a carrier on right."

"Cleo knows I'm not totally helpless," he asserted in protest, opening the door for her. He ruined his plea by continuing, "Besides, she had to run Matty to the doctor and thought Jared would be home soon."

"I never saw you as the family sort." She supposed she

might have, had she taken time to think about it. He was living near his brother, helping her because his sister-in-law loved it here. Inside the hard-ass image he liked to project was a man who might be worth knowing, if she dared.

She wasn't real good at risk-taking.

Now that she was here, she wasn't at all certain why. She couldn't do anything about the surveyors. She couldn't tell Clay about the bottle cap before she told her family. What had prompted her to come at his call?

Following him back to the bedroom, she saw that he didn't need her help with the kid. He arranged Midge in her crib as if he knew exactly what he was doing.

Admiring the colorful collection of butterflies and dragons hanging over the bed, Rory wasn't prepared when Clay straightened, caught her waist, and hauled her against him. Breathless, she gazed up at the bronzed planes of his face and tried to read his expression, but he was an un-fathomable man.

"I'm not the family sort. I was just handy. Don't get any ideas."

He didn't give her time to question. He opened his mouth over hers, and the world went away. She didn't care about bottle caps, surveyors, sleeping infants, or relatives who might walk in at any minute. Wrapping her arms around his neck, she wanted only the soul-stirringly deep intimacy of Clay's mouth taming hers. His arms enfolded her waist as if he would never let go, and his body pressed along the length of hers so she understood how it would be if he laid her on his bed and covered her with his weight.

Realizing how much she wanted to know how that

would feel, and how wrong it would be if she did, Rory whipped her head to the side so his lips merely grazed her ear, settling there to nibble. She pushed back but he didn't release her. "Let go," she murmured.

Clay released the pressure of his embrace to rest his hands on her hips. His kisses caressed her cheek. "Don't want to," he muttered. "You smell good. You *feel* good."

And so did he—feel good, that is—but she wasn't about to admit that. "You stink." She pulled back, out of his tempting hands. "What have you been into, skunk?"

"Baby puke." Without missing a beat, he stripped off his shirt, heaved it at a hamper of dirty baby clothes, and reached for her again.

Confronted with all that lovely bare chest, Rory hastily backed off. "We're not going there, McCloud," she warned.

"Yeah, I think we are, but I can wait. You taste too good for me to give up this soon." Catching her hips but giving her space, he nibbled her ear again, kissed her nose, then looked down at her with a wary expression. "You don't have some other guy waiting back in the big city, do you?"

Flustered, she inched out of his reach. "I don't have time for men. I don't have time for *you*. Take my word for it, McCloud, I'm outta here as soon as I have things back in order." Soon . . . if the cap was real.

"There's no harm in living in the moment," he said without a hint that her objection had made any impression.

Of course it hadn't. He didn't care if she left tomorrow, so long as he got what he wanted today.

She didn't sell herself that cheaply.

❊ THIRTEEN ❊

Aurora hung up Cleo's telephone with a sick feeling to replace her earlier joy. "I sent Pops out to talk to Iris. She thinks someone found out about Billy and he sold out."

From his position on the floor, Clay gazed up at her with an inscrutable expression, then returned to manipulating the controls of a computer game, entertaining a newly awakened Midge.

Rory paced the heart-of-pine cottage floor, fretting over the unfairness of fate. She might have a million dollars in her underwear drawer, but she *still* couldn't correct injustice. She should be dancing in the streets. Instead she was worrying about a *swamp*. Her friends back in the city would tell her that her head was definitely screwed on wrong.

Maybe a lifetime of habit had taught her caution. Money wasn't real until she had it in hand. Anything that appeared too good to be true probably was.

"The zoning meeting is Thursday night," she continued, thinking out loud. "This is Tuesday. If we can come up with some charts and statistics before the meeting, showing what overdevelopment has done in other areas—overcrowded roads, utilities, schools, whatever—

they might be concerned enough to put a moratorium on zoning changes. We may not be able to stop the auction, but if we can halt commercial zoning, developers might think twice about buying."

She tried to concentrate on the problem at hand, but Clay was too major a distraction. Sitting on Cleo's living room floor in front of a laptop with Midge slouched in his lap, he entertained the wide-eyed infant with spaceships that shot colored stars, mushrooms, and balloons at each other. Every once in a while, the game emitted a chiming version of "Love Me Do," Midge would coo excitedly, and Rory would swivel to see what new action crossed the screen.

Every time she turned to look, Clay was looking back.

She'd never had that much blatant interest focused on her. She didn't at all understand the thrill chasing through her every time she caught him looking. Just *looking* shouldn't generate such chills of excitement.

"I can feed statistics into a comparison program and set projections," he answered reasonably to her impassioned speech, his hands working the controller without regard to any result but Midge's contentment. "If any school officials are at the meeting, they'll cringe at doubling their population almost overnight."

She assumed he meant to generate the statistics from the laptop he'd been working on before Midge woke, although for all she knew, he could have been looking up her ancestry and credit rating. But she admired his ability and willingness to use the computer as a weapon to bring down the bad guys.

"Give me enough to create some charts," she said. "People like pretty pictures. I'll make copies of the petitions to hand out. Five hundred signatures in twenty-four hours is pretty impressive. Maybe we can get another five hundred before the meeting."

"We could easily collect thousands if we had time."

"We don't have time," she said impatiently, continuing her pacing.

Clay's controller produced a colorful explosion of singing birds. Midge didn't issue a sound, and he leaned over her little head to check on her. "I think that one sent her off to sleepy-bye."

With athletic coordination, he set aside the laptop, balanced the infant in his arms, and stood up. "Planning requires patience and persistence."

After shedding his smelly shirt, he'd apparently stolen one of his brother's. Aurora tried not to be distracted by the way the bright Hawaiian print fell open across his tanned chest, but she wasn't certain she remembered the argument. "I hate waiting."

"That's because you're a volatile cocktail," he said with a hint of amusement, rocking Midge lightly so her eyes closed again.

She stared as if the top of his head had blown off. "A what?" She supposed she should be insulted that he thought she didn't have patience, but he was probably right.

"Heady and explosive, but not lethal." His mouth curved in a little-boy grin that nearly turned her inside out. "We work well together."

That grin produced images of Cheshire cats, along with wistful wishes of a steady balance to her more explosive tendencies, but a car engine sounded far down the lane, saving her from any reply.

"There's Jared. I haven't gone into town to buy the steaks yet. Will you take a rain check?" Expertly holding the sleeping babe, Clay peered out the window to verify his brother's arrival.

"I'll find something," she answered, more aware of the tenderness he showed Midge than the fact that she hadn't been to the grocery either. She couldn't do this. No matter how many fascinating facets Clay McCloud exposed, he was still the worst thing that could happen to her.

She didn't want to imagine what the best could be.

"I'll create charts so pretty the commission won't know what hit them," he assured her, heading toward the nursery. "And then we'll celebrate because the commission is going to cave."

She could hear Clay's idea of celebration in the sensual lowering of his voice, and knowing what was on his mind heated parts of her best left cold. "You're doing this for the turtles, right? And your brother?" she called after him. And not for her, she reminded herself.

"Yep. And for Kiz and her family. That's their land the surveyors are tramping around." He disappeared down the hall, leaving her thoroughly rattled.

Damn, even though he'd just verified that he wasn't doing this for her, he made his intentions sound altruistic rather than selfish.

Clay returned to the front room just as a car door slammed outside. Without any show of acknowledgment that his brother would walk in on them any minute, he invaded her personal space by poking the frown forming above her nose. "It's not your responsibility to change the world."

"We need development." Attempting to disregard

Clay's broad chest and dangerous proximity, she stuck to her concerns. "I don't want condos, but I want the zoning only temporarily postponed until we have a plan."

"It's a crime to turn paradise into hot-dog stands, but we'll argue over that when the time comes," he acknowledged with lazy grace, twisting a strand of her hair around his finger again, his colorful shirt filling her field of vision.

They were still at odds, but Rory could almost feel flames flickering along her skin everywhere Clay touched her with his gaze. He didn't understand the island and its inhabitants, and he probably would be gone before she was. She'd better learn to use his expertise without any of this touchy-feely business. She spun on her heel to open the door.

Jared looked surprised, then concerned as he glanced over her shoulder to see Clay. "Where's Cleo? Is something wrong?"

"I have it all under control, bro. Midge is asleep. Cleo just called to say Matty is fine, and she's heading home. You can take up the baby-sitting duties. I have to see Aurora home."

Clay caught Rory's elbow, preventing her from fleeing the moment Jared walked through the door. She thought about pulling away, but she knew it would be futile. Besides, Jared didn't appear to be noticing anything except his empty house. She liked the way he looked a little shaken at Clay's insouciant recitation. Jared McCloud was a good family man, unlike his sex-god brother.

Except the sex god knew how to take care of babies.

"What happened to Matty?" Jared demanded.

"Playground accident. I said he's fine. Cleo just got a little rattled."

"Cleo called Aurora to look after Meg?" Jared turned toward the hall leading to the nursery, apparently listening for infant cries while attempting to sort out what had happened here.

"Nope, she called me. Aurora's here 'cause surveyors are tramping around the Watkins homestead. I'll fill you in later." With studied purpose, Clay urged Aurora through the open door. "Tell Matty I'll tell him a turtle tale when I come back."

"You'd better run that tale by me first!" Jared called as Clay attempted his escape. "I want to hear how Meg fits in."

"She's been fed, but you can have the dirty diapers," Clay called back, letting the screen door slam as he steered Rory down the porch stairs. "I'll never hear the end of this," he muttered. "Let me drive. I want out of here before Jared follows me out."

Still a little dazed, Rory handed him the keys. "He was just curious. Wouldn't you be if you came home to find someone like you baby-sitting your kid and the rest of your family gone?"

"Just because I'm the youngest, Jared and TJ think it's their duty to look after me. I'm not exactly a kid any longer." Clay opened the passenger-side door and held out his hand to help her in.

He certainly didn't have to tell her that, but she couldn't resist teasing him just a little. "I can't say I blame your brothers. I'd be afraid you oiled the baby and filled her up with gasoline."

She looked down at Clay's helping hand. He was always taking her arm or her hand and treating her as if she were a piece of dandelion fluff. "You know, you have an unusual flare for old-fashioned etiquette."

He looked down at his outstretched hand and shrugged. "Habit. Are you getting in or not?"

"Since I daresay you'll leave me here if I say 'not,' I guess I'll get in." Before the words left her mouth, he'd caught her elbow and all but shoved her into the seat.

He slid behind the driver's wheel and took off before she could decide whether to protest his manhandling. "I can do this without your help, you realize," she told him. "I only needed you to back off on giving the state the names of the landowners."

As the BMW shot out onto the highway, Clay grinned. "I have the list the bank, the state, and the developers would kill for shoved into my silverware drawer. If I'm foregoing monetary rewards for that list, I want to be around for the fireworks."

In his silverware drawer. Gads, they were a pair. She had the stuff dreams were made of stashed with her underwear. He had the means to blow her family's dreams sky-high hidden among his forks and spoons.

Unless, of course, Iris's brother, Billy, had definitely sold his share of the swamp. Then all bets were off.

"If Billy has sold out, the realty company will never give me what they offered the other day. We could be bankrupt." Cissy limped up and down the living room later that night after Clay left. "I've never lived anywhere else. How would I pay rent? I can't even find a job. Your friend McCloud could up and disappear tomorrow. That kind always does."

"Will you sit down? You're making me tired just watching you." Rory was sorry she'd brought up the zoning meeting during supper. It had been an otherwise pleasant evening until then.

Everything had gone so well—Clay didn't have to be more than his undemonstrative self to make Mandy shine and Cissy dote on his every word. When he exerted himself, he had them eating out of his hand. His masculine energy had been like a breath—more like a tornado—of fresh air in this all-female atmosphere.

Even Mandy had picked up a few pointers when Clay sat Cissy down in front of the computer and eased her fears. He'd had the sense to refrain from touching the keyboard himself. The way he manipulated those keys would have intimidated Cissy for certain.

But now he was gone and all that energy had dissipated with him. Cissy had reverted to fretting. Mandy had disappeared into her room. And Rory was more restless than she'd ever been in her life, and given her level of hyperactivity, that was going some. She really didn't need rampaging hormones and uncertain dreams for the future muddying her thought processes.

"If we sold to Commercial, at least I'd get a place nearby, where I know people," Cissy said. "If we go bankrupt, I'll have nothing. If you go to that meeting on Thursday, the realty company might withdraw its offer."

"I thought we'd decided not to take the offer?" Rory asked. She didn't like the bad vibrations she was picking up here.

Cissy threw up her hands in a gesture of despair and fell into the nearest chair. "I just can't stand this uncertainty! I *hate* living like this. I want a normal life with a job and money in the bank for Mandy's future. Tell me why I should care about turtles and our neighbors if no one else does?"

She had a point. A rotten one, admittedly, but in this day and age of "me first," who was she to argue?

The bottle cap in her drawer sang its siren song, and Rory fought a wave of guilt. If uncertainty was tearing Cissy apart, didn't she owe her sister a little bit of hope? Or would she only shatter her if the cap wasn't real?

"Do you hate staying here?" Rory asked, searching for clarification, terrified of revealing her secret dreams too soon. "If you had enough money to pay the bills, would you still want to sell?"

Cissy partially parted her hands where she'd buried her face. "I won't let you spend all your money on us. It's bad enough you're trying to sell your car."

Rory brushed that off with a careless gesture. "Forget me for a minute. Imagine you'd won a million dollars. What would you do? Sell out and move to Florida?"

Cissy rubbed her reddened eyes and leaned back in the chair. "You sound like Dad. He's always telling us what he'd do if he won the lottery. Daydreaming won't wish away the bill collectors."

"Ciss, this is *important*. I know Mandy's education would be first on your list, but after that? Do you hate living here?"

Cissy closed her eyes. "No. This is home. My friends are here. Dad is here. This land was Mama's and Grandmama's and I like having those roots. I like my garden, and the peach tree where we buried Old Bones. I like working with Grandma Iris. If I had a choice, I'd never leave. I'm not like you, Rora. I'm not curious about the world outside. I just want to feel *safe*."

Tears prickled behind Rory's eyelids. Cissy had lived in fear and uncertainty most of her life. That her sister's only dream was for safety struck Rory as heartbreaking. At least it was a dream she had some chance of fulfilling—if some developer didn't ruin it by sinking the island with condos and parking lots. If the bottle cap prize was real.

"I think we can have that, Ciss," she murmured, afraid to say it too loudly, afraid even a whisper of hope would attract the demons of misfortune. Living hand-to-mouth taught that kind of pessimism. Hope was a foreign creature to be wary of, but as the younger, more sheltered sister, she had more courage than Cissy. She hated taking risks, but she had to be the one to dream.

Cissy didn't even lift her head. "I have to have a job to pay the mortgage. I don't see it happening, Rora."

"Don't tell Pops, but I think we may have won a million dollars." Rory stated it as matter-of-factly as she could, keeping her voice low in case Mandy was still awake.

Cissy didn't move for about a minute. When she did, it was to eye Rory with suspicion. "Did your plate come up a few noodles short? Or have you listened to Dad once too often?"

Rather than argue, Rory crossed the room to her bedroom. She had a hard time believing it herself. She was itching for someone else to confirm that her plate wasn't short any noodles. Jittery with nerves, she returned with the precious bottle cap cradled in her palm and the bottle label with the prize instructions. "Look at this. You tell me."

In disbelief, Cissy glanced from her to the cap. Then, picking it up, she squinted at the writing on the inside. Still not believing, she got up and held the cap and the label under a reading lamp. Her hand was shaking as she closed her fingers tightly around the bit of plastic.

"Is this for real? Somebody didn't just manufacture this as a joke?"

Rory shook her head. "All I know is that it came off a bottle with that label on it this morning. I called that number, and they said I've won. I have an appointment to see a lawyer, verify its validity, and set up a trust. I didn't want to raise hopes until I knew for certain."

Cissy looked as if she wouldn't ever open her fist again. She held it against her chest, absorbing the impact. "I think I want to scream. Would it be more real if we jumped up and down and shrieked?"

Rory allowed a tiny bubble of joy to rise to the top. She'd been bottling up her hopes beneath a cork of disbelief all day. She was about to explode from the pressure. "We'd wake up Mandy," she warned with a grin. More little bubbles rose and fizzed like effervescent champagne. "We could go outside and do a happy dance— just in case it's really real."

Her family had lived so long on the edge, it was difficult to comprehend that solid ground might be in sight. But now that she'd shared the hope, Rory was ready to burst with it. Just seeing the light in her sister's eyes after it had been dead for so long erased her fears. The prize had to be real. God couldn't be so cruel as to disappoint Cissy again.

Shakily, Cissy held out her fist. "Take it. Hide it again. I'm terrified I'll lose it or someone will run in the front door and mug us for it. I'm not going to believe it until I see the money."

"Show me the money!" Rory crowed on her way back to the bedroom.

"Happy dance," Cissy cried, limping toward the door, cane in hand. "For once in my life, I want to know what it feels like to shriek in joy and howl at the moon!"

With the cap back where it belonged, Rory flew out the door after her. In the shadows of the moss-draped oaks, amid the frozen grinning statues, they screamed their jubilation to the winds, danced and hugged, hooted and laughed until they fell into the thick grass, howling at their insanity.

An owl flew off in noisy outrage at the disturbance. Fireflies skimmed the grass around them. And a particularly jolly old elf beamed down at them in delight.

"A million dollars," Cissy whispered to the moon. "Mandy can go to college."

"Pops can have insurance."

"We can buy a new truck, cherry red with an extended cab!"

"You can finally have that fire hazard of a toolshed taken out."

"Can we build a garage in its place?" As the dreams stacked dangerously one on top of the other, Cissy backed off. "And what about you? It's your money. You found it."

"Pops bought the soft drinks. I drank it. The house belongs to both of us. It's all one. I just don't want anyone to know until we're *certain*." Rory stared up at the moon, thinking they should have real champagne so they could be too high to come down to reality so quickly. Still, bliss filled her soul.

"Shouldn't we lock it up somewhere safe?"

"I called. The bank's safety-deposit boxes are full. I have an appointment with the attorney on Monday. He can put it in his vault until we check it out. It's going to be fine this time, Ciss. I know it is."

"I'll believe it when I see a cherry-red extended cab sitting in that driveway," Cissy said in decisive tones.

"I can trade in the Beamer for that," Rory said with a magnanimous gesture of her hand. "I'm not sure I'll believe it until I see Mandy wearing graduation robes from Duke."

"That's going to happen if I have to sell a kidney to do it. I think just seeing the bill basket empty would be enough."

"Make a list and attach all the bills to it. Maybe the lawyer can figure how to deduct medical bills against the taxes."

"This is just a little bit scary, isn't it?" Cissy whispered.

"A whole lot scary, but happy scary. Start imagining your new future, Ciss. I say we go to Charleston and celebrate with new shoes."

"Dancing shoes," Cissy agreed with glee. "I want to dance around the fire while we burn those bills."

"You got it."

Rory thought she'd spend her share on running shoes so she could run as fast and hard as she could from this narrow world where happiness meant having no bills to pay.

And faster still from a man who could break her heart and dash her dreams with one careless wave of farewell.

❧FOURTEEN❧

"I'm not going anywhere near the courthouse," Cissy protested the evening of the zoning meeting. "I'll stay here with Mandy and Dad, or you can drop me off at Iris's. She has basket-weaving classes tonight. You can tell me all about it when you come home."

Rory knew her sister was nervous. Even a million dollars couldn't save the swamp and their neighbors if the commission decided in favor of development. But she'd hoped Cissy would act as a barrier between her and Clay.

The messages from "Purple Knight" nagged at the back of her mind as Clay ambled about the living room, picking things up and putting them down. Remembering Clay's love of classic rock, she'd responded to the *starry, starry night* e-mail with *I can't get no satisfaction* in hopes of uncovering his identity. Purple Knight promptly replied with *Only the good die young*.

She knew enough about golden oldies to identify Billy Joel. Clay was the only man she knew who could quote rock songs for the purpose of seduction and get away with it. That he used computers for communication didn't bother her. That his idiosyncratic messages woke all her feminine instincts scared her to death. She didn't know enough about him to get involved. She had a family to take care of. A career to return to. She didn't have time for love. Or the courage to risk it.

Watching Clay study the brass clock from the knick-knack shelf as if it might reveal the secrets of time, she tried to believe this enigmatic man couldn't be the one talking about starry nights and planets, but she knew better. Aside from the distinctive rock theme, who else had the opportunity to filch her screen name? The man was just plain dangerous, in more ways than one.

He'd verified that Iris's brother had signed a sales agreement on his share of the swamp. Everything rode on tonight's zoning meeting.

"There's room for both of you in the truck," Clay offered, returning the clock to the shelf after resetting it. Although he'd behaved as if he hadn't heard a word of the family argument, he solved it in one fell swoop. "Jared and Cleo took the kids in the Jeep."

"I can take Cissy to Iris's and meet you in town," Rory said, hoping to wriggle out of spending time with Clay in the intimacy of the truck. Just standing in the same room with him had her nerve ends tingling, anticipating his touch or his kiss. After his promise of celebration a couple of days ago, her imagination kept veering down paths best left untaken.

It had been years since she'd necked with a guy in a pickup cab, but contrary to popular belief, she wasn't dead from the neck down.

She'd never necked with a guy who looked like Clay did tonight. He'd actually had his hair barbered so he came across as more respectable—and striking—than Jeff Spencer in his banker suit. Instead of a T-shirt and sandals, Clay had dug out a suspiciously Hollywood-looking collarless shirt and sport coat to wear with a pair of tailored khakis. "Funky business" might describe the style.

"Leave Cissy your car keys," he answered, rattling his own impatiently.

When Cissy's eyes lit with disbelief, Rory felt as if she'd been kicked in the stomach. It had never once occurred to her that her sister might like the freedom of her own wheels. How selfish could she get?

She'd been away from home too long, and controlling things had become a way of life she didn't like to recognize in herself. Digging the keys out of her purse, she offered them to her sister. "Keep 'em away from Pops," she said, grinning at Cissy's astonishment.

"Me? You want *me* to drive that expensive machine? Down Iris's dirt road?"

"Might as well get a little fun out of it before we sell it." Dropping the keys in Cissy's hand and ignoring Clay's invitation to take his, Rory stalked past him to open the front door.

Clay turned and offered his arm to Cissy instead, who accepted it without question. "At least one sister has a little sense," he commented.

"Rory doesn't trust men," Cissy confided as they stepped outside. "Back in high school she and Jeff Spencer used to date, until she decided to run for student council, and he ran against her. He won, of course. He could afford posters and beach parties. It's been downhill ever since."

"Thanks for sharing that, Ciss," Rory grumbled.

"Spencer?" Clay asked. "The suit you were arguing with in town?"

"We were both on the debate team. Maybe I should just take the Beamer in and leave the two of you to catch up on a lot of fun stories."

"No way, José," Cissy said, rattling the Beamer keys. "I'm not letting go of these babies. Besides, it's probably safer if you don't go into town alone if you're planning on upsetting whoever's surveying out here."

The last thing Rory was afraid of was physical violence, but Clay's accompaniment would make it look as if she weren't fighting this battle alone. Nervously she watched as Clay helped Cissy into the convertible's front seat.

"How much do you want to bet old Jeff has a stake in developing the Bingham property?" Clay asked as Cissy looked over the car's gauges.

"That's not even worth gambling on," Rory scoffed. "It's his bank that owns Commercial Realty. It's the biggest bank in town. They'd score huge in mortgages alone. And he's really not wrong. We *need* business out here. Farming isn't profitable on acreages this small."

"Argue this after I'm outta here," Cissy protested. "Debate isn't my gig. I just want everyone to get along."

"I'll find a catalog of happy dust just for you." Watching Cissy check the dials and the equipment, Rory lingered beside her convertible.

"I think happy dust is illegal in most states," Clay declared, catching her elbow and dragging her away. "Although I'm inclined to think that if we liquefied pot and poured it into a few corporate water coolers, the world would be a safer place."

"California dreaming," Rory muttered, but the image of bankers and CEOs skipping down the street arm in arm tickled her funny bone. She bit her lip to hide it.

"I'm supposed to be the cynic here," Clay protested. "You're supposed to say that's a jolly good idea and go looking for an organization to promote it."

Starting the car engine, Cissy chuckled. "He's got you nailed, Rora. Admit it. You're standing there wondering if pot would solve world peace."

Rory hated being judged and categorized and hated it worse when they were right. "I may be a dreamer, but you two are certifiable."

"Yeah, but we're cute," Clay insisted. "Never underestimate the power of cute."

Rory swallowed a laugh. He was impossible enough without encouraging him. "I can't do cute, so I'll stick with smart, thank you."

He stared at her in incredulity. "You're well above cute already. Let your hair down and wear something sexy, and you can do glamorous." Without giving her time for a reply, Clay opened the pickup door and all but shoved her inside.

As Cissy took off down the sandy drive, Aurora hid her flush in the growing dusk of the cab. Beyond cute? Glamorous! Was that how he saw her? She might be sturdy and practical and not half-bad to look at, but *sexy* or *glamorous* wasn't within the realm of possibility. The man lied through his teeth. He must be desperate for sex.

Watching Clay saunter around to the driver's seat, sun-bleached hair impeccably styled, bronzed features studying her warily through the windshield, she knew darned well a man that good-looking wasn't desperate.

"I don't want to do glamorous," she informed him the instant he took his seat. "My career is in banking, not

Hollywood. I want men to admire my mind, not my body."

He set his mouth as he turned on the ignition. "Look, let's not argue over this. I shouldn't have opened my mouth."

"Right." She crossed her arms over her chest before it sank in that he'd actually backed off. Sort of. Now his words nettled, and she wanted to pursue them further.

"Men don't take me seriously if I wear frilly clothes," she offered in the growing silence as the truck followed Cissy's dust to the main road.

"Then they're fools, and you may as well play them for such, but it's your choice, not mine. I like you fine in frills or suits. You don't have to be glamorous for my sake."

"Right, because you're a genius, not a fool." She was nervous and making an idiot of herself, but she thought he really meant what he said. He looked at her with admiration no matter what she wore. She just had a hard time seeing herself as he did.

He snorted. "I'm no genius when it comes to women. I can take a computer or a motorcycle apart and put them back together better than ever, but women I'll never figure out. I think they morph from one creature to another in between one sentence and the next."

Both Cissy and Clay turned right on the highway toward town, but half a mile down the road Cissy turned the BMW down the dirt lane leading back to the swamp and quickly disappeared in a cloud of dust.

Rory tried not to worry about the BMW or Cissy or the man sitting beside her. She had a million-dollar bottle cap in her underwear drawer, and her life seemed to be spinning out of control. She needed to get a grip on the reins again.

"Women think in terms of survival," she answered. "We may each have a different idea of what it takes to survive, but the instinct to protect ourselves and our families is basic. Grasp that, and you're halfway there."

In the shadow of the cab, Clay nodded his newly barbered head. "Excellent justification for theft, murder, and downright orneriness. Got it."

"Nah, we only need men to justify that. Survival is much more complicated." Relaxing at the foolishness— or because he wasn't staring at her as if she were the last piece of cake on earth—Rory leaned back and began to plot the evening's course.

Rory gulped when they entered city hall and instantly had an audience of well-wishers clapping them on the back. Others stood crowded in corners, pointing at her and Clay and whispering. These were her neighbors, people she hadn't seen in years and barely knew. But they all knew her and were counting on her to save their little pieces of heaven from the vast corporate world that had eaten most of the islands up and down the coast.

Like Don Quixote, she'd battled a lot of windmills without much success. She'd done it safely from within her secure corporate world without risking anything but her time. And her job, but she hadn't realized it then.

If she lost now, the realty company would rescind the offer for Cissy's share of the land, and their little acreage would be surrounded by condos within a few years. If she lost, most of these people would lose their livelihoods and their homes. What good would a million dollars do her then?

Her mouth tasted sour as Clay steered a path through the crowd to a seat up front. Out of the corner of her eye, she saw Terry Talbert signal her. He didn't look happy, but no one in here did. Skirting around the grim-faced officials in suits gathering at the front of the room, she let Clay claim their seats while she spoke with Terry.

"Rora, you can't fight zoning on the island," he whispered as soon as she came close.

"This doesn't have anything to do with the park," she explained. "We just want some planning before we turn into another Hilton Head."

"Golf courses make money!" he protested. "We *want* the park to draw in tourists and developers. That's the whole *point*. I can't believe you're fighting against everything the tourist commission stands for."

"I asked to be placed on the agenda as a property owner, not as a representative of the tourist commission," she said patiently. "I want tourists as much as you do. I'm not the evil force against development. I just want some planning first."

"We don't have *time* for planning. The state will acquire the property and auction off what they don't want to cover costs. Who will buy the land if they can't get zoning?"

Feeling vaguely sick to hear her fears laid out so plainly, Rory shook her head. "The state has a budget to buy the beach. They don't need more."

"If you go up there and delay the zoning, you're off the tourist commission, Rora. You're working against us and not with us."

Fired again for opening her big mouth. The sour taste turned bitter, but this time she figured all it cost her was a friend, and he couldn't be much of a friend if he wouldn't listen.

"Sorry, Terry, no can do. I'll send you my files in the morning." Turning her back on him, Rory walked toward Clay, who stood waiting for her to join him. Clay might not fully grasp her need to make things right, but he supported her desire to do so. He was the first damn man outside of her father to ever support her, even if all he wanted was to be in her bed. She'd give him half a brownie point for that.

Clay watched in admiration as Rory flipped open the last colorful chart succinctly conveying the impact of development without planning on the island. She summarized her report in a few powerful sentences, then returned to her seat to a round of applause. She should have been a lawyer. Her cautious, controlling nature concealed the power of her passion.

The commissioners looked more stunned than prepared to argue. Aurora had steamrollered them into their own swamp.

She took the seat beside him and Clay clasped her hand, feeling the acceleration of her pulse. "You spun their heads so forcefully, you didn't leave them any grounds to disagree on," he whispered.

She nodded but focused on Jeff Spencer, who stood to espouse the dry cause of tax bases and increased business. She didn't withdraw her hand but squeezed harder when Jeff finished up with a politician's smooth promise of a chicken in every pot, or the contemporary equivalent.

Clay had the urge to rearrange the banker's smug expression. People who thought that what they wanted was best for everyone had solidified his cynicism at an early age.

Aurora wasn't like that. She would give up her hopes of hot-dog stands if convinced they weren't good for everyone.

Shaken by that insight, Clay examined it while half listening to the commissioners argue among themselves. Aurora was here to espouse her cause, just like Jeff. She had a bee in her bonnet about condos, but she still wanted gas stations or peach stands on natural wetlands. So where the hell did he think she was different?

Because she wasn't thinking of herself so much as her neighbors and family.

She and Cissy could have taken the developer's money and run. Or they could hold out for a higher price. Or she could have gone his route, demanded total preservation of the wetlands, and had people kicked out of their homes and livelihoods.

Instead she was defending the property of people who didn't have the education or money to fight city hall.

Maybe—just maybe—he ought to start considering her side of things a little more seriously.

What would that entail? It wasn't as if he had much ready cash to help her fight. All he had was his software, and he wasn't letting any of his programs out of his control for love or money this time around. He wasn't fool enough to be burned a third time.

"All in favor of withholding a zoning change until after a planning study can be made, say aye."

Clay felt Rory hold her breath as each "aye" was recorded. Seven out of twelve. Did the majority win? Or
did they need two-thirds? He watched Rory close her
eyes and sit back with a smile of relief.

They'd won.

He liked winning, but this wasn't his home, and his triumph had far more to do with the woman beside him
blazing with exultation than in anything he had accomplished. Her joy shot through him like an aphrodisiac—
as if he needed any excuse to be turned on in her company.

"Celebration time," he whispered in her ear. "Champagne?"

"Chocolate malt," she whispered back.

"They still serve that stuff here?" With the meeting ad-
journed, he caught her arm and all but hauled her out of
the room before she could get into another public argument with the red-faced, furious banker, or the sulking
tourist commissioner. "Wasn't it declared a national health
hazard and banned along with soda fountains?"

He saw Cleo and Jared heading their way through the
crowd. With dexterity, he steered her out a side entrance
of city hall. He had romantic fireworks on the agenda
this evening, not the hotheaded kind that Cleo and Aurora could ignite in a room full of people. Although he
wasn't entirely certain Aurora recognized her power to
incite riots.

She laughed and sailed down the steps ahead of him, obviously knowing her territory and where she was headed.
"Malt is banned only in California," she asserted, "where
they eat snails and call it protein. Here, we know what's
good for you."

"Hamburger slathered in grease." Since he had no

idea where she was going, Clay didn't attempt to steer her, but followed along, all his senses zinging with anticipation. She was on a high, and they weren't fighting. Those had to be good signs.

"What did Timid Talbert have to say to you before the meeting?" That had been bothering him since he'd watched Aurora's expression go stone cold after that little discussion. She'd refused to tell him earlier under the excuse that she'd wanted to listen to the meeting. Maybe now that she'd won, she'd be a little less closemouthed.

"*Timid* Talbert?" she inquired with a lift of her eyebrows, diverting the question.

"All I have to do is growl, and he backs away as if I'm about to eat him alive. He made you angry. Why?"

Rory wasn't certain she was comfortable with Clay recognizing her anger, or in his feeling familiar enough to question her about it. But she was on a roll tonight, and he was part of the reason. Maybe she should experiment with being less controlling. "He fired me," she said with insouciance, stopping at the café.

Clay guided her inside with a proprietary hand at the small of her back. She decided she liked that old-fashioned side of him. Much too aware of heads turning, watching her with this striking man, Rory tried to look unselfconscious taking a place at the counter of her old high school haunt. Once upon a time she'd thought it the most important thing in the world to be sitting here with a hunk like Clay. Or Jeff. Surely she'd advanced a few stages of maturity since then.

"How could Talbert fire you?" he demanded. "You weren't being paid."

She shrugged and nodded at the approaching waitress.

"Not now," she whispered. "We're celebrating our victory," she reminded him in a louder voice. "Your statistics were fabulous. Now, if we could find the mayor's fabled U-boat treasure, we could give the city their funds and never worry again."

"Don't tell me you believe that story." Stella slapped the menus down in front of them. "Maybe the mayor's daddy shot those German spies like they say, but he spent every penny they carried buying up half the town."

"Not according to Brother Tim," Clay objected. "He thinks the late mayor died before he spent it all."

"And the town's sitting on gold?" Stella snorted inelegantly.

"Maybe he buried it in the swamp and Jeff thinks he can dig it up," Rory suggested.

"That's more like it. How did the petition go?" Stella switched the subject. "Are they paving the path to hell or not?"

"Not yet. Chocolate malt, please." Realizing they were attracting attention, Rory tried not to gloat, but she figured she was beaming from ear to ear.

"Delaying the zoning isn't the same as stopping it," Clay warned after ordering coffee. "Short of striking gold, we have no chance of convincing them to keep wetlands."

"Spoilsport." She pouted, and thrilled a little at the way Clay's gaze immediately diverted to her mouth. She was playing with fire here, but that was what celebrating was about, wasn't it? Dancing around a big old bonfire?

She wanted to do a whole lot more than dance around the bonfire that was Clay McCloud. He looked as if he could go up in flames at any moment.

"You'll have to persuade the committee that you can

bring in business without high-density zoning," Clay insisted, looking like a Hollywood star but talking like the genius he claimed to be.

"I don't want to hear about it." She dismissed his practicality in favor of celebration time. "I want a malt and happiness, and if you're going to be a downer, I'll do it without you."

She really didn't want him to go away. Right now she didn't care about the Terry Talberts of the world. She wanted to explore the excitement spilling through her, discover how much of it was over winning and how much was the man beside her.

"I am your bluebird of happiness," he agreed solemnly, accepting his coffee and sipping.

She raised her eyebrows at him, but busy slurping the first malt she'd enjoyed since high school, she refused to take the bait. She hoped the shiver down her spine was from the cold ice cream and not from anticipation of the night ahead, but she could feel his vibrations as certainly as her own.

Others from the audience drifted in, pounding them on the back or congratulating them, depending on proximity. Glowing with triumph, Aurora accepted the praise, knowing it could turn to scorn just as easily but not afraid. That much had changed since high school. She no longer feared disapproval.

Then maybe she should be brave enough not to fear the man who led her out of the café after they finished their celebratory snack. Clay was an intelligent adult male, after all, not a high school kid salivating to get his hands on her breasts.

Her sister might think it was the student council election that had soured Rory's attitude toward men, but
that had been only the tip of the iceberg, the part people
could see. Only Rory knew that Jeff had decided to run
against her when she'd swatted him for trying to remove
her swimsuit top. More than once. They'd ceased to be a
couple when he'd called her a prick teaser.

Her other encounters with men had pretty much been
fast-lane sex-and-runs, leaving her heart battered. She
didn't know if she was prepared to risk it again, not
when her life was already in a precarious position.

"Is your silence ominous?" Clay asked, handing her
into the truck.

"Nope. Maybe." Sitting this close to him in the small
cab, their knees nearly brushing, Rory was entirely too
aware of him. She would have to be dead to not know
that he had sex on his mind.

She simply couldn't decide if it was her brains or her
body that attracted Clay. And why should she care, since
she wouldn't be around long enough to become involved? She'd be leaving here as soon as . . . what?

The original plan had been to see her family on the
road to recovery. She could do that next week when she
cashed in the bottle cap, knock wood. But now she'd
opened a whole other can of worms. She couldn't leave
this zoning thing hanging unresolved while she pursued
her career.

"Am I that boring?" Clay asked warily when she didn't
expand upon her answer.

"Hardly. But you could be that terrifying."

"All right, that sounds promising." The pickup soared
across the bridge and onto the island. "Is it the biker

thing? Should I admit I never rode a Harley until I got here?"

Rory laughed and turned her attention more fully on him. "Really? You looked born to it."

"I like things with motors, and I always wanted a bike. Figured a place like this was a golden opportunity to change my image."

"Then let me congratulate you on your success. Must be living near Hollywood rubs off. Your acting is excellent."

"It's not an act," he insisted. "I like Harleys. Just because I can work computers doesn't mean I have to be a geek."

"I can assure you, geekdom is not what women think of when they look at you. I'd feel safer with a geek."

"No adventure in your soul," he griped. "You have to look outside the silk-necktie crowd once in a while, take a chance."

"I'm not a gambler." Maybe she should be. After all, she'd won a million dollars without even trying. "I prefer known quantities, and there's nothing certain about men and relationships," she added to remind herself as much as warn him.

He wiggled his shoulders inside his jacket as if it had become too tight. "I'm not good at discussing 'relationships.' My parents taught us it's bad manners to gossip, rude to talk about bodily functions in public, and feelings are best kept behind closed doors. Want to talk politics?"

Rory considered that a moment. He'd obviously been brought up in a much more sophisticated environment than her emotionally charged one. Grinning, she couldn't resist replying, "Ah've heard tell Yankees don't admit to needing pots to piss in, but Ah purely *loathe* speaking poorly of the uneducated."

In the light of the dashboard, Clay stared at her until his active brain kicked in and he laughed. "Gossip, bodily functions, and feelings all in one sentence. I want to introduce you to my mother."

At his warm laughter, interest flared so brightly she almost cringed.

Not until Clay exclaimed did she realize it wasn't her thoughts flaring brightly, but a roaring shower of flames against the night sky ahead.

❋ FIFTEEN ❋

The car shot past the drive leading to Jared and Cleo's. The fire soared brighter and closer, flinging sparks high into the heavens.

"Look at the top of that tree!" Aurora watched through the windshield in horror as the tip of a towering pine burst into flame.

"Pine sap burns like crazy," Clay muttered. Traffic slowed to a crawl, and he had to ease up on the accelerator. "Can you tell where it is?"

She didn't want to contemplate it. It was impossible to judge distances on flat land. She could hear sirens screaming from behind them, which meant the island's volunteer fire department had already sent out a call for reinforcement.

"The wells are unusually low." She murmured her fear aloud, as if that would dissipate it. "We've been in a drought for three years."

"Swell, surrounded by ocean and swamp and still dry. Surely they can pump it from somewhere. That marsh out there should stop it."

The cynic trying to be reassuring would have been amusing at any other time. Right now Rory grasped his encouragement and hung her prayers on it. "Pine straw," she murmured, hoping he could counter her fear. "All the houses out here use pines for shade and the dead needles for mulch."

"That stuff burns too fast to hurt anything else."

She nodded, not wanting to argue with that optimistic assessment, even if he was saying it just to shield her. His calm outlook gave her strength, forming a bond she didn't want to break.

They crawled past the peach stand at Iris's turnoff. Before they reached the road for home, police barriers blocked the highway. Behind the barriers the fire soared to new heights—in the direction of the trailer.

"Mandy," she whispered, trusting him with her worst fears. She waited for Clay to blow it off, but this time he had no reassuring words, and the terror multiplied. "Pops is in a cast. They only have the motorcycle." Would Cissy be home yet? Or was she still at Iris's, maybe stuck in this traffic, too?

His mouth forming a grim line, Clay jerked the steering wheel to one side, pulling the pickup off the road. He turned off the ignition and leaped out. "Come on, we'll walk."

Relieved that he understood and acted, Rory jumped out to follow. Pushing through the mob of spectators, they dodged vehicles and questions to reach the corner. A policeman ran up to halt them, but Clay didn't slow his stride. "Her family is down there," he shouted as he shoved past. "You'll have to shoot us to stop us."

Rory didn't know if she could have argued with an officer of the law, but Clay didn't seem to have any qualms about it. He shoved past the police officer and kept moving. She could learn to love a man who acted with confidence instead of hesitation in the face of emergency.

Another treetop burst into flame, and they broke into a run. Smoke choked the humid night air, concealing the fanciful mailboxes and colorful flower gardens in the yards along the road.

By the time they reached the curve in the long, flat pavement leading to home, bits of ash tore at Rory's lungs. Ambulances, fire trucks, and spectators littered the blacktopped lane, but Clay stayed outside the crowd, tramping through the grass and bushes. She wished she'd worn something more practical than high-heeled pumps and a business suit.

Clearing a path through a wax myrtle hedge ahead of her, Clay abruptly stopped. Turning, he grabbed her arm and steered her back toward the road. "Not this way."

He was bigger, heavier, and stronger than Rory, but she was far more terrified. With a burst of adrenaline she broke from his grip and raced back to the thicket. Pushing past a head-high shrub, she glimpsed the crumpled front fender of a powder-blue car.

Scorched ground and smoking trees surrounded it.

She opened her mouth to scream, but nothing came out. Her knees weakened, and she grabbed the branches ripping at her suit, trying to reach the car to see what was inside it.

"Don't, Aurora." Clay caught her by the waist, preventing her from tearing herself apart. "Let's go back to the road and talk to the policemen."

Heart racing, Rory ignored his admonition, elbowed him, and jerked free again.

Scraped by thorns and blackened branches, she forced

her way past the shrubbery to stare at the fire-blackened remains of her pride and joy.

The convertible top was down. The front end was totaled. Cissy wasn't in it.

Clay laid a comforting hand on her shoulder, but if she turned to him she would melt down into a helpless puddle. Instead she stiffened her spine and pulled free.

She and Cissy might never agree on anything, but she didn't want a world without her sister in it. Shaking, Rory stumbled in the direction of the road, determined to find her. Their ties ran root-deep. Cissy was mother and sister and best friend. She couldn't lose her.

The fire had destroyed the car and everything around it. Cissy had a pin in her hip and couldn't run, even if she'd survived the crash.

Panic surged through her, giving her the strength to keep moving.

This time Clay didn't stop her. Using his body as shield, he held aside branches, clearing a path to the road and the onlookers staring horror-struck at the night sky. Silence reigned as friends and neighbors watched the fire blazing down the road, spreading rapidly into the empty acreage of the Bingham swamp—roaring toward the trailer and the concrete factory.

Ignoring the fire, Aurora scanned the crowd for some sign of Cissy, praying her sister had somehow escaped. The fire must have started here, with the car Cissy was driving. Maybe there had been time . . . ?

They'd left Mandy home with Pops. Why weren't they out here?

Thoughts whirling incoherently, she fell upon the first

person she recognized when they reached the road. "Erly, where's Cissy?"

The elderly man, lined face creased even more with worry, glanced at her with dawning recognition. "Rora. I ain't seen her, hon. The firemen been goin' house to house. They'll get her out."

"That's her car back there." Panic rising, she turned from Erly to other neighbors, who heard the fear in her voice and turned to look. "Anyone seen Cissy? She was driving my car, and it's off the road back there."

"Ambulance took someone out," one woman shouted. "Didn't see who."

"I heard it was a car crash started this," a teenager called. "They took the driver into town."

"If she's walking, she headed home to check on Mandy and Jake," Clay murmured against her ear. "If she's in the ambulance, she's in good hands. Let's get closer."

Nodding because her tongue was suddenly too thick to talk, Rory followed his lead through the crowd. She needed his confidence to get her through this. She'd lost her own back there in that thicket. She clung to his hand, let him use his size to bully his way through the crowd, and prayed frantically.

Police stopped them at another roadblock, so Clay led her back into the shrubbery again. The fire had flashed so hot across the dry tinder, it had moved on without doing more than burning off the underbrush, carried by the east wind off the ocean. The stench of charred pine and wet charcoal choked the air.

"It's almost under control," he said, glancing upward at silver streams of water coursing into the trees.

He sounded positive and reassuring, but Rory figured

that was for her benefit. Flames roared through the tree-tops close to her home. Every twig around them smoldered and leaped into small fires with the slightest breeze.

Sheer terror had replaced her ability to plot a course of action. She simply trailed in Clay's path, praying as she'd never prayed before. She made wild promises to God as their feet found a grassy hummock barely touched by fire. Ahead, flames soared from two different wooded areas.

"There's not enough on the ground to feed it," Clay promised. She stumbled over the rough terrain, and he caught her waist and held her up. "The humidity is holding it in check over the marsh. It's only burning higher up where there's a breeze."

Maybe he fought forest fires in California. Maybe he knew what he was talking about. Maybe she wouldn't ask because she'd rather believe than question.

Where was Cissy? And Pops? And Mandy?

She broke into a run when she saw the weather vane on top of the house through a line of burned-out trees. Clay grabbed her, hauling her off her feet.

Rory kicked and squirmed, but this time he wouldn't let her go. Wildly, she fought his greater strength, not believing he could stop her if she'd made up her mind to go.

"Give it a rest, Aurora," he said with implacable finality. "We can't just run in there until we know if it's too hot to walk."

Too panicked to be reasonable, too frightened to fight, she collapsed against his chest. She could feel the heat, breathed the ashes and smoke, and she couldn't look. Clay's arms held her, his strength supported her, and she simply burst into helpless tears.

"I see your father." Holding her upright, he spoke

above her head. "We should go in by the road. He's turned a hose on the house, but everything else is scorched. Let me take his place, and you get him out, okay?"

Overwhelmed with relief that all might be well, she nodded against his chest, wiped her eyes, and tried to stand. Clay kept his grip on her waist as she pushed forward to observe the scene. She looked for blazing embers in the darkness, sought a clear path through the smoldering pine needles, but saw only her father in his purple cast, defiantly spraying any spark daring to alight in his vicinity.

If Pops was safe, then she'd have to believe Mandy was fine. If only she knew about Cissy . . .

Breaking free, Rory ran across charred grass, ignoring the heat and the smoke searing her skin and eyes. Hot embers burned through the soles of her pumps, water squished through the holes, but her shout of "Pops, where's Mandy?" caused her father to look up.

The relief on his bearded face was so blatant, she ran into his arms, weeping, getting soaked by the dripping hose for her efforts.

"I sent her to help old Annie out and to look for your sister. Figured the police would keep her away." Shakily he hugged her before glancing up at Clay. "Why the hell did you bring her back in here?" he roared with more than his usual force.

"You want to try to keep her out?" Clay asked, having followed in her path. "Give me the hose and you make her leave."

"I'll get the hose around back." Since they talked as if she couldn't hear, Rory ignored their commentary. "Pops, I think Cissy wrecked the car up the road. I can't find her. Someone said the ambulance may have taken her to town. You know the guys out there better than I do. Go find out what happened, please? It's killing me."

She could see the fear and uncertainty in her father's eyes. His leg had to be hurting. He couldn't run if the fire turned back in this direction. But he didn't want to be thought a coward for abandoning his daughters' house.

"Your family needs you." Clay took the hose from Jake's hands. "I can do this. I'll get Aurora out if it looks bad. I'll never budge her if you stay."

"Don't know how much longer the well will last," Jake warned. "The house ain't worth saving if the fire turns back this way. You haul her out the instant it does, y'hear?"

"It's chaos out there." Clay reached in his pockets and handed Jake his truck keys. "If you find Mandy, take her over to my place and wait for us there. You can start calling hospitals if you can't find Cissy. That way we'll know where everyone is."

A wave of relief nearly toppled Rory as Pops reluctantly took the keys and directions to the truck. Leaning on a crutch as he never did, he limped down the drive toward safety. She wanted to hug Clay in gratitude and cling to him for reassurance at the same time.

She didn't dare do either one or she'd break down and totally lose it.

"I'll go through the house, change, and get the hose out back." Without waiting for Clay's approval, Rory sprinted inside.

The house reeked of smoke but was blessedly untouched. Rory stripped off her wet suit and ruined pumps in favor of shorts and sneakers. The occasional patter of water against the thin roof reassured her that Clay had things in hand.

With a sudden terrifying thought, she jerked open her underwear drawer, located the precious bottle cap, and, with another prayer of thanks, shoved it deep into her pocket.

Having preserved the one valuable she could keep on her, she dashed outside, located the hose, and began to soak the shrubbery on the drive to her father's workshop. That he'd ignored his home and work and precious motorcycle in favor of saving his daughters' possessions brought another choking sob to her throat, but she fought it back. Tears could come later.

She kept a watch on the night sky and the flames flickering through the trees in the marsh. How well did cypress burn? Would Grandma Iris and the others back there be safe?

She couldn't tell the exact location of the leaping flames in the distance except that they seemed to be caught on the ocean breeze from the east and heading west.

Cleo's house and Clay's cottage were west of the Bingham swamp.

A smoldering ember caught in the pine mulch around the enormous azaleas camouflaging the old toolshed. Rory dragged the hose from the drive and back to the wooden structure, turning it on the flames licking at the dry bushes. The fire grew faster than she could spray, and she panicked. She tugged at the hose to get closer, but she had reached its length. The water pressure dwindled, dripping just short of the fire licking along the termite-riddled wood. If the fire reached the shed's roof, it could easily leap into the trees overhanging the house.

Apparently losing pressure in the front hose, Clay jogged around the corner of the trailer. Grasping her predicament, he grabbed a heavy concrete birdbath full of water, flung the contents on the low-lying flames, and ran for a nearby fountain. "What's in there?" he yelled.

"Old mowers, tillers, junk," she shouted back.

"Gasoline?" He dropped the birdbath he'd lifted and planted himself in front of her, apparently prepared to push her out of the reach of danger.

Rory shook her head. "Pops said the place is a firetrap. He keeps the gas with his bike." His expression of relief warmed her, giving her the strength to continue instead of giving up and getting out.

In silence they worked to combat the leapfrogging sparks, Rory with her trickle of water from the hose filling every available container, Clay lifting and emptying one concrete lawn ornament after another to the tinder-dry shack. The roof collapsed in a rain of flame and smoke, but the thoroughly doused shrubbery burned slower.

By the time Clay had climbed a fence to drop a Byzantine structure of spouting fish and mermaids on the last embers, Rory was crying tears of laughter as well as relief.

"I never thought that monument to Poseidon's bad taste would ever have a use." Her voice cracked and sounded hoarse. Abandoning the dry hose, she wrapped her arms around Clay's waist and kissed him.

He stank of wet smoke, and his fancy dress shirt was soaked in sweat, but he tasted more wonderful than strawberries and chocolate together. His mouth hungrily covered hers, not entirely in a sexual way, but seeking the same life-affirming reassurance she needed. Finding bliss in this mutual understanding, Rory was reluctant to release him when the kiss became something more demanding.

He pulled her roughly into his arms and deepened the connection with tongue and lips and an urgency that dragged her off her feet.

A hail from the driveway abruptly slapped them back to reality. "Everyone all right in here?"

With a curse, Clay set her back enough to break the spell. He lifted his smoke-smudged face to check the location of the fire, listened to the sirens in the distance, then watched her expression. "I think it's under control here," he called to the policeman on the drive.

In a lower voice, he added to her, "I'll talk to the cops, see what I can find out. Why don't you check the phone and see if you can call my place?"

Cissy. Without wasting time on words, Rory raced for the house. She had to know about Cissy.

Shivering, she flipped on a light, grateful the electricity still worked. Her fingers flew through the box of business cards and notes beside the phone, locating the index card she'd scribbled Clay's number on. Punching the numbers in, she collapsed against the counter while it rang.

"McCloud residence," a female voice announced curtly.

"Cleo!" Terror took root as she pondered the reason for Clay's sister-in-law's presence at the beach house. "This is Aurora. Is my family there?"

"Thank God!" Cleo's voice gained more animation. "We have two of them here, refusing to leave until they hear from you. Where's Clay?"

"Harassing policemen. My sister? Have they heard from Cissy?"

"Let me give you to your father before he pounds a hole in the floor with that cast."

"Rora?" he roared into her ear before Cleo could add any niceties. "You okay?"

"It's all okay. The well ran dry, we lost the toolshed, but I think we got all the hot spots. Clay's checking to see what else we need to do. Is Mandy there? Have you heard from Cissy?"

"Mandy's fine. We found Ciss. Your fancy car had air bags, so she's bruised up some, but she was walking, looking for us when the neighbors found her. They sent her in for observation. We were just waiting to hear from you before we catch a ride into Charleston. Are you gonna be okay?"

Exhausted, Rory knelt on the vinyl kitchen floor and pressed her forehead against the cabinet wall. Whispering silent prayers of thanksgiving, she couldn't immediately reply. Tears stung her swollen eyes, and she swiped at them while she tried to find words to reassure her father. "We can take your bike over, then drive in and pick Cissy up." She hoped she sounded sensible.

"Nah, don't you bother. You gotta keep an eye on the house. Never know what sumsabitches will be poking around, looking for trouble. Keep McCloud there until we get home. I figure they won't let Ciss out until morning."

She couldn't think straight enough to argue. Her father put Mandy on, and they exchanged encouraging words before hanging up.

Cissy was safe. Her family was all right.

Her life would never be the same again.

She managed to stumble into the bathroom, wash her face, and pull her tangled, smoky hair into a ponytail.

Clutching the bottle cap in her pocket, she blocked out all thought of more hospital and ambulance bills. Instead she worried over the neighbors, checked the night sky to see if more flames had cropped up, and walked the yard to search for hot spots.

When she recognized Clay's shadow jogging up the drive, she ran toward him, halting awkwardly just before she reached him. Ignoring her uncertainty, he wrapped one arm around her shoulders and hugged her wearily, then steered her toward the house.

"Cissy's okay," she said breathlessly, trying to spill all her news before her voice gave out. "They have her in the hospital for observation. Mandy and Pops are going in to see her."

He squeezed her shoulder. "Your sister's tough. She'll probably sneak out of bed and run away rather than face you over the damned car."

Rory hadn't thought of that. She didn't care about the car. Somewhere during the evening it had lost its importance. "I ought to go and talk to her, but Pops says we should guard the house."

"Let your sister rest. The cops have a patrol car driving up and down the road, but someone needs to stay here. The swamp halted the worst of it, but it's impossible to know if they've got all the hot spots. I told them I'd be here if the neighbors needed any help."

He'd be here. With her. In an empty house.

Rory tilted her head back to read his expression in the porch light.

Gray eyes returned her look, watching warily.

After all they'd been through, she couldn't turn him away. Didn't want to turn him away.

❦ SIXTEEN ❦

"I'll fix coffee." Rory held the door open for him to catch.

Clay supposed he should be relieved that she hadn't told him to sleep on the lawn after he'd nearly molested her in the backyard under completely inappropriate conditions. He wasn't a demonstrative man, but seeing her running toward him, unharmed and with open arms, had jolted awake a starving need he didn't recognize. He'd wanted to hold her and never let her go. And then he'd nearly devoured her until she'd had to push him away. Not precisely hero behavior.

Maybe her southern hospitality required that she invite him in before throwing him out. Or she wanted to pump him on what he'd found out about the accident.

He hoped it wasn't the latter. His suspicious mind had fixated on Aurora's car and destructive fires, and he wasn't liking his conclusions. The policeman hadn't been telling him everything. If she threw him out, he'd sleep on the lawn rather than leave her here alone.

"Water is fine," he replied, before remembering the water had run out. "You can't do either without water. Whatever you have will do."

"The house is on the water line. Only the hoses are on the well." She led the way back to the kitchen and removed ice cubes from the freezer.

He thought she might still be running on adrenaline and shock. She sounded hoarse. He could see where she'd attempted to wash the soot off her face, but it was ground into her hairline. She still brightened his world like sunrise. He didn't know how to deal with that feeling.

His stoic upbringing hadn't taught him to deal with rioting emotion. He really didn't want to be the one in the line of fire when Aurora's brain kicked in and she started asking questions. He'd much rather fall back on mind-melting kisses than face her fear and fury.

Kisses apparently overruled self-preservation. He stayed put.

He let the iced water slide down his parched throat. He stank to high heaven and probably looked like a chimney sweep. He needed a shower before he could think about being alone with the woman he wanted so much that he walked around with a permanent hitch in his stride.

Maybe he just had smoke in his eyes.

"If the water's working, would you mind if I took a shower?" Clay set the glass down on the counter. If he was staying here all night, he wanted her to be comfortable with him, but he wasn't certain this was the time or the place to ask for anything more.

She nibbled her luscious lip. He hoped he wasn't imagining the look of fascination in her eyes. If she would simply let loose of her iron-clad control, maybe he could see stars and soft violet nights, and they could wipe out this night of horror. His heart set up a jungle beat, and his palms were moist from something other than his glass of water.

"Not at all. You know where it is," she answered, her gaze dropping to his mouth.

"We could always shower together." He lifted one eyebrow in a leer, only half joking. The adrenaline high had hit both of them. He knew now wasn't the time to act on it. He just wanted the attraction between them out front and acknowledged. Maybe he needed to confirm that it was mutual.

She looked slightly shocked, then thoughtful. At least she hadn't socked him one.

"Yeah, but I won't." Crossing her arms over bounteous breasts outlined by her damp T-shirt, tilting her chin up, she backed away. "I'll use Cissy's shower."

Uncertain how to follow up on such a conflicting declaration, Clay held his ground. He didn't want a woman in his bed if she didn't want to be there. He simply wanted to understand. He waited, saying nothing.

She glared at him and rubbed a nervous hand over her disheveled hair. "It's just adrenaline and hormones. I'm not a kid anymore. I don't have to explore every urge that comes along."

The feeling was mutual. He could settle for that. For now.

"Neither do I." His voice sounded gravelly, even to him. Too much smoke, he supposed. "Just because a woman makes herself available doesn't mean I hop into bed with her. I prefer waiting for someone special."

Without trying to explain the inexplicable, Clay turned and walked away. He needed a shower, but he couldn't decide if cold or hot would work best in his current physical state.

After sudsing her hair a half dozen times in Cissy's herbal shampoo, and dawdling until the hot water ran out, Rory emerged from the shower and donned an ankle-length denim dress she'd grabbed from her closet.

She felt clean on the outside, but smoke still seemed to whirl and obscure the inside of her skull.

She fretted over Cissy. She worried the fire would return. She didn't know where to put her bottle cap. And Clay was wandering out there somewhere, wanting something she wasn't prepared to give him.

Just because a woman makes herself available doesn't mean I hop into bed with her. Did that mean he wanted her because she wasn't available?

She had to take her lust-stricken mind elsewhere.

Now that she'd stopped shaking, her thoughts tumbled back to the bottle cap in her dress pocket. It could have burned in the fire. A million dollars, gone, because she'd been too stupid to take it to a bank in Charleston.

Although, with her luck, the bank would probably have burned down.

But if she concentrated on her family and the bottle cap, she had less time to fret about the virile male pacing her front room. The way she felt right now, he could roar the mating call of a hungry tiger, and she would respond in kind.

Dallying, she twisted her damp hair into a braid and stuck a few pins in loose ends. She searched Cissy's drawers for cosmetics but couldn't find any suitable. When she ran out of excuses she returned to the main room.

She could start a to-do list while watching the smoldering yard. Surely she had enough crowding her mind to shut out the needs Clay's devastating kiss had awakened.

Instead of pacing the room as she'd expected, her guest had moved her computer in front of the TV. She could practically feel his vibrations across the room, but he was tamely sitting on the couch, shooting purple mushrooms drifting across the screen while keeping an eye on the big picture window behind him to be certain the yard wasn't engulfed in flames.

Weren't those games supposed to have guns and blood and other appalling visuals to relieve male testosterone poisoning? She'd almost feel better if he were noisily blowing up trucks on screen instead of smoldering quietly. And where had the game come from? She didn't keep games on her computer. Had Mandy been playing with it?

How could he appear so in control when she felt as if she might jump out of her skin at any moment?

He glanced up at her appearance, and the glow in his eyes leaped into flame, shaking her even more. She'd never known a man like Clay McCloud before. She couldn't call him a biker or a beach bum anymore. Without labels, she didn't know how to handle him. Just exactly who was he, anyway?

His damp hair curled against his strong brown neck. She'd given him an old work shirt of her father's that she'd borrowed years ago. Jake was a burly man, but Clay wore the shirt unbuttoned and still filled out the shoulders, although the rest of it billowed around him.

She'd not had any substitute for his damp and dirty khakis. He'd wrapped one of her big shower towels around his middle, so he must have dropped them in the wash. She could hear the dryer running—a man who knew how to do laundry! Much better to think about that than what the towel concealed.

She cast a discreet glance to his lap but caught only a glimpse of muscled thigh covered in golden hair.

Shivering at the level of arousal one glimpse could generate, she ignored the inviting lift of his eyebrow and began setting out fans to clear the air of the stench of smoke.

Shrugging, Clay returned to his game. She was too nervous to disturb him, so she raided the refrigerator. An all-nighter called for food.

Keeping an eye out the kitchen window for any re-igniting embers in the backyard while Clay watched the front, she boiled shrimp and cut up cheese and strawberries. She threw them on a platter with some grapes and crackers, added a dip and leftover shrimp sauce, and carried the tray to the coffee table. "Wouldn't the lounge chair be more comfortable?"

Clay didn't glance up. "Can't be comfortable and think straight at the same time."

He had long, arched feet and sinewy legs from running. Distracted, Rory turned to the TV screen to cover her nervousness.

"Playing games requires thinking?" She watched a dancing pink elephant walk over a smirking clown and fill the screen with exploding bubbles. She didn't see much thought behind that.

"This game does. Ever played?"

"Never had time to learn video games," she admitted. "I don't know where Mandy found that one."

"I loaned it to her the other day when she came over with Kiz."

Figures. "What would you like to drink?" She hadn't meant to sound curt, but Clay stopped what he was doing to turn his unfathomable gaze on her, so he must have caught the tone. The man might not communicate in normal fashion, but he listened—even when she didn't want him to. She didn't like being nervous. It made her even more defensive.

"Don't suppose you have wine, do you?" He checked out the tray and scarfed up a handful of shrimp.

"Nope. With teenagers in and out, we don't keep more than Pops's six-pack of beer. Will that do?"

"Even better. Thanks." He set the controller aside and strode off to check the dryer, holding the towel in place.

Rory felt somewhat better that she wasn't the only one suffering with this awareness. She'd probably self-destruct if she had to sit here much longer, waiting for the towel to shift.

When Clay returned, he was wearing a still slightly damp but much cleaner pair of trousers. She wasn't certain the damp trousers were an improvement over the towel. She politely kept her gaze on his face rather than the way the cloth clung to him when she handed him a cold beer. They were dancing around each other as if they were teenagers.

He dropped down on the couch beside her and helped himself to more shrimp.

She thought he'd focused all his energy on the game until he asked, "Why did you never have time to play games?"

That was when she figured out the game was just a

diversion, like the food, and she was his main topic of interest. Having all that intelligence aimed in her direction was almost scary.

She tried to shrug it off. "Pops never earned enough to buy more than groceries and pay the utilities. Cissy and I worked to buy our clothes and things. Games were way down on my list of necessities."

He sampled a dipped strawberry and, apparently approving, began making huge inroads through the fruit. He didn't notice what he was eating, though. Instead his full attention fell on her. "I'll teach you to play. It helps to unwind."

Admittedly she was curious about the colorful images still bouncing across the screen, but she was wary of his intentions, given the level of hormones buzzing around the room. "We probably ought to patrol the grounds every so often. Dry kudzu could go up in a minute."

"It's starting to rain. I don't think you have to worry."

She'd been concentrating so hard on him, she hadn't noticed. Surprised, she listened. The gentle patter against the roof was too rhythmic for tree branches. Still on edge, she rose on her knees to check out the picture window. It was hard to see anything in the meager porch light, but a dark puddle on the front walk glittered and reflected spreading drops.

Not realizing how terrified she'd been that the trailer would go up in flames, Rory pressed her forehead against the steamy window and expelled a huge sigh of relief. As a kid she'd hated her embarrassing home, but now that she'd almost lost it, she realized how much it meant to her. She'd grown up here. Her memories of her mother and laughing Christmases and birthday parties were all tied to this place. It was a *home*, not a trailer. Her modern condo in the city could never compare.

Turning away from the window, she was hit with the impact of the large man occupying the couch beside her, his sun-burnished hair gleaming in a pool of lamplight, his regard so intent on her that he forgot to drink from the can he was holding halfway to his mouth.

Her stomach did weird little twists as she sat back down. "We should get some sleep."

"Ain't gonna happen." Finally remembering the beer in his hand, he took a deep gulp, then set the can neatly on a coaster. When she didn't say anything, he reached for the game controller. "You can go to bed if you like. Unless you have a machine you want fixed, I guess I'll just play this."

"I'll be okay by myself," she said tentatively. "Maybe you could find the keys to Pops's bike."

The glare he turned on her positively bristled with male outrage. "The cops are patrolling the road for looters. Your sister is in the hospital, and you have no transportation. You think I ought to walk away?"

Every other male of her acquaintance would have. Especially after she'd refused his advances.

Clay didn't operate like normal people—probably because he lived on a vast plane above the common, giving him a broader scope than most. She had no right to believe that, but she did. Maybe she needed to right now.

Nervously Rory clasped her elbows and let the first whisper of fear into her universe. "Cissy is cautious to the max. I don't see how she could have gone off the road like that."

The look Clay gave her said he didn't want to talk

about this, but she couldn't help it. She'd almost lost everything tonight. She needed to understand why.

"Maybe a deer jumped in front of the car. Save it until you can ask her." He stared at the computer screen in seeming fascination, but she was beginning to understand the game was a reflexive action to cover up his rapidly spinning mental wheels.

"I thought cars only started fires in movies." She couldn't let it go. She didn't dare relax. She needed some *control* of the situation.

"It's dry enough out there for a spark from the bumper hitting a stone to ignite spilled gas," he insisted. "We'll know more in the morning. Find something else to do besides ask questions we can't answer."

Watching the pink elephant dance across the screen under Clay's manipulation, Rory surrendered. She wasn't ever going to sleep tonight. Rather than contemplate the alternative, she gave in. "Teach me to play."

She thought the devil looked back from Clay's deceptively clear eyes, but she took the hand he offered and slid down beside him on the plush green couch.

A man smelling of lemon soap couldn't be too dangerous.

"If the princess picks up the sword, she loses, but if she chooses a *fishing pole*, she defeats the monster?" Aurora asked in disbelief as her character strode triumphantly through the Gates of Gold. "Who the dickens comes up with these things?"

"Idealistic teenagers?" Clay suggested dryly. He'd finally convinced her to sit in front of him so he could show her how to use the controller, but she perched on the edge of the couch rather than make herself comfortable against his crotch. He liked an independent woman, but this one carried a good thing too far. His arms literally ached to hold her. Or maybe they ached from trying too hard not to brush her breasts.

"I'm in awe. I thought these things were all bloody battles. This is *fun*. What is she supposed to be doing in this cave?" She steered her character toward a dusty book on a shelf.

Clay brought his blue Karate Turtle character out of the rocks to poke around a conspicuous chest on the cave floor. "*Most* people look for treasure."

"That's too obvious," she scoffed, opening the virtual book. "Whoever created this thing had a devious mind."

Clay wasn't certain if that was a good thing or bad, but the herbal scent of red-gold tresses spilling down her back kept him from caring. Now that the game had captured Aurora's imagination, she bounced on the cushion like a gleeful child, braid swinging. He didn't care what the hell was happening on the screen. He simply wanted to bask in her eager energy, sink his fingers into soft, womanly flesh, and see where the moment took them.

Her tears earlier had pierced him in so many places that any word she spoke now slipped through his perforated hide to rub and irritate, or soothe and calm. She'd have him riddled to the bone if she kept this up. Her laughter softened him in dangerous ways.

It didn't soften the part of him that had been hard all evening. And he didn't mind that either. With some other woman, he might have become impatient, but this one kept blowing things up in his face, entertaining him on so many levels that he could wait until she was ready. Anticipate it, even.

She was a natural-born troublemaker in establishment disguise. He just wasn't certain she realized that. He wanted to be around for the fireworks when she did. He suspected he wanted more than that, but he would take it one step at a time.

"Oh, you dirty rat!" she shouted when his turtle won the Book of Wisdom by producing a golden key from beneath the princess's belt.

Aurora aimed an elbow backward at his midsection in retaliation, but Clay took the opening and dragged her back against him, sighing in satisfaction as his arms finally closed around her.

"To the wise go the rewards." He nibbled her ear until she turned her head. He had his arms full of woman, and he couldn't resist. He found her mouth with his, and electricity crackled.

He shut his eyes and drank in the flood of sensation—strawberry lips, rosemary-scented hair, searing hot kisses that he felt all the way to his groin—agony and ecstasy all rolled into one.

He fell back against the wide cushions, pulling Aurora down on top of him. She let him do it, feeding him with eager kisses instead of protesting as he'd half expected.

With her crushable breasts and belly cushioned against him, Clay rolled over, sandwiching her between the back of the sofa and himself. She had a way of tangling her tongue with his that blew steam out of his ears. His libido demanded that he take charge and conquer, win the duel of tongues and claim the prize.

He wasn't about to frighten her into backing off as he

had earlier. He desperately wanted Aurora in so many ways that he thought he might explode if he held in all these rampaging, conflicting tensions. He knew once he focused on a goal, his intensity could overcome good sense.

He searched his overheated—devious—brain for some means of holding himself in check while encouraging her, but an armful of woman kissing him with mind-melting ardor discouraged rational thinking. Her long fingers were wandering through his hair, and the pressure of soft breasts and hips crushed against him in all the right places sent any semblance of thought southward. The way he felt right now, this was anything but a casual encounter—a revelation that he wasn't prepared to explore.

With one last vestige of inspiration, Clay caught Aurora's hand, pressed a kiss to her palm, and placed it on his biceps. "Remember those old Atari games that had joysticks instead of controllers? Pretend I'm your joystick. Take me where you want to go."

If he put her in control, then maybe he wouldn't scare her away.

Rory's eyes flew open, staring disbelievingly into Clay's unwavering gray gaze. *Joystick?*

She didn't know anything about joysticks, and she scrambled for interpretation. A hard male body pressed her into the sofa cushions, a heavy thigh trapped hers, and she ached for so many things at once, she couldn't begin to name them. She could think of only one joystick on him, and she wasn't about to go there. Surely he wasn't so crude as to suggest . . . ?

Clay slid his hand through her hair, loosening the braid so it fell over her shoulders. "How about this? Do you like your hair undone?" He leaned over and nibbled her ear. "Does the turtle win the fair princess if he tastes her here?"

She chuckled in relief at his foolishness. Games were fun and nothing to fear. "The turtle is likely to land on his shell if he's not careful."

"Then the turtle will die. The fair princess wouldn't let the turtle die. He can show her many wise things. He's a very useful turtle," he said in a seductive rumble, kissing the tender place behind her ear.

He was very useful in more ways than this, but at the moment she could concentrate only on smoky kisses and simmering fires. She'd never been called a fair princess before. His whisper tantalized, but his hands were the prize she wanted.

Following his lead, Rory slid her fingers over Clay's cheek and guided his mouth back to hers. He accepted the offer so forcefully, she thought she might melt down to a pair of red shoes like the Wicked Witch of the West.

Aggravatingly, he didn't use his magical hands to touch her anywhere else. He clung to the sofa back behind her and leaned over to tease her with kisses and no more. She wanted his arms around her. She wanted his hardness pressed against her belly. Her breasts longed for attention—and she knew where that would lead and didn't care.

"Might I suggest . . ." He caught her hand and slid it under his open shirt so her fingers caressed the smooth skin over bulging muscles.

"The turtle has a broad shell," she murmured, liking the way his muscles rippled beneath her fingers so well that she explored his back and started on his front. He groaned as she addressed her attention to his puckered male nipples and stroked the light hairs over his pecs.

"The turtle may expire of pleasure before he pleases the princess." His breath was hot and seductive as he nibbled her ear. "He is at your command. Lead him, your highness."

She'd seldom played games as a child. She'd always understood that if she wanted to escape the tedium of poverty, she had to study and work hard and be the best at everything she did.

She'd thought of sex as another lesson to be studied and learned—and discarded when she'd found no advantage in it. Clay's teasing opened up enticing new views of this abandoned area of interest. She liked the idea of playing games with him. She liked the game he was playing.

She captured his wide, capable hand—his "joystick" if she lifted her mind from the gutter and interpreted correctly—and spread his fingers across her cheek, enjoying the rasp of calloused skin. "Touch me," she commanded in her best princess voice. Just saying the words shot a thrill through her. She'd never been so decadent in her life.

"Your servant will take much pleasure in doing so."

Clay's voice was low and beguiling, but there wasn't a damned thing subservient in his rapt attention. He traced his fingers across her cheek and gazed into her eyes as if she were the most fascinating treasure on earth, and he meant to claim her. He ran his hand to her nape and nibbled kisses along her jaw, testing for those places that made her moan. He brushed his lips across her skin tenderly, but with a hunger that drove her wild.

The intensity of his focus was too much to bear. She turned his head so she could meet his mouth with hers. It was easier this way, feeling, touching, not watching what was happening between them.

He kissed her slowly, savoring her mouth and tongue, letting the need build between them. His hand trailed down her spine, cupping her buttocks through the denim, stroking her hips—touching everywhere but where she wanted him most.

Servant, her foot and eye. He was the one in control here, and he was driving her crazy.

She kneaded his bare chest and nipples to show him what she wanted, but maddeningly he retraced the trail he'd already created. His kiss became more urgent, but still his hand remained on charted territories.

Every other man she'd kissed had gone straight for her breasts, but not this aggravating creature.

"Treat me as yours to do with as you wish," he murmured against her mouth, granting her a freedom of terrifying proportions—forcing her to admit she wanted this as much as he did.

She'd never taken command in sex before. It had never seemed the feminine thing to do, or she'd feared driving her partner away with her aggressiveness. But Clay was letting her know that not only were they equals in this, but she could call a halt at any time. The decision was hers.

"I'll make turtle soup of you shortly," she growled back, but she couldn't resist his game any longer. Taking command of his free hand, she placed it over her breast.

His reaction was instantaneous and dizzyingly gratifying.

Through denim and lace, Clay cupped and squeezed

and explored as if she were the most wonderful prize he'd ever won, when she was the one about to succumb to pleasure. She saw pure delight in his eyes as he studied her reaction to each touch and stroke. When he finally unfastened the buttons of her dress and slid his hand inside, Rory couldn't watch anymore. She closed her eyes and just let herself feel.

Feeling led to brainlessness, she knew, but Clay had shattered all resistance. She couldn't condemn him as selfish or greedy or interested only in her body, no matter how hard she might try. He concentrated on her pleasure and needs before giving in to his.

He had her completely under him and both hands inside her dress before she knew how she'd landed there. Hands that could take apart clocks and motorcycles wasted no time on bra hooks. He filled his palms with her bare breasts and brought her to the brink with just his touch. When he bent and applied his tongue to the places he'd aroused, Rory lost control, surrendered, submitted, and wept with joy until even his mouth on her breast wasn't enough.

She reached for his belt buckle, and he had his khakis unfastened before her fumbling fingers could work it out. His moan of pleasure as she took advantage of this new freedom released a frozen latch inside her, and she boldly went where she never had before.

She'd always been the compliant receptor of whatever her partners wanted, never reaching out for her own pleasure. Clay offered her the freedom to take as much control as she desired. Or as little.

She lifted her hips so he could drag her dress upward and touch her through her panties. She shoved at his trousers until he rose from the couch and dropped them. He grappled for his wallet in his pants pocket to produce a plastic package and tore it open, but she was too fascinated by the tent of his jersey boxers to pay attention.

Only when he remained silent and standing did she raise her gaze to his face. He was staring down at her as if she were a feast for the gods.

When he spoke, he confirmed what she saw in his eyes. "Do you have any idea how beautiful you are? I feel pagan enough to kneel down at your altar and worship you."

Her usual embarrassment at her overabundance didn't materialize. Clay's appreciation released her from all inhibition. "You make a good Jupiter to my Juno," she murmured, unable to hide from his shameless display of masculinity.

He towered over her, his gaze heating to smoking at her words. Playtime was over. She lay prone before a sex god of no mean proportions and obvious intent.

She no longer cared if this was for one night or forever. She needed now.

Rory opened her arms to welcome him, and Clay immediately knelt on the couch, covering her with his golden body. He lowered his weight until his erection pressed and rubbed where she ached for him. She couldn't stop him if she wanted to. She was too swept up in his kisses, in the magic of his hands on her bare breasts, in the murmurs of pleasure and nonsense he dispensed as he tugged her dress over her head and returned her to the peaks his abrupt departure had reduced.

"Tell me when," he demanded, his breath whispering against her cheek. They lay nearly naked together, the friction of their skin heating their blood. "Say the magic words."

Clay had turned sex into a game and taught her how to play. She didn't know if she was winning or losing, but he was offering her the next turn. She wasn't about to refuse it.

If she thought of what they were doing as a game, she could do this. She reached for the waistband of his boxers. "Do I win a treasure for setting the dragon free?"

"Magic wand," he corrected, maneuvering his underwear off with a single quick tug. "Insert with caution."

Laughing, breathless at the prize revealed, she corrected, "Magic club."

Ignoring her approving appraisal, Clay stripped off her panties while his mouth and tongue did things to hers that made words meaningless. Surrendering, she whispered "Alakazam" against his lips.

He took instant advantage, covering her with his weight, capturing her mouth with his tongue before taking possession of her body with his sex.

With a cry, Aurora accepted the thrust of magic, fell under the Purple Knight's spell, and let the potion of life bubble and lift her high in shivering sparkles of joy.

❧ SEVENTEEN ❧

Purple mushrooms exploded across the monitor to the tune of "Love Me Do."

Lying on his side, Clay awoke in such a cloud of contentment, he wondered if the mushrooms flashing before his eyes were hallucinogenic.

Then the scent of strawberries reached him, and he realized the soft cushion of breasts that had warmed him all night had disappeared. Missing them, missing Aurora's warm body next to his, he shifted position so he could see the end of the couch.

In the soft light of dawn, Aurora sat splendidly naked at his feet, absorbed in manipulating the game controller, trying to conquer the game that he'd created. It was such a glorious sight, he thought he might lie here forever and just watch. Fantasies of waking up like this every morning danced through his addled head.

Fantasies that encouraged more physical urges.

He stroked his toe against her bare hip to show he was awake and willing. She stopped playing to regard him cautiously. That wasn't the reaction he wanted, but it was better than some he could name. At least she hadn't wrapped herself up in armor again.

"Good morning, my queen." He propped himself on his elbow and inquired, "How soon can we expect your father to arrive?"

She didn't shriek or run, and hope ran rampant. Maybe he hadn't imagined they'd connected on a deeper level than the physical last night. Maybe she'd simply retreated to the game because she was shy of the intensity of that connection. It certainly made him nervous, but he was prepared to take risks. She wasn't.

To his regret, she apparently decided against extending their pleasurable interlude. In a fluid movement of breasts and hips and cascading hair that captured his admiration, she grabbed her denim dress off the floor.

Feeling a bit exposed, Clay grappled on the rug for his khakis. She dropped them on his lap before wiggling her dress on.

He wasn't adept at reading women, but he figured her continued silence didn't bode well. Last night hadn't been enough for him. He'd thought she felt the same. Maybe she wasn't a morning person.

He watched with regret as the denim slid to cover rosy nipples, supple curves, and, finally, the darker red of curls no longer concealed by panties. His Viking princess radiated the colors of dawn and the sensuality of an earth goddess. She grounded him in reality, and he wanted to keep her around longer.

He tugged on his khakis, and wadded his shorts up with the shirt he'd borrowed. "Coffee?"

He meant to make it for her, but she nodded and pattered off in bare feet to find the beans and fill the pot. Fearing anything he said would set her off in the wrong direction, Clay wandered back to her bathroom to make himself presentable—not an easy task without a razor.

He grimaced at his whisker-stubbled face in the mirror, took a quick shower, and ran a comb through his hair. Normally, the morning after, he just wanted the woman he was with to go away so he could get back to work. Strangely, he had no interest whatsoever in work this morning.

So maybe Diane had been right to leave him. She'd been good to look at, athletic in bed, but once he'd looked and touched, he'd wandered off to his own pursuits, and she'd gone after hers. They'd had no interests in common. Neither of them had been much on lazy mornings or playful nights.

He was just rediscovering the fun of fantasizing that had led him into game writing and programming. He wanted to fantasize about Aurora naked in his bed on a regular basis. She stirred his imagination as much as his body.

He pulled on the shirt that had looked expensive and businesslike when he'd dressed for the meeting last night. It currently resembled a refugee from a trash bin. Last night's fire had burned holes in the fabric, and his impromptu laundering had left it hopelessly wrinkled.

Aurora didn't seem to notice. Looking up from the coffee she was pouring when he returned to the kitchen, she didn't smile, but he thought he saw appreciation in her eyes when she handed him a mug.

She'd taken time to brush her glorious hair and tie it into a ribbon. The denim was no worse for wear after a night on the floor. She still looked like a goddess.

"Good coffee," was all he said.

*   *   *

Uncomfortable with the thick cloud of unspoken words between them, Aurora wrapped her hands around her mug and tried not to admire the man across from her too blatantly. No man had ever made her feel as Clay had. She ought to be ashamed of having fallen into bed so easily with a man who had no intention of hanging around, but she wasn't. Mornings-after were always a little strange, but Clay didn't make her feel uncomfortable with her sexuality or her looks or anything else.

She just didn't know where to go from here, and he offered no clues.

She wandered to the patio doors to look out on last night's devastation. The colorful array of flowers and the spring-laden vegetable garden they had mulched with pine straw had vanished in the fire. The oaks were charred but still standing, the leaves shriveled by heat. Some of the blackened pines still smoldered. The smoking ashes of the toolshed served to remind her of the tragedy that could have been.

She didn't know what to say. They'd behaved like a pair of adolescents last night, and it had been fun. A necessary release, perhaps. The morning recalled the dangers of childishness. At least he'd had the sense and maturity to remember protection. She wouldn't have.

Knowing he'd been the responsible one, that he'd taken care of her when she hadn't been thinking, lightened the confusion she'd experienced since waking. The night had been merely a life-affirming reaction to the earlier horror. It didn't have to mean anything serious. Sometimes people had sex just for the fun of it.

She turned and offered him a tentative smile. "I think

gaming could become addictive." Sex with McCloud certainly could be.

Wearing khakis and a wrinkled dress shirt, he didn't look like a biker anymore, despite the beard stubble. Leaning back against the table, crossing his legs at the ankles, he looked sexy, experienced, and almost as uncertain as she felt, which seemed odd. A man like Clay McCloud could have women begging at his feet. Shouldn't that lead to a measure of arrogance at times like this?

"Yeah, it probably is, but there are worse addictions," he agreed, after sipping his coffee.

The phone rang and, thinking of Cissy, Rory grabbed it.

"Aurora, this is Jeff Spencer."

Looking up at Clay's expression of concern, she narrowed her eyes and shook her head. Why would Jeff be calling her?

Before she could ask, he continued, "Is your sister there?"

Her eyebrows must have shot to her hairline. Clay closed in, but she didn't need his support—yet. "No, she's not. May I take a message?"

She heard the hesitation on the other end, and her stomach did a nervous jig. Cissy had taken an equity loan against the land at Jeff's bank to pay for Mandy's braces, but as far as she was aware, it was up-to-date.

"Your name is on the note, so I guess it's okay to talk to you," Jeff agreed reluctantly. "We've had our adjusters surveying the damage from the fire. Your place and a couple of others around there must have taken the brunt of it."

Still suspicious, Rory tried to figure where this was leading. She'd worked in a bank. Banks did not send out insurance adjusters. They expected property owners to do that. "We have a few trees that need removing. I haven't gone down the road yet, but the house is fine."

He coughed nervously, unlike his usual assured self. "Manufactured housing doesn't appreciate. Yours doesn't have any value left. We loaned the money on the value of the land. The adjusters say it's considerably diminished without the timber. We'll have to call in the loan as too risky."

Were she a violent person, Rory would gladly have reached through the phone and strangled Jeff. As it was, she was glad Cissy wasn't here to listen to this self-serving nonsense. Remembering the bottle cap, she grinned in glee.

She now had the means to take Jeff's measly loan and shove it down his throat. Spitefully, the knowledge tickled her all the way down to her toes.

"That's no problem, Jeff," she said in tones so dulcet Clay frowned. "I was planning on paying the loan off next week. Why don't you pull together a payoff figure as of next Friday?"

She'd planned on taking the bank interest off against her taxes, so she hadn't considered using her bottle cap to pay the mortgage. But if that was the way the bank wanted to play, she'd work it out. Mandy's braces couldn't have cost anywhere near the hundred thousand or more the hospital bills had reached to date.

She *loved* having a million-dollar pillow to fall back on. She could really get into scenes like this, jerking the rug out from under the feet of self-annointed VIPs.

Jeff coughed again, hemmed and hawed a few surprised pleasantries, then dropped the big one. "I'm showing the equity account with a balance outstanding of over two hundred thousand. If you need a little more time, we can take it in increments. . . ."

Dumbfounded, Rory didn't hear the rest of his speech. Two hundred thousand? Braces didn't cost two hundred thousand dollars. She'd known the equity line on the account when she'd signed the papers, but she'd never thought Cissy would use it for any more than a fund for emergencies.

Even if they sold the whole acreage, after the devastation of the fire they'd be lucky to get two hundred thousand—except from the bank's realty company.

Dismissing Jeff, Rory hung up the phone and sank onto a kitchen stool, trying hard not to fall off while her thoughts whirled.

"What did the bastard want?" Clay demanded.

She shook her head, frantically tabulating debts and taxes and plans for the future against the prize in her drawer. What if the prize wasn't real?

As the immensity of the debt sank in, she shivered. Panic doused her earlier glee. They couldn't possibly owe that much. They lived like paupers. This couldn't be happening.

She needed to talk to Cissy.

Cissy was in the hospital. She could have been badly injured last night. Her sister's overworked conscience would be devastated over the loss of the car. Rory couldn't explode all over her.

But two hundred thousand?

Taking a deep breath, Rory tried to remain calm, but her hand trembled as she reached for her coffee. Last night's terror had undermined her confidence. Clay's lovemaking had torn open her shields. She needed time to pull herself together.

Coffee slipped over the rim of the mug and burned her hand. She set the cup down too hard, and more sloshed on the counter. Before she knew it, tears were sliding down her cheeks.

She wrapped her arms around herself and rose to escape, but Clay caught her. Just the strength of his grip preventing her from running broke her last remaining thread of control. She buried her face against his shoulder and wept.

She shook with the force of her sobs, knowing the ridiculousness of it, knowing she should stand up and strike back, but simply not finding it within her right now.

"Is your family all right?" he demanded, stroking her hair. "I can go into the city, find a good doctor. . . ."

She shook her head, choking back tears, desperately striving for her usual control. "Fine. They're fine."

"Okay, then it's the banker. I can have him hung out high and dry. Just tell me what he did. I know people. I can make a few calls."

She gulped on a watery chuckle. She needed to pull away, to pull herself together, but it felt so *good* to have someone to lean on right now. She'd step away in a minute. She'd just like a moment to absorb and cherish this new experience. If she thought about it, she knew Clay wasn't really John Wayne, and he couldn't come riding to her rescue, but pretending helped. And his tough-guy assurances tickled her back to reality.

"You have an uncle Guido I can hire?" she asked with a hint of her usual humor, wiping her eyes with the back of her hand. "Maybe we could just pepper Jeff's ankles with gunshot and make him dance."

"You're dangerous, you know that?" Instead of backing away, Clay leaned against the counter and tucked her under his arm.

She thought maybe the gaze he bestowed on her was affectionate, sort of like the kind she'd give to an amusing puppy. She didn't want to disillusion him just yet.

"I try. What would you like for breakfast?" Now that she was returning to some semblance of control, she tried to pull away.

Clay was having none of it. He clamped both arms firmly around her waist so she couldn't escape. "Fix anything you like, but first you have to tell me why I'm calling in Uncle Guido."

"I haven't worked it all out yet. It's too early in the morning. I need sustenance first. Let me go."

He reached over to a bowl of fruit, grabbed a banana, and, holding it at her waist, began peeling it. "Sustenance." He offered it to her.

"If you turn into one of those controlling gorillas after a little sex, I'm outta here," she warned, snatching the banana and biting into it.

"I'm not the one eating the banana," he pointed out. "I'll slip back into turtle mode, if you like, but I'm not watching a stuffed-shirt banker reduce you to tears without striking back. So you might as well tell me what's happening."

"It's none of your business," she replied defiantly.

"Is so, too." He removed the banana, took a bite, and handed it back. "I'm not a dumbass bum who can't add two and two. Bankers . . . mortgages . . . land . . . fire . . . disaster. Am I getting close?"

She sagged against him. "Yeah, close. Let me go. I'll fix some eggs. Fried or scrambled?"

"Sunny-side up." He released her to sip his coffee and watch her move about the kitchen. "If he's working with whoever is surveying the Bingham property, he may be pressured into forcing you to sell. Is that what's happening?"

"Maybe. The amount caught me by surprise. Cissy's been borrowing behind my back. It's no wonder she was willing to sell Mama's land. She knew she could never pay her way out."

Clay regretted the millions he'd siphoned from his own funds to pay his company's investors, but she probably wouldn't take loans from friends anyway. She had that stubborn look about her. "You told him you were planning on paying it off next week. Do you have insurance money coming in from your father's accident?"

She snorted. "Pops never carries insurance, and we'd have to find an attorney willing to sue the guy who crashed into them. Since it was a drunk in a fifteen-year-old pickup, what are the chances we'd win anything?"

"So you were lying." That shouldn't bother him. He probably would have done the same if cornered. But she'd done it with such delight, he had to think she had experience. Somehow the knowledge that his Amazon warrior against social injustice had her human side disappointed him. Apparently he wanted to believe in angels. Stupid of him.

She flipped over her eggs and lifted his onto a plate

sporting a colorful rooster. "Put some toast in, will you?" She pointed out the bread cabinet.

Thinking his accusation had flown right over her head, Clay considered rewording it. Before he could, Aurora threw her gorgeous hair over her shoulder and looked him straight in the eye.

"I don't lie. I simply thought the amount was considerably smaller. I have an . . . unexpected windfall. I'd just about worked out how to best utilize it. Two hundred thousand will whack that plan to pieces."

The sound of a car door slamming interrupted any further questioning. Sniffing the beautifully fried egg with regret, Clay ambled to the front door, prepared to beat the wolves from the door if necessary. Not that it would be necessary if Aurora had her way. Fool woman thought she could hold off packs of wild animals with a spatula and a frown.

He had experience with wild animals, the money-hungry sort. Once they smelled cash, they went for the jugular. Nothing short of AK-47s or a few billion dollars would stop them. The banker's call proved the wolves were circling.

Mandy burst through the door as he opened it. Behind him, Aurora shouted with joy and caught her niece up in a hug. Wishing she'd hug him like that when he entered the house, Clay turned back to watch his brother assisting Cissy up the walk. Behind them trailed Jake, his expression a black cloud as he surveyed the damage.

Even the smiling gnomes had blistered with the heat. Instead of a colorful fairy-tale haven, the front yard had been transformed overnight into a blackened corner of hell, complete with demons.

Clay reached out to help Cissy up the stairs. She didn't look him in the eyes but limped toward the couch, defeat written in the curve of her spine.

She'd wrecked Aurora's pride and joy, apparently mortgaged their joint property to the hilt, and still Aurora raced up to hug her sister before she sat down. Clay had expected fireworks. Instead the water faucet turned on again. Both women clung to each other and wept.

He looked to Jared and Jake for some explanation of this curious phenomenon, but both men seemed to shrug it off.

"Is that eggs I smell?" Jake lumbered on his cast to the table, where their meal sat untouched. "Nothing beats Rora's fried eggs. I'll eat these cold ones, and she'll fix you up some hot ones."

"I'll fry some bacon. Jared, can I fix you some?" Mandy danced into the kitchen, all long teenage legs and energy. "I played that new version of 'Mysterious' some more last night, Clay. It's awesome."

Clay winced at his brother's inquiring look. The game's distinctive mushrooms still floated across the computer screen. Jared helped himself to an apple from the fruit bowl, took a bite, and, leaning against the counter, crossed his arms and ankles in obvious expectation of a long reply.

Maybe test-driving the new model on a couple of teenagers hadn't been a wise idea, but Kismet and Mandy had enjoyed the game far more than the graphics software. Clay shrugged and pushed the bread into the four-slice toaster. "Find any kinks?" he asked Mandy.

"I didn't get far. I'm still trapped by Bubbles the Clown."

"Bubbles? The clown's name is Bubbles?" Having

helped her sister to the couch, Aurora returned to break more eggs into the skillet. "That's why pink bubbles pop up when the elephant walks over him?"

Clay grinned. "Yeah. Obnoxious, isn't it?" Just being close to her made him feel better. He wanted the right to wrap his arm around Aurora's waist, but with family looking on, he figured that was a no-no. He didn't think Aurora would appreciate the proprietary gesture either.

"Tell us more," Jared prompted, chewing a bite of apple.

"Don't you have to get back to Cleo and the kids?" Smelling the toast burning, Clay popped the bread to inspect it. Deciding it wasn't too dark, he opened the jar of honey Aurora had set out earlier and proceeded to slather a slice. The rest he set in front of Jake.

"Nah. Kiz is looking after Meg and Matt. Cleo filled up the Jeep with buzz saws and stuff and is out with a crew down the road. Some of the places really took a hit. She'll have me whacking trees if I join her."

Shivering at the idea of his creative but not very mechanical brother aiming a chain saw at anything, Clay turned the toaster over the kitchen sink to examine its innards rather than say more.

"It's all my fault," Cissy said from the front room. "Rory, I'm so sorry." She started to weep again.

Momentarily giving up on the toaster, Clay leaned over to take the skillet handle out of Aurora's hands. With a grateful look, she surrendered the pan and raced to her sister.

"I was trying so hard to be careful," Cissy wailed. "I drove slow and had the lights on and braked every time I thought I saw something in the road. And then that car pulled out of nowhere! I'm a jinx, a total jinx. I should never get in a car again."

"Accidents happen," Aurora murmured. "You can't be blamed for what other idiots do. Did the other driver help you out? Who was it?"

Clay listened with interest. If the other driver was a neighbor with a good insurance policy, maybe Cissy could recover some of her losses.

"He didn't stop." Cissy lifted her head from her hands, and every face in the room turned to her at the tone of wonder in her voice. As if she were talking directly to him, she met Clay's eyes. "He sped away when I hit the brakes and lost control. It was a fancy black car. No one in this neighborhood can afford anything like it."

Aurora turned to stare at him as well. Clay knew they wanted him to confirm their suspicions. He wanted to argue just to provide balance, but he could think of only one good reason for a fancy black car to pull out in front of Aurora's very conspicuous BMW and speed away after it crashed—unless Cissy was lying. Aurora would cut his throat if he mentioned that.

No slowtop, Jake muttered an expletive that pithily expressed what everyone was thinking, and reached for the phone.

❧ EIGHTEEN ❧

Cissy duly made her report to the sheriff's department. The young deputy seemed fascinated at the idea of investigating a deliberate hit-and-run, and even more so at the possibility that Aurora may have been the target rather than her sister. But in the end, Cissy couldn't provide enough information for anything more than a shake of his head and a dubious promise to do the best he could. There might not be many fancy black cars in this neighborhood, but the rest of the county was littered with them.

Mandy ran off to check on her friends. Jared drove off with Cleo in the Jeep, leaving the pickup behind so Clay would have transportation. The rest of them remained inside, an air of gloom blanketing their collective mood.

In unspoken agreement, they didn't discuss the accident once they'd reported what they knew to the authorities. Cissy was still too rattled.

Rory didn't want to believe their speculation that it hadn't been an accident, or she'd start shaking all over again. Why would anyone think getting rid of her would resolve anything?

She finished cleaning up the breakfast dishes rather than fret. Clay spread the inner workings of a broken chain saw across the table while Jake looked on, offering useless advice. Cissy appeared to be napping on the couch, but Rory figured she was just closing out their problems and escaping inside her head, as they all were.

Cissy still hadn't called the real estate man and declined his offer.

Even Rory was starting to think twice about accepting it. It was a good offer, and they had Mandy's future to consider. But if they sold the land to pay the mortgage, how would she invest her prize so Cissy and their father could earn a living? What if she hadn't won? Monday couldn't come soon enough. She had to live through today and the weekend.

Mandy had turned off the video game and taken the CD with her, so Rory assumed she'd borrowed it from a friend. She kind of missed the purple mushrooms. Last night had been . . . elevating. Instead of the usual stiff dating conversation about careers and the latest Panthers game, followed by awkward kisses and rejection, they'd tussled like children over a silly game, and had sex with the passion and tenderness of lovers.

She still couldn't believe how good Clay had made her feel—not just in sex, but about herself. Her size had always made her self-conscious, but he didn't even seem to notice she was . . . more woman than most. But then, he was more man than most, in more ways than in size. That enormous brain of his never stopped ticking, and it seemed to operate from a fascinatingly broad perspective.

She glanced in curiosity to the table, where he painstakingly cleaned and put together each indistinguishable part of a saw that hadn't worked in years. Patience like that was a gift that provided many advantages for the receiver as well as the giver. When combined with intelligence, it created a formidable talent. Clay McCloud was no ordinary man.

She wanted him to make love to her again, to prove last night hadn't been a fluke.

Craving his touch, or even a glance from him, was a sure sign of imminent disaster. Neither of them had anything permanent in mind, so she'd better find some other outlet for her thoughts.

Remembering words exchanged earlier, Rory dried the last pan and put it away, poured a glass of lemonade, and set it on the table near Clay's hand. "Tell me more about Bubbles the Clown."

He glanced up in surprise. Just the sight of his clear-eyed gaze gave her goose bumps, but she had her shield safely in place again.

Apparently uncomfortable with the question, Clay shifted his attention to the glass of lemonade, sipping it while composing an answer. She'd noticed that about him. The things he said off the cuff tended to be irrelevant, aggravating, or humorous, and sometimes all three at once. But when he applied his mind to a question, she got straight answers, and not necessarily the ones she wanted to hear.

"Jared made him up," he confessed.

Rory waited, and when he didn't explain, she took the lemonade away from him. "Jared has connections with computer game makers?"

Laughter danced in his eyes as he reached up and snatched the glass back. "Yeah, you could say that."

Her father watched the byplay with more interest than

anything else he'd done that morning, and even Cissy sat up. Rory didn't mind distracting her family, but her focus now was on getting to the bottom of the puzzle that was Clay McCloud. A man with his patience and genius wasn't the party-hearty bad boy he pretended to be.

"I don't know anything about gaming," she said. "But I'm assuming the games are computer programs?"

"Someone writes a script first," he corrected. "Then there are visuals to put together and voices to plug in, and then the whole thing is processed into a program and film. It's kind of complicated." He returned to piecing the saw together. "Shouldn't you be replanting flower gardens or something? Can the statues be repainted?"

"Paint remover might take care of the worst blistering," Jake mused. "But tourist season has started. We ain't got time to repaint. We'll have to sell them cheap and bare."

"Rory," Cissy called from the couch, diverting Aurora's attention from the aggravating man who wouldn't tell her anything, "did your car have insurance?"

She asked it so tremulously that Rory knew she'd been worrying over it since the accident and had just now gained the courage to ask. Guilt tweaked Rory's conscience. She'd been wrapped up in herself again. That was what living alone did to her. "Yeah, it's covered. We'll get our cash out of it, sooner or later. But I want to hang whoever drove you off the road. You could have been killed."

Damn, so she'd been the one to say it aloud.

"You're going to need a car," Clay interjected, apparently as anxious as she to evade discussion of hit-and-run drivers. "Want me to take you into town to look for something?"

Accepting the more practical topic, Rory thought about it. They'd need ready cash to buy a car. She had no idea how long it would take for the insurance company to send a check. She had to get to the lawyer's office before she could cash in the cap, and she didn't have any transportation.

She took a deep breath and tried to pin all her whirling thoughts into place. First things first. While she had Cissy's attention, she gave up on Clay and faced her sister. "I had a call from the bank this morning."

Cissy turned even paler, if that was possible. "Why? I'm only a little behind."

"They say the fire destroyed the value of the land, and they're calling in the loan. I offered to pay them off—until Jeff gave me the balance."

Closing her eyes, Cissy dropped her head back against the high cushion of the couch. Rory tried not to think about what she and Clay had done on that piece of furniture not too many hours ago. She couldn't imagine it ever happening again, so it was better not to dwell on it.

"Your prize will cover it, won't it?" Cissy whispered.

That caught everyone's attention. Maybe there were a few too many unspoken topics clouding the air.

Before her father could jump all over Cissy's declaration, Rory spouted the question that had been killing her for hours. "Yeah, it will cover the mortgage, but then it won't cover the future. We'll be lucky to break even. What the dickens did you spend it on, Ciss?"

And then, seeing her sister's anguished expression, understanding dawned. With horror, Rory sank onto the nearest chair. "On us?" she whispered. Thoughts racing, she remembered the little surprises, the gifts at Christmas she and Mandy hadn't dared hope to receive, the unexpected pair of athletic shoes they needed for gym. "My prom dress, that's how you did it! And the gift baskets during finals and . . ."

Feeling guilty as hell now, Rory grabbed Clay's glass of lemonade and took a deep drink, searching her spinning mind for the impossible. "But why do we owe the bank for things that old? We just opened the equity account."

"I didn't know about equity loans until you took that one out for Mandy's braces." A note of defiance entered Cissy's voice, and her fists clenched against the green upholstery. "The bank said we could pay off the finance company and the credit cards, and keep the loan payment lower and the interest could be deducted from taxes. I thought it was a good thing."

"It was my loan at the finance company," Jake said gruffly. "I borrowed against the bike a ways back, and then again for the pickup. And every time you said I owed on the taxes, I had to borrow for that. The interest ate me up, and I never could get the balance paid."

"I got the credit cards back when Mandy was born," Cissy murmured tiredly. "Even her baby food cost a fortune. And there was that time I was laid off and had no insurance and she got sick. You were too young to pay attention to bills back then."

A huge lump formed in Rory's throat. "You mean you've been paying the minimum payment on credit cards for *fifteen years*? While continuing to charge on them?"

"Stupid, huh? But Mandy needed all kinds of things

my paycheck wouldn't cover, so I kept at it. And when I reached the card limit, they'd raise it for me. Or I'd get a new card. Once I borrowed from the finance company to pay them all off and swore never to use them again, but I did. It all kind of snowballed after a while."

Fifteen years of "miscellaneous" expenses, doubled and tripled by exorbitant credit card interest. The Girl Scout uniforms and the "special" birthday gifts that Rory had longed for with all her girlish heart and never expected to receive. The same for Mandy. Cissy had spent fifteen years lugging that burden, knowing the money would never be there, but determined to give her sister and daughter the things she'd never had.

Tears rose in her eyes again, but Rory choked them back. It was useless to tell Cissy that they were better off not buying prom dresses and gym shoes than to mire themselves in debt. As a teenager, she probably wouldn't have agreed. And Cissy had been a teenager, too, one who had taken great pride in providing the things their mother used to provide.

Cissy wouldn't care that each item charged ended up costing double or triple the bargain prices she'd scrupulously hunted down. She'd done it out of love, and Rory couldn't argue with that.

Fighting tears, she sat down beside her sister and hugged her. "I can't believe you never told me. You let me buy a stupid car when you were covered up in bills. I ought to shake you until your teeth rattle."

"Oh, I charged those, too," Cissy added with a watery half giggle. "Root canals and caps."

It wasn't funny, but Rory laughed out loud. "Let's tell the bank to repossess them!"

That struck Cissy as so hilarious that she began to laugh until tears streamed down her face. Rory joined in, and nearly doubled up with mirth when her father and Clay stared at them as if they'd gone berserk.

"Here, Jeff, take my teeth," Cissy howled. "They should be worth a few thousand. And the prom dresses! You can have them, too."

"The shoes! Let's give him the shoes. And if it's timber he wants from our yard, we can deliver firewood to his door." Rory rolled on the cushions with glee, imagining the impeccable Jeff Spencer faced with a semi load of burned, stinking pine trunks on the bank's pristine marble steps.

"We could hose down the two of them," Clay said thoughtfully in the other room. "Maybe we should haul them outside first."

"Nah, they get like this every once in a while. Beats crying all to pieces. Get used to it. They cook something fierce when they get done."

Fascinated, Clay accepted that. He and his brothers probably would have pummeled each other to death over subjects only half as explosive as years of unpaid debts. Diane had thought only of herself and had grabbed the money and run when she'd seen the company going down in the market crash.

Aurora and her sister thought of each other first. Clay guessed it was their upbringing, and he glanced at their father drinking coffee, a bit of egg still stuck in his beard. The old man didn't seem involved, but it had been his support that had kept the girls together and at home. He'd provided the example of unselfishness they'd needed to shape their lives.

Clay wondered how he would stack up in the father role. And then he wondered why he wondered.

Luckily Aurora recovered some of her senses and returned to the kitchen before he had to work that one out. As promised, she headed straight for the refrigerator. He hadn't bought groceries yet, and he'd better get on it. Their garden had been wiped out.

He was starting to feel much too at home here.

"You gonna tell us what prize you won?" Jake drawled laconically, as if he hadn't been chewing on that piece of information for the last half hour.

Clay noticed with interest that Aurora looked at him instead of her father while she worded her reply.

"I won't know anything for certain until Monday, when I see the lawyer," she said cautiously.

Clay had a feeling this had something to do with the unexpected "windfall" she'd mentioned. "Want me to leave? I'm almost done here. If it's a family thing, I can go."

He discovered he was waiting anxiously for her reply.

"It's not a family thing." Jake snorted. "It's a woman thing. They don't trust men."

Clay processed that while watching Aurora for her reaction.

"For good reason, I might add." Aurora rummaged in a cabinet and smacked a bowl down on the counter. "But this is kind of big and we don't like raising hopes until we know for certain."

She didn't even hesitate at including him in the discussion. Clay studiously returned to repairing the saw so he didn't intrude.

"You really won something?" Jake whooped with delight. "The lottery? Did you get a lottery ticket? How

much? A thousand? That could make a nice down payment on a truck."

"The BMW insurance will buy a new truck." Using a
crutch, Cissy hobbled back to see what Rory was doing.
"This will do a lot more."

Openmouthed, Jake waited, his expectation sweeping
away any lingering gloom. Unable to resist the sup-
pressed excitement in the sisters' voices, Clay leaned his
chair back on two legs, watching with amusement as
they exchanged glances and led the old man along. From
their cat-in-cream expressions, he'd think they'd won a
million dollars or something.

"Aurora was planning on paying off the mortgage until Jeff told her how much. So it's got to be more like five
or ten thousand," Clay calculated aloud for Jake's benefit. "Does the lottery pay that well?"

"Not often, unless they drove over to Georgia," Jake
said in awe. "Five, Rora? Did you win five thousand?"

Cissy grinned and began breaking eggs into a bowl.
"Rora says I can have a red F150 extended cab with a
moonroof and pinstriping."

"Hot damn!" Jake surged to his feet. "Them things'll
set you back more than ten. Are you crazy? We can pick
up a junker for a few thou and use the rest to pay bills."
He stopped on his way to the patio door, hesitated, and
all the joy fled his face. "But you said the bank wants
their money. That and the insurance ain't even gonna
dent the balance."

"It will if we have a million dollars," Rory said calmly,
unwrapping chocolate squares and dropping them into a
pot of butter.

A moment's reverent silence followed her announcement.

Then Jake let out a war whoop, Clay brought his chair legs crashing back to the floor, and Cissy laughed aloud at their astonishment.

"A million? You ain't pulling my bad leg, are you?" Jake recovered his senses and looked from one daughter to the other.

"Well, after taxes, we'll be lucky if it's six or seven hundred thousand," Rory said with a shrug.

Muttering biblical epithets, or maybe praises, Jake collapsed in his chair again, shaking his shaggy head in disbelief. "Where the hell did you win that much? And why ain't anyone heard about it?"

"A bottle cap from the soft drinks you bought for us, and because I wanted a lawyer to set up a trust fund to include all of us before we claimed it."

Clay started doing sums in his head as Aurora's family exclaimed and argued and laughed over ever-increasingly improbable uses for the money. Listening to them, just the basic necessities and outstanding debts would be met after taxes, he calculated. The few hundred thousand left for investment wouldn't produce enough income for things like her niece's education and her father's insurance and retirement. Now he understood her tears over the phone call this morning. They were as much of frustration as grief that she couldn't do everything her family needed.

And then there was the small matter of the land around them going for condos and tourist traps, destroying the turtle nests and the quaint neighborhood and the home they loved. The picture became increasingly gloomy as his natural cynicism kicked in.

"A million won't be enough, will it?" Clay asked into a sudden silence following Jake's appeal to build a gas station in front of his concrete-monument business.

Aurora rewarded him with a bleak smile before she shoved whatever she'd been mixing into the oven. "If it's real, it will be enough to cover the bills. That's far better than we could ever have hoped or prayed for."

But if the bank hadn't called the loan, they might have built Jake's gas station and a future. Clay couldn't believe he was even thinking about gas stations out here.

He understood full well that something serviceable like a minimart must have been Aurora's hidden agenda, not hot-dog or peach stands. Providing the neighborhood with necessities and her family with the income they desperately needed made sense, and much as he might want to, he couldn't argue with her logic.

Aurora needed a means of obtaining a fast return on her money so she could build that minimart and a future. Inside his computer, he had the means to produce what she needed. If they went together and sought third-party investors, they could multiply that million into many within months. He should know. He'd done it before.

"You need a solid investment with a fast return," Clay heard himself say. He knew better than to get involved, to let others have any form of control over his hard work, but even as he cursed his impulsive nature, he continued to fill the gap of their silence. "You'd have to risk your winnings all in one place, but I know a pretty sure thing if we don't foul up."

Clay knew he had their undivided attention, but he

focused solely on Aurora. He read the hope and skepticism in her beautiful eyes and called himself three kinds of fool for letting a night of fantastic sex turn him inside out, but with a sigh of disgust at himself, he offered, "Bubbles the Clown is mine."

❧ NINETEEN ❧

"This is insane. I can't believe I'm doing this. I *know* better than to trust sweet-talking men with their hands out," Rory muttered as Cleo's pickup roared down the highway toward Charleston with Clay behind the wheel. "And you don't even talk sweet that well."

"Actions talk louder than words," he answered predictably. "We're good together in bed. That ought to count for something."

"Oh, yeah, *count* on it," she repeated sarcastically, still mentally castigating herself. "I've had only one night to base that conclusion on. Bed and money don't walk hand in hand with Bubbles the Clown."

He chuckled, unfazed by her sudden panic. "The game is called 'Mysterious.' It made a fortune as a PC-generated game ten years ago. Jared and I share royalties, so I know the book version of the script is still selling."

"But the game isn't," she pointed out. "You want me to invest in a game that no one buys."

Clay waved away her objection. "While I was out in L.A., I played with updating it to bring in a whole new generation of kids who use PlayStations instead of the

236

computer. I've been wrangling to get the rights back from the PC people but they want money."

"And you really think a few hundred thousand dollars will persuade them to part with the rights they robbed you of?"

She still had a hard time believing his story. Okay, she believed an intelligent man like Clay could program computers. That wasn't too hard a stretch. And maybe a comic artist like Jared and a computer genius might put their teenage heads together long enough to produce the "Mysterious" script. But turning it into a computer game that made millions pushed the limits of her credulity.

Clay was a *millionaire*? Or had been. Past tense.

She fully accepted the part about the software company stealing the rights out from under their youthful idealism. She couldn't think of a lawyer good enough *now* to understand the industry contract. Ten years ago— nope, they hadn't stood a chance. Not if their family hired a hundred New York lawyers.

"The greedy pigs haven't kept up with the times," Clay argued. "The rights will revert shortly unless they're willing to produce a new version, and you can pretty much guarantee their marketing department has moved on to race cars and robots and gore. It's short-term thinking out there. They'll grab at our offer. We'll just need funding to produce a product PlayStation will accept. That requires a studio and technical assistance. I specialize in three-D animation and graphics, but there are other aspects I can't cover."

She still had difficulty grasping the extent of his genius. She'd known there was more beneath his pretty hair and denim vest than an immature gamer, but a software mogul?

A software mogul who played games and set her nights on fire. Surrounded by family, they'd been forced to be circumspect all weekend. She'd spent her lonely nights in bed reliving Clay's lovemaking. Sex, she reminded herself. There had been no love involved. Yet.

She was terrified of that tiny "yet." She had too soft a heart and needed to protect it before she destroyed everything she'd worked so hard to accomplish.

"You'd better hope other investors are as sure of this as you," she said gloomily, giving up on classifying him or anything else. "Venture capital went down the drain with the collapse of the tech market. I can call the entrepreneurial angels I know, but the market hurt them badly. You'll have to be mighty convincing, or we'll be out of house and home with half a video game to show for it."

"That won't happen," he said with such sureness that Rory almost believed him. "I'll borrow the money from Jared if I have to. He'll want to invest, too. Just call angels with teenagers, and I'll send them the latest PC version to test-drive. You've seen it. They'll invest."

She desperately wanted to believe him, but the events of the past few days had shaken her normal optimism.

But the program was addictive. Even she wanted to play it again.

"This could all be a waste of time if we can't stop the developers," she warned him, just to keep her feet firmly on the ground.

"One step at a time, my goddess," he said, sending her a warm smile that turned her into a pillar of sugar.

Resigned to this mad adventure, fearing she was in over her head, but knowing she carried her family's hopes and dreams with her, she valiantly focused on watching road signs. "That's the street there. It's number 1101. If I'd known I was looking for a corporate shark, I would have found a different lawyer."

"All he needs to see is the six zeroes after the one, and he'll find anyone you like."

A million dollars. She might have a million-dollar bottle cap in her pocket, and she was about to hand it over to a man who took wild risks and made and lost fortunes. She wasn't a gambler. She liked security. She was out of her ever-lovin' mind.

And terrified to the marrow.

Walking down the redbrick stairs of the attorney's old Charleston town house some hours later, Rory couldn't tear her gaze away from the fat manila envelope in her hand. "I exchanged a million dollars for this?" she muttered as Clay steered her past jasmine-covered wrought-iron fences to the parking lot. "I could have a fat stack of green bills to take to the bank, and instead I took meaningless paper?"

They'd won a million dollars! It was real. It didn't seem real. She continued staring at the envelope in incredulity with panic gnawing the lining of her stomach and ecstasy shaking her knees. Money certainly hadn't changed anything. Yet.

In the shade of a magnolia, Clay caught her arms and pulled her around to face him. When she glanced up in surprise, he kissed her.

Rory shut her eyes and reveled in the beauty and passion of his mouth plying hers. She tasted gratitude and excitement and a sexy undercurrent of hunger held in check. The electricity of power surged through her. This was more than just lust. This was mutual excitement and anticipation and joy in accomplishment. She could stand here like this forever, feeling the heat steam between their bodies, surrounded by the exotic smell of magnolias. If she could freeze a minute of time, this would be the one.

When she thought she would have to collapse against him and surrender to her blistering need, Clay abruptly set her back, still holding her arms but at a more sedate distance. The dazed expression on his face was priceless, and Rory couldn't resist stroking his chiseled jaw. He'd shaved for the occasion.

"We either find a hotel and continue this, or pretend we're respectable and walk back to the car." In his casual California business attire of open shirt and linen trousers, he managed to look not only respectable, but wealthy and influential.

She actually considered the first choice. She could imagine celebrating her winnings in a charming old inn overlooking the harbor, the breeze from an open window blowing lace curtains over a poster bed she and Clay would share in amazing ways.

But the papers in her hand involved them far more than she could manage as it was. Opting for caution, she shook her head, as much to clear it as to say no. "This is not a good idea," she said decisively, breaking away and heading for the car. "Business partners should never get involved outside the office. It's a recipe for disaster."

"Who are you trying to convince, me or yourself?"

Clay kept up with her long strides, jerking open the truck door before she could do it.

"Both. I've watched it happen. Give me some credit for experience. I worked with small businesses for years. Nasty, nasty stuff when families disagreed. Enough to explode a planet when lovers break up. Those papers in there are a powder keg. Let's not play with fire."

Slamming the driver's door and turning the key in the ignition, he backed the truck out angrily. "Are you saying we just gave up sex for money?"

"Why, were you planning on exchanging sex for money?" Crossing her arms, Rory glared out the windshield.

"I didn't even know you *had* money!" In a fit of frustration, he hit the car horn at an SUV turning left from the right-hand lane.

"Well, I didn't know you did either! I had sex with a mechanical god who sits on courthouse roofs and woke up with some kind of friggin' industry guru. You think I want more surprises like that while I'm scrabbling to save my family's future?"

"Mechanical god?" he asked, slanting her a look askance. Then, seeing her stubborn expression, he continued the argument. "You can't shove me into a little box, and it's making you mad. That's not my fault."

"Do you deny living in a sty on the beach with no discernible source of income?" she asked incredulously. "I thought you were a beach bum."

"I was working! You knew I was working. I just don't do it in air-conditioned offices anymore." He hesitated on a corner, switched lanes, and turned toward the harbor.

"You turned the wrong way. The interstate is behind us."

"So sue me. You have my life in that damned envelope. Rip it up and throw it out the window."

"*Your* life? You've already had your million dollars, buster, and now you have the only million I'll ever see, and we're talking about *your* life?"

"No, now we're talking nonsense." He slammed on the brake at a stoplight, glanced up and down a street of historic mansions, and, finding his direction, turned down an oak-and-Spanish-moss-lined lane.

"Where the dickens are you going?" Taken by surprise, she momentarily dropped the argument to gaze in awe at the towering, elegant homes they passed. She'd always loved Charleston, but she'd grown up in a trailer. These beautiful homes were about as real as a movie set to her.

"I figure we're already arguing about money, so there's no reason to deny ourselves the pleasurable side of it." He turned up a drive with a discreet B-and-B sign tucked among the azaleas.

"You what?" Stunned into near speechlessness, Rory gaped at the vine-covered stone turrets and portico of the mansion as Clay turned off the ignition and leaped out of the truck.

"Come on." He opened her door, caught her elbow, and tugged her out. "It's after three. We can check in."

She thought she ought to protest, but she was too busy admiring the shady stone terrace with a bubbling fountain and roses spilling across a sunny corner. Beneath the oaks, the day's heat evaporated in cool moistness. Towering philodendron-like plants protected tender hostas and colorful caladiums. Huge live bouquets of mixed pink impatiens lit the shade like sunshine. Wrought-iron tables and chairs adorned with comfortable cushions in a subtle blend of greens and beiges were already set for some occasion.

She'd dreamed of places like this. Someday she'd hoped to tour Europe and stay in quaint hotels, eat in neighborhood bistros, and pretend she was a sophisticated traveler. Her heart ached at this glimpse of what it might be like. Reluctant to leave paradise, but eager to see inside, she slowly followed her new partner into the lobby.

He was opening up terrifying new worlds. She'd placed her life in the hands of an ex-millionaire, and he had completely taken control. She resented his presumption and wanted his support at the same time. He had experience she could only dream about. She had thought she would learn about the world on her own. She hated being confused.

Clay was already returning his wallet to his pants pocket as Rory stepped into the ceiling fan–cooled interior.

A smiling hostess emerged from behind the desk. "If you'll follow me, I'll show you to your room. Do you have luggage? I can have Morris park your car and carry up your bags."

"I promised Aurora a shopping spree," Clay lied. "Just have him pull the truck out of the way."

"How delightful! If you need suggestions for shopping or directions, please check with Jane. She'll be happy to tell you anything you need to know."

"Like how to kill incorrigible men," Rory muttered under her breath, but there wasn't any anger in her words. He'd gone against her wishes, brought her here for the purpose of sex, and all she could do was stare in wonder at the surroundings.

The magnificent mahogany circular staircase had robbed her of temper. The crystal chandelier lighting the way suspended all thought. She'd always wondered what the inside of one of these homes looked like. She wouldn't ruin her chance to find out by pushing her domineering partner over the banister.

The turret room overlooking the harbor melted her into a puddle of love and lust and . . .

Refusing to be reduced to emotional tears, Rory touched the eyelet curtains of the antique poster bed and watched a sailboat outside the window reflect the sun in its billowing canvas.

She knew the instant they were alone even though she had her back to the door. She was aware of Clay's height as he stood at her elbow, watching the sailboat with her. She knew how his arms would feel around her, how his kisses would taste, and every cell of her body hummed in anticipation. She resented the reaction, but she couldn't fight it.

"How did you know?" she whispered.

"Know what?" With typical male cluelessness, he began releasing her sophisticated upswept coiffeur from its pins.

"The house. It's like a dream. You knew where to go. You had *reservations*. You planned this all along." She tried to hang on to the defensive shield of her anger.

"How many times in this life are you going to win a million dollars?" He filled his hands with her long hair, smoothed it around to her front, and began massaging her back and shoulders with strong fingers. "How many times do we have a chance to celebrate the formation of a company that will support us for life and potentially make a lot of people happy?"

"I just want to take care of my family," she murmured as the spell of his hands removed any lingering argument. "I need security, and I need to make my family's life easier. Gambling our lives on empire building is not my style. If I can help my neighbors along with my family, that's a good thing, but—"

"Quit trying to manage the future, and enjoy the present. The future is a series of moments like this, mixed with bad ones like the fire. Some you can prevent, some you can't."

His mellow mood and the beauty of this place won out over the stress of the past few days. She couldn't even remember why they were arguing. She'd never wanted to be with a man as much as she did this one. Clay offered emotional stability when her world spun into chaos. He balanced her flights of temper with logic, then countered her caution with recklessness. She needed his down-to-earth solidity to buffer her fears even as his creative impulses spun her head.

She needed his hands somewhere other than her shoulders.

"So now you're a philosophical cynic?" There was no rancor in her question.

"I've played in deep waters," he said with a certain amount of gruffness. "Give me credit for experience." He threw her words back at her.

"Can I credit one of your girlfriends for the massage experience?" She hated herself for asking. He was a striking man. Women would have flocked around him.

She knew that. She shouldn't compare herself to the California beauties he must have known. But she was having difficulty believing this was real.

"Nope. Took a course in college." His hands slid forward, finding the top button of her blouse. "I can surf and play poker, too. Didn't learn them from women either."

She leaned back against his broad chest as his fingers skillfully unfastened her blouse. "For a man's man, you know a lot about women."

"Studied them for years. Read books. Read newsgroups on-line. Didn't have much time to practice when I was starting out. I learned pretty quick, though, after they found out I had money."

He pulled her open blouse from her skirt, slid it off her arms, and located the back fastening of her bra without a hitch.

"Given the way you live, that must have taken a while for them to deduce," she said with as much equanimity as she could muster while his knuckles brushed her skin beneath the lacy elastic.

Clay chuckled. "Yeah, well, there is that, until the last one refused to enter my cubbyhole apartment, and I had to buy something respectable that she could decorate."

She heard the dryness in his tone and thought she understood another of the roots of his cynicism. "Did you lose the money?" she asked.

"Not exactly, but the woman I thought I was going to marry disappeared when she found out where it went. Same thing. So, yeah, I have some experience. Not any of it real good."

The bra fell away, and he leaned over to kiss the soft place behind her ear before he filled his hands with her breasts. Her arousal was instantaneous, and so strong she nearly cried out with it.

She didn't want to talk anymore, didn't want to empathize with a man who'd had all the material things but had never been offered the emotional ones that mattered.

Turning, she fumbled at Clay's shirt buttons. He hadn't bothered with a tie or jacket to impress the attorney, hadn't needed to. His knowledgeable questions and intelligent suggestions had won the man over within minutes. They'd impressed her, too, but right now she wanted to be impressed by something a little more physical. It had been three long, lonely nights.

Clay helped her discard his shirt. Before she could make further inroads into their attire, he caught her bare waist and lowered his head for a kiss.

It was as if they had never parted from the last one, except this time they were naked, chest-to-chest, and he warmed his hands around the curves of her breasts.

"My God, Aurora, you're like holding lightning and rainbows. I don't think it's possible to get enough."

His words melted her as much as his hands.

They had the bedcovers thrown back and were sprawled across cool sheets before she realized it. She aroused from her giddy daze when Clay peeled off her skirt and panty hose, and she had to lift her hips to accommodate the gesture. But only when the pleasure stopped while he pried off his shoes and stood to remove his trousers did she fully grasp what she was doing. Again.

The eyelet bed curtains were billowing slightly with the breeze from the open window, just as in her daydream. Clay stood tall and strong against the lacy background, the feminine surroundings only emphasizing his masculinity. For just this moment, he could be the warrior sea captain returned to his home after a long voyage at sea. And she could be the well-loved and pampered wife. Just for now.

She welcomed him with open arms, thrilled to his heavy weight sinking her into the feather bed, and wrapped her thighs around his hips when he returned to kissing her.

"Later we'll go slow," he promised huskily, accepting her invitation without hesitation.

Aurora cried out as he slid into her. The warbling of a mockingbird covered the lovers' sounds that followed.

Lost in the world Clay created, she followed his lead, releasing all control in exchange for the soaring pleasure of his body melded to hers.

❧ TWENTY ❧

"May I take the turret with me, please?" The next morning, Rory took one last, lingering look around the tower of enchantment before she picked up the manila envelope and walked out. Even with the breeze off the river, the room held a lingering scent of her perfume and sex.

"You like living in ivory towers?" Holding open the door, looking more like a pirate than a CEO since he hadn't shaved or changed, Clay waited patiently, wearing an appreciative expression while he watched her foolish farewell to the tower.

With the freedom granted by the intimacy of a night of lovemaking, Rory stroked his chest as she passed by him. "Towers are hard and round and very useful," she purred.

"I can give you that." Cocking an eyebrow in a leer, he placed a hand at the small of her back and provided impetus to get her moving.

Rummaging in his trouser pocket once he'd closed the bedroom door, he produced a palm-sized purple figure. "I can't do jewelry anymore, but how about something soft and squishy instead of hard and round as a commemorative?"

Rora laughed, and her foolish heart did a backflip as she took the purple turtle eraser from his hand. That he carried it at all told her it meant something to him. She thought maybe Clay related to turtles because they were loners, but she didn't think he really wanted to be one. He just hadn't learned to be anything different.

"Such a smooth talker," she teased. "I prefer erasers to jewels. They're far more useful." So maybe she didn't need romantic references to starry nights. She was very much afraid she couldn't learn to live without Clay if he continued causing this senseless quiver of her easily broken heartstrings.

"I make up in action for what I lack in words." Clay held on to her arm all the way down the circular stairs as if to shelter her from any fall. Or because he didn't want to break the contact any more than she did.

"So, then, what is our first action?" Determined to avoid the dangerous pit of sentimentality, Rory stepped into the humid morning air and breathed in the scent of magnolias. She refused to worry about anything until forced. She had a gorgeous man at her side, seven hundred thousand dollars in the bank—on paper anyway—a mountain of debts that could wipe out half of it, and the signatures to begin a spanking-new corporation designed to distribute a video game with bubbling clowns and pink elephants. What more could she ask for?

A good psychiatrist, maybe? She was investing her entire future in pink elephants! As a banker, she was the one who persuaded investors to take risks. She supposed it was poetic justice that she now walked in their shoes. Rory squeezed her turtle talisman for good luck.

"First we pay your bills." Clay held open the truck

door for her. "Next we contact venture capitalists so we spread production risks around. Whatever you have left after paying bills will barely buy back my game rights."

Seeing the truck woke her up, and ignoring his pragmatic list, she demanded, "First we buy a truck! An F150. Candy-apple-red extended cab, with pinstriping."

Clay caught her elbow and almost lifted her into the seat. "Used, in whatever color we find. The company needs to look good on a balance sheet, and F150s don't make an impression."

"Spoilsport." She crossed her arms and pretended to glare at him as he climbed in, but he was right. She just dearly wanted to make her sister as happy as she was. Rory opened the envelope in her lap. "Find a car dealer, Shylock. Then we need to go home and start making calls."

Clay roared Cleo's pickup into gear, and they trundled toward the highway, leaving the ivy-covered turret behind.

"It's red!" Cissy ran a loving hand over the shiny exterior of the miniature extended cab Aurora had parked in the drive.

"It's not an F150," Rory said diffidently, stomach churning as she waited for her sister's approval. "Clay said this one had the best engine and would last longer."

"There's room for groceries in the backseat." Even with her bad hip, Cissy was able to climb up and admire the like-new interior. "It even *smells* good." She sighed. "I'm afraid to drive it. Maybe we should teach Mandy."

Aurora held out the keys. "For now it's a company truck, but you're the driver. And the secretary. And the bookkeeper. And errand girl."

From the backseat, Cissy blinked and looked up into Aurora's face as Clay came to stand beside her. "What have the two of you done?" she demanded.

Aurora heard the sisterly admonition behind the question, but Clay chose to take out the personal and insert business.

"We're investing in the future. You are now part owner of Mysterious Productions, studio for 'Mysterious' video games."

"And cofounder of Turtles Unlimited, a nonprofit ecology-based group dedicated to saving the wetlands and promoting local industry," Aurora added proudly.

"This is going to give me a headache, isn't it?" Diverted from any further personal inquisition, Cissy stepped out of the backseat and took the front with Clay's assistance. She stuck the keys into the ignition and let the engine roar. "What about the mortgage?" She glanced up from examining the instrument panel.

"I'm ignoring Jeff until the end of the week, when I'll go in and either renegotiate the loan, or take it elsewhere." Rory would really like to take it elsewhere, but Clay had convinced her to let business rule and not spite. "We kept enough out of the corporation to pay the hospital bill. We'll start looking for health insurance for employees shortly."

"What about me?" Cissy asked, letting the engine idle, her gaze darting back and forth between them. "What do I do?"

"I have a list of Binghams back at my place," Clay said. "You'll start with writing letters to all the people on the list and keeping a file of their responses. We want to organize a counterproposal."

Before Clay could outline the discussion they'd pursued since their visit to the lawyer, Jake limped down the drive. His skeptical expression gave his opinion of the candy-apple-red truck, but Aurora had bought this one for her sister. Jake was his own boss and could find his own transportation. She loved her father enough to know he'd prefer it that way.

"This is what a million dollars buys?" he asked with a chuckle, sticking his head in the passenger-door window to check out the interior. "Price has gone up some since I bought one."

"We want to buy the Bingham land, Pops." Even as she said it, Rory knew it sounded insane, but Clay had convinced her it was feasible. She'd always dreamed of justice for all, but she would never have dreamed this big on her own. It took someone with a brain—and a soul— as big as Clay's.

"Do you now?" Jake leaned his arm against the truck hood and looked them both over. "I don't have no fancy college degree, but even I can see a million dollars don't buy that." He looked Clay straight in the eye. "I didn't figure you the type to mess with my girls. You walk out with their money, and I'll come after you and skin you alive."

Aurora blushed and huffed at the same time, but Clay intervened before she could let off steam.

"The lawyer has it all tied up tight. Either one of us can pull out with everything we put in and nothing more. But we'll need your help to make this wetlands thing work."

"You want a concrete monument to stupidity?"

"No, we want you to get together everyone you know

out here who might have an interest in the property or in selling their wares to tourists," Clay explained. "If we buy the land, and that's a big 'if,' we need some way of making it self-supporting."

He actually made it sound feasible. To Rory's ears, he spoke with knowledge and authority, as if he really were CEO of a multimillion-dollar company. Maybe this was one way actions spoke louder than words—he accomplished what she only dreamed.

Jake's expression brightened. "Grandma Iris could sell her baskets here instead of paying someone in Charleston? And Garnet could sell his whistles?" He began to look enthusiastic as the idea gripped him. "Erly could supply concessions. There's some others who do real good paintings. And that church the girls go to, they sell recipe books."

"We have to own the land, first, Pops. And to do any of this, we have to raise more money. Don't get too excited until we work a few more things out. We both have to start making calls. It could still all go down the drain."

"This is where I leave you to work it out," Cissy declared. "I have to buy groceries. Fetch that Bingham list, and when I come back, someone can teach me how to type letters on that fancy computer. I can learn and earn my keep at the same time."

She backed around Cleo's pickup and drove off in her red truck.

Leaning on a crutch as if his leg ached, Jake shook his finger under Clay's nose. "Remember what I said. You don't mess with my girls. I'll go talk to Iris and the others."

He limped off to the shed where he kept his motorcycle, leaving Aurora standing alone with the baffling man who had turned her view of the world around. She'd never deliberately stood on a cliff's edge before. She'd been pushed there more than once and had resolved never to come that close again. But here she was, on the edge, looking down, and the crevasse below looked paralyzingly rocky.

"Tell me again how this is going to work," she whispered.

"You have to risk something to win something," Clay answered prosaically. "We're gambling that the majority of the Binghams will side with us and accept our offer rather than let it go to the court and developers."

She knew that. She just needed to hear him say it. Clay made it sound more like a possibility than a fantasy, but they were gambling his future profits on his software as well. She had to trust him.

"Come on, let's retrieve that list from my silverware drawer. It's making me itchy just thinking about it."

A lot of things made her itchy just thinking about them. The Bingham heirs were way down on the bottom of the list, long after wondering what Clay expected of her after last night.

"I don't do things like this," she muttered a while later as the truck rolled down the road to his place. "I encourage *other* people to risk their money."

"You're a wimp," he scoffed. "You like the safety net of employment with benefits and retirement and corner offices. This will be a lot more fun."

"This is *insane*." She stared out the windshield rather than look at him. Everything seemed feasible when she looked at Clay McCloud. "I'm gambling against the bank and rich developers. I ought to take their money and run instead."

He slowed when they turned into the lane to the cottage and saw Cleo standing in her yard, waving them down. "You're gambling justice will prevail and the Viking princess wins," he said, turning up Cleo's drive.

"Yeah, like life is a video game." Seeing Midge in her stroller, Rory was more than willing to climb out of the truck and do something sensible, like coo at a baby, rather than start contacting an ephemeral list of Binghams to offer them pipe dreams.

"You have anything valuable in that shack of yours?" Cleo called out as they climbed out.

"Uh-oh." Aurora looked to Clay and saw the grim line form over his nose. She hastily knelt to play with Midge rather than watch the explosion. Her stomach twisted in tighter knots. She'd *known* this was a stupid risk to take. What had gone wrong already?

"The cottage was empty only one night," Clay protested. "What happened?"

"Jared saw lights down there last night and went down to see if you'd come home. The door was open, but we can't tell if someone was in there or not. The place is a wreck, but then, when isn't it?"

"Call the sheriff," Rory advised, looking up from Midge's wriggling fingers. She could tell from the way Clay clenched his fingers into fists that he had switched to battle mode. "Don't disturb anything."

"You sound like TJ. I have to check first. Maybe the door just blew open. Stay here." He jogged off without further ado.

If it made him happy to play Macho Man, by criminy,

this time she'd follow orders. Rory sat on the grass and let him steam off on his own. "Even *he* couldn't tell if someone wrecked the place."

"Frighteningly enough, I think he can." Cleo sat down on the other side of the stroller. "Jared already called big brother. If there's something missing, prepare yourself. Three McClouds in the same state are deadlier than hurricanes, and I'll bet TJ is already packing his bags."

Rory had never been swept off her feet before. She wasn't entirely certain if it was her or Clay who had gone off the deep end here. "Why would anyone in their right mind break into a trash heap, much less think there was something worth stealing? And why would his brothers care about a minor, everyday kind of break-in?"

"They tease each other unmercifully, but if something goes wrong, they all mysteriously appear to make it right again." Cleo caught Meg's pacifier and returned it to her mouth. "You really should see them in action. It's like watching one of those wrestling matches on TV, where all the good guys gang up against the bad guys."

"Do they wear funny costumes?" Conjuring up images of Clay wearing a purple shield and sword and little else, Rory gave up sensible thought.

Cleo snickered. "I think they'd like to. They grew up in this ultraconservative household wearing button-down collars and ties, but they think like Marvel comics. Where do you think Jared gets his ideas?"

"From Looney Tunes?" Grinning at the thought of three big McCloud men dressed in duck costumes, Rory stood and brushed the grass off her good skirt. "Maybe I'll sashay down and make certain Elmer Fudd doesn't shoot off his toe."

Cleo rolled her eyes. "You're going to fit right in with the crazies, aren't you? I think I'll call TJ's wife and tell her to come down. She loves crazies."

"In that case, tell her to bring her mosquito spray and a comfortable chair. It's going to be a lo-o-ong program."

Cleo laughed. "Lifelong, maybe?"

Rory's heartstrings hummed at the implication, but her mind quickly laid the possibility to rest. "Don't count on that. We're both hardheaded enough to kill each other first." Striding down the sandy lane toward the beach, Rory tried not to feel too effervescent over this exchange. She liked Cleo and Jared. She more than liked Clay. But she had a career on hold and a high degree of reservation about men in general and risk-taking fast-laners in particular. The future was too hard to see.

But for a fleeting moment, the vision of a future with Clay and his family in it shimmered like the fantasy of eyelet, turrets, and sea captains.

The image shattered fast enough when she met Clay storming out of the house, a wad of papers crushed in his fist. Judging by the virtual black smoke billowing from his ears, his privacy had been invaded, all right. Even in a business shirt and pleated trousers, he looked dangerous. She tried to smother a jolt of alarm. "What did they take?"

"Nothing." Crushing the papers tighter, he held them out to her. Realizing he'd all but turned them into trash, he loosened his grip. "They didn't find this list, so they weren't silverware thieves. They didn't take the Mac, but they played with it."

Without consciously thinking about it, Rory wrapped her arms around Clay's waist and rested her head against his shoulder. "Kids, then. Calm down. It's going to be fine."

He accepted her offer and held her close, but he didn't visibly relax. "Kids would have taken the video games. This one tried to get past my security system, and when he couldn't, he rifled all my hard-copy files."

"I refuse to let you frighten me. Did they find anything valuable, can you tell?"

"They screwed up my files." He kissed her quickly before she could give her opinion of his filing system. "I can tell. Take my word, okay? Just because I don't have file drawers doesn't mean I don't have a system."

"All right, I'll take your word for it. Just tell me how bad it is. Should we call the sheriff?"

"What's he going to do? Dust for fingerprints? Career criminals don't mess with paper files. I think someone took advantage of my absence to see what I've been doing. If they were after the list, it was too buried for them to find."

"If they were after the list, they'll be back," she whispered, glad to have his arms around her as she considered the ramifications of that wild assertion.

Maybe it wasn't so wild. Her sister had been driven off the road, her house had nearly burned to the ground, and now someone was searching Clay's home. She tried to stick to reality—she and Clay weren't important enough for these incidents to be more than coincidental. But fear won over logic, hands down.

"If they come back, it will be too late," Clay said with confidence. "Let's get the Bingham letters out and see how much property we can buy with a few hundred thousand and prospects."

And prospects. He was gambling that they would find investors to produce his software. And that the software would make enough money to cover all their expenses now and in the future. Gulping over how such a tiny word could cover such a huge gamble, Rory stepped away, straightened her shoulders, and marched back toward the main house.

She had telephone calls to make. And miles to go before she slept . . . should she ever sleep again.

❧ TWENTY-ONE ❧

Sunshine, lollipops, and Auroras are a few of my favorite things. Won't you come make beautiful music with me?

Rory smiled at the silly message on her computer screen. Remembering a song from the Blue Monkey's jukebox, she typed in, *My idea of beautiful music is a bridge over troubled water. Do you wanna dance?*

So it made no sense. Neither did his message. She simply wanted to connect with Clay, let him know she was thinking about him as she sat in her lonely bedroom, working up tomorrow's to-do list while Cissy took Jake into town and Rory stayed with Mandy. If she had a car, she might have given in to her longing and driven over to his place. Good thing temptation had been taken out of her hands.

She no longer had a hard time imagining Clay as the author of silly love notes. After watching him in action, she fully believed he could turn the moon blue and ask which shade she preferred if she requested it.

She was in very grave danger here, and it wasn't her future finances she was thinking about. Could she survive

without a heart if it were stolen by a taciturn, unpredictable computer mogul?

Clay grinned at the instant message crossing his screen.
He hadn't slept last night while working a marathon
session to fine-tune his script. His head ached, his eyes
blurred, and he probably hadn't eaten in twenty-four
hours. But Aurora's note had him grinning like a fool.

He'd known she was clever. She'd started the classic-
rock theme, so he hoped that meant she was connecting
the messages with him and not daydreaming of some
anonymous romantic hero.

He respected her insistence on staying in her own
place to provide a good role model for her niece. He had
to stay here and safeguard his files from any more break-
ins. But he really needed Aurora tonight. On his own, he
paid no heed to time or basics like food and sleep. He
wasn't a teenager anymore. He needed her here to drag
him from the computer, tempt him with good-smelling
meals, and seduce him into bed.

He needed a hell of a lot more than that, but he was
scared to analyze his expectations.

He sent off an e-mail resigning his position with the
state and offering to return their advance or the partially
completed program he'd created with their funds. That
should give a few people apoplexy and engender a few
weeks' worth of meetings before anyone acted on it.

He didn't like taking their money when he'd used the
list it generated for his own purposes. The program was
complete enough to do what the state needed it to do; he
just didn't intend to show them how. Of course, if he and
Aurora succeeded in obtaining the Bingham property for

the nonprofit trust, they would sell the state the part it wanted for a nominal sum, so the state would come out ahead.

Figuring he'd better go to bed if he wanted to think at all in the morning, he typed, *I can dance; love me do,* hit send, and turned off the machine.

Stupid to mention love anywhere around a female, but he was tired, and Aurora would know the messages were for fun. He hoped *he* knew that.

The phone rang and he winced. Surely no one was working in the state department at this hour. Grimacing, he wandered into the kitchen to grab the phone before the answering machine kicked in. If he was really, really good, maybe it would be Aurora willing to whisper sweet nothings in his ear.

"It's me," TJ said without preamble. "Mara and I have some time off and we're coming down. Want us to bring some real coffee?"

"Normal people aren't up at this hour of the night," Clay answered wearily, rubbing his forehead. His brother's casual announcement didn't fool him. TJ smelled trouble and was following his nose. Growing up in a family like theirs, they'd learned to communicate in cryptic asides rather than directly, as TJ's response proved.

"Yeah, I know, but you never were normal. We'll be staying at the B-and-B in town. Mara's attached to the place. They haven't built a Starbucks there since we've been down, have they?"

"I have no clue." He never went looking for coffee shops. He drank coffee whenever someone handed it to him. He wished someone would hand him some now. "I'm in the middle of something big here, so I won't have time to entertain." He really didn't think he was involved in anything important enough to drag TJ away from his new job. TJ was a forensic anthropologist and they hadn't uncovered any dead bodies yet.

Hearing another receiver click, Clay pictured TJ gesturing at his movie-producer wife to grab the line. Babealicious Mara was quiet Cleo's complete opposite, but then, so were Jared and TJ opposites. That was okay by him, but he really didn't want his brothers involved right now. He needed to work things out with Aurora without his interfering family breathing down his neck, offering advice and messing with his head.

"Oh, I imagine you're very entertaining without even trying," Mara breathed into the line. "Maybe we should fly down so you can work on the plane engine?"

"I'm flying Harleys these days. Look, don't come down for my sake, all right? Everything's totally under control." Or would be once he had the software under his belt and had time to go into town and knock a few heads together. He wanted to be there when Terry Talbert found out he wouldn't be doing the programming. Maybe he could tell the turkey that a committee that didn't have the sense to want Aurora didn't need him.

Or would Aurora have a fit if he said something like that? Probably.

Mara took the conversational ball out of his hands and ran with it. "But interfering is what families do best! Look, if we don't come down there, we'll have to visit our mothers, and my inclination is to ship them to you instead. So try being gracious and smile when we show up."

Clay smiled at the idea of shipping their problematic mothers anywhere. "All right, but you stand forewarned.

No one sits around and does nothing here. We have a major project going down."

"No skeletons," Mara demanded. "This is a vacation."

"I like skeletons," TJ reminded her from the other phone.

"I don't want any skeletons on our vacation," Mara warned.

Laughing as he pictured the two of them sending smoldering looks across the room, each with phone in hand while arguing long distance, Clay hung up the receiver. They wouldn't even notice he'd gone.

He wanted to have a relationship like that when he grew up.

Given his lifestyle and working habits, he had a fat chance of growing up, much less developing a relationship, but at least he knew a woman who liked him. The relationship element was where it fell apart. He'd have all he could do managing anything more than the business one—especially with his brothers and her family peering over their shoulders.

He thought being a turtle might have its advantages.

Composing herself, pretending she was simply walking into a meeting at her office where she would present loan proposals for a new business for someone else, Rory walked up the marble steps of the bank. She'd scheduled the meeting with Jeff for a Friday afternoon, when he'd be eager to escape for a round of golf. She wanted this short and sweet.

It had been only two days since the letters had gone out to the Binghams. The offer to set up the land in a nonprofit trust the family could control might already be stirring up talk among the local property owners. Soon they would have distant relatives talking to each other for the first time in their lives. Better that it was out in the open so the Binghams knew what was happening, and the bank and development companies couldn't steal the land out from under them for lack of knowledge.

Now, if only she could talk the bank into leaving her equity loan open, they'd have a few hundred thousand more to invest in Clay's software and, ultimately, an income for life, if "Mysterious" produced the astonishing profit Clay promised.

"Hello, Aurora! You're looking fantastic." Standing beside his secretary's desk as if he'd been waiting for her, Jeff Spencer greeted her with the enthusiasm he saved for his wealthier customers.

He was as handsome as ever, still single, and rich enough to build his own house in one of the town's McMansion neighborhoods. Rory figured any house Jeff built would have all blond-wood floors and white walls. Jeff never had possessed much imagination or color. As an insecure teenager, she'd seen that as steadiness. As a more secure adult, she recognized how boring that was—purple knights were much more challenging.

Boring Jeff could very well be behind the Commercial Realty ploy to buy out Cissy. She would have to play this one close.

"Thank you, Jeff," she said with just the right amount of frost while sweeping past him into his office. She couldn't believe that less than a month ago she'd stepped out of his way rather than rock the boat, and here she was now, ready to turn the boat over and shoot holes in it.

"I have the payoff calculated, as you requested." He

sat down at his desk and opened a file folder on his otherwise immaculate desk. "But you needn't be hasty about this, you know. If you can show substantial assets outside of the land—"

"We've had an offer of ten thousand an acre, and with thirty acres, that's more than sufficient to cover the current balance," she interrupted in the crisp tones she'd learned to use in the banking world. "I'm prepared to write a check for the entire balance."

No, she wasn't. The lawyer had collected the prize winnings and deposited them this morning, so the money was technically there. She just needed as much of it as she could hold on to. Experience had taught her that meant she must speak from a position of strength. "I would prefer working with the local bank, of course, since I see no reason to tie up liquid assets, but if you are uncomfortable with the loan, then I have no difficulty taking our interest elsewhere. What is the payoff balance?"

Jeff looked uneasy as she produced her checkbook and a pen and waited expectantly. "Now, Rora, let's not be so hasty. You know that ten thousand an acre is unlikely, and if you've really been offered that, you should grab it. We can come to some compromise—"

"No, I don't think so. Our land is on prime property along the access road to the new state park. Since you're so interested in developing a property tax base out there and the zoning commission won't be interested in anything less, then I see no reason why we shouldn't benefit from the ecological disaster that will result. That property will be worth ten times as much in ten years. I'm willing to take the risk. The payoff, please."

He managed to shutter a brief expression of alarm, but

his blatant self-interest couldn't be as easily disguised. "Then you'll quit fighting the zoning?"

Gifting him with her most dazzling smile and hiding the wolf grin behind it, Aurora put down her checkbook. "Why, Jeffy, if that's been your concern all along, you should have said so. I'm about to move a multimillion-dollar corporation in there. One-bank shopping makes sense to me. Are you interested?"

He fell for it, hook, line, and sinker. Rory decided she should have cut line and fished in deeper waters long ago.

She hadn't *said* she'd quit fighting zoning, now, had she?

Limping down the cracked sidewalk from Cleo's store, Cissy tingled with pride at the sight of her candy-apple-red pickup. She didn't care if it wasn't brand-new. Buying vehicles new was a waste of money. But this one was as close to new as she'd ever owned, with hardly a dent or scratch on it. She had a working tape player and room in the narrow backseat to transport Mandy and her friends. She wanted to take it out on the highway and test the acceleration, but she hadn't had an excuse to do so yet.

Sure, it was registered in the name of the corporation and not her name, and she hadn't paid for it. But Rora had showed her the corporate papers with her name on them, and part of the million dollars was hers, so if she carried the keys, she figured that truck was bought and paid for.

The idea of being part owner of a corporation was so far beyond her comprehension that she dismissed it. Owner of a truck, now, that she understood.

In the sack from the hardware store was a computer

cable. Cleo's Hardware carried computer parts, since the town was too small for a specialty store. Cissy now knew what cables did and even knew which one to buy to connect Rora's PC to the scanner Clay had brought over. She even knew what a scanner was and how to operate it. She'd be able to open her own computer store if she kept this up.

The warm fire in her belly at that thought was an unusual sensation. The maxim "With knowledge comes power" had always eluded her. How to find good clothes at the cheapest price and keep a grocery budget was knowledge, but she'd never considered it powerful.

But knowing all about computers could lead to a real future, a secure one, one that would make Mandy proud of her. Clay had been right: It was worth trading the opportunity for easy cash for the knowledge that would build a solid foundation.

A white Cadillac glided to a halt behind her pickup. Cissy glanced at her watch. Rora should be coming out of the bank any minute. They might have time to stop at the school and pick Mandy up so she didn't have to take that slow school bus. She didn't want to have to maneuver the truck out of a tight space if someone parked in front of her. She would move the truck and idle in front of the bank until Rora came out.

"Miss Jenkins, how fortuitous that we should run into each other!"

Distracted, Cissy glanced up at the business-suited gentleman climbing out of the Cadillac—Mr. Turner, from Commercial Realty.

Since rich gentlemen driving Cadillacs did not usually

acknowledge her existence, Cissy remained on the sidewalk, watching his approach with suspicion. Once upon a time she might have flirted with a man who smiled at her like that. These days she felt older than the hills, but maybe a little wiser.

"How do you do, Mr. Turner," she acknowledged his greeting politely.

"Have you given any thought to my offer, Miss Jenkins? I was surprised not to hear from you. It's an excellent offer, and we're saving that lot for you."

"I don't make decisions like that without some thought," she said stiffly. Even with her newfound confidence, she hated giving up such a tempting offer. Did she really need all that land? Did it matter if her mother's family had owned it for generations? Rory had asked how important it was to Cissy, but Rory hadn't indicated that it meant anything to her.

"We're quite anxious to start moving on this project," Turner said with bluff good humor. "If you're not interested, give your neighbors a chance."

What if Rory and Clay were wrong? What if Turner really meant to build something out there, and he took his money to their neighbors?

It took all the backbone Cissy had grown over the years, and her respect for Aurora's intelligence, to straighten her shoulders and look three hundred thousand dollars in the eye and kiss it good-bye. "I think you'd better start talking to my neighbors, Mr. Turner. My sister and I have other plans for that land, but thank you very much for your generous offer."

She walked away from his stunned expression, terror and a floating feeling of freedom carrying her past the truck and down to the bank, where she walked up the marble stairs as if she had as much right to be there as all the rich people did.

To Cissy's pride and dismay, Rory was just leaving Jeff Spencer's office, and the banker greeted Cissy as if she were a long-lost relative. Everyone in the lobby turned to stare, and she was wearing only her second-best jeans and a tank top.

But she owned a candy-apple-red pickup and had just turned down three hundred thousand dollars. Taking a deep breath, Cissy smiled and shook Jeff Spencer's hand. She was a millionaire.

❧ TWENTY-TWO ❧

On the Monday after Aurora's triumph at the bank, Clay locked the finished copies of his programs in Cleo's safety-deposit box with a sense of satisfaction. He had nearly worked himself to death this past week putting everything in order. Now he had time to breathe.

And think about Aurora. He glanced up at the courthouse roof, but he had no itch to tinker with the clock. His life had become a more interesting place since Aurora had walked into it.

It would become even more interesting if he could pry her away from her desk and her family and back into his bed again. But privacy and spare time had been in short supply since their trip to Charleston. Unlike the other women who had decorated his life, Aurora seemed to understand when he immersed himself in work. Would she have the same understanding of his need to play now? Could he talk her into running into Charleston with him?

Of course, she was juggling phone calls from Binghams and inquiries from investors. He couldn't expect her to drop everything just because he was ready to play.

And TJ had arrived last night. It might be easier to

park himself at Aurora's place and deal with sexual frustration than submit to his brother's questioning.

At least at her place he'd have the fun of listening to her deal with family and friends and Binghams and whatever else crossed her path. Every time he stopped by, Aurora was bubbling with energy, obviously in her element juggling half a dozen problems at once. She laughed away Cissy's timidity with the computer, teased Mandy into acting as receptionist, hugged her father when he blundered into the table, dumping off her worksheets.

Clay was the only one she walked softly around, and he figured that was because they set off enough electricity to light New York every time they got within three feet of each other. He'd stolen a few kisses behind the refrigerator door, but the trailer was way too crowded for anything else.

Thinking of those kisses, he dragged his gaze from the courthouse clock and its secrets to the florist shop next to the café. He used to send Diane huge bouquets of red roses when he'd spent the weekend working late. Would roses impress Aurora? Persuade her away from the telephone and the trailer and into somewhere private?

Or would she just swat him with them for wasting money? That was a new and not entirely comfortable question to puzzle out. The old Clay would have just spent money and called the problem solved. He hadn't quite decided what his new laid-back persona should do.

Spotting a small, balding man walking in his direction, Clay grinned. Yeah, he thought he knew what this Clay ought to do.

He stepped up on the curb in front of Terry Talbert,

nearly causing the tourist commissioner to walk into him. "Had any free MBAs walk into your office lately?"

Talbert glared up at him, swiping a flyaway hair back from his frowning forehead. "You're pond scum, you know that? You *promised* us that program! And now look what you've done—every Bingham in the county thinks he's a millionaire."

"Every Bingham in the country, more likely." Clay shrugged off the accusation. "They're not dumb. They'll figure it out now that they have the information to work with. You should have kept Aurora. She's handling the heirs beautifully."

"Do you have any idea what you've done?" Terry shouted, too furious for coherence, much less Clay's logic.

"Yeah," Clay said with great pleasure. "I have the smartest person in town working on my side because you threw her away. A word of advice—next time you choose sides, choose the honest one, not the rich one."

He left Talbert standing there, digesting that, as he strode off in the direction of the grocery store. He'd take the money he could have spent on roses and buy a tomato plant to put in the Jenkinses' ravaged garden, plus a lobster or two for Aurora to play with. And chocolate. She did the most amazing things with food. He might even learn to eat for the sheer pleasure of watching her cook.

"I've got it, I've got it!" Aurora ran screaming into the front room they'd converted into an office, waving a piece of paper at her audience of two. She and Cissy had spent a frantic weekend fielding phone calls from Binghams. Friday night Clay had started appearing for meals, sacks of groceries in hand. This morning he'd arrived with tomato plants and lobsters. She'd never understand the man, but she adored his thoughtfulness. Cissy had been ecstatic over the plants.

At Rory's triumphant cry, Clay glanced up from the laptop he'd brought over, and Cissy stopped frowning at the big computer they'd set on a television stand. They both waited expectantly, if somewhat warily, since Aurora tended to run in with excited messages several times a day.

"An angel! I have an angel."

Cissy snorted inelegantly and returned to frowning at the monitor and laboriously arguing with the word-processing program.

Understanding Aurora's cryptic cry, Clay raised both eyebrows in surprise, set the laptop aside, and grabbed for the paper in her hand. "Who's offering? Satan? The company who stole the first program? China?" "Angels" with money to invest were few and far between these days.

She danced away, holding the letter out of his reach, laughing. "Cynic! You didn't think I could do it, did you? You just like my cooking and wanted to keep me around to feed you."

He caught her by the waist and hauled her from her feet so he could snatch the paper. His strength always took her by surprise. She could get used to it quickly if the man overcoming her was Clay.

She wiggled against him and heard him growl, but Cissy was glaring at them again. They really would have to act on this attraction once things settled down. In the meantime, Rory nibbled Clay's ear, then shoved away when he held the note out of her reach to read it.

"One of the bigwigs at the bank where I used to work retired," she explained for her sister's benefit, "and he's looking for investments. He was one of the first people I sent a packet to last week. After I read his reply I called him, and he's definitely interested. He's already involved with another software firm, and they think this might work into their business plan."

"We keep controlling interest," Clay admonished, backing off as he read the name on the letter. " 'Mysterious' isn't leaving my hands now that I've bought the rights back."

"He understands that. He has grandkids, and he was impressed that they were enthusiastic about the game. I don't think he takes it very seriously. He's doing it because his grandkids told him to."

Cissy looked from one of them to the other. "Okay, I may sound stupid, but what are we talking about?"

"Money, lots and lots of money!" To the tune of "We Will Rock You" pouring from her computer's sound system, Aurora beat her fists in the air and danced across the room to the kitchen.

Clay caught her hand, spun her around, and bent her backward over his arm. "Turtles and sweetgrass," he reminded her.

Caught off guard as well as off balance, Rory squeaked in surprise when his mouth closed over hers. Sinking deep into the bliss of his kiss and the heady effect of his support, she flung her arms around his neck and let the moment happen. This was the way it should be, sharing happiness along with the burdens. She was bursting with joy in so many ways that kissing Clay was the only sensible way to express it.

"Take it to the bedroom," Cissy called.

"Whoops." Clay pretended to drop her, then pulled her upright again, brushing a kiss against her ear where Cissy couldn't see it. "Any chance of taking it to the bedroom?" he whispered into her hair.

"Not a chance." Still dizzy but conscious of her sister, Rory opened the refrigerator door and let the cold air blow away the steam that kiss had engendered. She didn't think her heart would ever be the same again.

She needed to think about turtles and sweetgrass and money and not sexy partners who blew her mind out her ears. Sexy partners who leaned over her shoulder and examined the refrigerator with her.

"Do you have any more of that banana pie?" he asked, reaching around her to push bowls out of the way.

"Banana pie isn't for celebrating. Chocolate is. With raspberries on top. And whipped cream. Should we start stocking champagne?"

"Lobster. Much better than champagne. And the pie will hold me until you've finished cooking up more calories." Finding the pie, he removed it to the counter with the air of a well-satisfied man.

"Company coming," Cissy called from the front room. "Know anyone in a white SUV?"

Rory watched with curiosity as Clay studied the banana cream pie with a glint in his eye that she'd learned to be wary of.

"Yeah, big brother is in town," he answered, setting the pie down and carving out a large piece. "His wife tried to talk him into renting something a little flashier than a Taurus, and he came up with that. TJ is not high on imagination."

Clay carefully placed his slice of pie on a dish he retrieved from the cabinet, but he didn't return the remainder to the refrigerator, Rory noted. Remembering Cleo's warning about the McCloud brothers, she decided to stay out of hurricanes. She emptied a cup of flour into her mixing bowl and waited for the doorbell to ring.

"Hi, my name is TJ McCloud," a gravelly bass voice announced as Cissy opened the door. "Jared said we might be able to purchase a fountain here."

Confused, Cissy glanced over her shoulder at Clay, who gestured with his head toward the back of the house. Shrugging, she turned back to the visitor. "If you'd go around to the rear, I'll send my father out to help you."

They'd had enough tourists wander to the wrong door to know the routine. That was why they'd lined the walk back to the factory with lawn ornaments. But why on earth was Clay sending his brother out back? Better yet, why was his brother asking about fountains instead of Clay?

Rory glanced surreptitiously at Clay's deadpan expression and decided this must be a McCloud thing. She cracked an egg into the bowl of flour as Clay carried the half-empty pie pan to the patio door.

"Do I call Dad?" Cissy inquired with equal curiosity. "Does he really want to buy a fountain?"

"No, he really wants to see what I'm doing. Since I locked him out of the cottage, he's come to snoop here. He needs a little reminding that snooping isn't polite." The glint in Clay's eye belied his impassive tone.

Siblings had issues. Rory knew that well enough. Maybe she ought to help him with his. "You know, I could just go out and meet them," she offered, hearing two voices coming around the trailer. "That's the adult, rational thing to do."

"What, and disappoint them? Nope. They came all this way because Jared told them I'm rotting away down here, not living up to my potential, and now I'm acting peculiar. So they'll get peculiar." He lifted an eyebrow in amusement as the voices came closer. "Not that peculiar is anything new in our family."

Rory tried to stifle a laugh but didn't succeed. She grinned the instant Clay slid open the patio door, and his brother's bass voice shouted "Duck!"

The pie flew from Clay's hand, probably with deadly accuracy.

Yelping and shouting ensued, but Clay merely folded his impressive biceps over his black T-shirt and leaned against the door frame. "Looking for someone?" he called.

"Thomas Clayton, I swear, you'll pay for this! This hairpiece set me back a hundred bucks, I'll have you know."

Rory couldn't resist. Leaning over the sink, she looked out the kitchen window to see a woman as tall as she was, but probably thirty pounds lighter. Their visitor picked an atrocious, banana-cream-smeared hairpiece off her head to shake it out. Beside her stood a bemused man more SUV-sized compared to Clay's race-car leanness.

Obviously torn between helping his laughing wife and maiming his brother, TJ rolled his eyes in frustration, and Rory cracked up. Neither of the pair seemed in the least startled by Clay's behavior. "Is this what Cleo calls a 'McCloud thing'?" she inquired through her chuckles.

Distracted, Clay lifted a cool eyebrow at her but didn't

blink until the ruined wig hit him in the face. He jumped in surprise, causing Rory to laugh harder. Yummy banana cream added to the appeal of impassive genius.

Wiping the worst of it off with the back of his arm, he bent to retrieve the hairpiece from the back step. "Sorry about that, Mara," he called. "I was aiming for Tim. You really should duck when big brother tells you, but you look too good to wear this ugly thing. I'll buy you a better one."

Watching from the window, Rory noted that once reassured his wife was unharmed, TJ greeted his youngest brother with the hint of a smile. "There are more civilized ways of saying hello," he intoned gravely, flicking at a speck of pie on Mara's shirtsleeve.

"Whoops, must have mixed my messages," Clay said in the same expressionless voice as TJ. "I thought I was saying, 'Get out of here.' My apologies. Want me to show you the water fountains? There's a really Byzantine one just past the magnolia. For you, I'll cut a deal." He tossed the hairpiece in the direction of the trash can.

Cissy wandered to the dining room window to watch. She eyed Clay with skepticism and started for the door, prepared to show their visitors fountains.

Deciding that if Clay's greeting was Yankee hospitality, she'd better show him a superior form, Rory shook her head at her sister. "Don't encourage them," she murmured as she brushed past. "McClouds are apparently not totally civilized in each other's company."

Tucking a proprietary hand beneath Clay's muscled biceps, wiping banana cream from his bristly cheek and licking her finger, Rory leaned through the doorway to smile at their visitors. "Hi, should I throw him out or are you coming in?"

Clay's arm tightened to hold her hand captive. She inched closer, brushing her breast against his side. Trying to carry on an affair beneath the eyes of family, especially her impressionable niece, had been impossible, but her body instantly responded to his touch. Not that she had to act on it, of course. They had visitors, after all.

The steam rising in Clay's eyes as they met hers warned that he considered visitors no deterrent.

A blush rose to her cheeks, and Rory hurriedly turned to greet their guests. Clay's attractive sister-in-law widened her eyes with interest, while his brother's narrowed, she noted. TJ looked just like Clay when he did that, although his hair was darker, his nose more prominent, and his face more rugged than striking.

"Hi, I'm Mara Simon," their willowy guest introduced herself. "And this is TJ. McClouds don't believe in introductions, maybe because they don't think they need any?" Appropriating her husband's arm in almost the same gesture Rory had used, she steered him up the garden path to the patio door.

"I'm Aurora Jenkins. Come in, there's still a piece of pie left if you want to get even, or I'll direct you to the bathroom so you can fix your hair. I think he missed the rest of you."

"We're standing right here, you realize?" Clay asked, not moving from his position while Rora and Mara exchanged pleasantries.

"Yeah, but if you remain silent, we can pretend you're invisible." Tugging, Rory toppled him back a step so

Mara could enter. "This is my sister, Sandra. We don't bite, even if Clay does."

Stepping up, TJ nearly filled the open doorway. He surveyed the interior, Aurora, and Cissy, before letting his wife out of his sight. Apparently unfazed by his protectiveness, Mara greeted Cissy and strolled down the hall with her, her hips swaying in rhythm with her blithe chatter.

"Iced tea, Mr. McCloud?" Slightly nervous before Clay's intimidating older brother, Aurora fell back on her upbringing.

"Call me TJ, please, and water will be fine. Excuse our intrusion. We really did want to see the fountains, contrary to what Clay may have led you to believe."

If Clay managed to fill the low-ceilinged room with his presence, TJ overwhelmed it. Rory busied herself with glasses and ice and keeping an eye on Clay's inscrutable expression for guidance. Stupid of her, but she had this unreasonable urge to defend him, as if he needed it.

Or was she feeling defensive because she feared TJ would scorn Clay's choice in befriending her and her family? Maybe that was why Clay resented his brother's interference.

If she judged on appearances, she'd say Clay's family came from a much more sophisticated, wealthier world than hers. Of course, ex-millionaires usually did. She'd never see him as a beach bum again.

"I told you, the fire destroyed the paint, and there's nothing for Mara to see except concrete." Clay closed the patio door and accepted the glass Rory handed him.

"And Jared told me Miss Jenkins's car may have been deliberately driven off the road to cause the fire, and that your place has been broken into. Having been through this once with the locals, I thought I might be able to add my expertise in finding the culprits," TJ replied patiently.

"Ah, now I see the reason for the pie. Clay didn't ask for your help, did he?" Rory handed a glass to TJ, but instead of politely retreating, she stared him in the eye, even if she had to tilt her head up to do so. She'd had about all she could take of superior attitudes, even from the family of a friend. "It's generous of you to offer, but you're overlooking the fact that *I* am one of the locals. If anyone has any expertise here, it's me and Cissy."

"There's no point arguing," Clay said, pulling her out of his brother's face. "He doesn't mean to be insulting. It's just that TJ's goal in life is to interfere."

"Cleo tells me that if TJ hadn't interfered with her, she and Jared might not be married now," Mara said, emerging from the hallway bathroom. "Interference is a *good* thing, even if you macho McClouds don't get it."

With a shrug, Clay took a stool at the counter and tugged Rory back between his knees. "If we promise not to set any more fires or report any break-ins, he might go away. I'd like to eat my pie before it melts."

TJ lifted an eyebrow in a gesture all too like his brother's. "He's eating pie? In the middle of the day? How did you pry him away from the computer long enough?" His gaze drifted to the front room, where both computers were flashing screen savers, Clay's with photo images from *Star Wars*, Rory's with dollar signs and a bank logo.

Clay reached behind him and stabbed his pie with a fork, savoring the bite while Rory scrambled for a suitable reply to a question she didn't quite understand.

"Don't most people eat during the day? Pie isn't totally unreasonable, is it?"

"Clay doesn't eat," Mara explained. "He's been known to forget to eat while an entire dinner sits before him. His idea of nourishment is beer and fries in front of a computer." She cocked her head and eyed the forkful of pie entering Clay's mouth. "Looks like you've found a way to his stomach, but I have a sneaking suspicion the way to Clay's heart is through his insatiable brain. Knock him over the head and see what happens."

Rory laughed, until Clay stuck a forkful of pie into her mouth, and she almost spit it out her nose.

Cissy collapsed on the couch and roared. Unable to resist her mirth, TJ and Mara grinned.

Shrugging, Clay took his pie outside and went looking for Jake, leaving the others to dissect his behavior without him.

"You mean you won a million dollars, and you're investing it all in *Clay*? A million dollars?"

Rory clutched her coffee cup and sat paralyzed in front of the computer screen. Mara McCloud's utter surprise struck at the heart of Aurora's worst fears. She had been given one chance to ensure her family's future, and she was gambling the entire thing on a man who made her heart go pitter-pat. *Gambling* it. Her stomach knotted, her brain froze, and fear washed over her with the force of a tidal wave. Bankruptcy loomed one step away if their venture failed.

She finally conquered her immobility long enough to glance at Clay. He'd been working on the recalcitrant toaster again, but he'd apparently heard enough to look in her direction. His stark features revealed nothing of his thoughts. A curl of untamed hair fell across a line puckering his wide forehead, his gray eyes met hers steadily, and reassurance flooded through her. He might have his eccentric methods, but she believed in him.

"We paid the outstanding bills first," she said with an insouciance she didn't feel. "I can find a job anywhere, so we're no worse off than we were if it doesn't work out." Well, Cissy wouldn't have a job, Pops would have no insurance, they would still have a mortgage, and Mandy would have to work to put herself through school. They'd weathered worse.

They'd never weathered enemies who indulged in bodily harm and breaking and entering. She was clinging to the hope that the black car had been an accident and curious kids had invaded Clay's home.

She'd wanted to secure her family's future, not endanger it.

Letting the flicker of appreciation in Clay's eyes bolster her flagging confidence, Rory shoved aside her doubts, pointed out the error Cissy had made in the bookkeeping program, and returned to the kitchen to taste the simmering gumbo.

Clay set the toaster on the counter, plugged it in, and tested it. Satisfied with the result, he leaned over her shoulder to inspect the gumbo. She was dying to have his arms around her waist, his mouth nuzzling her ear, all those intimate things men and women did together when they were a couple.

But they weren't and he didn't, especially with family looking on. Officially, theirs was a business relationship. She'd best remember that. It wasn't as if they'd discussed what kind of relationship they had. Or wanted. If they wanted one at all. She was a little confused on that point.

"What are you planning on doing with a swamp?" TJ asked with interest. "That's the land neighboring Cleo's, isn't it?"

"It stretches from here to there, yes. The state wants to build a park on the beach. We want to build offices for Clay's studio and a crafts village for local artisans along the highway. The rest we'd like to preserve as it is."

"And that's where the bad guys come in, isn't it?" TJ asked. "Someone thinks they can turn worthless wetlands into a contractor's heaven and make billions, and you're in their way."

Aurora exchanged a glance with Clay and knew he believed that, too. "No one knows or cares about this place but the locals," she protested.

"And the town doesn't have a bank or a realty company or a contractor who stands to make their fortune on rich homeowners?" TJ asked dryly.

"I can't believe anyone we know would hurt us!" But even as she said it, Aurora knew the answer to that. People hurt other people all the time.

And most often, it was the people closest to a person doing the hurting.

❦ TWENTY-THREE ❦

"Welcome, Aurora, Clayton," Grandma Iris said with dignity, gesturing for them to enter the crowded cabin. "We're all here, even that worthless Billy."

Clay stepped into the June heat of the airless room, uncertainty and a modicum of unease churning his gut as he scanned a sea of expectant faces. After a week of intense planning, this morning they'd finished negotiating the investment from the retired venture capitalist. They had money in the bank and serious prospects of more to come.

It was up to the Binghams to decide how it would all fall out.

So far there had been no further incidents of break-ins or accidents, although TJ had insisted on talking to all the suspects: the banks, the Realtors, and any unfortunate developer who crossed his path. Or perhaps nothing had happened *because* TJ had talked to them, and terrified the shit out of them. Clay let his brother amuse himself as he wished. He'd spent his time pulling together a product that could make this meeting happen.

He told himself abstinence was good for productivity, but he'd have to work twenty-four-seven and keel over dead before he could be rid of his hunger for Aurora. He had hopes that a successful conclusion to this meeting would lead to another of her celebrations, and this time she would choose him instead of chocolate.

Looking around at the cabin full of anxious faces, Clay knew his list of Binghams had produced this deputation of representatives from all across the country. On his own, he wouldn't have a clue how to address them.

Aurora didn't seem to have that problem. She spoke with those few she knew, shook hands with the ones to whom she was introduced, relaxed the crowd so they returned to sipping their drinks and fanning themselves while the inevitable southern small talk swirled around the room. Clay was ready to burst his seams with the impatience he'd accused Aurora of possessing, but he admired her ability to handle people.

He didn't catch the moment the socializing switched to serious business. He just watched expressions turn intent and gazes focus on Aurora while she spoke with a tall, elderly gentleman. Despite the warmth, the man wore a suit jacket that hung loosely on his spare frame. Silver curls cut close to his dark head gave away his age, but his gaze was alert and perceptive as Aurora explained their plans.

"The land would remain ours?" he demanded.

"The land would belong to the nonprofit trust, but the heirs would own the controlling interest," Aurora corrected. "Only, the way the trust is set up, the majority of the wetlands would have to remain undeveloped."

"We'd be giving up millions!" a rotund middle-aged man protested.

Clay had already noted that this was the notorious

Billy, the one who had already signed an agreement to sell out his family.

"You sold your share for five thousand," Aurora reminded him. "You've already given up your rights. If the developers take your contract to court, they'll force an auction of the entire property. As things stand now, the only buyer will be the developer who already owns your share. Without the nonprofit trust to bid against him, how much do you think he will pay?"

The tall man answered for everyone. "A dollar an acre. I've seen it happen."

A murmur rippled around the room, and the knot in Clay's gut loosened. They were going to make this work. Now all he had to do was see that "Mysterious" earned money. He'd done it once, but that had been for fun. Could he do it this time for Aurora and a community of trusting people?

And now that they had the developer against the wall, how would he strike back?

"Do you think we could sic TJ on the zoning commission and terrify them into granting our request?" Rory murmured as she and Clay walked the trail to the turtle nesting area after leaving the Bingham heirs to talk among themselves. The stars were already out, and they'd drenched themselves in insect repellent for the excursion.

"Not unless the members of the commission are criminals. TJ's intense, but his focus is pretty narrow."

"Unlike you," she added with a knowing chuckle.

"Is that sarcasm I hear from Miss Uptight herself?" Clay offered his hand to help her over a fallen oak propped high off the ground by its branches. "I'll have you know I have other interests. I'm learning all about turtles."

"So you can put them in another game," she responded. "Just like your 'other' interest in L.A. was 'Mysterious' when you weren't working on business programs."

"I had a girlfriend," he argued. "We went out."

"To restaurants. To discuss business. Did you ever go dancing? Watch sunsets? Meet her family?"

Rory took the seat Clay found for her between the vine-covered branches of the tree. This discussion had wandered a little farther down personal paths than she had intended, but now that they were there, she wanted to hear his answers. They'd spent a truly intense two weeks working on their business partnership. There hadn't been time, or privacy, for their personal one, but now that things were in motion, she wanted to know where she stood.

She longed for more of what they'd shared in Charleston, but she wasn't good at casual sex. And she didn't see how they could ever have anything else. Clay lived so far inside his head that he had trouble relating to family, and she had so much family inside her head, she had trouble thinking beyond their needs. Her career was all wrapped up in that somewhere. She didn't even know if Clay wanted a career or if he was just going along with her for lack of anything better to do. Maybe she was just another form of clock for him to tinker with.

Clay settled behind her, snuggling her against his chest and crotch, wrapping his arms around her waist as if they did this every day. His touch could settle all her doubts—until he got up and walked away, leaving her alone and wondering again.

She wasn't cut out for this. Relationships made her crazy. Maybe that was why she was so bad at them.

"Okay, so Diane is a bad example," he admitted. "I'm not much into socializing. I don't have the same kind of interests as most people. I don't seem to think like everyone else, and I just end up confusing them."

He was trying to tell her something. She wanted to understand, but it sounded very much as if he were saying he didn't want people around him. And she loved having people around.

"So you do everything yourself," she translated. "You don't want anyone else distributing your programs, and you don't want to get involved with any one person, and you don't want to commit to any one place. You think no one understands you, so you drive a Harley and live like a hermit, like some stereotypical James Dean."

She understood, she thought, but she didn't like realizing why. She'd gone off on her own career, leaving her family behind. She had had her own empty apartment and her own empty car. Clay just carried his isolation a little further because his family didn't need him as hers did.

"I don't get the connection," he said in bafflement. "I told you I don't think like other people. I'm living here because I don't like L.A. I'm riding a Harley because I don't want people judging me by my wheels."

"You just defined yourself by what you *don't* want," she insisted. "How will you ever know where you're going if you're only looking back to where you've been? What do you *want* to do?" She shouldn't be going there herself. Talk about the pot calling the kettle black.

But if he could reassure her somehow, tell her what she

needed to hear . . . Digging the hole deeper, she continued. "Where do you see yourself in the future? How are you planning on getting there if you shut everyone and everything out by thinking in terms of what you *don't* want?"

He sat silent for a moment, digesting this. "Okay, maybe I'm bad at the relationship thing. I'm open to learning. What do you suggest?"

He started nibbling on her neck, so Rory assumed he was merely being agreeable for her sake. Clay's brand of agreeable was downright addictive. She leaned back against him, encouraging his hand to stray higher. But they had issues here, and they were both avoiding them. "I suggest that sex is not the same thing as a relationship."

Oops. She hadn't really meant to say that, especially when his fingers instantly stopped their incredible massaging. Her nipples had already reached extreme sensitization, and she was ready for anything. Except stopping.

"I thought the sex was good."

Was that hurt she heard behind his gruff words? Surely she didn't have the power to wound a man granted every favor nature provided? "The sex is beyond good, and you know it."

"Okay." He hesitated, apparently uncertain where to hold her now. "If women don't want sex, then what do they want?"

"Lovemaking." She knew the answer, but she held her breath as she awaited his reaction. *Love* was not a word that most men wanted to hear. They seemed to think it was synonymous with *prison bars*. He'd jokingly used the song "Love Me Do" in his e-mail, but that was just his weird method of communication, wasn't it?

"Lovemaking isn't the same as sex?" he replied in surprise.

She almost giggled at his tone. Relaxing, she returned his hand to her breast. "That may depend on the participants' intentions. Women like sex well enough, although I hadn't realized how good it could be until you came along."

"Flattery will get you everywhere." His voice was bone dry against her ear. "So now that you have me where you want me, what do you want out of me?"

Stung by his implication that she wanted a return on her investment—like his former girlfriend, presumably—Rory stood up. It was high time she learned to assert herself in personal relationships as well as business ones. "Not casual sex."

She wanted sex, all right. Her whole body felt cold and empty now that they no longer touched. But she needed more than sex.

Clay looked suitably startled. Predictably, his confusion turned into a frown. "I don't know about you, but I'm not ready for rings and commitments."

She probably wasn't either, because they represented risks she wasn't ready to take, although a few soft words might have persuaded her differently. But as he'd pointed out, he wasn't good with words. Or people. And she didn't have the time or patience to teach him. Not when she was so confused that she hurt inside. "I don't think either of us knows what we want, so let's just leave it at that."

In confusion at her conflicting emotions, hurting more at his blunt rejection than she thought possible, she shoved past entwining branches in retreat. She hoped she wasn't scaring any turtles into not procreating just because her own ticking biological clock had started ringing shattering alarms.

She'd known all along that he just wanted sex. That was why she'd tried to keep this to a business partnership. But she no longer wanted just a business partnership, and it was killing her inside.

It wasn't within her abilities to teach him how to do personal relationships. She wasn't certain how to make them happen either.

Abandoned, Clay didn't follow. He couldn't see Aurora well enough in the moonless dark to know where she'd gone, but he sure as hell could feel the emptiness where she had been. The evening was sultry, but he felt cold.

She didn't want casual sex. How the hell was he supposed to take that? There wasn't anything casual about what they'd shared.

He'd thought they were getting along pretty well. She hadn't complained about his interfering brothers. She'd had an excellent grasp of the business contract he'd had the lawyer draw up, and she hadn't objected to his keeping all creative rights to his programs. She didn't even seem to mind his bad communication skills, until now, at least.

He'd tried to maintain a businesslike relationship in front of family, although he'd had some difficulty with that lately. It irked him every time she smiled and chatted up another man. That had never bothered him when Diane had done it. Probably because he'd thought the expensive rock on her finger was proof of fidelity.

He was walking straight into the same open pit again—

expecting a career-oriented female to have anything more in mind than the next step on the ladder to success. Maybe she was waiting to see if he was just a rung or the whole ladder. Who the devil knew? *Not casual sex* sounded like an invitation to commitment to him, and he wasn't ready to go there.

So maybe he was falling back into an old pattern of thinking. There was comfort in that. If he took the time to consider how much love Aurora possessed and how little she was like Diane, he'd have to reconsider a lot of things, most of them unflattering to himself. He was hurting too much to go there right now.

Wounded, he retreated into his shell.

The day after the meeting with the Binghams, Aurora answered the kitchen phone. Cleo's voice leaped through the receiver, conveying both concern and curiosity. "All right, what have you been feeding Clay?"

Aurora frowned, glanced at the front room, where Cissy worked alone, and shook her head. "He's not here to feed. I thought he must be involved in something at your place."

In truth, she'd been living in terror since he hadn't shown up at their door first thing in the morning, as he'd done lately. What if she'd insulted him and he'd gotten mad and caught a plane back to L.A.?

What if he had only wanted sex, and now he'd lost all interest in her and the company and the swamp and . . . ?

She had known better than to become involved. She had to go back to the city and work. She'd known Clay would—

"He's up on the courthouse roof taking the clock apart

again." Cleo interrupted her panic. "I thought maybe you knew what set him off. TJ's threatening to go up after him."

"Oh." Unwilling to let Clay's family know the extent of their involvement—if two nights of sex could be called that—Rory tried to keep her voice calm. "I just gave him some food for thought. If TJ's restless, tell him to threaten a few zoning commissioners. They've called a meeting next week in hopes of forcing our hand before we have enough Binghams on our side."

Business was something she understood, something that didn't involve emotional chaos. Maybe she wasn't any more ready for a relationship than Clay. But a cold terror ate at her heart at the thought of never seeing him again. She hoped the sinking feeling in her middle just had to do with the corporation and the future, not a relationship he obviously didn't want.

"As long as I can tell Jared and TJ that Clay's thinking and not blowing up the clock, I can arrange that. How many people would you like at the meeting?"

"Jam the house. The Binghams we've brought together are refusing to sell to anyone until they've had time to examine the issue. If the zoning goes for condos, then the Binghams might be better off selling out."

Saying good-bye to Cleo, Aurora hung up.

"Clay sick?" Cissy called across the room.

Of her, maybe, but Rory couldn't say that. Was she too forthright? Too bossy? She probably expected too much. She'd hoped Clay was different, but what would it matter if he was? He had his own agenda, and he'd done everything possible to show her that a relationship wasn't part of it. She ought to be relieved at his honesty.

She squeezed the turtle eraser in her pocket and tried not to place any sentiment on the silly gift. He gave her erasers and tomato plants and lobsters instead of romance. That ought to tell her something.

"He apparently got tired of the business end of the software," she said with a shrug, "and he's out pounding nails. Now that 'Mysterious' is in the hands of production, there isn't much he can do here anyway."

She needed to plan ahead. Clay had spent years reworking the game. Once it was safely in the hands of their new corporation, he had no reason to stay. He was a programmer, not a business expert. Once the problem was solved, he would go looking for another challenge.

Picking up the cordless, Aurora wandered back to her bedroom. She was glad they'd had that little discussion yesterday. He'd reminded her that she had more important things to consider besides mooning over a man like a sex-crazed adolescent. She had her own life to live. She didn't have to sit around waiting for Clay to decide how he wanted to live his.

She had a few contacts. She'd put out a few feelers. No sense in languishing here once her family's future was decided. If the zoning went against them, they'd need the money Rory's job brought in. If they got the zoning, then Cissy and their father would have plenty to keep them busy. They knew the community and wouldn't need her expertise any longer.

Feeling abandoned for no good reason, Aurora opened her address book and began placing calls.

* * *

Do you wanna dance? Put your red dress on and be ready to shake your tail feathers. Tonight, tonight. Seven P.M. Be there or be square.

Be where? What red dress? Her suit? And tail feathers? The man was surely insane. Maybe he'd baked his brains on the roof today. But her stupid heart did another one of its flip-flops of pure joy as she stared at the screen. They didn't have a relationship. He only wanted sex. But she'd missed him today.

She hadn't realized how much she could miss the way Clay listened intently, not interrupting until she'd had time to spew out everything boiling inside her, waiting until she was ready to hear what he had to say. She even missed his skewed perspectives that made her look at things in a new light.

She missed the heat of desire in his eyes when he looked at her that made her zing even when she was creating financial statements.

Straining her memory for old songs from the radio, she tapped out, *I can dance, but this devil wears a blue dress.* Let him figure out where she was wearing it. She was still too relieved at knowing he hadn't disappeared into the ether to care about details or to overanalyze her reaction.

Did the message mean he was taking her dancing? Did this mean he'd decided to date? Did she want to date? She didn't know what she wanted, she conceded. She just recognized after his absence today that Clay—in any form—was crucial to her precarious balance right now.

He was crucial to a lot of things, but she was averse to risk taking, and Clay was a risk wilder than spending a million dollars on hope and pink elephants. Money could be had anywhere, but her heart was irreplaceable.

That wouldn't keep her from dancing. She couldn't remember the last time she'd gone. She'd taken some swing lessons when that had been popular, but she'd never had much of a chance to use them. Would a busy man like Clay have learned swing?

Tonight! Irritating man. Did he think she ought to drop everything at his whim? She should have told him no, except she couldn't think of a musical reference.

She scanned her closet, frantically realizing she had absolutely nothing to wear dancing, especially if she didn't know where they were going. The blue dress was made for swing, with lots of swirly skirt. She couldn't think of a single place around here that it was suitable for.

"You're slamming drawers and doors like you have a big date." Mandy appeared in her doorway, watching with curiosity as Aurora threw the blue silk dress aside and tugged out a black one.

"Where do people go dancing in this town?" Of course, her niece wasn't old enough to go to bars, so what would she know?

"They have a deejay at the Monkey on Saturday nights. And they still have shag dances at the harbor pavilion. Old-people stuff."

She didn't need to be reminded that she would be over-the-hill shortly. Rory flung an old sundress that was too small for her at Mandy. "If you're not here to help, go away."

"Ooh, it *is* a big date! With Clay? That rocks. You have to wear something really kick-ass for a guy like that." Shouldering Rory aside, Mandy investigated the contents of her closet. "This stuff sucks, you know it? Don't you have anything besides suits?"

So her whole life was work. So shoot her. "Go away, little girl." Now she was talking in oldies. She was losing her mind.

Before she could shove Mandy out of the way, her niece reached in and grabbed a skirt shoved to the back of the closet. "This one! Do you have any halter tops?"

"To wear with shorts." Aurora held up the blue-flowered wraparound silk skirt and considered it dubiously. It was the next best thing to a sarong. She didn't know what had possessed her to buy it in the first place. It was too frivolous for work.

"Bare bellies are the bomb!" Mandy insisted. "I'll have something, if you don't. White or navy would work, don't you think?"

"If you're taking fashion advice from Mandy, my advice is, don't." Cissy appeared in the doorway to study the situation. "You have to weigh a hundred pounds and be ten years old to wear the stuff she wears."

"Mo-o-ommmm!" Mandy waved the skirt on the hanger. "This is not for ten-year olds. Aunt Rora will look bitchin'. Where's that white stretchy top Gladys gave you? The one you said is too big?"

Cissy raised her eyebrows, checked out the skirt, and disappeared to the other half of the trailer. Rory double-checked her closet, praying for something more suitable. She couldn't wear a sarong and a halter top. She'd look like an Amazon.

Cissy returned with a silky knit halter top. "You wear this, and his eyes are going to pop out," she warned.

"That's it, that's the one!" Mandy shouted with glee.

"A blue necklace. A choker? Or one of those big pendants with a blue stone? Where's your jewelry box? Or you can wear my beads."

Caught up in the whirlwind of advice, Rory showered, washed her hair, and let her sister and niece dress her as if she were going to the prom. What did she have to lose? The million dollars was already tied up, and if Clay didn't like prom queens, that was his loss.

If she repeated that to herself often enough, maybe she'd believe it.

They pulled her hair into a French braid, created a choker of a string of seed pearls and a fake sapphire from a pair of earrings, found a pair of dangling seed-pearl earrings, and Rory produced a pair of strappy low-heeled sandals that wouldn't require stockings. Casual, yet elegant.

"Whooeee, Clay won't know what hit him!" Mandy danced around, inspecting her handiwork, while Cissy propped her hip against the bed, nodding approval.

"What he thinks doesn't matter. What the two of you think is more important. Do I look like an idiot? Are people going to fall down laughing when they see me coming?" She felt safe encased in suits, but this outfit revealed all. She eyed her cleavage and exposed navel with skepticism, but it was the way the knit clung to her breasts that had her wishing for a bulky sweater.

By the time the doorbell rang, Mandy had them laughing and examining Cissy's closet. Mandy raced to answer the door while Rory tried to steady her nerves. It was just McCloud. She shouldn't read anything more into this than a night out and maybe a good time.

They were business partners. It wasn't as if they'd spoken words of love or commitment. A date. She could

handle a date. If that was what it was. Not a business
meeting or a farewell. A date.

Clay was waiting for her in the front room. She'd seen
him in here a thousand times, but this time he was a dif
ferent creature entirely. He'd attempted to force his thick
hair into a slicked-back style that any movie star would
envy. His blue raw-silk blazer whispered of understated
elegance, the stylish uncollared shirt with tiny pleats be
spoke Rodeo Drive, and the draping of his linen slack
shouted expensive tailoring. He looked fabulous.

And stunned. He watched her enter with such awe and
delight that Rory thought her head might swell to twice
its size. His smile was a wonder to behold.

"You just walked out of my favorite fantasy," he mur
mured as she approached.

When he held out a small florist's box containing a
tiny blue orchid, Rory forgot her fears and indulged in
teenage delight.

"This is absolutely perfect. I think I love you," she
cried, tucking the orchid into her hair, and swirling
around to check her image in a mirror.

"Partridge Family. That's a great song," he murmured
insensibly, touching her hair and not the orchid. "That's ex
actly how I pictured that flower. Better than I pictured it."

So many butterflies fluttered in Rory's stomach that
she was walking on air by the time Clay led her into the
soft evening light. She had to pinch herself and remem
ber they were just going dancing.

And then he opened the door to a sleek, black, antique
Jaguar convertible and flipped all her switches.

❧ TWENTY-FOUR ❧

On his best day Clay couldn't put together the kind of sweet words women wanted to hear. Under pressure to do the right thing so Aurora wouldn't walk out on him, he couldn't find any words at all.

He'd entertained the fanciful notion some time ago that the immense commitment the old Jag represented would show her that he wasn't a fly-by-night kind of guy, but he'd dragged his feet about bringing it out for fear he'd be disillusioned by her reaction. And he'd desperately not wanted to be disillusioned this time.

Aurora's astonished silence was worth every bit of the extortionate fees he'd paid to get the car out of storage and transported here. He opened the door for her, and she caressed the exquisitely painted and waxed exterior as if it were a precious antique. Standing close behind her, he inhaled a whiff of gardenia. She'd worn perfume for him.

She was treating this as a real date, not a business function.

"The top isn't automatic," he warned, testing to be certain she understood this was an old wreck and not a

303

fancy new car with automatic everything. "So if it rains, we'll get wet."

"I could drown in this and die happy." Climbing in, she ran her fingers lovingly over the polished wood of the dash. "Where did you find it? Doesn't it belong in a museum?"

Feeling as if he were on pins and needles, he climbed behind the wheel and started the engine. "It's not that old. I've had offers from collectors, but I put it together practically from scrap. I couldn't give it up." He could talk about machines, but what he really wanted to understand was the mechanics of relationships. From her responses, he thought maybe he'd passed the first step.

"You *rebuilt* this? I knew you tinkered, but I had no idea. . . ."

Clay didn't dare tear his gaze from the road to see her expression. Diane had been turned off by the mechanical aspect of his hobby. She thought he should have spent his millions *buying* cars, not building them. She hadn't understood the thrill of knowing a machine from the inside out.

"I like tinkering," he said defensively when Aurora didn't complete her comment.

"This is way more than tinkering." She reverently stroked the butter-soft leather, and there seemed to be awe in her voice. "Sitting on the courthouse roof playing with the clock is tinkering. This is genius and dedication."

Clay relaxed his painful grip on the wheel. He should have known not to let his prior experience color his opinion of Aurora. She had a mind of her own and wasn't afraid to use it. Or speak it. "It's going to take genius and dedication to make the courthouse clock work too. It's an old-fashioned balance mechanism and someone has replaced one of the balances with an inadequate weight. I'll have to figure out the mathematics to make it work."

"Can you do that?" Awe still tinged her voice, but she was returning to practicality. "I mean, it hardly seems worth your time."

He lifted one shoulder casually. He liked that she recognized his time as valuable, even if he spent it sitting on beaches. "Tinkering gives me time to think. I could just test weights until I get it right."

"And where did your thinking get you today?"

Hearing laughter and skepticism in that question, Clay braved a quick look. Aurora was so stunning with that long glowing braid over creamy shoulders and cleavage that—

He abruptly returned to watching the road. "It has me thinking that maybe some of my hobbies are a little unsociable."

Laughter did bubble out at that, but Aurora was always laughing. That was one of the things he liked about her. She didn't nag and complain and make life miserable for everyone around her when things didn't go right. She blew up, she cried; then she got over it and took matters into her own hands, smiling or cooking her way through it.

"You could always find partners to play your video games if you want to be sociable," she suggested. "There are probably kids out there just as good at them as you are."

"Most of them want the action games. I grew up on the Dungeons and Dragons things, and I like role-playing.

Not too many people are interested." Truth was, he wasn't
as interested as he used to be. As a kid, imaginary games
had given his overactive brain an escape when he'd
needed it, but he'd rather find a real-life role that suited
him better. Beach bum and biker had just been more role-
playing on a different level.

"They have sorcerers in those games, don't they? You
probably make a great sorcerer, knowing things way beyond the knowledge of most people."

A sorcerer. He liked that. Sending her another side-
ways look, deciding she wasn't laughing at him, he began
to relax and enjoy the evening even more. "Men like the
mystique of appearing omniscient. Gives the girls a
thrill," he teased.

She laughed again. "Just fixing our toasters gives us
a thrill. The strong, silent types are highly overrated.
Where are we going?"

"With you looking as hot as that? Probably Las Vegas.
But if you want to get home tonight, maybe we ought to
settle for the Monkey." She hadn't hit him yet, so he assumed he hadn't gone too far wrong. "Have you eaten?"

"Las Vegas is more tempting than the Monkey, but I'm
hungry and willing to settle for food. Did you have a reason for this evening out?"

He squirmed a little and didn't answer as he maneuvered the narrow town streets. She waited expectantly
while he found an opening and parked. "I don't know
how to do relationships," he finally said flat-out. He
slammed out of the car and walked around to assist her
from the low-slung seat.

"It's not something you learn in books or find in Help
files," she agreed sympathetically.

The open wrap side of Aurora's skirt flashed a tantalizing glimpse of shapely leg as she took his hand and climbed out. Clay almost lost track of the conversation until she spoke again.

"I figure relationships must be something you learn by doing," she continued.

"And failing," he said dryly, leading her into the Saturday-night bedlam of the bar. "That failing part is kind of rough."

"You're a sorcerer, make the magic work for you," she murmured beneath the chorus of greetings as they entered.

"I have a feeling you're not talking about my magic shirt," he whispered back, slapping palms with one of the other patrons while maneuvering Rory toward the booths and away from the slavering crowd at the bar.

"If you can keep Ed from bearing down on us with more tales of the mayor's daddy and German subs, I might believe in magic shirts."

"These days Ed's into believing the German spies left their treasure buried on the beach. TJ's been avoiding the bar, afraid Ed will ask him to dig up the beach again."

"Hey, Rora!" Terry Talbert called from the bar, his gaze darting from her to Clay. "Didn't know the two of you were hooking up."

"You belong to the wrong crowd then." Although he was getting a kick out of the winks and thumbs-ups he was receiving from his bar cronies, Clay disliked the way the head of the tourist commission eyed Rora in her revealing, non-banker attire. He was inclined to do something Neanderthal like kiss her cheek, wrap his arm around her, and stake his claim.

"Clay and I have mutual interests," Aurora replied coolly. "Right now our interest is in dancing. See you around, Terry."

She walked away from the man who had fired her as if Talbert were no more than a gnat in her tea. Grinning, Clay followed, admiring the view.

"Can you dance?" she asked abruptly, hesitating between the booths and the tables near the dance floor, where a couple was two-stepping across the floor out of time with the music.

"Never tried," he conceded, eyeing the dance floor with wary interest.

Rory wound her way through the booth crowd to the tables. "You listen to oldies but you've never danced?" she asked, intrigued.

He held out a chair for her, and she was entirely too aware of Clay's height, of the way he stood too close, of the seductive scent of his shaving lotion. She'd always been aware of the real man behind his many disguises, but she liked that he'd chosen his sophisticated persona for her.

"Dancing lessons are required education in our family," he admitted. "TJ dutifully took them as told. Jared got thrown out after he used the CDs as Frisbees, then decorated the dance hall with the teacher's favorite tapes in an impromptu game of Keep-away. After that, the teacher was more than willing to accept my deal of cashing my parents' check, giving me half, and letting me spend the time at the arcade next door."

"Afraid of girl cooties?" she taunted.

"I could apply myself to computers or to girls, not

both. I lost Jared's help on the script for 'Mysterious' when he got mushy over some female. Since I was skinny, with a nose that covered my entire face, the girls I knew wouldn't give me the time of day. After Jared's defection, I worked on the program alone. The sale of 'Mysterious' gave me my own IPO by the time I left college. By then I was working on three-D animation and several business programs. I didn't have time for a life."

"I think you grew into your nose," she said dryly. It was a unique nose that kept him from prettiness, giving his face the character that reflected the depths she had yet to explore.

She was amazed at the amount of information spilling out of him tonight. Sitting on the courthouse roof must have primed his speech pump. She was torn between learning more and getting up on the dance floor to work off some of the sexual tension smoldering between them. Although Clay didn't overtly stare at her cleavage, she recognized his awareness in the way he tried to stay focused on her face when she toyed with the pendant at her throat. Perversely, she wanted him to stare.

She wanted a whole lot more than that. If she was to survive the evening without jumping his bones, she needed to dance. "What they're doing looks easy." She nodded at the dance floor, where couples were rocking to some golden moldie she vaguely recognized. "Let's just imitate them."

She bit back a smile as Clay studiously observed the limited action on the dance floor while they ordered drinks and chose from the menu. His fingers were unconsciously tapping to the rhythm of the music, but he really

did seem to think he could study the dancers and discover a pattern to their movement, as if they were parts
of a ticking clock.

"How did you get into listening to classic rock?" she
asked. She knew she was in serious trouble when she
really wanted to know the answer.

Clay switched his intense focus from the dance floor to
her, and she nearly went up in smoke from the heat of it.
"Good beat and it went in one ear and out the other
while I was working. It just kind of wormed its way into
my head, and then into the program. Before I knew what
was happening, I started looking for more music my
game characters could dance to. The classic stuff worked
best. Paying for sub-rights on the songs made the game
expensive, but fun."

The beat was ringing her chimes right now. She could
feel the music in her bones. She could feel *him*. She
squirmed restlessly.

He turned back to watch the dancers. "They aren't all
doing the same steps."

"It doesn't work that way," she murmured, taking his
hand and standing up. "This is the kind of dancing you
feel."

"What I feel has nothing to do with dance floors."
With that enigmatic remark, he stood and drew her into
the growing crowd of dancing couples.

As luck would have it, the deejay played a slow song
the instant they stepped onto the dance floor. Despite his
protests, Clay knew the basics of slow dancing. He'd left
his jacket on his seat back. His strong arm wrapped
around her waist. His calloused hand held hers. He studied her face as he shuffled his feet in time to the music.

And they danced as if they'd done this a thousand times together, instinctively following the rhythm of each other's bodies.

Clay's angular features lifted in a study of delight upon discovering how the beat poured from the music, through him, to her.

Giddy with happiness, Aurora flowed with the man and the music and the movement. She didn't want to worry about anything while she surrendered to this moment of perfection. Clay towered over her just enough to make her feel feminine. His hands were confident as he guided her through the crowd, his fingers doing a subtle dance of their own at her waist. His body lingered every time his hips and thighs brushed hers. Had she really thought dancing would release some of the tension between them? She'd obviously not danced with the right man before.

Clay's steady hand rode her waist. The linen of his trousers brushed the silk of her skirt, and their gazes met and sparked with awareness. His palm at the small of her back guided her in a rhythmic sway as breast met chest, and their bodies pulsed to a beat that had more to do with their night together than it did to music. Had he asked it of her, she would have left the floor right then and looked for the nearest bed.

The song changed to a fast beat, and Clay hesitated, watching the other dancers. Caught in the spell of his embrace, Rory no longer cared about dancing, but her partner had a look of determination in his eye that fascinated her nearly as much as what the night promised.

She understood now that Clay could do anything he put his mind to, and that his mind was on dancing with her tonight. She had no words to express the thrill of that knowledge.

Other couples deserted the floor with the first pounding chords of the faster beat. Clay simply set his eagle eye on the remaining dancers, chose the pattern he preferred, and, holding Rory's hand and waist, loosened his grip and matched the rhythm of the music.

She laughed when he swung her beneath his arm and bent her backward as if he'd been doing this since childhood. As if she were made of fluff. She'd waited all her life for this—freedom to let go and be herself.

She began to see her smile reflected on Clay's face. His sharp jaw relaxed, and his eyes glittered with delight at her laughter. By the time their meal arrived, he was inventing steps of his own, and she feared other women would start swarming over him as if he were John Travolta.

"Food." She pointed at the table.

He studied the table, listened to the next song, and, apparently deciding food was preferable, returned her to her chair. She loved the way his mind constantly ticked, taking in everything, sorting through his observations, and working out solutions without a word being said.

She was in serious trouble here, thinking thoughts like that about a man who didn't think in terms of futures or careers—when she could never forget that her family depended on her career for their future.

"I've been thinking about what you said," he announced after satisfying his first urgent hunger pangs, pushing back in his chair, stretching his legs out, and watching her sip her wine.

"About what?" She wasn't certain she wanted to go wherever he was headed. But she did her best to appear together and calm. A man who actually wanted to talk wasn't a man to be taken lightly. She practiced his habit of listening.

He crumpled up his linen napkin and tossed it on the table. "About us. About sex. About relationships."

"Oh, that." Her heart kicked hard enough to hurt, and she tried not to wince. What had she said? Something stupid, probably—like not wanting casual sex when all she could think about right this minute was how soon they could find a bed not surrounded by family.

"I don't know how to date like a teenager," he warned.

He looked so serious. No, he looked like a Hollywood star being serious. Or a computer mogul who desperately wanted sex but was willing to negotiate a contract first. Aurora smiled at that.

"That's okay. I'm not a teenager." She wished she knew what she wanted well enough to tell him, but her life was too stressed-out and confused right now. "I haven't had a lot of experience at relationships. I just know the sex between us is good, but I need more than that."

It was hard to tell when a handsome man sprawled in a chair in a nightclub was tense, but Aurora calculated that the dent Clay's fingers were leaving in his trousers right now might be some indication. He didn't go up in smoke at her reply, though, so that was promising.

"Do people still go steady?" he asked warily.

"If that means agreeing not to see others, I suppose." She tried not to look too eager, but her heart was racing like a teenager's. She wanted him to figure out how they could have sex without the commitment they both obviously feared. She wanted it right now.

"If I tell you I'm not interested in any other woman but you, does that count as going steady?"

"That works for me. I can guarantee you're the only man on my agenda right now." *Be cool, Aurora. Businesslike. Don't send the guy screaming into the streets.*

"I hope you warned your family not to expect you home tonight," he said abruptly, standing and holding out his hand. "I'm willing to try this steady-dating thing, but I don't think I'll survive the night if I have to take you home afterward."

"You're such a hopeless romantic!" Accepting his hand, Rory smiled at the wary expression springing to his eyes at her teasing. "And I bet you don't even want to go over to the pavilion later and learn to shag."

"I'd say I already know how to shag, but something tells me we're not talking about the same thing." He still looked wary but interested. "If this is something you want to do, I'm willing. I'm opening myself to new experiences."

"Renaissance man, I like that. I like that so much I don't think I want to corrupt the innocent shaggers with the kind of shagging you have on your mind right now." Eagerly, she let him draw her close. The heat between them escalated to the temperature of a South Carolina August noon.

Clay threw a handful of money on the table. "Let's go."

"If I said I changed my mind and wanted to go to the pavilion, would you take me?" she jested, running to keep up with his pace outside the Monkey. Events were happening too fast. She needed to slow down. Or maybe she needed to know he was thinking about her and not just sex.

He halted. "Where's the pavilion?"

She'd experienced power trips before. She thrived on walking through a megabank with documents she'd put together to seal a multimillion-dollar deal.

That didn't begin to compare with having this much power over a man who flipped all her switches. Whatever this was between them, it was a two-way street. "What if I tell you I want to go home after the pavilion?"

"I'd tell you that you're insane and try to persuade you otherwise." Intelligently catching on to her little ego trip, Clay took her elbow and guided her toward the car. "Don't tease. I'm still working on that negativity thing. I want to see more of you. I'm working toward something positive, see?"

Since all her hormones were frolicking like little rabbits in an open field, she probably wasn't seeing anything clearly, but she liked the sound of this. She climbed into the Jag without further argument. Maybe they could figure out their emotions once they got this sexual frustration out of the way.

"And that's what you decided while pounding holes in the courthouse roof today?"

"I'm taking it slowly." He started the ignition and pulled into the unlit street. "Baby steps first. Dancing, wining, dining, flowers—that's all a form of lovemaking, isn't it?"

He sounded so sincere, Rory laughed. "You're a quick study, I give you that, though I don't know that I'd call it lovemaking."

His brow creased as if he were analyzing her comment for hidden meaning. "Will it pass for foreplay?" he asked with such studied gravity that Rory laughed.

"Very likely. So does the Jag. Want to try for sweet words next?"

"I think that's a little more advanced than I'm ready for yet. How about if I just try keeping my floor clean because I want my steady woman to make it up the stairs alive?"

Relaxing into the mood he created instead of fretting over this next step in their relationship, Rory admired the moon rising over the harbor as they crossed the bridge to the island. So maybe she was setting herself up for heartbreak. How many times in her life would she ever come across a man she enjoyed as much? How many men had she ever discussed sex with and still felt comfortable with without being pressured?

None. No man had ever met her on her own terms, then challenged her with his, stretching her viewpoint to encompass whole new horizons.

She didn't want to analyze what was happening to her, not when anticipation hummed inside her. The night was perfect, with a nearly full moon and a sensual warmth like silk against her skin. She would simply relish the moment and live with a broken heart later.

She darted a glance at him and smiled at the way he studied the road ahead, then the road behind in the rear-view mirror. Another man might have been looking at her or toying with the radio. Clay had a knack for applying seriousness to just the right things.

He abruptly swung down a road leading to the shopping center.

She blinked in surprise at the abrupt change in course. "Do we need something at the grocery?"

"See the headlights behind us?" He adjusted the rear-view mirror. "Watch and see if it's a black Lincoln when I turn off here."

He pulled the Jag into the parking lot and stopped under a streetlight. A black Lincoln slowed, rolled past, and turned into the entrance of a lot down the road.

"He's going into the office park." Rory eyed Clay with curiosity as he gunned the engine, hit the highway, and headed toward town. "The town is full of black cars. If you think that's the one Cissy—"

"Cissy couldn't even tell us what kind of car drove her off the road. I'm thinking that one followed us all the way from the Monkey."

"So someone left at the same time as we did. It's late, a lot of people were leaving."

"How many of the Monkey's patrons drive Lincolns?" Clay asked.

He had her there. "Tourists might. And maybe someone wanted to do a quick business deal over a drink. Not everyone does that at the country club."

"And that's why he's out here cruising the island in the dark?" His cynical tone said what he thought of that.

"Maybe he had to run back to his office for some papers and now he's on his way home."

"Then maybe the papers were hanging on his office door so he could grab them fast enough to be back on the road already, and his home is in town, because he's behind us again." Shadows sharpened the wide ridge of Clay's nose as he joined the traffic on the bridge and checked the mirror again.

She glanced over her shoulder, but all she could see were headlights. "Why would anyone follow us? It's not as if we'll lead them to buried treasure." Why would anyone run Cissy off the road? Or break into Clay's cottage? None of this made sense, but he was scaring her.

Clay unclipped his cell phone, punched a few buttons, and handed it to her. "Let's find out. Tell TJ what I'm telling you."

The reception in town was better than on the island. TJ's deep voice came through loud and clear. Embarrassed, Rory tried to think of a simple greeting. "Hello, TJ. This is Aurora Jenkins. I'm with Clay."

"We're leaving the bridge and driving down the highway going west toward the interstate," Clay instructed her.

She repeated that information to the quiet man on the other end of the phone line. He took Clay's dictation without any sign of agitation.

"Tell him to take his hulking SUV and wait in the lot at the bottom of the bridge. I'll be returning here in ten minutes. If he can rouse Jared, tell him we'll be heading his way."

TJ thanked Rory gravely and hung up. She stared at the phone and wondered if she'd stepped into a TV program without knowing it.

When Clay double-parked in front of the Monkey, she handed him the phone. She knew what he wanted her to do, but she wasn't buying it.

"I'm not getting out. It's very possible that if anyone is following us—and I'm not saying that I believe they are—they could be after me. I feel safer with you."

Without streetlights, she couldn't read Clay's expression, but she could see his hands tighten on the wheel and knew he was thinking furiously. She checked her seat belt and didn't budge.

He pulled back the shift and stepped on the gas. "Hold on to your hair, then, and let's see what this baby can do."

❧TWENTY-FIVE❧

The Jag could take sharp corners with astonishing swiftness, Rory learned. She couldn't say that Clay drove recklessly, but she'd never taken the tight corners and narrow brick streets of the old part of town at forty-five either.

They'd maneuvered only a few dark blocks when a squeal of brakes and Clay's grunt of satisfaction said their tail hadn't navigated the last turn. She checked behind them and couldn't see any headlights. She hadn't heard a crash, so no one was hurt. Sighing in relief, she leaned back against the comfortable leather and stretched her legs, letting the tension flow out of her. "Well, if you wanted to generate a little additional excitement out of the evening, you've succeeded."

"Depends on how dumb they are." Letting out the clutch, Clay smoothly took the machine through its paces down the highway. Then, checking his watch, he swung the Jag around in a neat three-point turn.

"No Lincoln could corner like this car. They can't still be following," she insisted.

"Not in that land yacht, for sure, and if they're car thieves, we've lost them. But think about it: If they knew who they were following, why should they bother endangering life and limb doing what we just did?"

"To see where we're going?" Although why anyone would care was beyond her.

"And if we kept on going, into Charleston or somewhere, they'd be cursing now that we've lost them. But I'm wagering they let us have our little joyride because they figure they know where to catch up with us."

"You think it's the police?" She definitely wasn't getting this. In the movies, wasn't it the FBI or private detectives who tailed cars? "The state and a few others are probably pretty riled at us about now, but it's hardly a police matter."

"We've 'riled' the state, the tourist commission, the bank, and probably half the developers within a hundred miles of us by delaying the zoning. You've told the bank we're building a multimillion-dollar business. Cissy has told the developer to piss off. No, I don't think it's the police out there."

Rory rubbed the goose bumps rising on her arms. She gaped as he drove straight toward the bridge and home. "If they're dangerous, you're driving right into their hands."

"Something like that." At a sedate rate of speed, he drove the Jag past the parking lot at the base of the bridge.

He was deliberately steering right into trouble! Wasn't he supposed to be avoiding it? Maybe those were car thieves out to carjack a Jag. If their followers knew they had to cross the bridge to go home . . . The man was insane. Reckless. Taking risks . . .

Risks that she wouldn't take. That didn't mean they

shouldn't be taken. Biting her thumb, she watched out the windshield. She didn't see any sign of TJ's white SUV. The convertible with its top down left her feeling overexposed. Nervously, she checked over her shoulder again. A long black car pulled out of the parking lot and followed at a cautious distance.

"I thought your brother was driving a white car."

"He should be." In the light of the dashboard, even Clay's jaw looked tense.

It relaxed a minute later as the headlights of a tall vehicle hidden in the shadows of a tree lumbered onto the highway at the last minute, falling in line behind the black one.

Feeling conspicuous, Rory quit looking. Holding her elbows and trying not to shake, she stared straight ahead. "This is not at all how I anticipated ending this evening."

Clay chuckled. Chuckled!

"I'm good at games," he reminded her. "I have the controller in my hands and all the points are on my side. Unless there's a trap that I haven't encountered on my other trips through gameland, the sorcerer wins."

She wanted to smack him. He was playing games with their *lives*. "You're certifiable, really, truly certifiable. This Viking princess wants a sword and shield before she plays any more."

She'd hate to see the antique Jag bubbling in the marsh. She'd hate worse to be inside when it did.

"It's brains that beat the evildoers, not swords," he declared.

"He could have killed Cissy," she whispered. That was the fear that had her skin crawling. Cissy had been forced off the road by a black car. And while Rory might not want to concede the implications of the accident, she couldn't ignore them either.

"Maybe. Maybe not. For an optimist, you sure see the worst side of everything." He glanced over at her. "Give the guy a thrill. Lift your hair and stretch as if you're enjoying the evening."

She kept her arms crossed. "The guy back there won't be the one getting the thrill, will he?"

"Nah, he can barely see you. But I can. How often does a real hot babe step off the screen and into my life?"

The comment was so jarring that she immediately reacted with fury. There was the difference between them. Cheap thrills made her miserable. She wanted certainties and safety. Whatever had she been thinking to even get in the same car with this unpredictable man?

She'd been thinking that he had a sound head on his shoulders. And she was just learning to acccept that he was utterly predictable in some things . . . like when someone needed protecting. "You're trying to distract me, aren't you?" And it was working. There for all of half a minute she'd wanted to bop him over the head instead of worry about flying headfirst into the marsh. Another piece of her heart melted at the idea of Clay trying to ease her fears.

Clay swung the Jag in another of his sharp turns, taking them off the highway and down the lane to Cleo's. As they slowed to bump over the ruts of Cleo's sandy lane, the black Lincoln turned off its headlights and rolled into the shadows of the overhanging trees.

Clay's cell phone rang. Stopping the Jag in the middle

of the lane, he picked it up. "Where are you?" he asked over the static.

"Blocking his escape. Jared should be pulling across the lane as soon as you pass him."

Satisfied, Clay glanced at Aurora. Clutching her elbows, she looked ready to bolt as he steered the car forward, past Jared's drive. It was too late to calm her nerves by explaining his intentions. He was too used to operating alone. His communication skills could use some polishing.

Cleo's battered pickup pulled out to park across the lane behind them. To avoid scratching the polished paint of the Jag on the bushes on either side, Clay simply stopped in the road.

"Stay here," he ordered, opening the driver's door. "Or better yet, go inside with Cleo and the kids."

He climbed out and noted in satisfaction that the driver of the Lincoln had recognized the trap. The big car tried to turn around in the soft sand of the road's shoulder but sank its rear wheels up to its hubcaps. The car wouldn't be going anywhere soon.

"That's the reason no one out here drives land yachts," a soft voice said from behind him. Rory.

Gritting his teeth, Clay waited for her to catch up with him. "I'm not speaking the same language as you, am I?"

"Nope. You're talking male gorilla. If you're not afraid to walk out here, then neither am I. I always feel better when I know what's happening." Rory didn't halt but continued toward the pickup.

"Some sorcerer I make. I can't even talk hot babes into behaving," he muttered, falling into step with her. Manipulating game figures was much simpler than real life.

Game figures could explode and come back to play again. In real life, a stray bullet could rob him of the precious gift that was Aurora.

Real-life responsibility added a level of tension that had his molars clenched.

"What if they have guns?" he demanded. "How am I supposed to save the day if you insist on taking the controller away from me?" Maybe if he made a joke of this, she'd walk off and go to Cleo.

Rory shot him one of her lifted-eyebrow looks as Jared stepped out of the truck to save Clay from himself.

"Cleo won't like a Lincoln for a lawn ornament." Jared nodded in the direction of the vehicle spinning its back tires. "Think TJ's hulking vehicle can pull him out?"

"TJ can pull it out once we take the lead weights out of the front seat." Clay watched as the tall silhouette of his oldest brother emerged from the darkness of the trees lining the lane on the far side of the Lincoln. "I don't suppose you know the magic words to keep Aurora out of the way, do you? They may have guns."

"They'd be shooting by now if they did," Rory said pragmatically. But Clay noticed she stayed out of the moonlight so she didn't make an easy target—although that white halter top sure drew *his* eye.

Apparently without a concern in the world, TJ walked up to the Lincoln and opened the driver's door. Not to be outdone, Clay leaned over and opened the passenger side. "Good evening, gentlemen. Lost?"

He noticed Aurora's gasp before he paid much attention to the man emerging. He studied the passenger's bland good looks and sheepish expression before identifying the banker she'd once dated. He glanced over the roof of the car to the balding, skinny driver, and it took a moment before he recognized the wimp who ran the tourist commission—the one who had greeted Aurora at the bar tonight.

"Jeff! Terry! What in the world?" Aurora propped her hands on her hips, and Clay's gaze diverted instantly to her bare curves. For a moment he couldn't remember why on earth they were standing out here in the road instead of falling into his bed.

"I told you the McClouds were in this together," Terry said with anger. "I did the research. Between them they have millions to blow on the swamp."

TJ crossed his arms and stared over the Lincoln's top at his brothers. "You guys holding out on me? Or maybe he thinks it's our wives with the riches?"

Jared shrugged. "Maybe he means baby brother's millions, and his sources are old."

Terry nearly turned purple. "Cissy would never have rejected our offer unless someone made her a better one! And Rora would be out of town by now if it hadn't been for you. Rich Yankees have bought up enough land down here. I don't see why you should have what little is left."

Clay contemplated straightening out the half dozen kinks in this logic, but glancing at the fury in Aurora's lovely face, he figured this was where he accentuated the positive and let her tear the morons into raw meat.

"What did you think following us would accomplish?" she asked in tones of utter disbelief that almost disguised her rage.

Jeff shrugged indifferently. "That was Terry's half-baked idea. He thought maybe you'd lead us to a meeting with the Binghams and that we could go in and speak for ourselves. Once he gets a few beers in him, it's easier to play along."

"That's bullhockey, Jeffrey Elmont Spencer. You always egged Terry on. What did Terry do—run right over to the country club to tattle about seeing Clay and me together? He probably thought we were celebrating a deal with the Binghams. And then the two of you sat there pouring alcohol down your throats, wondering where the poor white trash Jenkinses could have found enough money to pay off their mortgage, and you concluded it belonged to rich Yankees. You thought Clay was paying me? For what? Services rendered?"

Clay watched as Jared and TJ pretty much imitated him, backing off, crossing their arms, and staying the hell out of Aurora's way. He felt a confusing but comfortable camaraderie with his brothers as the three of them stood guard while Aurora ripped off heads. He had a feeling she'd just unleashed her inner rebel.

"It wasn't like that, Rora!" Terry protested. "I just told Jeff I saw you having a good time at the Monkey with McCloud, and someone mentioned that his family had money, and I was mad because he quit the state job and used the Bingham list against us, and one thing just led to another."

"Don't give me that, Terry. Was it you who drove Cissy off the road the other night and smashed my car to pieces? Cissy could have been killed! Crippled for life. What were you doing following her then?"

"I wasn't!" Talbert looked terrified. "After the zoning

meeting, I just went out to check the survey stakes. I saw
your car and didn't want you knowing I was there, so I
got panicky and hit the gas. It spun in the sand, and kind
of jerked out to the road. I didn't even see her go off, I
swear. I'd never . . . If I'd known . . ." He started stumbling over his tongue and shut up.

"You're supposed to be working with the state to
build a park for the public good, Terry. Why would you
want to steal the Bingham land? What possible use could
you have for a swamp?" Aurora demanded with escalat-
ing rage.

"You're not the only person in the world who wants
to make something of themselves!" Terry shouted back.
"The state park plum just fell in my lap. My construction
company could be on the ground floor of something really
big."

Aurora advanced on him like a prizefighter about to
throw the finishing punch. "You endangered my sister,
set fire to an entire neighborhood, threatened a way of
life and the ecology just so you could throw up a few cheap
condos that will get wiped out in the next hurricane—"

Figuring that sentence might never end, Clay finally intervened. "I suppose you were just checking up on me to
see if I'd finished my project when you walked into my
house in the middle of the night?"

Almost gratefully, Talbert turned away from Aurora's
fury. "I was jogging the beach and saw your place and
just thought to stop and see how you were doing." Sul-
lenly, Terry glanced around at Clay's brothers and left
Aurora's charges unanswered.

"Breaking and entering, reckless driving, leaving the
scene of an accident," TJ began reciting stoically. "I'd

have to look up the statutes on invasion of privacy, and there may be a case for threatening behavior."

"If there's any way of nailing him for the fire, Cleo will do a war dance, round up the natives, and have him hanged," Jared added helpfully.

"Oh, leave the jerk alone," Jeff said while Terry tried to unknot his tongue. "We've got everything we own tied up in making something out of this useless land. A man's got a right to look after himself. Aurora, I thought you told me you were with us on the zoning. If the McClouds are buying off the Binghams, did they buy you off, too? Where else could you get the money to pay the mortgage?"

"Go on, Jeff, say it again—you can't believe I'm siding with swamp rats and derelicts. I should be cheering on the rich white guys willing to cheat the poor out of their land so they can turn a swamp into a *profit base*."

Clay shot his gaze to her, fascinated. An MBA banker saying *profit base* as if it were a curse. It looked good on her. He'd known the rebel in her would have to come out sometime.

"Swamp rats—I can use that," Jared mused, leaning against the Lincoln's trunk and contemplating the moon. "We come crawling out of the murky waters to snap off the tails of what . . . toads? No, they don't have tails."

"Lizards," Clay suggested helpfully. "Now shut up and let's figure out how we can make these slimy lizards pay for the harm they've done."

"I haven't done anything," Jeff protested. "I was just along for the ride."

"You didn't call in Cissy's loan?" Aurora demanded. "You didn't sic your real estate vulture on her? And I bet anything that, even if I refused to sell after she signed, it never occurred to you that you could auction off my mama's property through the court, just like the state threatened to do with the Binghams."

"Rora, you are being unreasonable. This is business," Jeff argued. "You're standing in the way of the entire town's future. You would have been fairly paid for your property, just as the Binghams will be."

Clay was tired of this. He'd planned a much better end to this evening, and it would be dawn before this bunch stopped yammering. It seemed to him the script required a little action.

Catching Aurora's arms from behind, he gently set her aside. "I wager there is a major divide between the bank's idea of fairness and everyone else's. TJ, call the sheriff. We'll need a police report to file with the insurance company to cover the damages to Aurora's car, Cissy's injuries, and the results of the fire. And if I hear another word, I'll have them dust my office for fingerprints and press charges for grand theft. For all I know, they walked away with my copyrighted software."

Panic finally wrinkled the banker's brow. "That's ridiculous! You can't prove anything against Terry, and I'm just a bystander in all this. There's no law against doing business."

"Add theft, TJ," Clay warned.

"Clay, that's ridiculous," Aurora whispered beside him. "You can't ruin a man's career because he's a jerk."

He wanted to. A primitive urge for revenge had surfaced somewhere during this episode, and he wanted to wring the necks of both men for being the same kind of crass assholes who had stripped his company and his investors without thought to any larger principle than selfish greed.

Blind protective instinct wanted him to shield Aurora from their kind of menace. Or maybe it was a stupid possessive instinct, the "Me Tarzan, you Jane, lay your mitts off my woman" kind of thing that rose out of the primeval pools lurking in a man's soul.

Except with a woman like Aurora around, the big gorillas he'd have to fight off would be conniving powermongers like these. He could handle that with both thumbs tied together.

He stepped in front of Aurora, crossed his arms again, and watched in satisfaction as Jeff backed off. "The Binghams would like to present an alternative development plan to the zoning commission, but they need more time. You'll arrange it so that they get that time, won't you?"

"The sheriff's line is busy," TJ called from the other side of the car. "Want me to keep trying?"

Clay bit back the urge to laugh as Talbert's face grew whiter. He was beginning to like this role, especially since Aurora had wrapped her fingers around his biceps and was hanging on with both hands while he was practicing the communication skills he needed for her world.

He had walked away from the corporate life with a bad taste in his mouth, but now that he knew it was just another jungle, he could learn the game, for Aurora's sake. "I haven't heard anything to change my mind yet," he called back to TJ.

"Wait a minute!" Terry shouted. "Let's be reasonable here. If we have to go to court, it will be only your word against mine. Let me talk to the insurance companies, get some damage estimates, see what I can do. I'm not a rich man, you know. I might have been," he added bitterly, "if my construction company could have built those condos."

"You don't have to be a rich man; you just have to be a reasonable one," Clay offered, generously, he thought. "You can work with us, or you can go to jail. Fair enough?"

"I want him to apologize to my sister." Aurora stepped out from behind him. "I want him out there helping all those old people cart off dead timber and fixing up their burned yards."

"Hey, Talbert, you want us to keep trying for the sheriff?" Jared asked helpfully. "You might be better off with him than Rora."

"I'll bring my crew in," Terry agreed with a weary swipe of his hand over his thin hair. "We'll fix things up. I didn't mean to hurt your sister, Aurora. I'll see if I can find her a job. I don't suppose she can do budgets, can she?"

"No, but she can run your office better than you can," Clay intruded. "I'm not sure we're ready to part with her yet, though."

Clay let Aurora and his brothers take it from there. His goal had always been to protect the work he'd spent his life developing. The unsettling feeling that he wanted far more than that now had him longing for the courthouse roof so he could sort things out.

He wanted to protect Aurora and her family from corporate gorillas. Aurora's admiration had made him prouder than working the kinks out of an inoperable program. What he felt right now was a real thrill and not the virtual one provided by his computer.

He recognized the kick of anticipation zinging through him. He was ready to take a risk again, step outside his isolation and into Aurora's life, if she'd let him.

Only, now that Talbert and his cronies were out of her way, did Aurora need him anymore? The company was in production. Her investment was secure. She had her career, and she had made it plain that she couldn't wait to kick the dust of this town off her heels and move on.

So where did that leave him? Like the turtle, swimming back to sea, alone?

❧ TWENTY-SIX ❧

As the various cars departed, taking with them Clay's brothers and two angry ex-friends, Aurora opened the door to the Jag. "Take me home, please."

Clay was already beside her, reaching for the door, offering his hand, performing all those little courtesies with which he betrayed his bad-boy image to make her feel as if she mattered to him. Clay might want to pretend he was an island, but she didn't think he wanted to be. She loved both sides of him, the tough one and the loner who wanted acceptance.

She loved him. She ached with the bittersweetness of the knowledge. He'd stood up for her, protected her as if she were precious to him, and her heart had nearly burst at the seams with joy and love.

It hurt her more than him when she asked to go home. She didn't want to go back to her childhood bedroom. She longed to go forward to the man of her dreams, physically ached with the need of it.

Unfortunately, he hadn't offered the future of her dreams, and her job here was done.

He'd talked about going steady, but given their disparate personalities, that moment of magic couldn't last any longer than the arc of a perfect moon on a perfect night.

She not only knew better than to rely on a man to provide her happiness; she knew better than to stand in the way of someone else's. Clay could have any woman he wanted once he decided where he wanted to go next. He hadn't made that step yet, and she wasn't languishing out here, waiting until he did, endangering her fragile heart any more than she had.

He touched her arm, almost a placating touch that made her want to weep, but she climbed in the car before she could fall victim to her hormones again. Sure, she could do the easy thing, go to bed with him now and walk away later. But she wasn't a risk taker at heart. Clay thrived on taking giant leaps into unknown waters. He could splash happily here today and be gone tomorrow.

Going to bed with Clay the way she felt now would be to risk never wanting to get out of his bed again. She would crumble into nothing and lose herself when he walked away. Going steady was for teenagers. She wanted a grown-up relationship involving family and kids and vows never to part. Or none at all.

Just admitting that she wanted family and kids scared her enough.

"We could go back to my place for a cup of coffee, talk about how this changes things," he suggested, climbing into the driver's seat. "I've even bought a filing cabinet."

It took her tired mind a minute to make the connection. Filing cabinet . . . papers . . . he'd cleaned up the cottage in anticipation of bringing her home.

Even though she was shattering inside, she smiled.

"That was thoughtful of you. Thank you, but I need to go home."

"It's that controlling thing I do making you mad, isn't it?" He turned on the ignition and carefully backed up in the driveway. "I got in the way of letting you flatten Jeff into roadkill."

"No, believe it or not, I was glad you stepped in. I wasn't running on rational. I have control issues of my own, so I can relate."

The silence thickened inside the dark car. Rory loved the hum of the powerful engine, the sleek feel of the luxurious seats. She wanted to sit here beside Clay and take off for some unseen future.

But he hadn't offered to share his future, just his bed. And she had a family who needed her support. She didn't believe in placing all her eggs in one basket, especially a basket as unpredictable as Clay.

"I'm not any good at analyzing motivations," he warned. "If I did something wrong, you have to tell me."

"No, you did everything right. Sort of. It's me who has problems. Let's just sleep on it, okay?"

He said nothing but turned down the fire-blackened road to her house.

In the moonlight, all the colorful flowers, painted mailboxes, and cheerful gnomes were scorched and sad against the charred leaves of trees and shrubs. Aurora thought the scene more than reflected her mood. She'd brought their destruction by stirring up trouble—again. She'd make it go away if she did what she was supposed to do—build a career.

She'd invested her prize money wisely. She trusted Clay to take care of it. "Mysterious" would sell a billion copies and generate tons of franchise licenses for toys and games. Even if he didn't keep his studio here, her investment should show a profit. It was time to move on.

"What do you mean she's in Chicago?" Clay paced with the telephone glued to his ear, afraid that if he didn't pry every detail out of Cissy, he would lose something vital. "She said nothing about it last night."

He stared down at the newly uncluttered boards underfoot. He'd never realized the cottage floor was yellow pine.

"She had a call last night after you went out, some bank up there confirming an appointment. I thought it had to do with your investors. I haven't learned that much about big business yet," Cissy explained through the receiver. "We took her to the airport this morning."

"We don't have any investors in Chicago." That was the whole point of not going public this time around. Between Aurora's money and her banker friend's money, they had enough to put the game in production. Soon the corporation would generate stacks of cash. Aurora needed to hang around to help him make some decisions. He'd *trusted* her to do that.

They needed to talk to the Binghams, tell them no one would fight whatever zoning they chose, that they were free to do as they pleased now that Jeff and Terry had backed off.

Cissy and her father could do that.

She had no reason to stay here any longer.

His breath caught in his throat, but he must have managed something dismissive, because Cissy hung up. He set the phone down and continued pacing, more rapidly now.

Aurora was leaving. She hadn't told him. Was their relationship that unimportant to her?

What relationship? He'd asked her to go *steady*, for heaven's sake. What woman would bank her future on that?

Panic set in. His last corporation had failed because he'd listened to his MBAs. His ignorance had almost lost him "Mysterious" the first time around. He couldn't afford any more failures. He'd trusted Aurora to see this one through. She had the business acumen he lacked.

So had Diane. She'd seen the collapse coming and gotten out, taking care of herself and no one else. If Aurora turned out to be like Diane . . .

Aurora wasn't Diane. He'd hidden behind that excuse too long.

It had been easy buying into the isolationist theory, thinking turtles had the right idea, swimming around in that whole big ocean out there, not needing anyone. Why risk hanging around, making homes, raising kids, and losing the protective shelter of his shell?

Aurora had shown him the fallacy of his theory. He'd loved shedding the heavy burden of his shell and walking into the bright kaleidoscope of her world. It hurt like hell thinking he needed to crawl back into isolation.

Dammit! Didn't Aurora understand what he'd been trying to tell her?

Of course she didn't. How could she understand when even he had no idea what he thought—or felt? It wasn't about the damned computer—it was about *living*.

He'd been holding back in so many ways he couldn't begin to count them all. If he wanted Aurora instead of computers, now was the time to act on it—lay his pride and his future on the line for real.

Ignoring the siren call of his laptop and the tool belt hanging over a chair, Clay reached for the telephone. He could climb up on the roof and think about things until his dying day and never really classify the way he felt about Aurora. He just knew not having her in his day was akin to losing sunsets and dawn.

No more hiding. He was about to communicate in a big way.

By the time Aurora returned, she'd have to understand that he was ready for a real relationship.

Rory listened to the CEO espousing the benefits of working with an up-and-coming bank situated in the heart of the city, while she glanced around the office that could be hers for the asking.

Chicago had a fabulous skyline, far better than Charlotte's. Her modern chrome-and-glass furniture would fit right into one of those high-rise apartment complexes across the way. She had several college buddies here, and she'd been wined and dined since arriving. She'd spent the last few days in interviews and her spare time finding trendy little restaurants, nightlife, and art galleries. She could have all that, if that was what she wanted.

If that was what she wanted.

She *wanted* a future with Clay. She would take the Monkey's jukebox and Clay over bankers and Chicago's most sparkling nightclubs any day of the week. But if Clay didn't want her . . . She had to decide what was best for *her*, not anticipate a future she had no reason to expect, based on a man who might be in Tahiti tomorrow.

As the CEO's spiel wound down, Rory offered her hand. "You've made an excellent case for transplanting to Chicago, thank you. May I get back to you in a few days?"

Rushing for the elevator and the airport limo waiting for her, she couldn't believe she'd said that. She could handle anything that affected her family's financial future from Chicago, probably better than at home. She'd have access to more funds, more people, more everything. She could find loans for the Binghams to develop the swamp, more distributors for Clay if he continued developing software, scholarships for Mandy. She'd have sources at her fingertips.

She should have sealed the deal, signed the contracts, and offered to go to work right there and then. The money and benefits were fabulous. She could support her whole family without their ever having to earn another dime. She could build a garage for their new truck. She'd have all the security she'd ever craved. She could have the fast-paced city life that had been her dream since childhood.

She was no longer that child.

She argued with herself all the way back to Charleston. She cried, and hid the tear tracks by staring out the airplane window. She could have it all, everything money could buy, including the security her impoverished childhood demanded.

The words to an old song immediately trilled in her mind: *Can't buy me lo-ove* . . .

But that was what life was about, wasn't it? Choices. She could take a risk on the man who offered everything her heart desired, or she could have the security she craved. She couldn't have both.

She didn't bother dissolving into the old protests of "It isn't fair." One made choices and paid the consequences. Risk everything for happiness, or take the safe road and be satisfied. Cissy had risked and lost. Rory had learned from her and always chosen the safe road.

Loving Clay enough to throw away her career in *hopes* that he might love her back someday was the height of idiocy.

She was still arguing with herself when she boarded the airport van in Charleston. For her family's sake she needed to take the safe road, she reasoned as the car drove away from the airport. She had invested a lot of years in becoming a woman of the world. She no longer belonged in the rural town where she grew up.

But her heart belonged there. It wept as she rode toward the clear blue skies and open marshlands of the coast. She craved a steaming bowl of crab gumbo, a brisk walk on the wet sand, and the familiar drawl and welcoming hugs of her neighbors.

She craved the security of love as much as money.

Maybe more. If it had been only her family's love she craved, she might work this out. But she'd go crazy longing for the love of a man she couldn't have. She didn't dare take that path while her emotions scraped her raw. She had to think clearly, and Clay turned her thoughts into passionate sunsets and moonlit nights. Thinking wasn't what she did around him.

She had to take him out of the picture if she wanted to make a decision based strictly on known factors. Still, she couldn't tear her gaze away from the courthouse clock as they drove through town. What had he done when he found out she'd left? She didn't see anyone on the roof.

Watching the crystal blue of the harbor out the car windows, she tried not to wonder what Clay was doing or thinking now. If she walked away, she would never have to wonder again.

She blinked back tears as the driver turned the car down the road toward home. A convoy of trucks carrying balled and burlapped trees and shrubs blocked half the road. No one bought landscaping out here. People just dug up what they needed from the fields.

"Looks like the highway department's been busy," the van driver said, gesturing toward a mountain of wood chips. "That used to be all burned trees last week. They even hauled out the roots so the land can be replanted. Someone has clout."

Jeff and Terry? Rory had a hard time believing that, but they'd promised, and here it was. She smiled at the sight of painters restoring the bubbled finish on Erly's fence and more men crawling up ladders on his neighbor's house. Perhaps the insurance companies had all gone together to start repairs at a quantity discount.

Brand-new rosebushes bloomed all along the next fence. She was certain that stretch had been burned out as well. With fascination and a growing joy that her home was being restored better than new, she searched for more changes, finding a painted gnome among newly planted petunias in one garden, a new gaudy gold mailbox amid a circle of young azaleas at the bottom of a drive lined with tender willow oak saplings.

There were still telltale signs of the fire here and there: a scorched tree trunk with branches trimmed back to new leaf shoots, a blackened field just beginning to shoot up sprigs of green, a telephone pole that hadn't been replaced. The usual beds of rampant flowers and shrubs and eccentric lawn ornaments hadn't been completely restored, but the half bathtub with its concrete Madonna was freshly painted, and the rosebushes around it would be full of blooms in a week or two.

Miracles happened. Her heart was pounding harder than her chest could contain it as she climbed out of the car at her front door and handed the driver a tip well beyond the expected. She was afraid to go inside, afraid her bubble would burst once she heard the real reason for all these changes.

Her father's concrete statues had been stripped of their burned paint. Someone must have hauled in an entire tank of paint remover and dipped them en masse. She could see stains of color here and there, a little red on a dwarf's vest, a bit of gold in a fairy's wings. One of the massive fountains had been given a white base coat, and several of the ducks and turtles already sported new paint jobs.

Burned shrubs had been ripped from the fence rows, and the ground had been tilled, ready for replanting. At the sound of hammering, she peeked around the corner of the trailer and saw a wood frame going up where the toolshed had been. The frame was far larger than the old shed, big enough to be a garage. She didn't recognize the carpenter.

Work trucks littered the drive, but the candy-apple-red extended cab was nowhere to be seen. Maybe nobody was home.

She was hit with the realization that she had been ea-

gerly anticipating entering a house spilling over with life
and laughter. She would never enjoy an empty apartment
again, no matter how fashionable. She wanted to share
Mandy's shrieks of triumph when she received her driver's
license and scholarships. She wanted to help Cissy get
back on her feet again. She wanted her father's hugs and
earthy advice and bottle caps promising prizes.

She wasn't a rebellious child wanting the respect
money bought anymore. She'd seen the world and knew
what was really important.

Tears threatening to stream down her cheeks again,
Aurora dared the front door. A telephone rang as she entered. A computer announced someone had mail. A sorcerer dressed in robes with moons and stars waved a
magic wand on the TV screen. Stacks of paper covered
the once pristine carpet, and filing cabinets lined the wall
where the knickknack shelf had been. The big green sofa
had been shoved aside to make room for a desk and computer table.

Cissy jumped up from an office chair at Aurora's
entrance—or jumped as best as she could with her heal-
ing hip. "You're back, thank goodness! We were afraid
you'd moved up there. Here, you need to talk with the
banker. I have no idea what he's going on about." She
shoved a message slip at her.

Hugging Cissy, taking the pink piece of paper, Aurora
felt something shift into place. Still too overwhelmed by all
the changes, she didn't analyze the feeling as the back door
opened and her father stalked in. Behind him trailed Clay.

His eyes met hers over Jake's shoulder. Aurora tried to
read his blank expression, but Clay had his turtle act
down to perfection. He merely threw a file folder on the

kitchen table and waited while Jake shouted his welcome and began a spiel about the new mold he'd installed that would make his fortune.

At Aurora's congratulations, Jake grabbed a bottle of beer from the refrigerator and wandered out again, satisfied that she'd arrived home safely.

Clay remained. Unable to make sense of all the changes and still read his mind, Aurora focused on what she could. "Wait a minute, if you're all here, where's the truck?" She was terrified they'd tell her someone had wrecked it. Mandy? Mandy wasn't here.

As if understanding her panic, Cissy stepped in. "Mandy got her beginner's permit. She and Erly have gone out to Grandma Iris's. The Binghams are gathering out there before the zoning meeting, and we promised to give them all our charts and research."

Somewhat shakily, Rory nodded her head. She'd have to remember that having family around would always mean living with fear as well as joy. Her safe, sane—lonely—existence would be transformed into one upheaval after another if she stayed here.

She couldn't stay here. Glancing around the littered front room, she knew this wasn't her home. Just as she'd outgrown childhood dreams, she'd outgrown the trailer as well. Cissy was welcome to it. She didn't belong. She needed her own space. If she stayed on the island . . .

She turned back to the man who possessed the power to keep her here or drive her away. Her heart raced a little faster as she looked for some signal, some sign of hope from him. But he offered none. She supposed he was waiting for an explanation.

"I've been offered a job in Chicago," she said nervously. Since Clay wasn't inclined to talk, she had to be the one to get it out in the open. She didn't know what he wanted from her, if anything, so she had to make him understand where she stood. "If I take it, I'll help you find someone else to deal with the business end of the company."

His flat nose didn't twitch. She thought she saw fire erupt behind the gray glass of his eyes, but he banked it quickly.

"Thanks, but no thanks. If you want to go to Chicago, I can buy back your share. Just let me know how you want to handle it." With those cold words, he walked out the back door. Before Rory could run after him and attempt to explain, a Harley roared into gear.

Cissy sighed and shook her head. "Damn, Rora, you sure know how to kick them where it hurts."

"Where? How? He didn't even give me time to finish!" Sick to her stomach, she stood there, bewildered, uncertain where she should turn next. She could get back to work; she still held the message slip from their banker, but she thought she'd just been fired. Again.

Cissy looked at her pityingly. "You may have school smarts, kid, but you've got a lot to learn about men. Clay's turned this place upside down these last few days, trying to prove something to you, I guess. I take back any comparison to Dad I may have made. He's chewed off chunks of Terry's ass to get his equipment out here. He's called every insurance adjuster in the book, pulling them together to move in construction crews. And when he isn't yelling into the telephone, he's meeting with the Binghams and the Nature Conservancy and the state and who-knows-all so they'll have it all together for the zoning commission. He even talked to your banker friend about distributing some other software he's developed so we can generate cash faster. I think that was akin to laying his life on the line for that man."

Clay had exploded from his shell, and let his genius drive him, just as it had when he'd become a teenage millionaire. He was practicing his corporate skills to the max.

For her?

Dizzy with the possibility of it, afraid to take the leap of faith it would require to believe that Clay had decided to rejoin the real world for her sake, Rory took a deep breath. "Do you know where he just went?"

Cissy shrugged. "Could be anywhere, but when he wants to think about things, he takes apart the clock."

She knew that. Shedding her fear, regaining her confidence and, with it, her fury that Clay hadn't waited to hear her out, Rory started for the back door. If they meant to build a future together, the damned man would have to learn that not everyone possessed his intuitive instincts and had the courage to leap blindly into the fray. She needed to logically work things out, one step at a time. "Does Pops still keep his bike keys in the saddlebag?"

"Far as I know. Wait a minute—"

But Rory didn't have a minute. She'd waited far too long already.

With determination, she ran for the motorcycle parked under the lean-to at her father's warehouse.

❊ TWENTY-SEVEN ❊

June was a lousy time for sitting on roofs. Heat simmered off the old tile. Clay threw off his shirt, took a swig from his water bottle, and returned to unscrewing the hands of the clock. This was the last damned time he would do this. He'd found an antique counterweight on eBay that ought to match the one in here. If that didn't work, nothing would.

When he first started this project, he'd had some fantasy of finding the mayor's lost German gold in the clock and using it to rebuild his software company. Fantasizing had been better than sitting on the beach, feeling sorry for himself.

It wasn't gold he sought now.

His brain was thudding louder than the clock. *Tick-tock, tick-tock.* He zapped a screw with the electric screwdriver, adding a roar to the thud. Rora was returning to Chicago. He needed a hammer. Reaching into his tool belt, he pulled one out, hit the stubborn screw with a satisfying *wham, wham,* and didn't feel any better for the act of frustration.

Chicago! How could she go to Chicago? She had it all here—family, home, sun, sea—and him.

She had him. Ex-millionaire CEOs ought to know better, but he thought he'd finally found a place where he belonged, and a woman who could keep him there. Aurora didn't mind when he didn't want to talk. Maybe others placed more importance on his computer genius than his mechanical abilities, but Aurora understood his need to do both. He'd thought he'd found a woman who wouldn't care if he sat on his porch for days on end while grappling with a new idea, one who wouldn't waste time looking over his shoulder, nagging him to do something useful. He'd thought she *understood*.

Since coming here, he'd learned a lot about living with others. He had been willing to expand his horizons so he could spend more time with Aurora. He'd learned how to cope with Jared's teasing, Cleo's panics, and the tumultuous emotions of the Jenkins family. Even baby Midge had taught him to hope.

He'd gotten *involved* and done his damnedest to rebuild Aurora's fairy-tale world so she'd want to stay. Because *he* wanted to stay. And he wanted her to stay here with him. He'd thought that if he built his company here, she'd be happier staying with her family and running it, fighting social injustice without fear of being fired. Had he asked her what she wanted?

For a boy genius, he sure had his head on backward. He'd known all along she wanted to return to the city. He should have just waited until she chose a city, then showed up on her doorstep.

Snorting at his incredible stupidity, he turned on the battery-operated screwdriver, bored another screw out of its hole, and propped up the internal mechanism of the clock so it wouldn't fly off the roof onto the lawn below.

The roar of the motor continued well after he turned the power tool off.

He had to drag his thoughts back from Chicago—and women who didn't understand what a man was trying to tell them—before he recognized the roar of a Harley.

He glanced down, hoping no one had decided to steal his bike. He needed to sell the thing to pay for the expense of shipping out the Jag.

A golden-red flag of hair waved from beneath the Harley driver's helmet as the bike thundered down the tree-lined street to the courthouse. Clay's gut flipped like a pancake.

Aurora!

She knew how to drive a Harley!

She looked like an Amazon warrior roaring to a halt on the sidewalk and glancing up in his direction.

She was wearing one of those prim black banker's skirts hiked nearly to her hips. She'd probably left a slew of fender benders in her wake as heads swiveled to follow those wicked thighs. If he had to guess, he'd say she'd traded her suit jacket for her father's leathers.

His gut tightened in anticipation of the battle to come. He'd never been much at interacting with others, but he loved sparring with Aurora. Her brainpower matched his. They just ran at things from different directions. He had to admit that opened whole new worlds of exploration.

Separate worlds—hers in Chicago and his here on the island.

The wind carried the sound of his name, but Clay saw no reason to listen. If she was willing to walk out on all their hopes and dreams . . . What hopes and dreams?

His? It wasn't as if he'd mentioned them to her. He shoved down a surge of guilt.

He'd trusted her with his software. He thought that meant something. It had, to him. Those programs were his life, and he'd committed himself to a future of working with her when he'd handed them over. He'd *trusted* her. Obviously she hadn't understood the gesture. Maybe he was too slow at these relationship things. He should have given her a diamond instead.

She would have thrown it at him, he was pretty sure. So what the hell did she want of him?

He tried to argue that if she was willing to walk out just because of some damned job offer, she wasn't the woman he'd thought she was. But she had come uncomfortably close to being the woman he'd always wanted. Damn close. So close she'd walked around inside his heart and made a home there.

Ignoring her shouts, he diligently removed the ancient weight mechanism and looked for a place to put it. He decided the windowsill of the louvered attic window was safest and leaned over to lay it there.

He couldn't hear Aurora anymore. Good. She'd have the whole damned town staring at them if she kept it up. He liked his privacy. Or he thought he had.

He didn't mind everyone staring when Aurora walked beside him. He'd felt like a movie star, a conquering hero, and the Magic Man she'd called him when he'd walked into the Monkey with her on his arm.

She made him feel as if he might be human after all. That he could love and be loved. He'd tried to show her that he could build a life outside his computer screen. In his head, everything he'd done had shouted commitment. He just hadn't said it out loud. He'd talked about sex and going steady when she'd wanted to hear kids and marriage. A fine time to learn caution.

"Thomas Clayton McCloud, I'm talking to you!"

She'd climbed the stairs again. He tried to scowl at the sound of her voice through the louvered window, but he loved the flaming orange tone of it. He'd never realized sound had color until Aurora walked into his life.

"Talk away," he shot back. So he'd never been much at snappy repartee.

"I'll be damned if I'll shout it from the rooftops. If you intend to hide up here every time we need to talk, I'll install a telephone."

"I'm not hiding. I'm right out here where you can find me." Where he'd hoped she'd find him, he had to admit. He supposed it was about time he admitted to something.

"If you're mad because I wouldn't have sex with you, then I don't want to talk with you anyway. If it's the job, then we need to talk. Want me to climb out there with you?"

The image of Aurora tumbling off the roof scared him so much Clay nearly dropped his favorite screwdriver. "Don't you dare!" he yelled back.

"Why? *You're* out there. Why can't I risk my neck if you're risking yours? Isn't that what this is all about? Who takes the first risk?"

Maybe. Probably. But the minute she rattled the louvers to climb through that window, he had heart failure. "Get down out of there this instant," he ordered.

"You're not my boss, McCloud. If I want to climb out there, I will. Or you can come down and talk to me."

He heard her banging on the warped shutters, trying

to pry them open. His heart in his throat, Clay gathered up his tools and started for the rope ladder he'd secured to the clock tower. "Aurora, don't! I'm coming down. Meet me—"

The shutter slammed open. The clock's old counter-weight flew off the ledge where he'd left it, bounced against the roof with a firecracker bang, and rattled over the tiles to the ground two stories below.

Stricken, they both gazed down.

"I don't think anyone's down there," she murmured guiltily.

"If they are, you planted time in their brain," he muttered, confirming her observation while trying not to stare at the wondrous dawn that was his Aurora.

His. Every cell of his body screamed it. The prim banker he'd first seen had metamorphosed into a blazing sun goddess. The ride here had blown her hair into a halo of red-gold. She'd doffed her father's leathers in the attic heat, revealing a flimsy silken gold thing that sparkled like sun drops over her magnificent curves, revealing more cleavage from this vantage point than she probably realized. He liked that she didn't flaunt her curves for all to see, but he also liked seeing them. In broad daylight, he could see the scattering of freckles between her breasts. He suffered a sudden throbbing in his groin that nearly crippled him.

In his eyes she was the dawn of his future. She offered fireworks to light his life, surprises and laughter to provoke him, understanding and trust to keep him moving forward. She offered the love he craved more than the food she cooked or the air he breathed. He wanted Aurora lighting his nights and challenging his days. He wanted to give her sunshine and rainbows in return. And maybe someday, if things worked out between them, kids.

Without her, he would have no life at all. How in hell did he tell her that?

"Get out of there, Aurora," he growled. "Now."

She shot him a look that ought to kill, but he was in too much pain to notice. His entire future rested on these next few moments, and he was suffering heatstroke and couldn't think.

Bystanders had already begun to gather on the courthouse lawn as Clay climbed down. He wasn't a public person and disliked making a spectacle of himself.

He was a private person who loved a woman so striking her very presence lit up the whole damned lawn when she emerged from the courthouse.

They met in the middle of the grassy yard.

"I didn't say I'd taken the job!" she shouted at him without regard to their audience.

"Why would you go if you didn't *want* the damned job?" he asked, to cover his otherwise senseless reaction to her approach.

"Because it's the intelligent thing to do," she shouted back, even though they were only a few feet apart. "You can hire a dozen people I could name right offhand to run your business. You don't need me."

Was it his imagination, or did a question mark dangle at the end of her statement? *You don't need me . . . do you?*

Clay was aware of people wandering out of adjoining businesses to see what the shouting was about, but he had his focus now, and he wasn't letting anything distract him from Aurora. Standing toe-to-toe with her, he stared down into her upturned face with that glorious, kissable mouth. "Who the hell said I don't need you? Do you think for one damned minute that I'd have stayed here and fought fires and worked for nothing and listened to arguments about *swamp* development if I didn't need you?"

"The swamp's important," a voice argued from the crowd—Jake. Hell, that figured. He was probably charging admission for ringside seats to the fight. Mandy's voice cheered Rora on. She'd probably arrived home just in time to haul the whole family in to watch the circus. If he weren't so pissed off, he'd laugh at the absurdity his life had become.

He'd had some idiot idea he could learn to handle involvement and people a little at a time. She was heaving him into the middle of the pond without a life jacket, showing him what to expect if he stayed here.

Paddling hard to keep his head above water, Clay concentrated on the fury gesturing beneath his nose and not their growing audience.

"You needed *sex*," Rora shouted. "You can have that anywhere." A few female cheers rose from the crowd, but she wasn't diverted. "We're talking about *me* here. You don't need *me*. You can fight your own battles, make your own millions, write your own future. Don't you think I ought to be able to do the same? Or do you think I ought to sit here and wait for you to do it?"

"I want what you want," he heard himself saying. He didn't even think about it. He simply knew the answer.

"I want to stay here," she said defiantly. "Or maybe Charleston. I want to work. I like my career. I want to save the swamp. I want people to have jobs and decent housing. I want ten thousand things!"

She was shouting again. So was the expanding crowd. Clay processed all her demands silently while a cat-caller jeered and women hurled insults. Jake and Mandy shouted encouragement. He had to learn how to handle this kind of confusion if he wanted to do more than sit in front of a computer screen for the rest of his life. Aurora would never be a restful, complacent partner.

"I don't want ten thousand things," he said carefully, hoping he'd understood, that she would understand. "I've *had* ten thousand things. I can have them all again tomorrow. But I don't have any interest in things. My only interest is in you, and you're one of a kind."

Clay's declaration jammed any reply back down Rory's throat. She devoured his determined expression, seeking any sign of insincerity. There was no room in his irregular features for insincerity.

When the catcaller started defending himself with shouts of, "She's just a swamp rat from the island, what the hell are you gettin' on me for?" she jumped on the distraction. Maybe she wasn't prepared for Clay's unexpected candor, but she was wound up right for a rip-roaring fight.

And if she were to come back here to live, she needed to straighten out a few misconceptions. The whole *county* was going to know that she'd stand up for her family. Her days of running away from her origins had ended.

Swinging to face their audience, she planted her hands on her hips and sought the loudmouth. "I'm a Jenkins. I live in a double-wide. I'm meaner than a junkyard dog, more ornery than a gator, and I have more brains in my little finger than an air bag like you has in his whole inflated head."

"Only island trash causes a scene on the courthouse lawn," the voice from the crowd shouted back.

Might as well administer her first lesson. "If you didn't have your nose up your ass—"

She gasped as Clay caught her waist, moved her behind him, and blocked her access to one of her old high school foes. With one hand, Clay jerked the clod from his feet by his shirt collar.

"You're causing a public scene," Clay pointed out reasonably, although swinging his captive back and forth until he gagged on his own collar wasn't precisely an act of rationality. "Apologize to the lady."

A thrill shot straight to Aurora's toes at Clay's instant defense. If he was showing her how it would be if she stayed here, he was doing a fine job of it. The idea of not having to fight alone anymore excited her more than if he'd given her diamonds and gold.

"That's no lady . . ." the heckler started to argue.

Aurora sighed as Jake pushed his way through the crowd to aim a punch at her tormentor. "Pops, no! That's just Walter. He hates his own mama. Clay, let him down. I don't need to be bailing both of you out."

Clay released Walter before Jake could take a swing. Walking away from the pair as they tumbled into the dust, he occupied Aurora's space by placing his lovely flat nose next to hers. "We don't have to live here and put up with this crap. I'll go where you go. You just say the word."

He was much better at recklessly jumping off high cliffs without a parachute than she was. Her heart skipped erratically at his wild assertion. She needed detailed promises written in stone. Or concrete. He made brash declarations without saying the words she longed to hear.

"Just what exactly are you proposing?" she asked to hide her nervousness.

Oops. She hadn't meant to phrase it quite that way. But she had Clay's full attention now. As deputies spilled out of the courthouse to settle the battle on the lawn, he let down his defensive shields, and his gaze flared so hotly he could have scorched her.

"Marriage, if that's what you want," he shouted. Then, obviously studying her reaction for a better response, he amended, "Or if that's too fast for you, I can try old-fashioned courtship."

Grappling with his unpredictable reply, Rory watched his eyes dance in reaction to her stunned silence. "You haven't taught me how to shag yet," he reminded her.

Laughter tinted his voice now—not the cynical bitterness she'd heard when they first met, but the joyful noise that reflected hope and confidence and awoke warm butterflies in her belly.

She ought to swat him for being so certain of her answer, for standing there like a shirtless sex god who commanded all he surveyed. He hadn't said the magic words yet. They hadn't known each other long enough. . . .

She saw the challenge rising in his eyes and realized she was fully back in her old non–risk taking mode. She could follow her head, or take the chance her heart begged for.

"She started it," Walter yelled in the background. "Arrest her! And him. He assaulted me!"

With a slow smile, Rory lifted her arms and wrapped them around Clay's neck. "Love is going to jail together," she murmured foolishly as he grabbed her and held her tight.

"I know a good lawyer." Capturing her mouth with his, he ignored the apologetic deputy walking up behind them.

"Sir, you've been charged with assault. . . ."

Aurora giggled against his mouth. "Magic Man forgot the magic words."

"Will the words make buzzing gnats go away?" Continuing to ignore the young deputy, Clay rearranged her more firmly against him and began nibbling her ear between murmurs. "Abracadabra." Nibble. "Alakazam." Two nibbles. "Love, marriage, hearts, and flowers," he continued as the deputy read him his rights.

She'd have to chew his ear off for being so perverse in not saying the three little words she wanted to hear until she'd said it first, but the love spilling from her heart included the whole world right now, and she could afford to be gracious. Sort of. Leaning back so Clay could no longer nibble on her, she smiled at the deputy. "Tell Wally if he presses charges, I'll tell his mama who egged her house on graduation night."

The deputy looked startled. Clay laughed out loud. Rory was so tickled to hear his laughter that she stepped back to admire the sight. Shirtless, with his jeans riding halfway down his hips under the weight of the tool belt, Clay was a bronzed magician who had every woman in the crowd sighing with lust. . . .

And he was *hers*.

This was no risk. This was heaven. Clay had the single-minded focus of a hound on the hunt, and he wanted *her*. A man with the patience and steadiness of this one would never change his mind when waters got murky. And he *loved* her. She had no doubt that a man of Clay's strength of character would ever say words he didn't mean. Or sort of say them.

But she wasn't about to celebrate her joy out here where everyone could watch. When he reached for her again, she took another step backward and tripped over an object on the grass. Clay grabbed her arm, but the unexpected brunt of her weight as she went down caught him off balance. Together they tumbled onto the lawn.

He broke her fall, yelping as he rolled over the object that had caused her to trip. Shifting, Clay lay her safely back on the ground again, then leaned over her, grinning. He smelled of masculine sweat and a musk that stirred fantasies of what they ought to be doing right now instead of making spectacles of themselves.

"I love you," he murmured as the deputy hovered over them. "I want you, I need you, and if you want to hear the lyrics to a lot of corny love songs, I can summon them in a second. Just give my addled brain time to translate what I'm feeling."

Turning red, the deputy wandered off to pass Aurora's message on to Walter.

"Until the mountains crumble and the rivers dry," she agreed, her heady joy summoning more old lyrics. "I love you so much it's scaring me half to death." She hated admitting that, but he had to know what he was doing to her.

"I'll take care of that," he said reassuringly. "If we stand together, you'll never have to be afraid again. We'll grow old together, sharing whatever life has in store for us."

He ran his fingers into her hair and looked at her with such joy and wonder that Rory believed him. Clay McCloud was one scary man, but love was a powerful emotion, one she'd avoided because she'd been afraid of losing control, of sharing her heart. She thought she was strong enough to live with love now, trusting Clay to cherish and protect it.

"Maybe I'd better hold out for old-fashioned courtship," she murmured, shaken by the depth of her emotion. "Shagging sounds like a good start."

At Clay's burst of laughter, she regained some of her senses. Deciding they'd better take this out of the public eye, Rory started to edge away, then noticed the object she'd fallen over.

"Is that the thing you took out of the clock?" she asked in wonder, not certain she was seeing what she thought she was seeing.

Reluctantly releasing her hair, Clay pushed up on one hand to look over her. His silence said he saw what she did.

"The sorcerer found the key to the treasure?" she whispered in incredulity at the glitter in the grass.

"Or the late mayor's hidden assets," Clay said with his normal cynicism, reaching over to dump a treasure of diamonds from the clock's old counterweight.

Rory erupted in laughter and delight. The ex-millionaire had just discovered millions when he no longer needed it. She thought it even funnier when Clay's brothers wandered up with their wives to see if they'd lost their minds.

"Well, guess that solves the mystery of where the old mayor hid the rest of the spy hoard," TJ said with a degree of satisfaction.

"Man, you're millionaires," Cleo whispered in awe.

Which sent both Rory and Clay into further paroxysms of laughter.

❄ TWENTY-EIGHT ❄

"Courtship," Clay insisted, leading Aurora up the inside stairs of his beach cottage. "You need to know exactly what you're getting. I'm no million-dollar prize."

"You're better," she asserted.

They'd spent a hectic day surrounded by crowds of the curious. It was heaven to finally be alone, listening to the surf outside the windows, feeling her pulse beat as Clay clasped her hand in his gifted fingers. She hadn't had time to fully appreciate the words they'd exchanged, much less absorb how she felt about them.

He didn't smile at her, but on the landing he tugged her into his arms and rested his head on hers. "I'm better than a million dollars?"

Another woman might have thought he was teasing. Rory knew he asked for reassurance. Wrapping her arms around his waist, she reveled in the way his embrace tightened. "Better than all the diamonds in the world."

He chuckled and relaxed as he snuggled her against him. "You could have kept at least one. Then I wouldn't need to buy one for you."

"For a smart man, you have a lot to learn, mister." She brushed her lips along the strong column of his throat to

361

show she didn't mind teaching him. "With those diamonds the town can afford new schools without needing condo developments or golf courses. I don't like diamonds. They're cold and hard."

"They're not for a soft, warm woman like you," he agreed, pulling the pins out of her hair so it cascaded over her shoulders. "A gold ring, then, to show you're taken. Otherwise I'm likely to make a habit of defending my territory. I don't seem to be entirely civilized around you."

She heard the smile in his voice as he led her toward his bedroom. She shivered as Clay stroked her nape and his hand strayed down her spine. She liked this gentle, smiling side of him. She liked Clay's magic fingers even more. Standing beside his bed, he pushed her silk shell up and over her head and skimmed his hands over her breasts. She was instantly aroused and ready for him. "Who needs civilization in the bedroom?"

"A lady after my own heart." He kissed her then, a slow, seductive, mind-melting, knee-jellifying kiss that toppled her into his bed without care for anything but the flood of need rushing through her.

"Sometime we have to discuss babies," he murmured between kisses.

He said that as he was tugging off her panties, so Rory didn't completely register his suggestion until they lay naked together, kissing and touching and causing enough friction to light fires.

"Later," she murmured, her mind more on muscled male and the freedom to fully express the urges his love unleashed.

When he didn't act fast enough to suit her, she pushed

him onto his back and climbed on top to show him how she felt.

She loved it that Clay accepted her aggression by turning it to his advantage, fondling and stroking in new and different ways. But when she was ready for more, he caught her hips and prevented what they both wanted. "The drawer in the nightstand," he said with a gasp, "unless you want to start talking babies right now."

She didn't want to talk at all. She wanted him inside her. She needed him now, and he was preventing her from it. "I like babies," she said, rubbing at him with her hips.

"Good." He grabbed the back of her head and pulled her down to slant his mouth across hers.

With joy Rory sank into his kiss, letting his tongue and hands plunder as they would. She surged against him when he filled his hands with her breasts. Love offered a freedom she'd never known in this act, a safety net that allowed her to be who she was without second-guessing every move. There were so many things she hadn't done and wanted to try, and with utter happiness she knew Clay would gladly offer her all of them and invent more of his own.

When she couldn't tolerate being separated from him by even this degree, she rose up on her knees and took him inside her.

Clay shouted with delight, caught her hips, and flipped her back to the mattress, pinning her beneath him.

Laughing, Rory wrapped her legs around his hips and surged upward. "There's no risk in forever," she murmured.

"Together forever. I love the way you think. I love

everything about you." In approval, he bent to suckle her breast.

Rory's hips surged off the bed, driving him deeper, driving them both to frenzy, as if this were the only outlet for the powerful emotions penned up inside them. After weeks of denying themselves, they climaxed quickly and together, already one, with only one driving need.

Once satisfied, physical urgency ebbed to a quieter place, resting while they caught their breaths and redis-covered their surroundings.

Sprawling his long body next to hers, Clay rubbed his fingers over the moisture he'd left on her thigh. "A small ceremony in Vegas, tomorrow."

Unprotected sex . . . babies . . . marriage. Following the unspoken path of his thoughts, Rory smiled at the mosquito netting over their heads. Inside that complex brain of his, Clay carried old-fashioned morals and cour-tesy to their limits. She liked that in a man. That didn't mean she had to be an old-fashioned girl. "A huge cere-mony, here, when I have time to pull it together."

She liked the way he stroked her with familiarity, as if they already knew each other so well they could read each other's thoughts. They could, she realized. She knew exactly what was going through Clay's head right now, as he did hers. The thrill of knowing someone else understood was even headier than sex.

His fingers squeezed her thigh. "I've waited too long to find you. I don't want to wait any longer to have you in my life on a permanent basis. I want to wake up with your head on my pillow in the morning, and I want it properly, so you won't be ashamed in front of your family."

She wanted that, too. She liked turning her head and meeting Clay's serious stare, or his amused smile, and knowing he was thinking about her. She liked lying here, talking about the future with a man who understood her ambitions. "Mandy will just have to be corrupted. I don't think I can leave this bed anytime soon."

When Clay smiled, the sun rose in the sky and the birds broke into song. Aurora sighed in thanksgiving. Life had been kind to give her a man with the intelligence to look and listen and think for himself.

"There may not be much time for fancy weddings once 'Mysterious' hits the shelves," he warned. "The company could get pretty big, pretty fast."

"So could I," she said with laughter, turning on her side because she loved looking at him. Clay's need for physical activity to offset his intense mental work habits had developed nicely defined abs and shoulders to die for, but it was his eyes that held her gaze. Surely they were windows to the soul, as the poets said. Trusting the love she saw in his, she revealed one of her fears. "I could turn into a blimp in months. Are you ready for that?"

The ex-millionaire who'd had everything life had to offer smiled like a kid in a toy store, his whole face lighting with joy. "You wouldn't mind? Having kids is kind of problematic for careers. I'd understand if you didn't want—"

"I want one just like Midge," she declared happily, snuggling closer. She shouldn't have doubted that Clay would think of making babies as a wonderful new process he could explore. He would be a fantastic father simply because he'd have to figure out how kids worked. Love poured through her at the thought of how his mind operated. "But I'm not small."

He deliberately lowered his gaze to her breasts. "Oh, yeah, I noticed. Your point?"

She laughed in relief at his foolishness. When he looked at her, he was seeing *her*, not her clothes or her attitude or her size, but the woman she was and would be. Just as she didn't see the man who'd had it all but a man who wanted to understand how the world worked so he could fix it.

"My point is the same as yours." She jiggled a little, just to keep him looking. She could see that more than his spirit was rising to the occasion. "Banks might not want blimps on their staff. Babies need mothers. I can work on your company and take care of myself and babies at the same time. Am I following your thoughts close enough?"

Clay abruptly sat up, arranged her on his lap, and leaned his back against the headboard. Gently cupping and lifting her breasts together, he returned his focus to her face. "Will you mind? Your career is important."

She squirmed into a more comfortable position and basked in satisfaction when she succeeded in diverting his focus for a fraction of a second. She'd never liked men looking at her breasts until Clay came along. Now she reveled in it. "My career is in financial management. I help businesses grow. Can we have an office in Charleston?"

She had his full attention in a nanosecond. Understanding lit his bronzed face, and she could almost see his brain kick into gear. "How about a house with a tower overlooking the water, where we can spend the day making love?"

"And locking out the world." She wrapped her arms around his neck and rejoiced in the crush of his muscled chest against her. Understanding ran deep. He needed time out from the world, and she could give him what he needed. In return, he would enthusiastically support the place she would build in the community because he didn't need the money for himself. Who could ask for anything more?

"We could lock our families out," he agreed with a touch of dryness at the sounds of pounding on the front door and voices rising from the porch interrupting their interlude.

"Lots of guest bedrooms so they can come visit us anytime they like," she countered.

"Vegas tomorrow and a big ceremony later?"

"I'm feeling lucky," she murmured against his neck. "Let's gamble on it."

It took nearly a week to reach Vegas.

They couldn't skip the zoning meeting. When the Binghams announced they'd sell a third of their acreage to the state for a park and an equal amount to the Nature Conservancy for a wildlife preserve if their descendants were allowed to remain on the land, the entire audience stood up and cheered. The commission voted unanimously to allow restricted commercial use on the remaining third along the highway for development of small businesses.

Clay talked Aurora into running off for a quick wedding and returning to tell their families later so they wouldn't have to make a big production of it. But she hadn't been able to hide her engagement from Cissy, who promptly told Jake, who immediately told the entire world.

Mara called on her Hollywood connections to rent a casino. TJ and Jared notified family and arranged the logistics. Cleo organized entertainment and caretaking for the kids.

By week's end, their entourage could have filled the plane to Vegas if they'd been efficient enough to catch the same flight.

"It's better this way," Clay intoned solemnly in imitation of his big brother as he gazed around the casino filled with their wedding party, still a little in awe at how quickly his private wedding had turned into a circus, and a lot in awe at how good it made him feel. "They'll be much too busy gambling to know when we leave."

"I think it was the Vegas part that decided it." Tucking her arm around her husband's, Aurora leaned against him to watch Cissy laugh and flirt with a poker dealer. As her maid of honor, Cissy had had her hair styled and tinted, and even consented to let Rory buy her a new dress. She looked fabulous, and the handsome poker dealer seemed more than interested. "Pops has always wanted to do Vegas."

"He's doing it in style." Clay gazed over the glittering lights of the casino to locate the older man in his tux, his graying hair pulled back in a neat ponytail, his beard immaculately trimmed, and two women clinging to his arms as he punched the buttons of an electronic slot machine. "You're not worried about losing him to the bright lights?"

He liked Jake's down-to-earthness. He hoped he could

rely on his new father-in-law to teach him the balance he needed in dealing with family. And kids. He glanced down at his gorgeous wife—Clay noted the solid gold band on Aurora's finger with a good deal of pride and satisfaction—and tried to imagine how she would look carrying his child. Good. Very good, he decided. She snuggled closer and almost purred with his attention. He enjoyed knowing that the more he indulged in looking, the more she liked it.

She'd chosen a sleeveless, cream-colored gown with a heart-shaped neckline that he couldn't help studying—in pure intellectual interest—to see what held it in place. The amber sunburst dangling between her breasts distracted him into remembering last night, when she'd worn only the amber he'd given her and nothing else.

"Pop's already designing a set of gnomes for the baby's room," she informed him, her eyes crinkling with laughter as she watched him consider this.

Since it was much too soon to predict babies, Clay pondered the image of cribs and dancing concrete gnomes. A burst of laughter diverted him to his own family competing at the blackjack table. TJ and Jared were teaching their wives the finer points of losing money. Cleo's sister, a teacher who ran a day-care center, had taken Mandy and the other kids under her wing. The teacher's husband already had a tall stack of winning chips in front of him.

"Concrete gnomes?" Clay finally asked, since even his creative mind couldn't picture concrete Dopeys in juxtaposition with cribs.

Aurora laughed and tugged him toward the door, where their limo waited. She didn't have to tug very hard. "Wooden ones. He's decided to expand his inventory with woodworking. Not all the pines burned in the fire, and he figures to make lemonade out of what's left."

That made absolute, perfect sense, probably because his brain had checked out the instant she pressed a kiss to his cheek. He'd already learned that once Aurora felt safe, she was a creative and enthusiastic lover. The honeymoon suite at the hotel—in Reno, out of range of their families—had a mirror over a whirlpool bath. He may have grown up in highbrow, wealthy surroundings, but he was learning to appreciate popular taste. He was learning to play, and Aurora was teaching him. He was looking forward to Reno.

She was looking forward to Paris. He'd promised her that, as soon as the game was making enough money so she felt comfortable spending it.

He looked forward to lots of things, but right now he was learning to live in the moment. He had the woman of his dreams on his arm, and the future was too bright to see.

Behind them, before they reached the double glass doors, red and blue lights flashed frenetically, sirens shrieked, and bells clamored, accompanied by wild cheers and shouts.

Turning, Clay and Aurora watched as silver coins poured from the slot machine Jake was operating, cascading into the bucket he held as he yelled in surprise and exultation. More coins tumbled onto the carpet to the tune of "We Are the Champions" on the speakers.

"Perfect," Rory murmured. "It's only fair."

Laughing, they escaped before anyone noticed they were gone.

Read on for a sneak peek at
Patricia Rice's
next historical romance,

THIS MAGIC MOMENT

Coming in August 2004
from Signet Books.

April, 1755

"Lord Harry has made an appointment to see your father this afternoon," Cousin Lucinda announced excitedly, entering Christina's bedchamber without knocking.

"The Most Noble the Duke of Sommersville, you mean." Christina plopped down on the edge of the bed and began to pry off her boots. "Or His Grace, the Duke of Sommersville." She dropped the boot on the faded carpet and pried off the other. Then she shimmied out of her half-brother's breeches and stockings. "I expect he's come to cry off."

"Christina!" Shocked—not by her cousin's breeches but by her assertion—Lucinda tucked the outlandish clothes into their usual place in the bottom of the armoire. "He cannot do that. You have been betrothed for *ages*."

With the ease of expertise, Christina untied the old skirt that hid her breeches. She'd spent these past weeks exploring inside London's inner city walls looking for the ghost of Hans Holbein, the artist Lucinda most admired. It was much easier—and less conspicuous—to skulk about disguised in boy's clothing.

"Sinda, my dear, do you remember when all London whispered in astonishment after you painted the portrait of the earl's daughter in her casket—before the child died?"

Lucinda clasped her talented fingers and looked nervous. "I thought they'd ride me out of town on a rail. I want my work to be recognized, but not in such a fashion. I don't mean to do these things," she murmured, "but if anyone notices this latest. . ."

"You really should quit doing portraits and work anonymously," Christina chided her. "One of these days, there will be no one about to rescue you from these muddles. I'm sure I can get you out of this one if I could only speak with Holbein's ghost. He persuaded society that his artistic fantasies were fashionable and not dangerous."

"I'm not *dangerous*," Sinda insisted. "I didn't even know Lord Pelham. I couldn't know he'd die. I just painted what I saw in my head."

"You see people die before they do. That's dangerous. I found Holbein's grave in St. Andrews, but his ghost doesn't haunt it," Christina offered. "If I only knew which house he died in, it might help. If he could draw all those macabre pictures of people dying and be celebrated for it, I don't know why you can't."

"Because he was a man and not a Malcolm," Lucinda said with a touch more acid than was her usual habit. "Besides, even if you found Holbein's ghost, he'd speak German. You have too much imagination for your own good. I thank you for your efforts, but what has any of this to do with Harry?"

"The reason you weren't run out of town last time was because Harry laughed at the gossips," Christina said matter-of-factly, unhooking her too-large bodice to slip out of the man's shirt she'd worn under it. "Harry told everyone he met that Malcolms were always good for a little amusement, and he poked fun at their 'superstition.' He is such a popular fellow that everyone was too embarrassed to condemn you after he belittled their fears."

"Oh, how thoughtful of him! I had no idea." Sinda watched Christina with curiosity. "But that means he's perfect for you."

"Sinda, you aren't *listening*. He doesn't believe in our Malcolm gifts. He takes nothing seriously. When I tell him about my ghost hunts, he calls me his 'imaginative little creature.' I vow, he asked for my hand because it kept us both from having to seriously engage anyone else. He never intended to marry me."

"But he's a *duke* now," Lucinda protested. "He must marry and raise heirs, and he's betrothed to you. He must take that seriously."

Christina dropped a lacy chemise over her head and reached for a white silk stomacher, ignoring the corset Lucinda held out. "And raise *heirs*, Sinda. Just listen to yourself and think for a change, will you?"

"Oh." Lucinda dropped to a tapestried chair seat and looked pained. "Malcolm women don't marry dukes who don't already have heirs."

"Right. Malcolms always have daughters, never sons. That's why there are dozens of us girls and no little boys running around."

"Ninian had a boy," Lucinda pointed out.

"To an Ives, who are a race of demons of their own. Harry isn't an Ives. If both our mamas had nothing but girls, what are the chances I'll be any different?" Christina stepped into her rose silk skirt and pulled the bodice sleeves over her arms.

Lucinda leapt up to fasten the hooks in back. "But he can't call off a betrothal," she wailed. "It just isn't done."

"He's a duke worth thousands of pounds a year. He can pay my father off and buy any woman who catches his fancy. Can you imagine me as a duchess? His ancestors would fall out of their noble picture frames."

Although she did her best to sound pragmatic, Christina's romantic nature wished it could be otherwise. She probably didn't love Harry, but he was the only man she'd ever met who didn't scold her for her antics. Since her favorite pastime was chasing ghosts and other creatures invisible to the normal eye, this required a certain degree of open-mindedness that the rest of mankind did not possess.

She and Harry didn't spend much time in each other's pockets, but they saw each other regularly at London's entertainments. One of her favorite memories was of the night at the Grosvenor's ball when she'd grown weary of the overheated, smelly ballroom and had wandered out to the garden, certain she'd seen a brownie under a tulip leaf. She didn't know if Harry had been conducting a liaison or if he'd followed her, but he'd found her sitting on a tree branch in her ball gown, waiting for the brownie to reappear.

He'd looked quite refined in his embroidered vest and plain ruffled cravat, when all others wore lace frothing from neck and cuff. Harry had a knack for dressing simply and looking richer than any other man in the vicinity. He'd leaned his elegant shoulders against the tree trunk, propped one polished shoe against the bark to display a splendidly sculpted leg in evening breeches, and twirled a rose in his fingers while he located her amid the leaves.

"I hadn't realized nightingales wore silk plumage," he said, as if he came across maidens in ball gowns sitting in trees all the time. "The yellow suits you."

"Thank you," she answered a trifle crossly. "If you came out here just to tell me that, your mission has been accomplished. You may leave now."

"And return to that noxious ballroom? Do you despise me that much to banish me there?"

She could never be cross with Harry for long. Kicking her feet so that her petticoats bobbed, she gave up her pursuit of brownies in favor of dallying with a charming man. Just looking at Harry gave her pleasure. Out of respect for the occasion he'd powdered his hair and tied it in black silk to accent the white lawn of his jabot. Since he normally wore his thick blond hair in the same manner, it did not seem pretentious to see him so now. But it was his laughing eyes that always held her captivated.

"I cannot despise you," she replied saucily, "but you have chased off all the brownies in the garden for the evening. They know they cannot compare to your magnificence."

His deep rich laugh warmed her because she knew he wasn't laughing at her but at her description of him. Harry did not suffer from an ounce of vanity.

"I apologize, my fairy lady. I did not know I surpassed

ᴜrownies in elegance. Shall I attempt to be more shabby next time we meet?"

Enchanted by his romantic gallantry, she forgot brownies or auras or any of the other things with which she entertained herself. Instead, when he stepped up on the bench to help her down, she held out her arms to him and allowed him to swing her from her perch.

Standing there on the bench beside him, she probably whispered something unutterably foolish in reply, but Harry wasn't listening any more than she was. He kept his hands on her waist, and she kept her hands on his shoulders, and it had seemed the most natural thing in the world for her to lift her face and for him to tilt his head down and for their mouths to come together.

It had been bliss, pure bliss. His lips had been soft and warm and respectful, but she'd opened her eyes and seen the red aura of his passion heating when she returned his kiss with all the fervency she possessed. He'd stepped away then, just at the moment when she thought to learn more. Always cautious was Harry.

She'd spent many a night reliving that kiss, wondering where it might have taken them had they been anyone else but two people who preferred independence to the marital state.

"Christina! You haven't heard a word I said."

Jolted back from her lovely daydream, Christina ran her hands over her face and into her hair, spinning to find the looking glass. Her lamentably light hair flew every which way, and she hastened to pin it into a respectable coiffeur.

"If you'd wear a corset, you'd have a smaller waist

than any lady in town," Lucinda observed with her critical artist's eye.

"In other words, I'm skinny and you'd have me skinnier. Isn't it enough that I'm tall enough to be a boy?"

"A short boy," her cousin scoffed. "What will you do if Harry calls off the betrothal?"

"Congratulate him on his intelligence, of course." Having spent the better part of her life stumbling into one adventure after another, Christina had learned how to put on a brave face for all occasions. She just didn't think she'd ever faced such a crushing pain in her heart before.

Harry was hers. He'd always been hers. Even as youngsters, they'd played in the park together. She'd thought when they grew old and tired of playing, they'd eventually marry and settle down into old age together. She couldn't imagine doing the same with anyone else. She was twenty-two years old and well beyond looking for another mate. Her rosy picture of the future had been knocked cock-a-hoop, and insecurity crushed her usual optimism. What would become of her?

Putting on a brave face, she dismissed her foolish fears with a cocky smile. "I shall tell him I'll dance at his wedding and ask who the lucky duchess might be."

Christina's father was a marquess, and Lucinda's father was a duke—both men having taken Malcolm women as their second wives after their first wives gave them heirs. She and Lucinda and their sisters and cousins traveled in noble circles and were not mightily impressed by titles.

But they were expected to marry well and wisely. As a respectable second son of a duke, Harry had not been a grand match, but a sensible one as far as everyone was concerned. Christina's boyishness didn't "take" with most gentlemen, no matter how her would-be suitors had pretended otherwise. She could see it in their auras when they thought her foolish or sought her dowry out of avarice. Harry was the only man who adored her for herself.

And for his own sake, she would have to let him go.